"The moon is bleeding," Drusilla said, looking out at the night. "The girl has ghosts all around her; they're her family, and when she holds the sword all their hands are upon the hilt."

Drusilla hugged herself, then rocked forward on her toes and ran her fingers up to her shoulders and then back down again. Spike laid the rifle down and rose from his chair. She turned to meet him.

"What girl?" he asked. "The one we're after?"

With her eyes drifting from side to side, face titled demurely downward, Drusilla looked lost. Then her smile slowly returned.

"Not that one, though I saw her, too. She's a dancer, the girl we're after. We'll find her, Spike. But we aren't the only ones looking. The Slayer, that one that hurt you, with her blond hair and cold lips, she's coming here. Coming home."

"Home? You mean she's from Copenhagen?" Spike asked.

"Oh yes. They all know her 'round here. All the dark things do."

Spike grinned.

His mood was improving.

Buffy the Vampire Slayer™

Available from ARCHWAY Paperbacks and POCKET PULSE

Available from POCKET BOOKS

SPIKE & DRU
Pretty Maids All in a Row

A Buffy the Vampire Slayer ™ Novel

CHRISTOPHER GOLDEN

**An original novel based on the hit TV series
created by Joss Whedon**

POCKET BOOKS
New York   London   Toronto   Sydney   Singapore

This book is a work of fiction. Names, characters, places, and incidents are products of the author's imagination or are used fictitiously. Any resemblance to actual events or locales or persons, living or dead, is entirely coincidental.

POCKET BOOKS, a division of Simon & Schuster, Inc.
1230 Avenue of the Americas, New York, NY 10020

™ and © 2000 Twentieth Century Fox Film
Corporation. All rights reserved.

Originally published in hardcover in 2000 by Pocket Books

All rights reserved, including the right to reproduce
this book or portions thereof in any form whatsoever.
For information address Pocket Books, 1230 Avenue
of the Americas, New York, NY 10020

ISBN: 0-7434-1892-1

First Pocket Books paperback printing June 2001

10 9 8 7 6 5 4 3 2 1

POCKET and colophon are registered trademarks of
Simon & Schuster, Inc.

Printed in the U.S.A.

For James Marsters

Acknowledgments

Thanks are due, as always, to Connie and the boys, to my agent Lori Perkins, my editor Lisa Clancy, and her team supreme, Micol Ostow and Liz Shiflett, as well as Sally Partington and all the people at S & S U.K. who gave me such a warm welcome. I am grateful, also, to Joss Whedon, Debbie Olshan, George Snyder, and (as always) Caroline Kallas, for saying yes. Thanks to my friends at the Bronze on both sides of the Atlantic.

SPIKE & DRU

Pretty Maids All in a Row

Prologue

New York City, U.S.A.
March 9th, 1940

New York City. Center of the universe.

He stood on the corner at Sixth Avenue and Thirty-sixth Street and looked north. Night had long since fallen but the lights of this extraordinary city still burned. People milled about in fancy dress searching for more of the nightlife now that the evening's shows had all let out. It was still early in 1940 but the Depression was long since over. Prohibition was over. In Europe a dark cloud hung over every nation. The German invasion of Poland the previous September had prompted France and Britain to declare war, but there had been little action in Europe since then. Still, it was inevitable. War would come. Its specter loomed ever larger, ever more imminent in Europe. But here in America there was a pride and a confidence that was unlike anything he had ever seen.

Were they ignorant, these Americans, or simply arrogant?

Whatever the answer one thing was clear to him: with its vibrant color and electric crackle of life America had become the new empire, and none of the European nations—neither the home of Hitler nor his critics—was truly aware of it yet.

As he watched the people walk past, the men in their striped suits and bowlers, the women in their expensive dresses and wraps, he wondered if even these Americans quite understood the shift in the world that had come since the Great War had devastated Europe twenty years before.

With a snicker, he shook his head. *Why go to America?* the love of his life had asked. He had led her to the window and drawn back the curtains to reveal the gray pallor of an anxious London below.

"Have a look, pet," he had told her. "Do the poor sods down there look like they're havin' even a bit o' fun? They're so grave and frumpy these days, it's almost enough to make me pity them before they bleed. Let's have a little fun, shall we?"

The savage smile that played at the corners of her lips then enticed him, and he fell upon her there in the wan light from a cloud-shrouded moon. They made love with a furious abandon and she hurt him, tearing at the skin on his back with her talons. Even now he shivered at the memory of that delicious pain.

New York had been everything they had dreamed. Parties and music and young debutantes flush with red life and exuberance. A hunter's paradise.

Four months later she was bored.

"You'd think living forever would give the girl a bit of patience," he whispered to himself as he stood in the cool breeze that swept down Sixth Avenue, as if someone were there to appreciate the irony in his voice.

The wind blew again. He was exposed where he stood on the corner, and he turned up his collar to stave off the chill. With a quick tug he set his hat more firmly on his head; it had once belonged to a gray-haired gentleman who had not wanted to part with it. There were only two small drops of blood staining the brim.

At that moment the object of his loitering appeared on the opposite corner. Adrienne Montclaire was a devious old bitch with the face of an eighteen-year-old and the heart of a killer. He admired her for it but trusted her not at all. Her blond hair flew behind her, much longer than the cultivated bob so fashionable among Manhattan's female population. With the wind pasting her scarlet cloak to her body, Adrienne had a sultry vitality that their kind so rarely exhibited.

She looked so very alive.

Just a short way down the block she crossed the street and went into a restaurant and pub called Keen's Chophouse. He watched to be certain she had not been followed. Their meeting was to be private. No observers. Well, none other than the humans, who would have no idea what they were seeing.

Two minutes after Miss Montclaire entered Keen's, he followed. The door swung open before him and he descended a few steps to the foyer. Smoke billowed around him. Keen's was famous among New York's elite for its steak, its wood-and-brass atmosphere, and for the thousands of corn-cob pipes that hung from hooks on the ceiling. Each pipe had a number and each number corresponded to one of the restaurant's regular patrons.

Theodore Roosevelt had dined here and there was his pipe to prove it. Buffalo Bill Cody had left a pipe behind when he died.

The roar of men speaking of their fortunes, blathering about their businesses or their wives or mistresses, about baseball or the tensions in Europe; it would have been amusing if not for the cloud of smoke.

He was grateful that he did not have the burden of needing to breathe.

The maitre'd snapped to attention as he removed his bowler.

"May I help you, sir?"

"I'm to meet Miss Montclaire for dinner," he replied.

The man stood a little straighter, chin a little higher, though whether the reaction had to do with respect for Adrienne Montclaire or the dignity he had found most Americans associated with his accent, he could not say.

"Right this way, sir."

Adrienne's table was at the back of the restaurant against the wall opposite the entry. A private booth, though not so private that other patrons would not send curious glances at the young man dining with one of the city's most notoriously wealthy debutantes.

She smiled as he approached, her teeth perfectly white.

"Hello, William," she said, voice as raspy as he recalled, eyes dancing with sinister intent.

Miss Montclaire offered her hand and he took it, held it up to be kissed. The maitre'd hurried away as he sat across from her.

"Adrienne. Lovely to see you. How long has it been?"

"Thirty-five years, William. You're as handsome as ever."

"And you as ravishing, love," he replied. "But let's skip the niceties, eh? You know bloody well I don't use that name anymore."

A petulant pout re-formed her thick red lips. But it was insincere. "You know I hate that sobriquet of yours. Spike. Wherever did you pick up such a crude nickname?"

He grinned at that, his thin face appearing almost skeletal in the dim light and the smoke. "Let's just say I used to work on the railroad."

A silent moment passed between them, and Adrienne's expression was grave. At length she sat up a bit straighter, but remained silent. A waiter came and they ordered drinks. He was back swiftly, but when he departed she only looked at her drink.

"Are you going to tell me why you wanted to see me, or am I meant to guess?" she asked, a bit curt.

Spike sipped from a pint of warm beer. Not quite like home but not bad either. His gaze darted around, glancing at the other patrons, wondering if anyone nearby was not what he appeared to be, if there was anyone else there who would understand what they were speaking of enough to benefit from it.

Eventually he decided there was nothing to be done for it.

"I want to do something for Drusilla," he said.

"Are you still with that cow?" Adrienne asked, playful and cruel as a kitten.

Spike narrowed his eyes, gave her a look that told her another such remark would cost her her life. Adrienne only smiled obtusely, pushed her luxurious hair away from her face, and tilted her head as she regarded him.

"How can I help, *William?*"

"She's been a bit, well, bored lately. I've set my heart upon a gift for her, and I believe that you know where I could find it." Even before he spoke the words, he could see awareness in her eyes. She knew what he was after.

"Freyja's Strand," he confirmed in a low voice.

She frowned. "You're insane."

"Now come on, love. It's dear old William you're talking to. Don't tell me you don't know where it is, because I know better. Always been a bit of a hobby for you, hasn't it, keeping track of such things? I want the necklace of the Brisings for Dru, and I'll have it, with or without your help."

"A grand quest for your lover, then?" she teased. "How romantic."

"Something like that," Spike snarled.

Adrienne regarded him steadily. "And how am I to benefit from this information; a bit of knowledge which, as I'm certain you know, could get me killed?"

"Do you still hold a grudge against the Master?" Spike asked, well aware of the answer.

She froze. Stared at him with profound suspicion. "Nest? You're going to tell me where to find Nest if I tell you where to find Freyja's Strand?"

"Exactly."

He watched her turn the offer over and over in her mind. When the moment of her decision arrived, he saw that there as well. But he had known from the start what Adrienne would say. He had made her, after all.

"The demon Skrymir has it," she revealed.

With a grunt, Spike furrowed his brow.

"You know of him, then?"

"Heard of the bloke, yeah. Who hasn't? Wasn't sure if he was real, or still alive if he was."

"Oh, he's real," Adrienne told him. Her smile was even more condescending than her tone. "He has been alive since the time the necklace of the Brisings was forged by the gods of the North country."

"I don't believe in gods. Not of any country." Spike sniffed.

"As you will. Whatever those creatures were, they were as real as the trinket you seek. I can tell you how to reach Skrymir, but he will not relinquish it to you. Your journey will be hard and will gain you nothing."

Satisfied, Spike leaned back into his chair and gazed levelly at Adrienne. "I'll make a bargain with you, girl. You tell me how to find the crusty old bastard, and I'll worry about getting the bloody necklace from him."

Her eyes grew stormy a moment, but then the storm passed. The lineage behind Spike was long, but the Master was a part of it. Adrienne had tried, once upon a time, to use that bloodline to become a part of the Master's circle, the Brethren of Aurelius. He had spurned her. Hurt her. Left her to die in the sun.

But she had escaped, and she had been hunting him ever since. It would not be long, Spike knew, before Adrienne discovered the Master's whereabouts on her own. For now though he turned her ignorance to his advantage.

She told him how to find Skrymir's lair. Though they had no map between them, her instructions were very precise. He committed them to memory. As she spoke, he watched those lovely full lips move, remembering why he had turned her in the first place. Not for love, of course. He loved no one but Drusilla. But those lips had their attractions.

"Now, where do I find Nest?" she demanded.

Spike smiled. "All right then, pet. I'm a bit parched yet. Just give us a moment."

He held up a hand to gesture to the waiter, who had been keeping a respectful distance. The waiter noticed and began to approach, unaware that the signal had not truly been meant for him.

In the foyer of the restaurant a woman screamed and began to faint, her skirts flying up in revelatory fashion. Her black tresses cascaded across her pale features and she convulsed on the floor, tearing obscenely at her breast.

"Dear God, she's having a fit!" the maitre'd shouted, and ran to kneel by her.

Every single patron turned from their dining partners and their red and bloody meat to stare in fascination at the scene unfolding near the entry way.

All save Spike.

Adrienne glanced away only for a moment. Long enough for Spike to withdraw the long, thin, tapered wooden stake from inside his sleeve. She began to turn back toward him just as he thrust it across the table. Her perfect lips formed a stunned little O as it plunged into her chest and punctured her heart.

She exploded in a cloud of ash and dust. It smelled of damp wood and spices.

He paid for their drinks, stood, and walked up to the foyer. The maitre'd nearly fell backward, so shocked was he when the contorting woman simply sat up, grinning madly.

"There were bleeding children in my wine," she said, her smile impossibly wide; the smile of a hungry tiger. "I was choking on them. But I'm better now."

Spike bent to help her to her feet, dusted her off, and kissed her full on the mouth. "Off we go, then, love."

They went out together, all the patrons of Keen's staring after them.

Outside, with the cold wind still blowing, they ran together, laughing wildly.

"She told you, didn't she?" Drusilla asked. "The birdy whispered in your ear?"

"That she did, love. That she did. We're off to Norway."

Drusilla paused on the sidewalk, an almost comical expression of concern on her features. "Ooh, Spike, are you sure it's safe? There will be war, you know. A real one, not all this posturing and chest-beating. Any day now. I had a vision of tin soldiers on fire, and the sky was raining babies. I told you, remember?"

"Don't give it another thought, poodle," Spike said happily. He pressed his face to her cheek, then nuzzled into the nape of her neck, nipping her there with his teeth. "You're the cream in my tea, Dru. Always. My sweet one is going to have her heart's desire, and that is simply that.

"If it's to be war, all right then. Let's go to war."

Chapter One

Spike stood on the deck of the *Aberdeen*, cigarette clenched between his lips, and leaned perhaps too much against the rail. It was twilight, and the last of the sun's rays lit the tips of the waves on the western horizon. The ocean was rough and beautiful, ephemeral turbulence on the surface belying the eternal calm below.

The boredom was killing him.

The engines rumbled loudly below the thrumming deck, their smell inescapable for anyone who actually *had* to breathe. In the dining room each night Spike and Drusilla sat and ate the slop that was served to them. They did not have to eat for sustenance. On this trip, however, if they dined with others aboard the ship it was for the sake of appearances only and almost not worth the trouble.

Monotony. The same faces passed by on the deck each night. Three British airmen returning home to do their duty for His Majesty. A young lady and her governess en route via England to an elite Paris boarding school. The filthy crewmen and anxious-looking stewards. The fat American woman whose pinched features threatened at any moment to explode in a torrent of abuse poured upon her bespectacled, quavering husband. He represented an American firm that hoped to introduce new techniques in steel welding and shipbuilding to the British for the war. Apparently no one had explained to him that the British were not bloody likely to be taking advice from the Yanks, if anyone.

Nearly every one of them had been the object of his homicidal fantasies during the voyage. Most had escaped unscathed. It would not do to have the truth about his and Drusilla's nature revealed to a passenger ship full of humans already on edge because of the outbreak of war. Particularly not in the middle of the Atlantic.

Spike took a long drag on his cigarette, the ember at its tip glowing in the dark, and leaned out across the rail to stare down at the water churned up by the *Aberdeen*'s passing.

"Careful there, mate. This old girl's in good shape, but the rail might not hold."

The voice was gruff, British, and by now familiar. It belonged to Jack Norton, one of the grimy men responsible for keeping the old vessel's engine running. He often walked the deck to stretch his legs after a shift below and was among the very few living souls on board that Spike had no immediate urge to kill.

Smoke drifted in twin streams from Spike's nostrils, quickly sucked away into the cold spring night. "I can think of worse things, Jack. A little bit of a dip, some chaos aboardship, 'man overboard,' all that. It'd be a bloody joy about now. How do you do this all the time without going out of your mind with the boredom?"

Norton stroked his gray mustache, unmindful of his dirty hands. "Who says I'm not out of me mind?" he said, expression quite serious. "Tell the truth, lad, it don't really bother me. I'm down below, me mind on me work. Don't have much time to think about it."

The crewman paused, studying Spike closely. "You and the missus have a fight?"

Spike frowned. "I don't think I like that question."

"No offense, sir," Norton replied, unaffected by Spike's apparent annoyance. "It's only that yer on yer honeymoon here, ain'tcha? Makin' yer way home. You've spent near every waking moment in yer compartment, celebratin' like."

"Well, that's what newlyweds do, isn't it?" Spike snapped. "We've come out for meals and walks around the deck and the like."

"Aye. But this is the first time I've heard ye sayin' how bored you are. None of my business to be sure, but I've a feeling if I was on me honeymoon with that pretty bird o' yours, I wouldn't be bored, or at least I wouldn't act it. Just a friendly bit of advice, as me ol' mum used to say. Worth what you make of it."

The impulse to kill Jack Norton just then was quite strong. Spike resisted it. Instead he took another puff of his cigarette, felt the burning in his throat, and then snorted plumes of smoke back into the air. He shook his head.

"So you don't think I should go for a swim, Jack? That's what you're saying?"

"That's what I'm saying," Norton agreed. "I expect you knew that, but we're all feeling a bit dodgy these days, aren't we? What with the U-boats prowling about down there . . ." He gestured toward the water. ". . . and three people lost on this trip already."

Spike raised an eyebrow. "Three?"

Norton glanced about to make sure no one else was within listening distance. "The captain don't want us talking about such things with the passengers, but aye, the count's up to three now. The first one was that doctor from New York. Hastings was his name I think. Same night one of the nightwatch went missing. A piece of the rail give way. He were up there watching for subs, so he might have gone over by accident. Might have."

"But then in the storm last night . . ."

"Aye," Norton said gravely.

As if on cue, the fat American woman and her ratlike husband ambled by on the deck, out for an evening stroll. Many of the passengers stayed belowdecks as much as possible, uncomfortable with the roll of the ocean and the openness around them. Not this pair. The woman visibly flinched as she walked through the trail of smoke from Spike's cigarette. She turned up her nose as she paused to regard him.

"Pardon me, sir, if I might inquire? What manner of tobacco is it that creates such an awful stench?"

Norton grumbled something under his breath and tried to diminish his large frame somehow. He was uncomfortable around passengers other than Spike. Only the stewards were meant to have contact with them.

For his part, Spike pinched the cigarette in his fingers, put it to his lips and drew in a lungful of smoke. He did not need to breathe, but could duplicate the process at will. With a devilish grin, he exhaled smoke into the woman's face. Her husband blinked behind his glasses as his wife began to cough.

"It's Turkish," Spike told her. "A bit exotic for you, dear, but you should get 'round to that part of the world sometime. Like as not they'd slit your throat for being such an obnoxious cow."

The woman had the imagination to glance at her husband as if he might have the temerity to offer some retort. He seemed frozen, rooted to the spot, and managed only to look flustered and fiddle with his spectacles as if he were warming up for some tart rejoinder. None was forthcoming however. His wife marched away in a huff and her mate followed as though she held his leash.

Spike turned his attention back to Norton who was staring at him with an expression of amazement. "You were saying?"

"Now see here," Norton said stuffily. "I may only be one of the blokes stoking the engines 'round here, but it isn't proper for you to speak to a woman that way."

"Spare me." Spike sighed. "You'd like to see *her* overboard next, I'd wager. You were telling me about last night."

The crewman seemed about to chide him again but then chuckled and shook his head. He glanced about once more, then slipped into the conspiratorial tone he had been using before the Americans had approached.

"Coulda been the storm, right enough. But Webley, the man went over last night, had eleven years at sea. Not the kind of man ye expect to fall overboard, even in a real guster."

"So that makes three," Spike noted. "But if they weren't accidental, then what? Does the captain think you've got a killer on board?"

"Worse," Norton said, his voice barely a growl. "Nazi spies."

Spike brightened. "Oh, right! Now there's a bit of excitement."

"Keep it down, mate. You'll have me in a fix if anyone finds out I let it slip."

"Not to worry, Jack. Ol' Spike can keep a secret," he reassured the man. With a grin, he flicked his still burning cigarette overboard and watched it spin down into the raging sea.

"Do a chap a favor though. Give us a shout if you hear any more, right? If there is a Nazi spy on board, I'd like to get a few licks in myself. Break a few bones for His Majesty."

Norton's expression became grave, his jaw set grimly. "Will do, sir."

They said their good-byes and Spike shoved his hands in his pockets and went back belowdecks. He bumped into an older British couple, the Bracketts, he thought he recalled, and nodded an amiable enough greeting. Not much farther along, he came to his stateroom. When he pushed the door open, Spike found Drusilla brushing her long raven hair and singing softly to herself. A violent little lullaby whose lyrics were never once the same.

She turned to pout at him. "You were gone too long, Spike. Hurt my feelings. The ocean hissed and I was afraid at first. Then I grew angry and it slunk away."

Spike went to Drusilla and kissed her silent. Then he stroked her face lovingly as he regarded her. "The bloody fools think they've got spies on board, Dru. Think there are Nazis killing the crew."

"Spies!" she exclaimed, her eyes flashing. "How exciting."

As he often was when around her, Spike was overcome suddenly with the intensity of his feelings for Drusilla. He stared at her, glared even, almost angered by how deeply she affected him. Lights seemed to dance in her eyes, and the corners of her mouth turned up in a mischievous, seductive smile. Overwhelmed, he kissed her again, harder this time, and ran his hands over her body. His tongue flickered into her mouth, and Drusilla bit it hard enough to draw blood. Spike hissed with the tiny pain, but did not withdraw. He felt her curves beneath his hands. His fingers trailed up to her throat and he untied the little bow that held her shift in place. It slid down her pale body, alabaster skin veined with blue ice.

They made love in a brutal frenzy on the floor next to the corpse of Webley the steward, whose dead eyes watched with blank jealousy. Later they drank of him again. In the small hours of the morning, the lovers slipped out together to dump his body over the side and into the tumultuous waters below.

The submarine sliced the rough ocean surface, the light of the moon gleaming off the imposing armor of its conning tower.

Kurt Raeder sat deep within its bowels and wished for a shower. Not only that, but he wanted every other member of the crew of U-28B to have one as well. He sat with the submarine's other petty officers in their quarters and ate what passed for food after four days at sea. The four men sat in silence on the lower bunks in the U-room, heads bowed to avoid striking them on the metal frames above. A grim air of disappointment mixed with their stink to contaminate the entire vessel.

A convoy had passed within forty nautical miles of them and they had missed it. U-29 and U-5 had reached it in time and done a great deal of damage but they had been out of the action. They had sunk only one vessel—a merchant ship—since the outbreak of war.

"Damned convoy," Petty Officer Walther grumbled, dropping his spoon into the slop in his bowl. "What is the sense of a convoy of ships? They make a larger target traveling together. I have never understood it."

Kurt frowned. "It is a big ocean. Ships traveling together are less likely to run across one of our patrols and even if they do they have armed escort. It is all about the odds."

He might have said more but the others all glanced at him distastefully and then went back to their meals. Jaw set angrily, Kurt put down his bowl. He ought to have known better than to respond to such a question. It proved Walther's ignorance but attempting to correct one of the other petty officers was fruitless. Kurt's uncle was Grand Admiral Erich Raeder, commander in chief of the German navy. Kurt could have had any job on the ocean, but he chose to serve under it. U-boat crewmen were valiant and clever. Their clandestine operations required courage and stealth and were vital to the Führer's plans. Uncle Erich had attempted to dissuade him, but Kurt was steadfast. Submarine service would be everything he had ever imagined.

Or so he had thought.

He lived, now, in a Type VIIA U-boat; crammed into the steel cylinder with forty-five other men. From outside, the sub was the size and shape of a passenger train car. Within, however, the size was revealed to be an illusion. The vessel's interior space was filled with machinery; it was one long gangway along which the men moved during shift changes. Even the captain had only a desk hidden by a curtain. There was no privacy aboard a ship like this. No room to move save to sleep or do the job that he had been sent to do. Nobody washed or changed his clothes. When the U-boat was submerged the toilets did not work. The stink of men and oil and mold was thick enough to choke on.

Kurt had chosen this. He might not even have regretted it, for there were benefits as well. The things he had imagined about U-boat service were true. For other subs. But U-28B had sunk a single merchant ship, nothing more glorious than that. And the other men hated him because he was so obviously their intellectual superior and because his uncle was Grand Admiral Raeder.

The others all dropped their spoons. Mealtime was over. Kurt's shift would begin soon. It was still night above and he and others on his shift would shepherd the boat through the night and into the dawn hours until the captain awoke. By then they would turn for home. A day for rest and refueling, and then out to sea again. It had not turned out to be all he had dreamed but Kurt would not allow himself to become further discouraged. He would do his job and speak to his uncle about advancement. If word spread and bitterness trailed in his wake, so be it. He realized that the only way for him to prove his worth was as a captain with a U-boat of his own to command.

"Your turn, Raeder," Walther grunted.

Kurt made no response as he picked up the bowls and spoons from the table in the middle of the corridor. The others folded down the table's leaves. With them up, no one would be able to manuever along the passage. Kurt carried the bowls toward the galley, squeezing through other crewmen's quarters and past the captain's desk on his way. Before he reached his destination he heard shouts echoing down the passage all the way from the command center.

A target had been sighted.

Kurt grinned even as the submarine—which had been running on the surface to conserve time and fuel—began to dive. He stumbled with the pitch of the U-boat but regained his footing before he dropped any of the bowls. As U-28B dove he rushed to the galley, shoving men aside, and dumped the bowls in a sink.

Quick as he was able, he manuevered back along the ship's single corridor until he reached the command center. His clothes were always damp aboard U-28B, but now they were damp with sweat as well. The sweat not of fear but of anticipation. Within the command center all was now silent. The chief stood motionless between the men of the bridge watch. In the small space between the periscope shaft and the interior wall of the conning tower, the commander sat on the periscope saddle, feet on the controls that would rotate the entire mechanism, hands on the levers that would raise or lower it.

The periscope motor hummed. The periscope rose. The commander spun around the shaft on the saddle as the men watched quietly.

"There," he whispered. "A passenger ship under British flag."

"A passenger ship, Commander? Shall we move on?"

The commander froze. Took his eye away from the rubber ring of the periscope to turn slowly and glare at the chief. "Move on, Haupt? We're at war. The Reich does not move on. We have only one vessel sunk to our credit. Now that we have this opportunity in front of us, I won't return to port with that on our log."

"But, sir, if the ship has no military use—"

His words were ignored. At his post, Kurt Raeder allowed himself a tiny smile. Men like Chief Haupt did not understand blitzkrieg, did not realize what war meant to the Reich.

The commander put his eye to the periscope again.

When he spoke, his words were guttural and low. Precise. They were obviously lies for the benefit of those with a conscience about such things, but no one would question him. It was his vessel to command, after all.

"There are deck guns on the ship," he said. "Torpedoes ready. Fire at will."

Spike was asleep on the floor of their cabin aboard the *Aberdeen*. When the ocean was particularly rough, he preferred the floor to the bed for some reason. Drusilla did not argue. There was nothing they could do on the bed that she was not equally happy doing on the floor— or anywhere else for that matter. When he slept, Spike looked like a corpse. All of their kind shared that attribute. His flesh was cold and his chest did not rise and fall with even the false semblance of breath.

It aroused her to look at him that way. She was tempted to wake him but changed her mind. Instead, she sprawled luxuriously across the bed, nude and lascivious, and simply enjoyed the sounds of the ocean. Her head was at the foot of the bed and she stared at the porthole on the wall above it. With a coquettish smile, Dru issued a mental invitation to the gods and sprites of the ocean to come and ravish her. Though she did not expect an answer, she hoped for one.

Should Poseidon himself come up from below to take her, Spike would wish his sometimes cantankerous nature had not prevented her from waking him to satisfy her. Drusilla relished the thought and arranged herself on the bed to be more attractive should even a selkie or merrow hear her mental call or sense her craving.

Close by she heard the aching echo of carillon bells tolling in time with a mournful voice singing "Danny Boy." Drusilla was aware it was a voice only she could hear, but enjoyed it for its music nonetheless. It was made even more special by the knowledge that this performance was solely for her.

She stretched and shuddered with pleasure. When she glanced at the porthole again she giggled, a playful smile caressing her features. There were fish outside the little window. Their room was far above the surface of the water, but the fish swam beyond the glass just the same, creatures of all stripes and sizes.

Drusilla frowned in alarm. The fish were frightened, she could feel it. They began to scream. She recoiled, her momentum causing her to slide off the bed to land on the floor beside Spike. Hands over her ears, she sat there and screamed her lover's name.

Spike sat up instantly, alert, scanning the room for any sign of danger. For a moment, she saw in his eyes that he would kill for her, and she loved him for it.

Then he scowled. "Bloody hell, Dru, stop that racket. What's the matter with you?"

Drusilla lowered her gaze, wrists crossed in front of her face so that she might hide her face from him.

"A voice sang me a beautiful dirge. Then the fish danced at my window and began to scream."

He frowned. "A premonition, pet."

"A nasty whisper, Spike. So much water."

"We're *surrounded* by water, Drusilla. Think you might be a bit more specific?"

The first torpedo struck the *Aberdeen* just then and the sound of the explosion was nearly blotted out by the noise of tearing metal. The ship rocked.

Spike sighed. "Oh, bollocks," he muttered, as the second torpedo struck and the ship began to tilt in the water. "Just my bloody luck."

* * *

Several torpedoes from U-28B had hit their mark. The passenger ship would go down quickly, Kurt knew. The British had not yet learned properly to armor their seagoing vessels, nor how to compartmentalize them so that the hull might be breached and only one section flooded, allowing the ship to continue its course.

Kurt hurried from the command center toward the hatch that would take him onto the deck. He heard the chief shout his name and turned angrily.

"Petty Officer Raeder," Chief Haupt said gravely. "You will return to your post immediately."

"No, sir. Langsdorff is ill. Someone must take his post at the deck gun."

Haupt knew this, but no one had given Kurt the command to take Langsdorff's post. The chief wore a look of bitter contemplation. He would not want to reward such a breach in the chain of command but he would also not want to offend Grand Admiral Raeder. On the other hand, they both knew quite well that there was every chance Kurt would be driven overboard by the sea or the gun's recoil.

"Very well," the chief snapped. "Move along."

Elsewhere in the U-boat another torpedo was fired. It would likely be the last. The British ship was sinking and undefended. The artillery and flak gun on the deck would finish her off. In the petty officers' quarters, Kurt pulled on a thick sweater knitted by his mother and a heavy rubber jacket. He turned the collar up and slipped binoculars around his neck. When he at last climbed the ladder up to the open hatch he could hear the guns firing.

U-28B's engines were still. She was nearly stopped in the water. The waves thrashed against her hull and washed over the deck. Kurt grinned wildly as he fought to keep his footing. Heinrich Gort was at the flak gun. It was meant as an antiaircraft weapon, but Gort fired upon the passenger liner regardless.

The British ship was on fire. It slid into the water slowly and inexorably, but the fire burned on those sections not yet submerged. Kurt imagined he could hear the screaming but knew, sadly, that it was merely wishful thinking. He reached the primary deck gun, an 8.8 centimeter artillery weapon. Others were already there. Together they turned the gun on the sinking ship, loaded the weapon, and fired.

The shell hit the deck of the other ship and exploded. Even with the spray in his eyes, Kurt knew he had seen several bodies fly. He laughed as they prepared to fire again.

Then he noticed something else. The British had put a lifeboat over the side. Perhaps more than one. There were people in it, rowing away from their sinking ship.

"Johannes," he said to the man beside him. "Go below. Bring guns."

The other looked at him with alarm, but Kurt set him with a hard look and after a moment Johannes complied. Even as he fired the deck gun at the devastated vessel again he kept his eye on the lifeboat.

Spike and Drusilla had waited patiently as their room flooded with water. Dru had even closed her eyes for a few minutes, enjoying the sensation of the water lifting her. Spike was furious beyond rationality and could not let go of that rage as the ocean invaded. Electricity sparked and the room was thrown into near total darkness. A human would have been unable to see at all, vampires could see better in the dark.

When the flow of water into the room had ceased he

pushed off the wall and floated to Drusilla. He tapped her arm and her eyes opened instantly. She grinned, seemed almost to laugh. No bubbles escaped her mouth.

Together they swam out into the corridor. Debris floated in the water; perhaps the largest bits of debris were the corpses. The elderly British couple Spike had thought were called the Bracketts were among the drowned dead, though from the look on Mrs. Brackett's face he judged that she, at least, had died from fright.

The pressure of the water on his ear drums was uncomfortable. His clothes were saturated, of course, and that made swimming more difficult. But he had taken the time to pull some clothes on and he'd be damned if he was going to take them off now. Drusilla, on the other hand, was still completely naked. When the water had first begun to flood their compartment he had suggested she dress, but she was simply having too much fun to bother. Now as they made their way underwater toward the ship's sunken deck, she flitted about like some sort of sea sprite.

Despite himself, Spike smiled. She was mad, but he loved her. To see her enjoying herself so much, exalting in the chaos that surrounded them, reminded him of the way she had behaved in Prague decades before on a night when they had both nearly been killed by maddened crowds.

The memory would have made him shudder were it not for the pleasure Dru took in chaos, even now. To her, life and death were both ecstasy.

Mad old thing, he thought, watching her.

When they swam from the *Aberdeen* out into the open ocean he was still smiling. Then they breached the surface and the silence of the ocean was torn apart by the chaos above. Screams ripped the night air and echoed to the stars. Spike faced the ship, half-sunk or more by now. The fire was bright enough to light the surface of the ocean all around. People clung to the portion of the vessel that was still above water and crew members shouted for passengers to jump. He spied Jack Norton, feet and hands on an outer deck railing as if it were a ladder, and thought it a pity that the man was fool enough to save others through some twisted sense of human nobility rather than save himself.

Gunfire sounded behind him and Spike turned in the water. He was tossed by the rough surf so he did not see right away the source of the shooting.

"Oooh, bad, bad men," Drusilla said, her voice barely audible over the cacaphony around them, though she treaded water beside him.

Spike saw it then. A German submarine. There were two lifeboats not far from it and dozens of people in the water attempting to put enough distance between themselves and the *Aberdeen* that they would not be drawn down into the ocean in its wake. On the deck of the U-boat, Nazi seamen stood fast and fired upon the humans in the water.

"Fun as it's been, love, this whole sinking is quite an inconvenience," Drusilla said in a little girl voice, as though she were sternly reprimanding one of her many dolls. "I think we should kill them."

"Bloody well right."

They began to swim. When they were in range of the German machine guns, Spike saw the fat American woman who had so annoyed him on deck throughout their journey. She had a bullet hole in her right cheek and a large section of the back of her head was gone. Already the ocean water was washing the gray matter from within her skull. It floated beside her on the surface of the ocean, roiling with the waves, spreading like a tiny oil slick.

The old cow had more brains than I'd've given her credit for, he thought.

Right about then the first bullet tore through his shoulder.

"Kill them!" Kurt screamed.

An enlisted man named Scharnhorst stood before him, holding tight to a deck rail, flinching as Raeder's spittle flew into his face. "They are civilians," Scharnhorst argued. "Their ship is sunk, no longer a threat. We must rescue them."

Kurt fumed. "You were posted to a battleship before this, weren't you, Scharnhorst?"

"Yes sir."

"Battleships have room to carry prisoners of war. U-boats do not, you fool!" Kurt told him. "If you kill them now you are merely saving them the misery of drowning. Now do it!"

Scharnhorst hesitated. Kurt was astonished. The man was going to refuse once more. He opened his mouth.

"Just give me your weapon then," Kurt demanded.

Relieved, Scharnhorst did as he was told. The other half dozen men on deck were systematically executing those who had escaped the sinking ship. The gunfire blasted the air, pounded their ears, chopped flesh and water.

Kurt slammed the stock of the MG34 machine gun into Scharnhorst's face, shattering his nose and driving him off the deck into the water below. There, in the ocean spray, he was just another face in the water. Kurt cut him in two with a strafing of bullets from his own weapon.

From off to his left there came a great deal of shouting. He fired at a floundering man who was just slipping under the water, killing him before he could drown, then he carefully walked the deck to see what the noise was about. What he saw stopped him dead in his tracks. He nearly lost his balance.

A beautiful woman with raven hair stood completely nude on the deck of the submarine, ocean water splashing her body and washing only the tiniest drops of blood that slipped from the many bullet holes in her flesh. Even as he watched she pitched Johannes overboard, then pulled Heinrich Gort to her. Her face changed suddenly, became grotesque and evil, and she sank her teeth into the flesh of the man's throat. Gort was powerless to stop her. His legs quivered and he dropped his weapon to the deck.

"God in Heaven," Kurt muttered to himself.

Some kind of demon. It has to be. He shook off his fear and raised his weapon. A hand clamped on his shoulder from behind and spun him around. He would have fallen into the water if not for the fingers that gripped his throat, crushing it. The weapon was torn from his hands.

He stared into the face of a monster. It walked like a man and wore human clothes but its features were twisted and hideous and its eyes glowed with an evil yellow light.

It was annoyed.

"I'm so bloody tired of asking this question," the monster said, its British accent stunning Kurt as if someone had struck him. "Does anyone on board this floating scrap heap speak even a word of English?"

Kurt frowned.

The thing's protruding brow shot up in surprise. "You understand me, Gerry? You do, don't you?"

Kurt's mind reeled. *The British have monsters on their*

side, creatures of Darkness fighting the war for them. The Führer doesn't know. How can we combat such beings?

They could not.

"I speak English, demon," Kurt confirmed.

The creature grinned, then looked past him at the naked woman. "We've got one, Dru," he said, tongue flicking across the fangs that protruded from his mouth. Then he studied Kurt closely. "You sank our transportation. We're going to need yours. We just had to find one of you who could soddin' understand us."

"Then you need me alive," Kurt said firmly.

The demon gave him a doubtful look. "Don't flatter yourself," it said.

It yanked his head back by the hair and sank its fangs into his throat and all the strength went out of him. Kurt could not even scream as the vampire drained his blood, ocean spray striking his face.

By the time his dead eyes opened the following night every man on board the U-28B was dead. He was among five members of the crew who had not been allowed to remain that way. Of those who rose from the dead, he was the senior officer. The vampires had given him his command even faster than the Grand Admiral could have managed.

In exchange, all they wanted was transport to their destination.

With Spike and Drusilla on the bridge of the command center, Captain Raeder and the bloodthirsty crew of the U-28B set a course for the western coast of Norway at ten knots. The diesel engines growled. The mariners drank the cold blood of their dead fellows before it could become completely stagnant.

Chapter Two

Copenhagen, Denmark
April 1st

The flowers in Kongens Have were dead. The King's Garden around Rosenborg Palace had been designed by Christian IV in 1606 and from late spring through early fall it was nearly as beautiful as the tulip gardens at Tivoli. But the thermometer hung this long night at five below zero centigrade. By the calendar it was spring, but the grounds were cold and hard and the sky unrelentingly dark.

Only the stars shone above. The moon hid its face, as though it sensed the things that were afoot and could not bear to watch.

The royal family was safely ensconced in their winter residence at Amalienborg Palace. There were only guards at Rosenborg Palace, in the heart of the city. Guards and the crown jewels they had stood sentinel over for ages.

In the dark above the palace the wind whipped the *Dannebrog*. The flag flapped loudly, like the wings of some enormous bat. It was after three o'clock in the morning and the sounds of the city had diminished to almost nothing. Under the pinpoint starlight, nothing moved that was not moved by the wind.

Almost nothing.

They slipped soundlessly along the grounds, moving from low lines of shrubbery to press themselves against the brown stone-and-mortar of the palace walls. Its elegant domes and spires spoke of a magnificence and authority within; Rosenborg Palace was a beautiful but intimidating structure. But *they* were not intimidated.

A wide cobblestone path led to the main arched entrance of the palace. The creatures that slipped through that arch were silent and deadly, but not afraid to be seen. Not afraid to be caught. They went right through the front entrance.

Vampires were an arrogant breed of monster.

There were three of them, and likely dozens of guards on the premises. But it was late and the guards tired and used only to dealing with thieves who were merely human. The courtyard was dark in the starlight, despite the lanterns set out for the guards. And the thieves could see better in the dark.

The four guards walking the interior perimeter of the palace courtyard died as swiftly beneath the fang as had those walking the outer walls. Their killers were meticulous, drinking only a bit for pleasure and moving on. Blood was a luxury that night, for they had not come to feed but to steal. Their master had given them explicit instructions. He wanted what he believed was rightly due him—the crown jewels of Denmark—and he meant to have them.

They were expert, these killers. None of their victims made the slightest sound, save for a bit of clanking as they were laid to the ground—or the corridor floor within the palace—after their necks had been broken. Blood stained pristine marble floors, spreading with the inevitable creep of death. In no time at all, more than a dozen men lay broken and lifeless.

Sophie Carstensen had known that Gorm's acolytes would attempt to steal the jewels tonight. But she had not known how or precisely when they would make their way into the rooms where the jewels were kept. If she had watched the palace from outside, they might have found a way to slip past her. The only way for her to guarantee that she would stop them was to enter the palace herself, to use all her stealth, both natural and that which had been one of the gifts she had received upon becoming the Chosen One.

The Slayer.

The one girl in all the world chosen by higher forces to fight the darkness, upon whom had been bestowed powers and abilities that made her far more than human. Just as the vampires were less. Disgusting, horrid creatures. That much was obvious.

But they had never made her cry before tonight.

From somewhere in the palace there came a tiny yowl. A small shout of pain, but not enough to bring the other guards running. Anyone close enough to hear was already dead. Sophie gritted her teeth, forced herself to remain silent and motionless. The only way she could be certain that she would stop them from stealing the jewels, and that she would be able to kill them all, was to stay precisely where she was.

A tear formed at the corner of her left eye. Much as she detested it, the tiny drop of salty water cut its way down her cheek with a heat that seemed impossible.

It was cold inside the palace. Even colder now, with death slithering about, visiting men who had families, wives, and children. Men who served the crown and did so with honor and dignity. Sophie had been born not far from Copenhagen, and she felt a loyalty to the king that sometimes surprised her.

"King and Council," she often told her watcher, Yanna. But in the presence of anyone else from the Council of Watchers, she reversed the order.

It was an odd sensation, simply waiting there in the dark. There were glass cases all around her. Within them were jeweled scepters and crowns, swords and tiaras. Wealth unlike anything she had ever known. As the Slayer, she had been able to slip into this place unnoticed. It made her think of Greta, a friend from home she had not seen in three years. Greta would have urged her to take the jewels for herself. Sophie could not even imagine doing such a thing.

She had a higher calling. She had been gifted with these abilities for a purpose—to fight the forces of darkness.

Yet sometimes those forces were too dark. Brave as she was, much as she had seen in the eight months since she had become the Slayer, skilled as she might be after seven years under Yanna's tutelage, Sophie was still merely a girl. Sixteen years old.

A naïve girl who had assumed that because she was stealthy enough to break into the palace unnoticed, the vampires would do the same. Out in the darkened corridors and on the grounds, men were dead and dying. She knew that she could not have saved them and been in place to stop the vampires in time, but that was little comfort.

The barest whisper of movement sounded in the darkness to her right. Sophie turned, eyes gazing into the shadows. A switch was thrown. Someone had attempted to turn on the lights in the display room but the dark remained. She had cut the electricity to the room upon her arrival. It had been a risk—the guards might have noticed before she could do what she had come for—but she had no regrets.

Now they were all in the dark.

Taking a slow, deep breath, she closed her eyes. Two of them. No, three. *Simple enough,* she thought.

Inside the long, heavy jacket she wore there were two finely carved wooden stakes in pockets sewn specially to fit them. Sophie did not reach for the stakes. For within her jacket she also wore something else. From a leather belt that went over her shoulder and across her chest there hung a scabbard. Within the scabbard, a Danish cavalry sword, crafted in 1734, had a double-edged blade and a shell-like guard on the hilt to protect her hand. It had been in her family for two hundred years. Her father had left behind the blade issued to him and worn the sword of his ancestors as a soldier for the king.

Hans Carstensen was dead now. So was Sophie's mother. Taken by the vampires when Gorm learned that she was the Slayer. But with sword in hand she fought for them both. For them. For King and Council. And for herself.

"It's incredible," whispered one of the vampires. "The jewels . . . even in the dark they seem to glow."

Another, nearer to her, began to reply but stopped himself. He glanced sharply in her direction. The corner of a glass case separated them, and the shelves within, and the jewels thereupon. But neither they nor the darkness hid her from the vampire.

"We are not alone. Ssshow yourself girl," the creature hissed in sibilant tones. "I can feel you. I can sssmell your fear. I can sssee you there, pale in the dark."

A shudder of revulsion burned through her, but Sophie allowed herself only one. She focused her disgust and her hatred and with a move so quick and fluid it defined the power of the Slayer in a single motion, she drew the sword from within her jacket. It slid from its scabbard with the sound of pouring salt.

Something moved behind her.

Sophie twisted, swung the sword above her head at an angle meant to save the glass all around her. The blade was silent as it descended. She followed through on the motion with her entire body, blond hair flying, long legs nearly crossed in a dance both elegant and bloody. The vampire who had attempted to fall upon her unaware flinched but had no time to withdraw before her father's sword cleaved his head from his shoulders with a crunch of bone and a tiny spurt of blood it had only just stolen from a palace guard.

Then it exploded in a cloud of dust.

She turned again, almost a pirouette, for she had always been a graceful child and was now a tall, powerful, lithe, and dangerous young woman.

"Ssslayer," whispered the vampire closest to her.

Sophie could make them out in the dark now. The one who hissed when he spoke was short and broad, a jagged scar across his hideous, demonic features. The other was thin, but bent like a wolf sniffing after prey. It looked feral, vicious but stupid.

"Why do you want the jewels?" she demanded, her tone imperious.

"They belong to our massster."

The scarred vampire regarded her cautiously, yellow eyes darting back and forth. Sophie thought he must be wondering how well she could see in the dark. *Not well,* she thought. *But well enough.* She did not rely only on her eyes.

"Your master was king almost one thousand years ago. But he died. He is no longer the king of Denmark," she said firmly.

Every muscle in her body was tense. Thrumming with energy. Her fingers flexed around the hilt of her sword. She felt the inside of the steel shell on her knuckles.

"What do you really want here?" she asked, wishing she could see the vampire's eyes more closely. Surely they would give him away. It was not mere pride that drove Gorm, she was certain. One of the artifacts encased in glass must have some other value to them, perhaps some magical property. She and Yanna had agreed upon that much.

"Only our massster's due. He will reward us handsssomely. Even more ssso, when we bring him your head, girl. More than once he hasss told me how he relishesss the feel of a Ssslayer's eyesss between his teeth. He likesss to taste what you've ssseen, or ssso he sssays. He hasss even claimed he can sssee the sssunrise as he sssswallows. I tried it once. It didn't work for me."

Sophie shook herself. Even in the dark, the vampire had been trying to mesmerize her. It was a rare talent, but some had it. She stared at him again, and then noticed the darkness behind him. The shadows within shadows.

And yet one shadow was gone.

She sensed the movement out of the corner of her eye, and turned just in time. The thin, hunched vampire crashed through the glass case to her right and Sophie recoiled. Glass shards cut her skin and she tried to duck, held up her sword hand in an instinctive attempt at defense.

The vampire grabbed her wrist. Its strength was incredible. She could not bring down her blade. She had no idea where the other was, and knew she was dead if the second one reached her. Her attacker yanked her by the hair, pulled her head back to expose her throat. It gazed into her wide, ice blue eyes and she gazed back up into its sickening yellow orbs.

With inhuman speed she reached inside her jacket with her free left hand, withdrew a stake, and drove it up into her attacker's chest. It grunted once as the wood pierced its heart, then exploded in a blast of ash.

The other was almost upon her. Sophie turned and with one fluid motion decapitated the stout, scarred vampire. Then it too was nothing but fine powder, eddying in the draft that swept across the floor.

The palace erupted in shouts of alarm. She could not know if the guards' bodies had been found or if the shattering of glass had drawn the attention of the surviving guards but they would all be converging upon her in a moment. If there were intruders in the palace, there was only one place that could possibly be their destination.

Cursing under her breath Sophie sheathed her sword and replaced the stake within her jacket. She had killed the vampires, yes. Slain them as was her duty. But she felt in her heart that she had failed. She would have to return to Yanna without the information they had needed. They did not know what Gorm was planning, nor where his new lair was.

Along a corridor off to her left Sophie heard more shouting and the sound of heavy boots running. With a quick glance around, she slipped into the shadows herself, her own boots crunching glass shards on the floor. Then she was gone, just as stealthily as she had come.

Copenhagen
April 2nd

Sophie did not cry out for the vampire to stop. There would have been no point to it. She planned to kill the creature, as it well knew. Of course it would not stop. In silence, she pursued it along the Vesterbrogade. There were still many people out on the street, despite the lateness of the hour. The crowds were thin this time of year in Tivoli Garden. Its flowers and amusements and music were not so alluring with the weather still very cold. Yet there were people about regardless.

The vampire sprinted through the front entrance, knocking over an older woman on the arm of a man who might have been her son. Sophie brushed past the man as he bent to help his mother up. Someone shouted after her. She was not surprised, of course. The sight of a young girl in a dark, loose dress chasing a powerful-looking man through the front entrance of Tivoli was sure to raise a few eyebrows.

Better not to slow down, not to let them get too close a look.

Yanna was somewhere behind her, but Sophie did not dare wait for her Watcher to catch up. There were clouds in the darkness above, blotting out the stars. Even the many lights of the garden and the amusement rides did not truly illuminate the park. Sophie ran, eyes searching for the vampire ahead. It had only beaten her inside by mere seconds. No way could the creature have escaped her notice so quickly. There were small clutches of people wandering within, mostly couples. She heard laughter.

Another shout as she ran past, long legs flying, heart pumping. She leaped a long row of tulips.

The lake. Then nothing.

Sophie stopped and spun around. She had lost the vampire and was now furious. Another chance at forcing Gorm's location out of one of his acolytes, and once more she had let the opportunity slip her grasp.

With a series of sudden pops, the sky lit up with multi-colored fireworks. Sophie recoiled for a moment, expecting some sort of attack. When she realized what had happened she cursed her foolishness. She felt the thundrous booming of the fireworks reverberating within her. They were a frequent event at Tivoli. Those souls who had braved the cold stood staring up at the sky, green and red and orange flickering across their faces.

She studied them. All looking up . . . all but one.

At the far edge of the cluster of people, one man, trying not to be noticed, trying to hide within his jacket. Not watching the fireworks at all. It was the vampire, Ernst. He was not looking at her.

Swift as she was able, Sophie moved to her right and behind those gathered to watch the spectacle. The colors flickered across the sky, across Tivoli itself. She moved in and around the people, as inconspicuously as possible. Moments later she reached the spot where she had seen Ernst.

But the vampire was gone.

Sophie cursed under her breath just as a hand touched her shoulder. She spun, reaching into her jacket for a stake, but it was Yanna. The Watcher's brow was furrowed.

"He got away?" Yanna asked.

The Slayer could only nod. She tried not to look at her Watcher's face, at the deepening lines around her green eyes. They were both frustrated, but Sophie could not bear to disappoint her again.

Yet when she looked up, Yanna was smiling. "It's all right. We'll find Gorm. And you'll have another chance at Ernst as well."

"I've let you down," Sophie said, voice low.

"You did your best," Yanna reassured her, trying to pat down her hair, which was wild from the chase. "We have had this conversation several times, Sophie. Your level of skill and accomplishment far outstrips all but the greatest Slayers on record. And you're just getting started."

Yanna was not yet forty, relatively young for a Watcher, but her eyes were old. Sophie looked down at her—the older woman was much shorter than she—and sighed, letting out a long breath she had been unconsciously holding. Yanna smiled warmly and slipped her arm inside Sophie's, and the two walked out of Tivoli and onto Vesterbrogade again.

"I only wish we knew what Gorm was after," Sophie said. She shook her head in frustration. "He thinks he can rule Denmark again. He wants to make it a kingdom of the dead. Whatever he's looking for, he must think it can—"

"I know what he's after," Yanna said simply.

Sophie froze. She turned to stare at Yanna. "If you knew what he was after—"

"I've only just learned. I had a communiqué from the Council today. They've determined that Gorm must be trying to find the Helm of Haraxis," Yanna explained.

Sophie continued to stare, brow furrowed.

"Haraxis was an ancient warrior and sorcerer. It was said that he wore an enchanted helm with his armor, and that with that helm he could command all manner of supernatural creatures."

They were out on the cobblestoned street now. As they moved away from Tivoli there were fewer and fewer people on the street. Even the lights of the city seemed dimmer.

"Oh my God," Sophie whispered. She felt as though all the energy were draining out of her. "If Gorm were to get his hands on it, he could . . . raise an entire army of demons. He would truly have the power to transform Denmark into a kingdom of the dead."

Yanna smiled. "He could. But he won't."

"How can you be so calm?" Sophie cried, her voice ringing along the cobblestoned street, off the stone faces of buildings.

An older man walking with a cane paused half a block up to turn and stare at them.

"One report, more than fifty years ago, hinted that the Helm was part of the collection of Denmark's crown jewels. Gorm obviously believes it, but it isn't true. The Helm is in a cave on the west coast of America, guarded by wood spirits and other forces of nature and order," Yanna explained.

Sophie allowed herself to smile. "He'll never find it."

"Not before we find him, at least," Yanna said firmly. "And we *will* find him, Sophie. If not tonight, then tomorrow night. When we destroy Gorm, Copenhagen will be far safer. Then we can move on to other places, other monsters. I have every confidence that decades and centuries from now, when the Council discusses the greatest Slayers who ever served our cause, you will be among them."

"You flatter me," Sophie said, blushing.

"Not at . . ." In midsentence, Yanna seemed to drift away. Her gaze became blank and unfocused and she swayed a bit on her feet. After a moment she shuddered as though with revulsion. Her eyes went wide, her body rigid, and a tiny gasp escaped her lips.

"Yanna?" Sophie said in alarm. She bent so that her face was mere inches from that of her Watcher. "Yanna come back."

The older woman blinked, her gaze regained its focus. Her countenance, which had been blank mere moments before, transformed dramatically. Her expression hardened, her breathing sped up, her jaw tightened. She might have been furious if not for the ashen color of her skin and the moisture at the corners of her eyes. Sophie had never seen the Watcher cry.

"What is it?" she asked, voice timid and girlish. "What did you see?"

"War," Yanna replied firmly.

She glanced around to see if anyone could hear them, but the streets had cleared completely. Sophie thought it was eerie when there was not a soul to be seen on the streets of Copenhagen. The city was normally so alive, even late at night.

"The Germans are going to attack." Yanna's eyes had dried but her expression was grim. "Soon their soldiers will sweep across Denmark. They will conquer."

Sophie shook her head, angry herself now. "That can't be. We . . . there's a treaty. And they're too busy with

Poland and . . . why here? Why would they attack us? What have we done?"

"Nothing. Hitler wants all of Europe. We're just a stop along the way. A treaty will mean nothing to them. I have seen it."

"Are you sure?" Sophie asked, almost pleading. "This is . . . this is my home, Yanna. Are you *sure*? Your visions are sometimes quite vague."

"Not this one."

A chill ran through the Slayer, but she stood a little straighter. Not far off a church bell began to chime midnight. "We'll stay. We'll fight. I won't allow it."

Yanna grabbed her hand and squeezed it. Sophie swallowed hard but refused to look at her Watcher.

"This is an *army*. Even if you could fight them yourself I have seen it. There's nothing you can do. I don't know when the attack will come, but it's soon. We'll go back to our rooms and pack our things, and we'll go to England. The Council will want to decide how best to utilize you during this time."

"I won't leave," Sophie said grimly.

Yanna stood up a little straighter, chin tilted up so that she was at her most dignified. "As the Slayer, you have certain responsibilities. One of them is to stay alive and active as long as possible. You know the risks of your duties as well as anyone. You might well die. But if you do, it will not be because you threw your life away."

Sophie felt as though she were deflating. "What about Gorm?" she asked, half defeated.

"The Germans will kill him, or he will still be here when we return. We won't forget about him, Sophie. But we must withdraw now."

"Could we warn the king at least?"

"How would you propose we do that?" Yanna asked. "There is a treaty, as you said. Shall we tell them I had a vision?"

"There must be something we can do!" Sophie cried. In one of the homes a bit farther up the street, a dog began to bark, alarmed by her outburst.

"Yes," Yanna agreed. "We can survive."

As they hurried back to their boarding house—where they were thought by landlord and boarders to be aunt and niece—Sophie retreated within her own thoughts. Copenhagen was her city. Her father had fought for Denmark, but now she was expected to abandon her king to safeguard her own life. She knew it was more complicated than that, knew that her duties to the world were more important than her duties to her homeland, but those thoughts weighed heavily upon her. The idea that she would be running—and leaving her home unprotected—was an ache in her soul that Sophie did not think she would ever be able to cure.

For her part, Yanna also kept silent. Sophie was torn. But as always, she would do what must be done, no matter how much it pained her.

They left the cobblestoned streets at the center of the city. The paved roads in the rest of Copenhagen were almost as deserted, save for several automobiles that rumbled by them. Some time later, they turned into Madvigs Alle and walked halfway down the block to their boarding house. Their rooms were on the fourth floor at the back of the building, at a corner where the gabled roof was accessible from the windows. At least, for the Slayer they were.

For other things as well.

When they entered their apartment, the smell wafted over them. Sophie nearly retched it was so putrid. Holding her breath, she drew her father's sword from its scabbard and motioned for Yanna to stay back. The Watcher had her hands over her face, eyes watering from the stench. Despite the noxious odor, Yanna closed the door. Whatever was about to happen was for them alone to deal with.

At the end of the short hall, Sophie pushed open the door to her room and lunged inside, sword at the ready. A Quetz demon—all quills and fangs—sat on the wooden plank floor feasting on the remains of a large dog. The mutt had been dead for quite some time. The window was open and the chill wind blew in, but even that could not erase the smell.

"Tycho!" Sophie snapped.

Yanna appeared in the doorway. "Good lord," she said. "How long has that animal been dead?"

Tycho, the Quetz demon, glanced up at them. "Hello," he said amiably, mangling the Danish tongue. "I could smell this fellow in the back alley and the longer I waited the hungrier I became."

"It reeks," Sophie said curtly.

"Sorry." Tycho offered her a sheepish look. "I have good news, though."

"You've been gone three weeks," Yanna scolded him. "We thought you were dead."

Tycho shrugged. "I get distracted. You know that."

"The dog, Tycho," Yanna said, and coughed as if to punctuate her disgust. "Get it out of here."

The Quetz demon's quills ran all down its back and arms. Now they lay down flat and looked almost as though Tycho were wearing a coat of some sort. Despite his fangs, when he pouted Tycho looked pitiful.

"I said I was sorry," he whined. "I'll take it out now. I just thought you would want to hear my good news."

Sophie could not help but feel bad for the lonely, somewhat simple demon. He had certainly not meant any harm.

"What's your news then?" she demanded.

Tycho brightened. He looked from one to the other of them expectantly, apparently hoping to build a certain amount of suspense that, in the presence of the stench of long-dead dog, Sophie certainly did not feel.

"Well?" she asked impatiently.

The demon apparently took her impatience for suspense, and finally gave in.

"Gorm," he said. "I know where his lair is."

Sophie's breath caught in her throat. Heart racing she looked over at Yanna, whose expression was grimmer than ever.

"Yanna," she said, the one word heavy with import.

The Watcher closed her eyes, pursed her lips tightly, thinking. When she opened them, she shot Sophie a grave look. "I will pack. We are leaving in the morning. I will make all the arrangements. I expect you back within an hour past dawn," she said.

Tycho was using his three rows of fangs to tear into the dead dog's leg. Sophie stood over him and glared down, her displeasure obvious.

"Get rid of the dog. Now," she instructed him. "Then you can show me. If I must leave, so be it. But now that we know where he is, I won't leave while Gorm is alive."

Chapter Three

Bodø, Norway
A.D. 837

The night seemed to last forever.

Gudrod reveled in it. For without the dreaded sun, he could walk the frozen earth unimpeded. He stood upon the crest of a snowy hill, looking down upon the fjord below. The ship was moored in the shallows but this far north the men were forced to break the ice around the vessel almost constantly to keep it from being locked in.

It would not do for them to be trapped here after all this time. After working so hard and killing so many to discover the secrets of this particular fjord.

The world was night and ice. The half-dozen men he had brought with him onto the land carried torches, which guttered in the chill winds with the shuddering of the men. Even beneath their heavy clothes and their mail, the men were cold. Gudrod did not feel it. Where the breath of the others plumed in the air around their heads, Gudrod had no breath to give.

"We go," he announced.

They obeyed in silence, these Viking warriors. Though they were merely human, he knew that they would persevere. Once, he had been one of them. Now they were together again, following him for the promise of power undreamed of, for the secrets of the gods.

The men he had chosen to accompany him did not balk at the job set out for them. Those left behind on the ship were another thing entirely. Despite Gudrod's nature they had accepted him as simply another form of berserker. In battle, they had no leader who was his equal, none as skilled or as bloodthirsty. But if they knew their purpose in this expedition, they would have killed him themselves.

"Come," he grunted to the others. "The wealth of the gods shall be ours."

He set off along the ridge overlooking the fjord, oblivious to the wind. His axe hung at his right side and his sword at the left. His long black hair flowed over his shoulders and his beard was stiff with ice. Many of the others wore caps of fur and leather, but just as he did not bother with a helmet for battle, he had no use for a cap now.

For hours they walked and the long night wore on. They lost sight of the ship quickly enough, and traveled deeper and deeper into the fjord, much farther than the ship could ever have gone. Several of the torches burned down to nothing and were left behind to sizzle in the snow. Still Gudrod led them on. He did not need a flame to see by.

The pass was exactly where he had been told it would be. The craggy path that descended along the inner wall of the fjord would have been invisible from top or bottom and he only found it because he knew exactly what he was looking for.

With a triumphant laugh, the Viking leader started along the hidden pass. The way was treacherous, the wind gusting fast enough to bend them over. Ice and snow lashed at their faces, kicked up off the ground by the wind. Gudrod glanced back and saw that his warriors were shivering, their teeth chattering, their skin blue and stiff. The path in the fjord wall was so narrow in some places that they had to stand with their backs to the jagged stone and hold on with each gust of wind to be sure they were not dashed upon the rocks below or tossed into the icy fjord at the base of the wall.

But still they kept on.

All for the sake of plunder.

It was only when they came upon the cave entrance that they hesitated. The opening in the wall was narrow and shallow and only by stepping into it was it possible to see that the cave did not stop half a dozen feet in. That was illusion. Rather, it *turned*. After which it widened and became a tunnel large enough for two large men to walk abreast.

His warriors, Vikings all, savage men with a taste for rape and riches and fire, paused at the opening of the cave, fear etched on their faces. The man in front, a huge, red-bearded man called Stig, seemed most reluctant of all.

"Come on, you fools, out of the wind," Gudrod assailed them. "You knew where I was taking you. It is too late to stay behind with the others."

Stig's gaze hardened. "It is one thing to hear of it and another to see it," he said. "I am not certain I have ever believed in the gods, but if this is here . . . then the other things you said might be true."

"They *are* true."

"Woden will destroy us," Stig countered, still unwilling to go any farther into the cave.

With a snarl, Gudrod changed. Ridges erupted across his forehead and nose and fangs sprouted from his mouth. He reached for Stig, hauled the man to him with impossible strength, and yanked his chin back to reach his throat with such ferocity that the human's neck broke with a grinding of bone. He tore a chunk of flesh away and drank the blood that gouted from the wound, even as the other warriors looked on.

The warm ichor splashed his face.

Gudrod knocked Stig's cap away and held him by the hair. His legs were still kicking, limbs still twitching.

"Drink with me, all of you. Anyone who does not drink dies just the same way. Then we enter the tomb of the old gods, and we take whatever we can find. I know not if any others lie here, but I have been told that Freyja's bones lie within, and her magicks as well."

"Who told you thus?" demanded Jarl, the one he trusted the most among them.

"The one who killed her, and lay her here," Gudrod told him.

Jarl drank. So did the others.

Together they entered, in search of the bones of the goddess Freyja and a great deal more besides.

Galdhöpiggen, Norway
April 2nd, 1940

It hurt to move.

Drusilla had been cold before. For the most part, it never bothered her. Her mind was so often away from her body that her skull barely felt like home anymore. But this was different. She and Spike had been forced to swim ashore outside Bergen several days before. They had needed warm clothing and transportation and had killed for both. But even the heavy wool sweaters and jackets they now wore were not enough to protect them from the elements.

They were halfway up the side of the tallest mountain in Norway. The wind that swept the face of the mountain cut through them without mercy. Initially Drusilla had paid it little attention, though Spike had complained a bit. When it had grown cold enough that even she could not ignore it, she studied her physical reaction to the temperature with curiosity. She was dead. The cold could not kill her. But vampires did not have any internal body heat save for what they stole from the blood of others and it had been too long since they had made a fresh kill. When she moved, climbing the mountain, her bones ached as if she were not only still human, but old.

Interesting. But only enough to hold her attention for a few seconds at a time. There was no danger in it, after all. Spike seemed to have grown depressed, however, and Drusilla wanted to cheer him up. He was her special boy, after all.

"Look at the stars, Spike." Drusilla sighed happily. "The moon is hiding from them; they're triumphant. It's so beautiful."

"Yeah. Bloody magnificent," he groaned.

Her eyes went wide, her lips opening in the tiniest pout. "What's wrong, pet?"

"I'm cold, that's what's wrong."

"Ohhh, my baby," she cooed, reaching out to stroke his cheek. "Don't worry. Next time we see some people I promise we'll eat them, all right? Lots of hot sticky blood for you. We'll make it sing."

Spike allowed a thin smile. "You always know just what to say, Dru."

They were both quiet after that. The mountain seemed to breathe beneath them, and Drusilla studied the sounds it made, the way the snow *shush*ed beneath her boots, and the secrets the wind told as it caressed the peak above. From time to time Spike would grumble, and the noise of him, his nearness to her, would remind her what they were doing there on the mountain. She tended to be a bit forgetful.

Her anniversary. Eighty years as a vampire. Her *birthday*. It wasn't too far off now, later in the year, and Spike had asked her what she wanted. Drusilla was lucid enough to realize that most vampires did not receive gifts on that day, but it was a tradition begun for her by Angelus even before she had made Spike a vampire.

Angelus.

He always wanted to celebrate her rebirth to the darkness, and would shower her with special things. All the rest of the year she had whatever she wanted, the finest gowns, the most sparkling baubles. But her birthday, that was different. Then Angelus would give her something completely unique, one of a kind in the world. A painting. A sculpture. An object of power. Once upon a time he had given her Rasputin's Eye, magickally preserved. With it she could control the will of any living creature. Truly one of a kind. A piece of history, and of powerful sorcery. Dear Angelus had not even been angry with her when she had given it back to Rasputin. The demon had simply been too pitiful for her to say no, and quite sweet in his way.

Angelus.

Even after he had decided she should not be so reliant upon him, and had brought Spike to her, a wild young man to feast upon, and to make her lover, Angelus would never forget her birthday. Spike bristled at the attentions Angelus gave her, and got unique trinkets for her as well. Angelus would disappear for months, sometimes longer, but he never forgot her birthday. Until the first time he did. After that he never remembered again. Drusilla did not know what year that was or how long it had been, for it was all quite fresh in her mind and she had never been very good at keeping track of time.

After Angelus had abandoned them, Spike continued the tradition. Always something special, something unique. Perhaps he did not even realize it, or perhaps he merely pretended he did not, but Spike was competing with the shadow of Angelus's memory. When it came to what Spike thought was a milestone, the fiftieth, sixtieth, seventieth anniversary of her blood-drenched nativity, his gift would be even more magnificent.

But this was the first time Drusilla had thought of something she *wanted*. The first time ever she knew what to ask for. Ages ago, when she had first heard of Freyja's Strand, the necklace of the Brisings, she had been told that it would allow whoever wore it to take on the appearance of anyone. A powerful glamour, to change one's face at will, a giddy little game to play, and a useful tool if one had enemies.

It made her curious, but not for long. Few things did.

Then, only a handful of months ago, she had heard another story about Freyja's Strand, a little known side effect of its glamour and magick.

If the one wearing it was a vampire, she would be able to see her own reflection as long as she had it on. The reflection of her own face, or whatever guise she might use the necklace's power to adopt.

Sometimes Drusilla forgot she was really there, a tangible creature and not some ghost of a memory, drifting about the world, only observing. That was one of the reasons she loved Spike so much. He was her anchor, kept her rooted, stopped her from drifting away forever. When they made love, and they hurt each other, it made her feel like *flesh*. But seeing herself again . . .

In the eighty years since Drusilla had become a vampire, she had forgotten what her face looked like. If she could see her reflection, it would help her feel more real.

Less like a whisper.

Whispers . . .

Drusilla frowned, then glanced around curiously. They were not alone up there in the snow and the frozen wind. There were whispers all around and they drew her attention now. She listened with growing wonder, though also with a bit of sadness. They were grim whispers, and she was drawn to them, wrapped up in them and carried off just a bit.

The stars were dead by now, but their light reached her, there on the mountain. Just as the sound of those whispers reached her, though the whisperers themselves were as extinct as the stars. She drifted and could no longer remember what she had been thinking so much about only a moment before.

Spike loved Drusilla more than anything. He could deny her nothing. But he had long since begun to wish she had asked him for something a bit simpler to acquire than Freyja's Strand. Still, he had promised, and he was not about to let his baby down.

With the wind whipping at him, his body temperature still dropping, Spike hunched over farther and continued to climb. From time to time he stopped to check the map he had marked at the start of their trek. Adrienne had given him coordinates and landmarks, but at a certain point they would simply have to simply keep their eyes open and hope. This far north the days were still incredibly short, but if they failed to find Skrymir's lair by dawn, that would not matter at all. A few minutes of daylight or many hours, it did not matter. The sun would kill them just the same.

Only moments after that thought went through Spike's mind Drusilla stopped abruptly. He had been following her and nearly knocked her over.

"Dru?" he asked, concerned.

"I can hear the clang of axe on bone. It echoes. Can you hear it, too?"

Spike nearly uttered an automatic reply, a denial, of course. Drusilla spoke so frequently in mad little riddles, insanity turned into lilting poetry. It was one of the things he loved most about her, the way she perceived the world's beauty and horror so much more keenly than anyone else he had ever met. She was sane enough to realize that most of her perceptions were hers alone, and did not usually ask if he shared them. When she did, he never lied.

The words *of course not* were on the tip of his tongue.

But then he saw the tumble of gray stone that lay ahead of them, set within an enormous crevasse that seemed cleaved out of the mountainside by some colossal blade. They had reached their destination. The stronghold of

Skrymir. Once, centuries upon centuries before, it had been a Viking castle. Now it lay in ruins.

It was not a castle, but the ghost of one.

Somewhere beneath, in the bowels of those ruins, the demon Skrymir made his home. If the legends were to be believed, Skrymir had been there when the Vikings still roamed the land, and even before, when the gods of Norse mythology thrived, when giants and dark elves and hideous dwarfs populated the northlands. Spike had seen enough in his life to believe anything, but he knew he did not believe in gods. There had been a time when monsters stalked the long nights, and then there had come a time of heroes, men and women brave enough to face the things in the dark.

Not gods, just humans.

The monsters, though, he certainly believed in those. If legends could be believed, Skrymir was one of them. Spike did not know if he had ever met a creature as old as this demon was supposed to be. He wondered about it, those ages past, and what the demon's eyes had seen.

It echoes, Dru had said. *Can you hear it too?*

Staring at the gray stone corpse before him, Spike paused.

"You know, love, I think I can," he whispered.

"So much blood," she told him. "Old blood."

Together they carefully started to climb down into the crevasse toward the devastated stronghold. Spike found, to his amazement, that he did not feel cold anymore. Not at all.

Dawn was hours away, but Spike was anxious. They were still on the snow-covered side of an enormous mountain. The ancient, crumbling stone stronghold around them offered little by way of shelter, but it was going to have to be enough. Even if they could not find a surviving chamber or even a bolthole into which they might withdraw, the tumbled walls at least would provide shade from the sun.

They had to.

"You still hear anything, Dru?" he asked, and flinched as his own voice echoed back to him from the crevasse around them.

Drusilla was perhaps thirty feet away, caressing the smooth edge of stone that might once have been part of a window. She touched the cool rock surface as though it were her lover, and gazed at it as though at any moment she expected it to speak, and she dared not miss a word.

Spike frowned at her lack of response, and kept looking. The place was a shambles. Snow had piled up on the floor and across the rubble, though there were a couple of spots where enough roof remained to cast the illusion that they were still inside. The ruins extended much farther than they had appeared to from above. Entire portions of the foundation—where the walls had fallen down completely—were covered by snow. Shattered arches and other supports had not been visible from above and even down among them the snow obscured detail.

They searched every corner, moved stones away to reveal tiny hollows in the rubble, trod every inch of snow, even along the perimeter of this structure. According to Adrienne, it had once been Skrymir's stronghold. Which might well have been true at one time, but certainly was not now.

"That little trollop," Spike grumbled to himself. He wished he hadn't dusted her so he could go back and hurt her first.

"Spike?"

Drusilla was out in the snow, meandering among the portion of the stronghold that had been completely leveled. He realized she must have heard him speak. Frustrated, he realized that it would do neither of them any good to dwell on it.

"Nothing, poodle," he called.

The wind had picked up, and snow was whisked right through even the standing portions of the structure. It swirled and eddied inside, where the breezes fought for supremacy. Spike looked around again. He had noted several spots where they might hide themselves away during the day. Nothing substantial, but enough. As he examined them he concluded that the best was a spot between an extant stretch of wall and a fallen stone column. There was a strip of roof above the spot still. They would be forced to move several times during the day, more than likely. But at least they would not fry.

Spike shuddered with the wind. The cold was getting to him again. Down inside his bones. He knew that if they slept, they would wake with frost crusting their eyes closed, perhaps clogging their nostrils. It would not be the first time such things had happened to him. Just to open their eyes, they might have to build a fire to thaw out.

Where they would get the wood was another concern entirely. He had flint and matches and other things small enough to stick inside his pockets. Cigarettes and a battered metal lighter. But lugging firewood up a mountainside . . . he had expected that the ruins of the stronghold would contain some wood but all he had seen so far was stone. And snow.

"Spike?"

He turned, frowning. There was a strange tone in her voice. Even for Dru. In retrospect, he thought it had also been there the first time she had called out for him. A kind of darkness swept over him, thicker than the night that surrounded them. Something touched him in the depths of his demon soul. It was an uncommon presence but he recognized it.

Fear.

Dru might be alarmed, even frightened for him. In her own cold, dead heart, though, there was no fear.

Yet now there was something in her voice which quavered with something near it. Perhaps not fear. He thought he could place it now, that tone. It was dread.

Spike ran. He tripped over some rubble beneath the snow and stumbled, went down hard. His left knee banged into something and he cursed loudly. But he ignored his pain and pulled himself up on the edge of a large chunk of stone that looked as though it had once been a statue. With growing alarm he rushed out past the wall, beyond the limits of the stronghold's original foundation. The sky was lightening to the east. Dawn was not more than half an hour off, but for once he was not thinking about the sun.

Only of Dru.

He saw her, and came to a sudden stop up to his calves in snow where it had blown and drifted deeper.

Drusilla was about twenty feet away, sitting in the snow. Her legs were thrust out from her at odd angles as though she were a marionette dropped there by its owner. Her head hung down and to one side, completing the image. She was silent and unmoving and Spike's mind concocted any number of horrible things that might have happened to her.

Then she moved. Her raven hair had been across her face like a veil, but now that she looked up it fell away to reveal her vampiric features beneath. Even with the brief distance between them, her eyes seemed to glow yellow, which Spike guessed was only reflected moonlight.

Her face proved it. She would not have shifted her appearance unless she felt threatened somehow.

"Dru, what is it, love? What's happened?" he asked, still moving toward her. Spike fell on his knees in the snow before her. "What's got under your skin?"

Spike touched her cheek. Her flesh seemed even more like marble than ever, cold and pale. Snow blew across her face. Drusilla tilted her head to one side and ran her tongue over her fangs as she regarded him.

"We're not alone."

Simple as that. Spike blinked, looked at her. "Is it Skrymir?" he asked. "You've figured out where he is?"

"I don't think so. Do you remember when we slept in the morgue with all the pretty children, with their bows and their naughty faces and their cold, cold blood?" she asked, utterly sincere. "They're here with us now, dancing on the snow, waiting for the mountain to fall."

"That was in Chicago, Dru. Right before the World's Fair. Half a world away," Spike told her, and stood up again. Drusilla was all right, but she had clearly sensed something. Not the ghosts of slaughtered children, certainly, but something cold and slow and cruel.

"They don't want us here," Drusilla said, her voice certain. Then it changed. She stood and went to him, her face smooth and lovely again, her eyes wide, her voice like a little girl's. "Let's taunt them, Spike. Oh, can we? Let's tell them we're having a party and they're not invited. Tea and scones. Is it all right?"

Spike turned slowly, his boots cutting through the snow. With the sky lightening, he stared at their surroundings more carefully. The ruins were a dead end. He felt that strongly, and Drusilla's moment of prescience had not come within the stronghold but here, on the snow. They were down inside the crevasse, and there was nothing else down there with them, save for the rubble. Nothing but ice and snow that had built up on the craggy walls of this cut into the flesh of the mountain. Spike studied the walls and found that his gaze kept roving back to one particular spot, where an odd outcropping from the wall beneath had provided the foundation for an even stranger formation of ice and snow.

It was beyond Drusilla perhaps thirty yards and a bit higher up inside the crevasse, closer to the heart of the mountain.

"They don't want me to have my prize," Drusilla whispered petulantly behind him.

Spike trudged across the bottom of the crevasse. The snow deepened as he got closer to the wall. It was above his knees when he came close enough to the ice formation to reach out and touch it.

The wall began to rumble as though an avalanche were about to occur. The formation cracked down the center and snow spilled off it along with shards of broken ice. The ice was splintered, cracking all around the bizarre outcropping. Separating.

It began to move.

Spike staggered backward, staring at the ice formation. It cracked and surged as though something beneath it were trying to break free. He had moved back a dozen feet, peering at the ice in an attempt to see what was behind it.

With a pop that resounded throughout the crevasse, the top of the formation finally split. The left side of the shattered ice broke away from the stone beneath . . . and turned to look at him.

Its eyes were blue and cold and its mouth was filled with jagged white shards.

"What the f—"

It reached for him then, one arm breaking away from the frozen body to strike impossibly fast. Spike was only just out of range, but he felt the wind of its icy claws pass by his face, impossibly cold. Sub-zero. It made the air around him feel balmy by comparison.

Still up to his knees, Spike turned and thundered through the snow toward Drusilla. For her part, she only stood staring at the creature, a tiny smile playing at the corners of her mouth.

"Dru, run!" he shouted. "Get inside the ruins. Hide behind a wall. Just go!"

But Drusilla did not move. Spike could hear the crackling behind him, the tinkling of tiny bits of ice sliding down a frozen surface. He stared at Drusilla but her eyes were locked on the creature behind him. *Skrymir,* he thought. It could be. But if so, they needed the demon calm before they could talk to him.

"They're beautiful," Drusilla said suddenly. "All prisms and sharp edges. And they make music like wind chimes."

Spike paid little attention to her observations, save for one. A single word, in fact. *They.* "Oh, right," he muttered to himself. "Why the hell not. More the merrier." Then he looked back and saw that Drusilla was right. The ice formation had split down the middle to produce not one but two enormous creatures. Their bodies were jagged points and ridges, their heads covered in spikes that might have been icicles if they didn't look so deadly. The first of the monsters to emerge was roughly eleven feet tall. This new one was even bigger, and broader across as well.

He cried out again for Drusilla to find shelter and he ran as fast as he could manage in the snow. It was not as deep now—halfway to his knees—but it was still deep enough to slow him down.

They were almost upon him.

"Right, that's it then," he grumbled.

He stopped short in the snow and turned to face them. The lumbering ice creatures came on, thundering toward them. Snow kicked up by their massive feet sprayed all around. The sky continued to lighten, dawn twenty minutes away at best.

"That's far enough!" he shouted at them.

The larger one faltered. The smaller came on without the slightest pause. Spike swore under his breath.

"Just hold on now, boys," he said loudly, trying another approach. "Look, we're here to see Skrymir. Maybe that's one of you—"

The ice monster barely slowed. Ice and snow spattered Spike's face as it approached. As it reached out and batted him away the frozen skewers on its knuckles tore into his face and made him cry out in pain and anger.

Spike hit the snow, rolled, and was up instantly. His face and flesh were so cold that he did not bleed even a drop. He felt the contortion of his features, the elongating of his canines.

"Round one to you," he said.

"Trespasser," rumbled one of the giants, its voice like an avalanche.

"Shut your gob," Spike snapped.

The two of them moved on him, slower now, edging around to trap him between them. He bumped something behind him and jumped, startled. It was Drusilla. Her eyes sparkled with glee.

"This is fun. Like having enormous pets. They're not very bright, though, are they?"

"Fun?" Spike asked, eyeing the monsters. "They'll likely kill us in a moment, Dru. To my mind, killing's only fun when *we're* doing it."

She looked sad at his scolding. Then she brightened. "Perhaps you could drop a wall on them?"

He glanced at her, but only for a single eyeblink. Then he grabbed her arm and they were running together for the ruins of Skrymir's stronghold. She ought to have run before, but he was glad she had not. Spike was certain the monsters would catch them before they reached the stronghold, but they somehow managed to get there ahead of the ice giants.

It was a pitifully simple plan. They moved inside the ruins, waited until the things had come in after them, then slipped back out and rammed their bodies against one of the walls that was still standing. There was no give, not even a loosening of mortar. The creatures were moving, coming around to the other side. Together, Spike and Drusilla tried a second time.

Spike dislocated his shoulder and roared with the pain. He bit into his lower lip and found a bit of blood that was not frozen.

"So much for that," he grunted. "We're dead, we are."

Even as he said it, what remained of the ceiling of the stronghold cracked and then collapsed under its own weight and that of the snow on top of it. Enormous chunks of rubble rained down onto the ice giants. Spike darted around to one side of the wall to see them being smashed to thousands of shards of ice. A moment later, the rumble had subsided and the creatures were no more.

Drusilla fixed his shoulder with one powerful tug on his arm. He roared with pain, but when it was over, he laughed and shook his head.

Spike grinned, face transforming once more, becoming as close to human as he would ever appear. He turned to Dru, pulled her to him and put his hands on her body, rough as she liked it. With a deep kiss, he explored her mouth and found surprising warmth there. When he pulled back, she watched him with mischief dancing in her eyes.

"In the snow," she whispered, her chest rising and falling in an aroused imitation of life.

With a laugh, filled with exhilaration from the luck of their survival, Spike nipped her lower lip.

"I am your humble servant, milady," he growled. Spike pressed his forehead against Drusilla's, grinning. Then he frowned thoughtfully and glanced over at the shattered remains of the creatures. "Any idea what those things were, then?"

"They were Frost Demons."

The response came from behind him. Spike whirled, ready for a fight.

"You seek Skrymir," the demon said. "I am he."

If Spike had not seen Skrymir move and speak, he would have thought the demon a statue or some kind of sculpture in ice. Jagged shards of ice hung down from his arms and long talons. When he opened his mouth it appeared that Skrymir's teeth were also ice. A ragged, frosty formation suggested hair and pointed ears. Green energy like fire crackled around his eyes. Long wings fluttered behind him, somehow without cracking their icy coating. With the lightening of the horizon signifying the approaching dawn, he could see that there was color beneath the ice, but unfocused and changing as if he were looking at the demon through a faceted window or a fishbowl.

"Ooh, Spike, look at him. He's all sparkly," Drusilla cooed.

Spike ignored her, though she was right. The effect of the light reflecting upon the ice coating Skrymir made him appear almost to be an enormous gargoyle carved of diamond. The demon crouched on frozen hooves before an opening in the wall of the crevasse that must have been the entrance to his lair and watched them expectantly.

"Well?" Skrymir asked, his voice deep and resonant. "Surely you did not come all this way to admire my grandeur."

Sarcasm. Spike liked him already. Might have to kill him, of course, but liked him just the same.

"Grandeur? That what you call it?" he prodded. "Look like a bloody ugly snowman, y'ask me. So you're him, eh? Truth is I was half convinced you were just a myth."

Drusilla's eyes were wide, watching Skrymir, as she slipped up next to Spike. He casually put an arm around her waist. The demon rose up on his hooves a bit, extending his wings as he glared down upon them.

Then he laughed, and the sound was like boots crunching on hard snow.

"You are crude and insolent. But I have come to expect that from vampires. I am a myth, leech. But *just* a myth?

Hardly. As for my appearance, perhaps you are right. Perhaps I place too much value on pageantry."

With a sudden crackle and a cry of delight from Drusilla, Skrymir shuddered and transformed. Large shards split off from his huge form like splinters calving from an iceberg. His frozen wings shattered. Mere seconds after it had begun he stood before them, entirely new. Where previously he had the aspect of a huge gargoyle he looked now almost like a man, but taller and thinner, and yet still with that covering of ice that only hinted at the color beneath. But that color churned and swirled like smoke or flowing mercury.

Spike would not say it, but he was startled. Whatever sort of demon Skrymir was, it was nothing Spike had seen before.

"Nice trick," Spike drawled. "A little surprised you know how to speak English actually." Unmindful of the sun crawling ever nearer the horizon and their obvious need to hurry, he took a cigarette out and lit it.

Skrymir walked toward them, eyes on Drusilla now, taking her measure and quite obviously appreciating what he saw.

"I know a great many things that would surprise you, Spike," the demon said, almost sneering. He reached out with his frozen talons and brushed Drusilla's hair away from her face. "And you must be Drusilla. As lovely as I have heard."

Drusilla made a tiny noise of pleasure in her throat. "Aren't you something?" she whispered. "I saw a little boy frozen in ice once, eyes staring up from under the lake. His tiny arm broke when I pulled him out, and his skin was blue. I gave him a lick. Vanilla ice cream with fear sprinkled on top. I can still taste him."

"What an intriguing thought," Skrymir said.

Spike bristled, stepping between them. Drusilla grunted as though an electrical current had been broken between herself and the demon. Spike glared at him, the smile on his features enhancing, rather than hiding, the jealousy and anger in his dead heart.

"Enough playing around here. We came to talk. Let's talk. You gonna stand out here and watch us burn or you gonna let us in?"

Skrymir smiled, and the doubling effect of it, the suggestion of the face within his icy visage, was haunting. "By all means come in. You've killed my door guards. The least I can do is show you some hospitality."

The demon turned and walked toward the hole in the side of the crevasse. Sunlight broke over the top edge of the crack in the earth where they stood. It would not be long until it rose high enough to spead its killing light down upon them.

"Your guards attacked us," Spike retorted, still angry.

Just inside the icy cave entrance, Skrymir turned to shoot Spike a withering glance. Evil shimmered off him in waves, but more than evil. Danger. Polite, yes. But as he had already proven, there was far more to this demon than Spike had expected.

"You are not guests here, leech," Skrymir warned. "You are intruders. You still live only because I realized who you were and was intrigued to find you here. Beware your own tongue."

Several nasty retorts occurred to Spike but he amazed himself by remaining silent. As Skrymir disappeared into the tunnel that led down into his lair, Spike at first began to follow, but then paused. He *felt* that Drusilla was not with him any longer. When he turned he saw that she was still in the crevasse, gazing at the line of daylight on one wall as it crept lower and lower with the sun's rise.

"Come on, pet. We've come all this way. Let's get your prize, shall we?"

Drusilla was mesmerized by the sunlight creeping across the frozen ground toward her. Ice sparkled in the heat of its touch.

Spike shook her a bit. "Dru? Come on."

Swaying a bit, she turned to him, feeling as though she were in a dream. "Wouldn't you like to see it, just once? Feel it? The night's a gentle lover, filled with caresses and tender kisses. But the sun would be violent and blindingly cruel."

"Right." Spike sighed. "For all of three seconds. I know you've got higher standards than that." He gave her hand a tug and moved into the tunnel to follow Skrymir.

Drusilla glanced once more with longing at the deadly, brilliant yellow light, then she moved after him into the tunnel. The demon had gotten far ahead of them but the way was clear enough. The tunnel turned down and to the left and just as the slope became precipitous there were stairs hewn from the bedrock of the mountain. Torches burned in sconces on either side of the tunnel. Forty steps down and the tunnel turned again and became a wide landing. It was a junction of some kind with passages stretching out on either side of them as well as ahead.

Spike grunted angrily. "Bloody hell. Invite us in and leave us to find—"

He was interrupted by the sound of metal clanking against metal, off to their right.

As Drusilla peered into the darkened passage a torch roared to life. The creature that held it was not more than three and a half feet tall. It was hideously ugly. The dark and leathery flesh of its face protruded in whorled plugs of skin like the knots on an old tree and it was covered with layers of filthy cloth over which it had some sort of metal breastplate. It had a helmet atop its head from beneath which scraggly strands of matted hair hung. At its hip, a small double-bladed axe with gleaming edges hung from a leather thong.

"My master awaits," it croaked in halting English, words it probably did not even understand. "You will follow."

Drusilla studied it curiously. She smiled at it, but the creature seemed to ignore her.

"Well, aren't you an ugly little git," Spike said, chuckling. "You look like the arse end of a Vahrall."

"Now, Spike, be polite," Drusilla chastened him. She flounced a bit as she moved toward the dwarf and knelt in front of it. "You're like a little doll," she crooned to it. "The kind only bad girls get. You've just eaten, haven't you? I can smell it."

She turned to look at her grumbling lover, knowing he could never resist her.

Spike smiled thinly and nodded. "Go on then, munchkinland. We'll follow."

Without a word or glance the dwarf turned and led them along the passage, torch held high. Spike paid close attention to their path. Drusilla realized he must have been concerned about possible routes of retreat in case they had to find their way back out of there quickly. Drusilla thought it all a bit silly. It was a grand adventure, going down into the demon's lair.

"He knew our names," Spike mumbled to her.

"Well he should, shouldn't he?" Dru replied. "We're a spectacle, we are. I want all the things in the dark to know our names."

The passage was wide enough for them to walk side by side, and Drusilla's fingers entwined with Spike's as they followed the dwarf. She hummed as they went, an old nursery rhyme.

They came to another set of stairs and went down them to find a thick wooden door. The tunnels were made of ice and stone but this was the first they'd seen of wood, and of metal save for that worn by the dwarf. The little beast rapped on the door and a moment later it was opened.

"Bugger all," Spike muttered.

Drusilla gasped in admiration.

The room was enormous. Pillars of ice and stone stood high enough that their peak could not be seen in the light thrown by the many torches in the room. At its center stood an ornately carved wooden chair on a dais around which were the skulls of humans and other things. Skrymir sat there, an impatient expression upon his face, talons tapping on the arm of the chair.

What appeared to be a gryphon lounged beside the dais, tethered by a chain so unimaginably thin it seemed ridiculous. Dozens of creatures languished on pillows on the floor of the chamber, drinking from iron cups and eating from platters of fruit and cheese, bread and meat. Some of them were eating what appeared to be human viscera—Drusilla confirmed the thought with a single whiff of the aromas in the room—and she spotted the source on the far side of the room. Five round, thin iron cages, each with a human inside. Two were recently dead, but the other three were alive, strips of flesh torn off their bodies. One had been blinded, eyes gouged from their sockets. None could speak, since their tongues had been removed.

There was a sixth cage, much larger than the others. The thing inside had no head but mouths and eyes all over its trunk, six arms, and a prehensile tail that thrust out through the bars at anything that passed close by. Even as Drusilla watched, one of the armored dwarfs had to step quickly to avoid it.

The dwarfs were the guards, that much was clear. The creatures on the floor—demons, monsters, whatever— were apparently guests. The servers who meandered about with platters and cups and who carved flesh off the writhing, caged humans were also new to her. They were tall and thin, humanoid but not at all human. Their flesh was almost green, their eyes wide and completely black. No pupil, no iris, just black. They appeared harmless, or she thought so until one of them smiled at her, lips curling back and back so she could see the rows of impossibly long teeth that seemed to grow as she watched.

Drusilla smiled back. The creature was beautiful.

Then she turned to Skrymir. "Lovely what you've done with the place," she said pleasantly.

"You've got a nice setup here, no doubt about it," Spike agreed. "Got your friends over, too, which is nice and sociable. They must be dedicated to come all the way up the bloody mountainside for a visit."

Skrymir laughed. "They live here, vampire. I have other agents, all around the world. But these friends of mine are always here."

"Vampire," Drusilla said, echoing the demon and lingering on the word. "Leech. I notice you don't have any of us about, Skrymir. From your tone, I'd almost believe you don't much care for our kind. Which wouldn't be very nice at all."

"You have your uses," Skrymir replied. "I think we'll find out what yours are. Both of you. I presume you've come here for a reason. You want something of me."

"Course not," Spike grunted. "We climbed the bloody mountain to pay a social call. We're big on myths, Dru and I. Scholars, we are."

Skrymir regarded them both coolly.

"I promised my baby a little prize for her birthday, see. A trinket, a token of my affections, like. She never asks for anything, but she asked for this, and I'm determined she's to have it. The necklace of the Brisings."

Skrymir flinched, surprised. Drusilla was pleased to see the creature startled for once.

"See how my baby loves me?" she asked, swaying a bit and gazing at Skrymir from beneath her long lashes. Then she turned her back on him, leaving the business to her man, and began to walk about the room, whispering greetings to some of the guards and servants, particularly to the animals.

"Freyja's Strand," Skrymir said appreciatively. "You two are nothing if not ambitious. And what? You planned to steal it from me, perhaps?"

"Kill you for it maybe," Spike agreed. "Maybe not. I was hoping we could work something out. Maybe there's something we can do for you."

"Perhaps," Skrymir replied, a kind of hush to his voice.

The demon stood up and stepped off the dais. Drusilla stood staring into the cage with the blinded man, her head tilted to one side as she studied him.

"I think he sees me," she whispered.

Skrymir slipped up behind her and reached out to touch her hair again with an icy hand. With a deep frown she turned to regard him, her mouth twisted into an angry pout. Beyond the demon, she saw Spike's features twist and re-form into the face of the vampire. He started for Skrymir, but two of the dwarf guards nearest him reached for the axes at their sides.

Skrymir's talons touched Drusilla's cheek.

Her hand whipped up faster than the eye could follow. With a snarl, she twisted those frozen digits and they snapped off in her grasp. Where blood ought to have flowed there was only a bit of green mist. Skrymir grunted but Drusilla did not stop there. With a growing snarl that built from deep within her chest she drove him back and back until he slammed against the largest cage, the one with the six-armed demon in it. Ice shavings—Skrymir's flesh—scraped raw and fell to the ground.

"You take liberties, my poncy boy," Dru scolded. "It was naughty of you to leave us back there in the dark. Rude. I simply cannot abide rudeness."

The dwarfs began to move in. One of the thin, needle-mouthed servers dropped a platter and started for her as well. Dru saw Spike grab the nearest dwarf and snap its neck with a single twist, then pick up the dirty beast's axe.

Drusilla's nails cracked the ice at Skrymir's throat. The demon in the cage roared and its tail whipped out between the bars and wrapped around Skrymir, who had started to shudder. She had been offended and now she would be appeased.

"Dru, back off!" Spike suddenly yelled, voice thick with concern for her.

She glanced up and saw him bury the small axe in the back of another dwarf's head. It cut right through the helmet and pulled out without any resistance at all. The sharpest blade she had ever seen.

Spike called out to her again, but Dru only frowned more deeply.

The ice seemed to appear from nowhere as if formed from the very air itself, and yet at the same time it nearly bubbled off Skrymir's body, enveloping Drusilla so quickly that the frown was frozen on her face.

Skrymir dug the regrown talons of his once-injured hand into the demon's tail that was wrapped around him and ripped it off. The thing screamed from all of its mouths, a savage sound of agony that deafened all those in the room. Skrymir only laughed. Laughed while Drusilla stood frozen in a block of ice.

"You bloody bastard!" Spike roared, and charged.

A dwarf tried to block his way and Spike kicked it in the head. One of the servers flashed its rows of teeth at him. Spike swung an axe sideways into its open mouth and lopped off the top of its head.

Then Skrymir was before him. Spike raised both blades.

"Don't be an idiot," the demon whispered, the menace back in its voice. "She's in no danger."

Spike hesitated.

"She hurt me," Skrymir continued. "She's lucky I did not kill her. I could have done so, quite easily I assure you."

"Why didn't you?" Spike demanded, still in battle stance, blades at the ready.

Skrymir reached out and touched the ice surrounding Drusilla. With the cracking sound it had made earlier, the ice began to fall away. The demon shuddered as it returned to him, built upon him so that the humanoid appearance he had briefly worn was gone and the frozen, winged, hooved gargoyle they had first seen had returned. This close Spike saw that he was well over eight feet tall. That greenish mist within his frigid form spread out through the demon's icy form, filling it, and Spike wondered if that little bit of smoke—the gas that had leaked out when Drusilla had snapped off his fingers—if that was the real demon.

With the ice removed from around her Drusilla collapsed into Spike's arms. She leaned against him, eyes pained and angry, mouth twisted into a petulant grimace.

"You saw what he did, Spike. Why is he still alive?"

Spike ignored her.

"I'm waiting for an answer," he told the demon.

Skrymir's hooves clacked on the stone floor. He waved a hand and servers moved in to drag away the dead. The revelers on the floor had paused to watch the melee but by now they had already gone back to their indulgence.

"You said it yourself," the demon rumbled. "Maybe there's something you can do for me. Though I warn you, Freyja's Strand is priceless, an arcane artifact older than man, and one of a kind. I will ask a great deal from you in exchange for it."

Spike smiled. "Name it, old man. Not a thing in the world I wouldn't do for my baby."

At that Drusilla's pout disappeared and she nuzzled her face against his neck, nipping the flesh there just as he liked it.

Skrymir began to speak, explaining to the vampires what he would require of them in exchange for the necklace of the Brisings. The more he talked the better Spike liked it. All in all it sounded like fun.

Hell, if he'd thought of it first, he would have done it all for free.

Chapter Four

Copenhagen, Denmark
April 5th

Christiansborg Palace was cursed. The origins of that curse were shrouded in mystery, but no one doubted that it existed. The massive, rambling configuration stood proud against the night sky. Its core building was a regal, stone, U-shaped structure with a spire stretching up from its center. The palace was the seat of Danish government and parliament, but it was cursed. The location had originally been the site of the castle of Bishop Absalon, built in 1167 and subsequently destroyed. King Christian VI built his palace upon the ruins of Absalon's castle, and it was razed by fire in 1794. Frederick VI built anew upon that spot, but that palace burned to the ground in 1884. The current structure had been completed in 1928, but though the curse went unspoken, the older residents of Copenhagen, in their secret hearts, knew it was only a matter of time.

It might have been that the land was tainted. Common wisdom held that it was something to do with

Bishop Absalon and his castle, with unspeakable horrors that had been performed there in secret. Others imagined that the clergyman had been righteous and faced the forces of darkness within that castle, and it was they who had laid the curse upon the grounds, and any stone laid upon them.

Whatever the truth, there was a sort of energy there, both in the palace above and in the ruins of Absalon's castle below. A dark and ugly energy, resonating with the taint of blood and shadows.

Gorm loved it down there. Most of the time.

Torches blazed in sconces on the stone walls, flaring and guttering with each draft and eddy that shuddered through the air of the crumbling ruins. Shattered history lay all around them, chaos bent into some form of order by Gorm's will alone. Tapestries and paintings, jewels and weapons, even contemporary furniture, though the ancient king of Denmark had balked at first at including such modern things in his lair. The others had respectfully pleaded, and eventually he had relented.

Still this was his place. His *palace*. While the machinery of governing the kingdom of Denmark rumbled along in the modern palace above their heads, Gorm and his followers plotted its destruction, and planned for the time when darkness would reign over the land. For the moment, the hated sun had long since risen, and so Gorm was left only to brood in the stone bowels of Copenhagen, awaiting the night once more.

Something moved in the shadows cast by the torch-light.

"Who comes?" Gorm demanded.

One of his subjects slithered into the light. The vampire's features were scorched, his clothes burnt at the edges, even still smoldering. Gorm frowned and stared at him, hoping for some spark of recognition to ignite in his brain. He had trouble, at times, remembering the names and faces of his subjects. The old king knew he was probably half-mad, but madness had never bothered him. Rather, it freed him.

"Your name?" the king snapped.

The vampire stared at him wide-eyed, then dropped to his knees in obeisance. "B-but, you told me never to speak my name in your presence, Majesty."

Gorm glowered at the stout creature menacingly. He was a large one, and the king did not like that. Gorm himself was rail thin, almost a wraith, but savage and fast, and stronger than any who had ever dared challenge him. Thus he still lived. But this one . . .

"I don't like the look of you," he snarled. The old king stood up from the velvet-shrouded wooden chair that had been his throne for some years, and started across the room toward his subject. "Tell me your name."

The stout, charred vampire flinched, eyes to the ground.

"Christian, sire."

Gorm's eyes went wide, and then he began to laugh. It was an awful sound, even to him, coming up from his guts, churning the air with his fetid breath. Moments after he began, the king stopped laughing. He hated the way it made him feel.

"What news, *Christian?*" Gorm demanded.

The vampire remained on his knees. "You sent me to find Ernst, Majesty. He has disappeared."

"The Slayer," the king growled.

At last Christian looked up and met his sire's gaze. "I think not, Majesty. Others have seen him, not long before dawn. He escaped the Slayer, but she must have frightened him, for it seems he has betrayed you."

Rage erupted from within Gorm in a roar. His face changed, long fangs jutting from within his mouth. Acid bile burned the back of his throat.

"Find him and bring him to me," Gorm snarled, storming back to his throne. He sat, fuming, before he blinked suddenly and looked over at Christian again. "No. To hell with him. Find him and kill him."

"But, sire," Christian wheedled, "dawn has come. I nearly burned this morning, bringing this information to you. The sun grows high."

"Cover yourself, then, fool." Gorm sat up on his throne, stroking his leathery, pitted face with long, razor talons. "Find Ernst and kill him."

Christian stood, bowed deeply, and began to withdraw from the throne room. He moved backward, eyes to the ground. "As you command, sire," the stout vampire said. "Ernst will die."

With a wave, Gorm dismissed him, mind already moving on to other matters, specifically the Helm of Haraxis. Without it, he might never create the dark kingdom of his dreams.

He heard a noise, then, like the sound of someone biting into an apple. It was followed by a low grunt of pain. King Gorm knew those sounds all too well. Lips curling back from his teeth, yellow eyes shimmering in the torchlight, he peered at the shadows where Christian had disappeared. A draft blew dust and ash, whipping it into the air and then sweeping it along the stone floor.

Past the Slayer's boots. She came farther into the room, blond hair cast with an orange hue by the torches. The girl, Sophie, was tall and lithe and moved with extraordinary grace. Gorm admired her for that. He had wanted to drink of her since the moment he had first seen her in front of Grundtvig church, while it was still under construction.

"Slayer," he hissed. A tiny smile played around his sharp teeth, but it did not bother Gorm the way laughter did. There was nothing good in that smile, only pain.

"I would not worry about Ernst," she said. "He spoke to the wrong people last night. I missed him once, but I found him again this morning. He is in the wind, now."

"I am grateful," Gorm sneered. "I suppose I owe you something for disposing of my garbage."

The Slayer paused, looked at him, and returned his smile. Gorm shuddered. He did not like that, for her smile seemed even crueler than his own.

There were other entrances into the throne room. Already, shadows had begun to cluster in them. Vampires, Gorm's subjects, bringing violent death for she who had dared to intrude upon his presence. With the Slayer disposed of, Gorm knew, his quest to find the Helm could proceed at a far greater pace.

"You've come to die?" the vampire king asked.

"I have come to share information," Sophie replied sharply. "First, I should tell you that I am leaving Copenhagen, perhaps forever."

Gorm grunted in surprise. It was not what he had expected to hear. "You will never leave this room alive," he promised her.

"You underestimate me," she said, her voice so low that it was almost a whisper. "I am here to kill you. To exterminate all of the vermin in this little nest of yours. Before I do that, however, there's something you should know. The Helm of Haraxis—"

The king stiffened. With a flash of teeth and talon, he practically leaped from his throne and crouched on the stone floor, muscles crackling with hatred and violence ready to be unleashed.

"What do you know of the Helm?" he demanded.

"Very little," she said. "But I know this. It isn't here. Not in Copenhagen, nor in Denmark, nor even in Europe, for that matter."

"Tell me where it is!" he shrieked, unable to control himself.

The Slayer smiled again. He hated it, wanted to tear her face off.

"Make me," she said.

Sophie felt the crackle of evil energy in the ruins. She stood ready, in a stance Yanna had first taught her just after her tenth birthday. There had been years of training even before she had been Chosen as the Slayer, and even more intensive instruction since. All for this.

"Die," Gorm snarled, his voice so low and confident that it sounded almost as though he believed he could kill her with just a word.

When the ancient king's vampire subjects sprang from the shadows and boltholes, and from the two other entrances into the throne room, Sophie almost believed it as well. But almost could not kill her. Neither could a word. She had staked seven vampires as she made her way down into the ruins of Absalon's castle. There were none behind her. But that did not mean she was alone.

"Tycho!" she shouted.

Her demonic ally let out a war cry his species had not used in seven thousand years of peace. Sophie felt it resonating in her own heart. Then the vampires were upon her. She drew her sword so quickly that it almost felt to her as though she had skipped forward in time. Her blade whisked across the air before her. The room was so filled with vampires that she decapitated two of them with that single stroke.

She had a stake in her left hand, and she plunged it into the chest of a girl she thought she recognized from her youth. A childhood friend, perhaps. Moving on, she forced herself to forget that face. It was not the first of her memories to die, and she had no time to mourn.

Tycho's war cry tore through the air again. Sophie drove the point of her sword through the right eye of the vampire in front of her. The blade punched through the beast's brain and out the back of its skull. She cursed herself for having missed the throat and drew the sword out. The vampire was blinded and she kicked it down in front of several others, buying herself several precious seconds.

A quick glance up and she saw Tycho, the razor spines on his back and arms raised, tearing his way through a rabid pack of vampires. No stake, no sword, no interest in dusting them. He would rather simply tear them apart. Before she looked away, she saw Tycho open his massive jaws impossibly wide, his mouth seeming to unhinge, then clamping shut on the throat of a vampire. His three rows of needle teeth chomped cleanly through the thing's neck and its head fell to the stone ground with a thump before both head and torso exploded in a cloud of dust.

Sophie grinned madly.

Her stake was knocked from her left hand. She beheaded the vampire that had done it, then cut down another one as she lunged for a torch on the wall. With a roar of her own, the Slayer turned and shoved the burning torch into the gut of the nearest vampire. Its clothes caught fire like kindling and she kicked the creature back toward three others. Their clothes began to burn as well and they screamed and panicked, trying to put the flames out.

Side by side, Sophie and Tycho hacked and slashed and burned their way through the vampires in service to old King Gorm. Minutes after the bloodshed and death had begun, Sophie held her sword at the ready, barely breathing hard, and watched as two of the creatures turned and ran from her, willing to take their chances in the sun rather than face her.

She actually laughed.

But she was not the only one.

"He was your friend, this one?"

The voice was Gorm's. Sophie spun, sword in one hand and torch in the other, ready to attack, to do whatever was necessary. But it was too late. Gorm had remained at the edges of the battle. Not so, now. He stood at the center of the room, holding the slumped form of Tycho by the hair. The muscles in the vampire's arm were taut with his power as he held the demon up off the floor with one hand. In the other, Gorm held Tycho's black and bloody heart, trailing thick, torn blood vessels.

There was a gaping, ragged wound in Tycho's chest.

Sophie whispered her friend's name.

"They have two hearts, you know," Gorm said slowly. "Quetz demons."

As if to prove the point, Tycho's eyes fluttered open.

"Sophie," he grunted, voice a hoarse ghost of itself.

"Watch, I'll show you," the old king snapped. He dropped Tycho's heart into the swirling eddies of vampire dust on the castle floor, then thrust his hand back into the wound, rooting around, snapping bone.

Tycho opened his mouth to scream but could not. He was already dead when his second heart was ripped out through the hole in his chest.

Sophie screamed for him and dropped the torch to hold her sword in both hands.

Gorm was faster than any vampire she had ever seen. He moved like a snake, his entire body fluid and deadly, built to kill. His long talons swept out to tear Sophie apart.

She dodged.

Her father's sword impaled him, and Sophie drove him back with all the strength of the Chosen One until Gorm stumbled and sat down hard on his velvet and wood throne. The point of the sword had punched out through his back and she could hear it splinter the wood of the chair, lodging there.

Pinning Gorm there.

Chest heaving with her fury and grief, Sophie stood away and watched as Gorm cursed and spat, slamming forward, trying to free himself. He had the strength, certainly. It would take seconds.

"I will have your blood, girl!" he screamed. "I am Gorm. I am king!"

Sophie picked up the torch she had dropped and set the throne alight. Gorm screamed and glared at her as the blaze roared up and engulfed his dead flesh in seconds. His wide, insane eyes were fixed on her until they melted in his skull.

Gorm exploded in a cloud of burning embers and the sword that had been her father's clattered to the stone. Sophie picked it up. The metal of the blade was warm from the fire. She said a silent prayer to her father and resheathed the weapon.

When Sophie emerged into the sunlight and walked away from Christiansborg Palace, her thoughts were of London. She and Yanna would be leaving, possibly that very day, and she would never see that palace again. She would miss Copenhagen, but not that place.

It was cursed.

London, England
May 18th

A pall hung over London, a shroud of dread. Yanna had never seen anything like it. After months of warnings and flag-waving, the invasion and partition of Poland, the buildup of German troops and armaments, the Nazis had invaded Denmark and Norway in April, only days after the Slayer and her Watcher had left Copenhagen. The British somehow seemed surprised.

There was irony in it. From the day she had arrived in London she had watched the shifting emotions of the people. They were filled with righteous anger at Hitler and his forces, and yet not overly concerned about the fate of the nations on the continent. Should the Nazis reach their shores, why the people were cocksure of the supremacy of the British Empire.

But the whispers and the shouts had already begun. British industry was not ready. His Majesty's treasury was low on funds and simply could not afford to defend the whole of Europe. But the decision had been made. Despite all the warning signs there had been almost no preparation for war. The arrogance inherent in that fact was astounding and yet once into the fray not a single voice would confess to having been caught napping.

None of that mattered. The dread existed, yes, but as a low current running beneath the emotions that surged to the fore. Foremost among them was pride. This was not some new war for the freedom of Europe but merely a continuation of the Great War begun decades before. Hitler was a new face but the enemy was the same. The same.

But stronger. Faster. More brutal.

Still it did not matter. The British Empire would rise to the challenge. Ill-prepared, poorly financed, undersupplied, somehow they would triumph.

Every day that passed Yanna became more torn between her love and respect for these fierce, courageous people, and her despair that they simply had no idea what they were dealing with. Poland had fallen in eighteen days. Norway and Denmark in no more time than that. Here was a conqueror unlike any the modern world had seen, a crisis of unfathomable proportions.

Yet somehow, in the building at the far end of Great Russell Street, the Council of Watchers managed to pretend that there were still no greater concerns than their own.

It was raining outside, just a light drizzle but enough to bring a chill upon the day. There were high windows in the fourth floor chamber where the Council's directors met, but they were tightly closed and locked. There were things that could fly, of course, and things that could scale stone walls with bare feet and hands. All of them had ears and, in this room, the Council would not allow its wishes to be overheard.

The room covered most of the fourth floor. Comfortable leather chairs and small side tables were in the corners closest to the windows. The directors might retreat there in pairs or trios to have a sherry and a smoke, or perhaps tea. But the business was done around the mahogany table on the other side of the room. There were fourteen chairs around the table. At the moment only nine of them were taken; seven by Council directors, one by Yanna herself, and the ninth by the Slayer. For her part, Sophie sat quite respectfully and answered the questions posed to her.

Harold Travers sat at the head of the table. For the purposes of this meeting, and several others they had attended since their arrival, Mr. Travers spoke for the Council.

"You're certain?" Mr. Travers inquired again, almost impishly pleased with his question. "In the past week not a single vampire?"

"None," Sophie replied.

She had been required to learn English when she had first begun her training; a product of the arrogance of the Council, Yanna thought. They were based in Britain and so the Slayer must be able to speak English.

"Two minor demons only," Sophie added, her accent thick. She had not been practicing her English much.

Yanna studied Mr. Travers as he glanced around at the other directors gathered at the table. Several of them nodded meaningfully. One, a bespectacled, gray-haired woman Yanna did not recognize, leaned over and whispered in Travers's ear. With a puff of his chest, Travers straightened his tie and sat up in his chair.

"I had hoped we could put off this discussion until Mrs. Giles returned from her research in South America, but with the war on we cannot know for certain when that might be," Mr. Travers explained.

Yanna frowned. What was this about?

Sophie shifted uncomfortably, the chair poorly suited to her lanky frame and long legs.

Gray light reached across the wood floor as rain pattered on the thick glass. Elsewhere in the building a door slammed and then Yanna heard someone laugh. A light, easy sound; a rarity in that building and, in recent days, in that city. Around the table the Watchers sat up expectantly, importantly, and Yanna felt the dread that hovered over London settle deep within her own heart.

"Our operatives have been investigating this phenomenon." Mr. Travers leaned forward in his chair as he spoke, as if to impress upon Yanna and Sophie the weight of his words. "Since the Germans overran Belgium and Holland eight days ago, and began their attack on France, the vampires have left Brittania in droves each night."

"Left?" Yanna asked, startled by this pronouncement. "To go where?"

Travers smiled as if in appreciation of his own cleverness. "Why, to war, Miss Narvik. To war. What easier prey than the fallen soldier? What better hunting ground than the front lines of a war in which thousands of men are slaughtered every day? Western Europe is a veritable banquet for the fiends. They have gone to war.

"And the Slayer will follow."

Yanna felt Sophie stiffen beside her, and she reached out and placed a calming hand on the girl's arm.

"You're mad," she told Travers, who flinched at the word. "What could you be thinking?"

A ripple of dismay, even anger, went through the gathered directors, summed up by the glare Travers gave her now.

"You forget yourself, Miss Narvik," he said. "As you also forget the duties of the Slayer. She is to protect the world from the forces of darkness; that is her calling, that is what she has been Chosen for. That does not mean she may sit at home and wait for the darkness to come to her. There may never be a higher concentration of the vampire population in one place as we will see in France in the next several weeks. Logic dictates—"

"Logic be damned!" Yanna shouted.

She stood up, unable to contain herself, and glanced down at Sophie. The Slayer's eyes, so cold and blue, were wide and searching as though she were lost. It was an emotion Yanna had never seen on the girl's face before, and she never wanted to see it there again.

Reasserting control over herself, Yanna took a breath and met the angry gaze of her superiors directly. "Mr. Travers. Fellow Watchers, I respectfully request that the Slayer be dismissed at this time so that we may speak more freely—"

"You cannot speak freely in front of the Slayer, she whom you trained and is your charge and responsibility?" demanded the gray-haired woman who had whispered in Travers's ear.

Yanna ground her teeth together. "Not in this instance, no."

Mr. Travers's gaze ticked once to Sophie, then back to Yanna. "Then this meeting is adj—"

"I am reluctant to speak in Sophie's presence on this subject because I think it is unkind and unnecessary to discuss a young girl's death in front of her," Yanna snapped. "But if you insist. Even if Sophie can find a way to keep herself hidden, how long can that go on? The vampires are her natural enemy, but thousands of soldiers on both sides of this conflict have guns with real bullets. Bullets cannot kill vampires, but they will kill the Slayer. If you send her to war, she will die there."

"You don't know that," Travers scoffed.

"I do. And so do you," she insisted.

Mr. Travers cleared his throat. He reached up and fixed his tie again, smoothing it. "It is my considered opinion, having conversed with our Miss Carstensen several times, that she is well aware of her duties as the Slayer. Do I speak true, miss?"

Slowly, Sophie turned her eyes to him. She held her chin high, nostrils flaring with both pride and anger. "You do, sir."

"Excellent. I thought so," Mr. Travers said, much pleased with himself and with Sophie. He turned to Yanna again. "You see, Miss Narvik. Our Slayer knows her destiny. To find the evil in its lair and root it out. What you seem to forget is that the Council of Watchers, and the Slayers who have served us, have been at war for centuries. It is nothing new to us. If the worst happens, as it very well may, there is certainly no shortage of well-trained candidates in line to be Chosen. One Slayer dies, another is called. You leave tonight."

He said this last with a wave of his hand, a dismissive gesture that was a blade in Yanna's heart.

"You heartless—"

"Miss Narvik," Travers scowled. "One more outburst and you will be relieved of your duties as Watcher. A replacement for you can easily be found as well. Though perhaps that is your goal. I wonder if it isn't your own vulnerability to bullets that concerns you here."

Yanna was speechless. She stared gape-mouthed at him, horrified at the mere suggestion.

Sophie stood, her chair scraping the floor. Without pause she walked the length of the table, Watchers turning to see her pass, and slapped Harold Travers in the face hard enough that his teeth clacked together and blood and spittle flew from his mouth.

"No, Sophie," Yanna said, finding her voice at last.

But the Slayer was clearly enraged. She had sat and listened to Travers so callously speak about her death without response. No longer.

"How dare you?" Travers sputtered.

"How dare *you?*" Sophie spat at him. "You send me to my death. If that is my fate, then so be it. If there are as many vampires there as you say then it may be worth dying to have a chance at them. But I was Chosen, not Yanna. This is *my* destiny. Her courage is greater than mine because she chooses to go with me. You will apologize."

Attempting to regain his composure, and his control over the situation, Travers actually managed a sneer. "I'll do no such thing."

Sophie smiled. It was a vicious smile, cruel and gleeful. Yanna had seen it on her face before, but only with demons nearby.

The Slayer grabbed Mr. Travers by the tie and hauled him up to his feet. She was taller than he, and he was forced to stand on the tips of his toes to avoid choking.

"I will go to France," Sophie said calmly, even happily. "And I will take a Watcher with me. But if you do not apologize to Yanna, then the only way I go to war is with *you* as my Watcher."

She let him go. Travers smoothed his suit and straightened his tie. He ran his hands over his thinning brown hair and cleared his throat.

"Right," he said very softly. "Sorry."

Chapter Five

The English Channel
May 18th

The water in the Channel was rough and Yanna marveled that Sophie was able to sleep. They had not had any conversation about it but she imagined that the girl must have realized how little opportunity there would be for rest in the coming days and weeks. Yanna knew it as well, of course, but could not have brought herself to sleep even if the choppy sea would allow it. The duties of the Slayer were sacrosanct. As the Watcher it was her obligation to keep that certainty foremost in her mind, yet she found that she could not. The only thing that truly concerned her now was keeping Sophie alive. The girl could handle demons and vampires. Most were too arrogant to fight with conventional weapons. But this . . .

Yanna was hungry as well. There had been food in their private car on the train to Dover, but her stomach had felt queasy. Now she wished she had at least taken something with her. Ironic, she thought, that the rough sea did not make her nauseated, particularly given the size of the boat. It was a fishing trawler, privately owned, though it smelled only faintly of fish. She suspected that it had rarely been used for its stated purpose and more frequently for functions not unlike that it was serving tonight.

The captain and two crew members were silent save for shouting instructions back and forth to one another. Yanna sat on the floor of the cabin with Sophie curled up under a blanket beside her. A wide passage was open to the deck of the boat without a door or even a curtain, but the cabin was protection from the elements nevertheless.

At the back of the boat, spattered by sea spray, sat Mr. Rubie and Mr. Haversham, the two Council operatives who had been assigned to aid them in their journey and in establishing a suitable base from which to operate in France. Haversham was tall and thin, neat and stylish. Beneath his great coat he wore a dark suit and spotted tie, a round-collared shirt and a silk kerchief in his breast pocket. Rubie was his opposite, a stout, cherub-faced man whose rumpled, pin-striped suit and bow tie seemed an almost purposeful echo of the style favored by Winston Churchill, the former Lord of the Admiralty who had just replaced Chamberlain as British Prime Minister. During their time in London, Yanna had seen his picture in the papers nearly every day.

Neither of the Council operatives was forthcoming with their plans, but Yanna had learned certain bits of information through constant prodding. Mr. Haversham had arranged for transport upon their arrival at Calais, France, and for two sets of papers—one that would identify them as British subjects and one that would offer proof that they were Danish and traveling with the permission of the conquering German army. Both sets of papers were real. The agenda of the Council was not defined by regional politics, even at war time. Their influence was widespread.

Mr. Rubie spoke French more fluently than either Yanna or Sophie and had spent some years living on the continent. His connections were more personal. He had—with the help of friends in France and England—worked out an entire system of safe houses along the French–Belgian border and south to Orleans and Dijon, among others.

Yanna's only concern in regard to these arrangements was whether or not those houses would still be there when they were needed. Belgium had been quickly overrun and the Germans were relentless in their attack upon France. Their papers would likely allow them the ability to act no matter whose hands the territory was in, but the entirety of western Europe was becoming a battlefield. There was no way to know if a village or town that had stood the week before would still be intact a week later.

A swell raised the boat suddenly and Yanna banged her head on a wall inside. The captain turned to see that the women in his care were well but said nothing before turning back to peer through the glass and the spray at the dark horizon beyond. The Watcher glanced at Sophie to be sure she was all right and then pulled herself up to move out of the cabin. Mr. Rubie and Mr. Haversham saw her coming immediately. They looked quite stiff in their damp greatcoats, hands thrust in their pockets even with the black gloves both wore.

"Can we help, Miss Narvik?" Haversham asked politely.

"I don't suppose either of you has a cigarette," she said grumpily.

"I'm a cigar man, I'm afraid," Mr. Haversham apologized.

Mr. Rubie smiled as he reached inside his jacket and removed a thin silver cigarette case and a lighter. "It might be difficult to light here. Why don't you take them into the cabin. You can return them to me when we arrive at Calais."

"You have my thanks," Yanna told him.

She moved carefully along the deck to the cabin and stood in the doorway to light up. The cigarette's tip flared with orange flame and she drew the smoke into her lungs. The lighter made a satisfying metallic click when she snapped it closed; then she slipped both case and lighter into the long black jacket she wore over a white blouse and gray skirt. Both she and Sophie would return to attire more appropriate for their vocation when they had settled in the first safe house.

Yanna drew another lungful of smoke and her eyes went to the floor of the cabin, where Sophie had pulled herself into a tight ball in her sleep. At her height, it seemed impossible that she could ever be so small or look so vulnerable, but in that moment, she did.

Bastards, Yanna thought angrily as she exhaled. The wind took the smoke away in an instant.

The trawler rose up on another swell and Yanna braced herself, then stiffened. The cigarette dropped from her hand and she grabbed the frame of the door with both hands. Her mouth hung agape and the world around her disappeared, to be replaced by another.

A vision . . .

. . . under the water. The current is strong and Yanna can feel it pulling at her. It is dark below and the taste of salt is in her mouth. Her jacket and skirt are sodden and

hamper her movements but she feels no fear. Instead there is a warmth and safety to the feel of the water as it rocks her like a mother cradling a newborn. She opens her mouth ever so slightly as a shudder of pleasure runs through her. Yanna is drowning and it is bliss.

Her eyes begin to flicker, to close. Through slitted lids she looks down into the impenetrable depths, and something white glimmers in the light from far above. White and cold and moving so swiftly. A shark. It must be. A frisson of fear replaces her pleasure and then somehow they merge, her heart beating more rapidly as those emotions entwine. The beast cuts through the water, rising toward her.

Its skin is pale and its ridged brow set and determined upon having her for its feast. It comes for her, mouth open and ready, fangs impossibly long.

It is not a shark.

Its body is wiry but powerful and dangerous. Its hair is so blond it is nearly white, like an albino's.

It is a vampire.

It is pursuing her. No ocean will stop it, nor the land between. It will have her, given time. With another shudder, Yanna finds that the thought does not frighten her at all . . .

Until she shook herself awake from the dream.

"Oh God," the Watcher whispered.

Above her, Sophie called out her name, voice broken with concern. Mr. Rubie and Mr. Haversham were there as well, looking down upon her where she lay on the floor of the boat's cabin.

"Miss Narvik! Are you all right?" Haversham demanded worriedly.

"She's a seer, Kenneth. An inopportune time, but not life threatening certainly. Don't you read your assignments anymore?" Rubie chided him.

Yanna flinched at his words. Being a seer might not be life threatening, but that did not mean there were no dangers involved. Ever since she had first developed the gift of prescience—vague as many of her visions were—Yanna had been sternly instructed about keeping her wits about her. Her own father had warned her about that gift when she was quite young.

"Most every seer I've ever known or been told about died a lunatic," the old man had said, big white eyebrows tufted over his intense, black eyes. "Take care, girl. You see beyond this world, see past it. After a time it may be that the things that bind you here begin to shatter, those bonds break, and your mind becomes unfettered by what is real. Madness, Yanna. Only the strongest-willed of seers can avoid it."

Yanna remembered, and the memory frightened her. For though she lifted her chin high, kept her gaze clear, pulled her hair back tight and severe, she did not feel as well put together as the image she tried to present of herself. Indeed, with every new vision, she felt herself unraveling more and more. It was something she had worked hard at hiding from Sophie. The Slayer knew the possible fate that was in store for Yanna, as a seer, but Yanna did not want the girl to lose faith in her.

She would fight it. Control it. Keep her mind firmly tethered to the world around her. Yanna was determined.

Or she had been, before this vision. It chilled her to the bone, made her see the faces around her almost as though they were gossamer spirits or the last strands of a dream she was waking from. Her heart thundered in her chest and she felt tears threatening. Above her, Sophie and the Council men still watched her closely.

Yanna wanted to speak to them, but could not make her mouth work.

She felt as though she were drowning, could still taste the water in her mouth, still see the image of that vampire burned into her mind, could imagine the feel of his fangs in the soft flesh of her throat . . .

. . . and yearned for it. *God help me, I want to give myself to him.* But no, that was in the vision. That was not her own mind, her rational self. *But which is in control? The power within, the sub-conscious voice of the seer, or the other, my true self?*

Which is my true self? How can I be certain?

Despite the thoughts that tormented her, Yanna managed to focus on the world around her once more. It took longer and longer for her to do so after each vision. When Sophie saw that she seemed to be feeling better, she helped Yanna to sit up, though she still leaned against the door frame.

"You're all right," Sophie said in Danish, her relief obvious. "You struck your head when you went down."

Now that the girl mentioned it, Yanna found that the back of her skull was throbbing slightly. She imagined that if she reached around she would find that a bump had begun to form there.

"You had a vision?" Sophie asked, still in her native tongue.

"I did," Yanna agreed in Danish, searching Sophie's eyes for a sign that the girl had noticed her distress. She was relieved to find none.

I am the Watcher, she thought, firmly scolding herself. *My duties to the Slayer and the Council must come before any concern for myself.*

Yanna switched to English and spoke to the Council operatives as well. She explained the ominous clairvoyant episode, but not the feelings she had had during and after it.

"The water is our current adversary. It's possible there is no more significance to the vision's setting than that," she explained. "The core message is more important. Somewhere out there, for whatever reason, there is a vampire who is hunting . . . us."

She had almost said *me,* the intimate feelings aroused by her vision still lingering in her. But even in the vision she had felt that the vampire was not truly after her, but out to remove her as an obstacle standing in the way of its true goal.

"His name is Spike," she added. "He's very dangerous."

Mr. Haversham cleared his throat. "You got his name from a bloody vision?"

"No," Yanna confessed. "I know his name. It isn't the first time I've seen him."

London, England
May 19th

In her years with the Council, Marie-Christine Fontaine had served in nearly every position available. Her father had begun her training in 1894, on her eighth birthday. There had never been any doubt that she would become a Watcher, for Jacques Fontaine had no sons, though he would have unquestionably preferred to be able to induct a male child into the ranks of the Council. Marie-Christine carried decades of bitterness toward her father as a heavy burden on her soul that she could never find the strength to expunge.

In spite of that, or perhaps because of it, she had become a veritable institution at the Council headquarters. As a Watcher she had trained dozens of Slayers-in-Waiting, as she thought of the potential candidates the Council had identified. There was no precise way to tell which girl would be the next Chosen One, but they had gotten better over the years at reading the signs that would identify a candidate. Marie-Christine had helped with that, as well as with organizing past Watchers' Journals into some semblance of order. She had unearthed many diaries that had once been deemed unimportant and thus not copied outside the main collection in the vaults at Great Russell Street. Several of them had proven vital and were now part of the duplicate collections available at other Council offices worldwide.

As a Watcher she could not be an operative, but as a young woman she had spent some time in the field with them. She had whispered into the ears of members of Parliament and traveled to the chambers of ancient sorcerers, and yet also performed more mundane tasks such as bookkeeping and making funeral arrangements. In some ways, Miss Fontaine was the essence of the Council of Watchers. She had risen so far that she was now a Council director, and yet she was unfulfilled.

None of the Slayers-in-Waiting she had ever trained had been Chosen. It was her life's one great regret. Or it had been. The previous day she had, for the first time, taken an action in the name of the Council and their mission that disturbed her profoundly, one that resounded within her like an echo. She had supported her fellow directors in their plan to send the Slayer to almost certain death in greedy pursuit of a high kill ratio. A chance to thin the herd had presented itself, though one with unacceptable levels of risk. It was suicidal and yet they had sent the girl regardless. And why not? Thanks to her own good works in early identification of candidates by signs and portents, there were more than enough well-trained girls waiting in the wings.

Miss Fontaine was disgusted with herself.

But she had not let that stop her from endorsing their plan. For the sake of the Council, the Slayer had gone to war, and she would likely die, but if Sophie Carstensen's past accomplishments were any indication, she would kill a great many vampires before then. The great work of the Council would go on, as it always had.

It was raining again. She sat in a high-backed leather chair in front of the fireplace in the study at Great Russell Street and pretended, even to herself, that she was reading from the book on her lap. It was Dickens, whom she loved, but she could not focus on the pages. The fire roared. Two of the Watchers-in-Training, including Travers's son John, were about somewhere. They had been tending the fire as well as handling communications that night. John had brought her cocoa, and Marie-Christine was appreciative. His thoughtfulness was not necessary, and yet she had the impression he was a genuinely kind boy, not merely attempting to win her favor because she held some influence over the Council. Young Travers was certainly more amiable than the other boy, Marco Giampa. Miss Fontaine planned to keep her eye on Giampa. She did not like the boy at all.

Behind her, she heard someone clear his throat. Miss Fontaine turned to see that Harold Travers, John's father, had not left for the evening after all.

"Mr. Travers. What news of our girl?" she asked.

"They reached their first safe location with no surprises," Travers replied. "Reconnaissance begins, and then a roving patrol each night over the ground won or lost on the battlefield. It is only unfortunate that we do not have one hundred of her. We might go a long way toward wiping the blight of vampirism from the earth completely."

Marie-Christine smiled. "We will one day, Harold. Perhaps not in my lifetime or yours, but one day."

Travers returned her smile. Theirs was a quiet affection built up over years of acquaintance that had never quite blossomed into friendship. She had never married, and Harold Travers was a widower. It had always seemed to her best to keep him at arm's length, for she could not afford any silly romantic entanglements within the Council. Particularly not at her age.

"Tea, Marie-Christine?" he asked.

"No," she replied. "Your kind boy brought me some cocoa earlier. But thank you, Harold."

He might have spoken again but the door bell chimed far away, echoing down to them from the front of the house. Mr. Travers frowned and Miss Fontaine imagined it was an accurate reflection of the expression on her own face.

She rose from her chair, sharing a silent exchange with Mr. Travers. It was very unusual for them to receive visitors who felt it necessary to ring the bell, particularly this late at night. Together, they started down the long hallway toward the front of the house. The walls were decorated with ancient weapons and portraits of some of the Council's most famous members. No Slayers here. They were honored in other areas of the house, but the main hall was a place to remember Watchers, not the girls in their charge.

Voices drifted to them from the front door. Anxious tones and clipped words. Marie-Christine heard someone say *please,* and alarm bells went off in her mind.

"Harold," she whispered.

He nodded and they picked up their pace. Already the conversation had become more clear. A man's voice, British, speaking with Marco Giampa. The Italian boy's accent was immediately recognizable.

"Look you've got to let us in. The bastards who did this to her are right 'round the corner. They'll be on your doorstep in a minute. Phone up Scotland bloody Yard if you want, just give us five minutes and your phone to call a doctor. She'll die otherwise."

Miss Fontaine heard Marco sigh as they came around the corner and into sight of the foyer and the front door. On the stoop a man with white-blond hair cradled a raven-tressed woman in a blood-spattered dress in his arms, a pleading expression on his face.

"All right," Marco said. "You may—"

Mr. Travers screamed.

The bloody girl surged from her lover's arms like an uncaged beast and landed on top of Marco, driving him back against the stairs. The sounds of her teeth tearing his throat were all that could be heard in that moment save the ticking of the pendulum in the grandfather clock against the far wall.

"No!" Marie-Christine shouted. "Don't let them—"

The blond vampire crossed the threshold and slammed the door behind him. He smiled, face both angelic and mischievous.

"Thanks ever so much for the hospitality," he said. "I'm Spike. That's Drusilla. We've been sent with a message to all you bloody annoying wankers up here."

"Unclean thing!" Travers shouted. "You have no place here!" He kicked a baluster out of the main stairwell and hefted it, aiming its splintered end like a stake as he ran at Spike.

The vampire dodged, reached out a hand with incredible speed and grabbed Mr. Travers by the back of the neck. He propelled the man faster and faster, using Travers's own momentum to drive him headfirst into the wall. The man crumpled to the ground with a grunt, the makeshift stake clattering to the wooden floor.

"You don't want my message?" Spike asked.

Marie-Christine was frozen, uncertain what to do. She did not know who else was in the building. It was late enough that those who had homes of their own were long gone, and yet early enough that others who lived on the premises had not yet returned.

On the stairs the female, Drusilla, sat up and drew an already bloody sleeve across her mouth, smearing red life across her cheeks like soot on a chimney sweep. "That's not very polite," she said in a singsong voice. "Not polite at all. You don't want to be rude and offend us, love."

"Oh no, not that," Marie-Christine said, managing to scoff. "Then you might try to kill us."

In response, the vampire girl giggled and spun into a mad pirouette. Her feet were bare and she slid in Marco's blood without losing her balance at all. She seemed to relish it, lifting her emerald velvet skirts and flowing like a reed on the breeze.

Suddenly she stopped and stared at her lover in a pout.

"What is it, Dru?" Spike asked worriedly.

"That one," she said, suddenly seeming almost afraid, filled with disgust. She shuddered into a kind of revolted tantrum. "He's still alive, Spike, and he's staring at me."

They all looked at Mr. Travers's still form on the ground. His chest rose and fell. He was indeed alive, but lay on his side, quite unconscious.

"He's out cold, Dru," Spike protested.

She shuddered even more as if she might have a fit of some kind.

Spike sighed, rolled his eyes, then bent over Travers's body.

"No, please stop!" Marie-Christine screamed.

Tears sprang to her eyes as the vampire snapped Harold Travers's neck without another word. She ran back down along the main hall to the first weapons display she came to. There was a sword there, but she was too old and weak to be able to decapitate even one of the creatures, never mind both. Her only choice was the crossbow. There were bolts there as well and she grabbed them off the wall. When she turned to head back to the foyer, the vampires were already coming for her. Slowly. Spike with his hands clasped behind his back, watching her curiously. Drusilla closed in upon herself like a frightened child, red-stained hands fluttering in front of her as though they had a language of their own.

As she watched, Spike's face changed. From angelic, it became the visage of the devil himself. He opened his mouth and hissed and Marie-Christine found she could barely control her old bladder.

"Don't you want the message I bring? Hear it and we'll go," he promised.

"Murdering . . . vile . . ." she muttered, nocking a bolt in the crossbow.

There was the thunder of heavy footfalls on the stairs. Young John Travers must have been elsewhere in the huge house. Now he screamed as he came upon the sight of Marco's ravaged body, and the broken corpse of his own father.

"John, no!" Marie-Christine shouted. "Run. Call for help!"

Spike glanced back at the youthful Watcher as he stood in the foyer glaring at them. Young Travers bolted, running out of the room for a moment.

Drusilla giggled. "He looks yummy," she said, and then she went after him.

Marie-Christine had had all the time in the world to concentrate, to focus her aim on Spike's chest. On his heart. But she was twenty feet away when she let the bolt fly. It struck Spike in the center of the chest, inches away from his heart. He grunted and took a step back, then flashed his fangs and yellow eyes at her in a fury.

"Tell me, you silly cow, what the hell do you do when the postman comes with a bleedin' package? D'you stab him in the throat?"

She tried nocking another bolt but he was there too quickly. Spike batted the crossbow from her hands and she simply wilted in front of him. Humiliation flooded through her. After all the years she had served, the demons she had fought, the vampires she had destroyed, how could the fear have gotten hold of her so deeply.

The answer came to her with brutal simplicity. *I am old.*

Spike slammed her back against the wall and pinned her there. He glanced back down the corridor to see Drusilla dragging John Travers by the hair. She let him flop there on the ground and Marie-Christine prayed that he was still alive; though in truth she had not much hope for either of them. The side of Drusilla's face was blackened and charred in the shape of the cross. The smell of burning flesh lingered in the air. She knew what had happened right away. John had been smart. He had run for the cross on the wall in the parlor. But it had availed him nothing.

"Are you hurt, poodle?" Spike asked tenderly.

"A little," Drusilla replied, as though it were a thrill. "Though I'd rather you had done it to me."

The mad vampire girl poked at her burned face with a long fingernail and began to tear a strip of charred flesh from her cheek. Marie-Christine winced and looked down, unable to watch any longer.

"Now you'll kill me too, I suppose." She loathed herself for her inability to meet Spike's gaze.

"Are you daft, or just deaf?" he shouted at her.

She flinched and looked up. The vampire sighed in frustration.

"First thing, boy's not dead," he said. "Second, I told you we were here with a message. Message is, quit. Just stop. All of you. You been hunting us long enough. We can do the same. Call off your girl."

A perverse grin split his features, his lips curling back around his fangs. "Let my people go," he said gleefully. "I'm the bloody Moses of vampires."

Then he struck her across the face hard enough to knock her head into the wall. The nearest portrait fell to the ground, splintering the frame. She was lost to the darkness.

Spike stood looking down at the gray-haired lady Watcher.

"You think she bought it, Dru?" he asked idly. "I mean, you think I was convincing enough?"

"Oh yes," she said, dancing up beside him.

They kissed, nipping each other's tongues, and Spike licked the burned portion of her cheek. Drusilla winced, then moaned just a little. He wondered if the boy had been too quick with the cross, or if she had simply not cared if he burned her or not.

"Right then," he said, turning around and looking up the stairs. "You stay here. Make sure they don't wake up but don't kill them. No point to our 'message' if there's no one to carry it, is there? Anyone comes in though, you can kill them all right. I've got to find what we're looking for and copy it over. Shouldn't be twenty minutes."

Drusilla was eyeing the weapons on the wall in the main hall.

"Take all the time you need, Spike," she whispered. "Mommy has some new toys to play with."

He shook his head indulgently. "All right, pet," he said. "Do whatever you want to the dead ones. But I'll only tell you one more time. Don't touch the ones that are still breathing, right?"

"I'll be a good girl," she promised.

Spike had been wrong. It took him nearly forty minutes to find what he was looking for, copy it, and return it to its place so that no one would notice that it had been disturbed. When he went back down to the foyer, Drusilla was still playing.

The River Somme, France
May 21st

In the burned-out shell of a French troop carrier, the Slayer crouched in darkness and stared at the young soldiers at rest atop a tank not fifty yards away. The German Panzer was a massive metal beast with shuttered viewports, a riveted steel face, and a short turret gun whose truncated appearance gave it an air of additional brutality. Yet with the quartet of grim boy soldiers who surrounded it, sitting on the turret or leaning against the treads, cigarettes burning in their mouths, the scene almost seemed absurd.

They're no older than I am, Sophie thought. *Or at least not much older.*

It was far from the first time the thought had occurred to her but she continued to be astonished by it. The German army had thundered down the center of France like lightning splitting the trunk of a tree. North and south were separated now and still the Nazi soldiers came, pressing the lines of battle farther on every side. Here, in the south, the French had managed to stall them at the River Somme, but only briefly. The Germans had taken the river and even now the front lines had been moved south of it. More ground was being lost.

Sophie could not afford to be seen during the day, not by either side. French or German, the soldiers would not want a girl running about the lines. At night, though, she was able to slip among the regrouping troops when necessary. And it was necessary, in order to get to the dead and dying. That was where the scavengers were found, the vampires who lurked on the battlefields after dark like Valkyries collecting the souls of fallen warriors.

For the moment, she and Yanna had a safe place north of the river, a place only a little damaged by the war. She would rather have been on the French side of the battle than the German, but it seemed that in short order there would no longer be a French side at all. Even with their allies from Britain and elsewhere, the French were losing ground too quickly to face anything but conquest.

Sophie told herself that this was not the war she had come for. But it was not easy to keep her focus.

Until the vampires showed themselves.

The Slayer remained perfectly still in the husk of the vehicle. The moon was a bright sliver above and the stars glittered like jewels. *Beautiful,* she thought. But little more than pearls before swine for all the appreciation they inspired among those who perpetrated the slaughter below—the killers on all sides, Nazi, Allied, and the other, of course. The vampires.

The celestial illumination was limited, but enough that Sophie could see the five—no six—scavengers as they slowly surrounded the tank, keeping to the shadows, moving among the metal corpses and the fresh human dead as well. The vultures had likely been seeking those not quite dead on the battlefield, the young boys bleeding out on the soil of France or lying on the banks of the Somme with their life trickling into the water. The tank crew had drawn the wrong sort of attention with their talking and smoking.

As Sophie had suspected they might.

As she had hoped they would.

They were bait.

The scavengers were fast. One of the soldiers was dead almost before the others realized they were under attack. A second one screamed as his head was yanked back, leaving his throat exposed. He scrabbled for his sidearm even as Sophie bolted across the stretch of blasted earth between them, long legs flying in the regulation British army pants she wore, stake in hand.

The sharpened length of wood made a satisfying thunk as she rammed it into the chest cavity of the nearest vampire. The monster exploded in a cloud of ash that the wind did not even have time to catch before a second of the scavengers was dust.

Sophie was swift and deadly as she moved among them, yet still all four members of the tank crew died before the last of the vampires had been eliminated.

A grim set to her mouth, Sophie stared down at the dead boys, four more in such a long procession of them in recent days, and an infinite number to follow. *Not much older than I am,* she thought again.

Her priorities were clear. Her war was with the vampires. It was not her place to choose sides in this one. And yet these boys were part of the army that had trampled her own homeland and subjugated her people.

She had not *let* them die. Sophie would not, could not have done such a thing.

But she had to wonder if she could have moved faster.

Chapter Six

Liverpool, England
May 22nd

"Hello, what's this? Ain't you a pretty bird?"

The voice came to Drusilla as if a whisper and she stretched her arms out languidly as though she had been sleeping. Lorries and rattling autos chugged by, blasting horrid exhaust. Nearby someone was singing badly to a melody played on an out-of-tune piano. Raucous laughter exploded behind her and she blinked.

"Eh, girl, I'm talkin' to yer."

Lashes fluttering, she turned to the brute who had spoken. He was a fetid beast of a man with both brawn and bulk, as evidenced by the breadth of his shoulders and the paunch of his gut. He smelled as though he had been swimming in ale, and something brown had dried on the long brush of a mustache that hung over his lip. His brows were furrowed and angry as though he had a tiger inside.

But he had eyes like a ferret, frightened and suspicious.

"I'm talkin' ta yer!" he said, loud and slow as though she were stupid.

Drusilla was not stupid. She smiled at the man, unmindful of those who might be watching through the filthy windows of the pub behind them. Eyes wide, lips open suggestively, she began a serpentine swaying that brought first a lascivious grin and then an uncertain quiver to his features.

She moved nearer to him, still swaying, and his eyes were only on her. There were whores out on the street, girls he might have had for the change in his pocket. He was a mouse, this man, and he had made the mistake of drawing the attention of the cat.

"What a specimen you are," Drusilla drawled. She touched his chest, pushed herself against him. "A skulking human animal. Are they afraid of you, the women? Can't they smell the fear on you? It's like cinnamon and offal."

Mesmerized, he only swayed along with her, subject to her every whim. Laughter thundered from the pub again and a glass shattered somewhere. The man's face had changed. He had the aspect of a hog now, wild and tusked and snorting. That was how she saw him. The putrid stench of his fear, sickly sweet with cinnamon, filled her with both pleasure and disgust. She heard horses' hooves thundering close by and knew that it was death riding for the slobbering hog before her.

"Think we'll take a walk," she said, snickering deep in her chest. "Lovely night for a walk."

She began to lead him toward the alley beside the pub, but Spike stepped up behind her and laid a hand on her shoulder.

"Hold on, pet," he said, his voice low and musical. "Our girl's here."

Excited, Drusilla turned, eyes wide again as Spike gestured to the short, pale girl walking beside a silver-haired man of perhaps fifty. Grinning, a flutter of crawling insects in her belly, Drusilla threw her arms around Spike and kissed him deeply, though both of them remained completely aware of the girl and her Watcher as they passed.

Her name was Kate Hutchins.

"That one?" Drusilla asked, a bit surprised, as Kate and her Watcher went into the door that would lead to the rooms they had taken above the pub. "Might be the Slayer someday?"

"No," Spike said, nostrils flaring dangerously. "No, she won't."

Drusilla's lips were set in a thin, mischievous smile as she and her lover went to that door and followed the pair up to their rooms. On the curb in front of the pub, the rancid drunk shook his head, blinked his eyes, and headed back in for another pint.

Above the laughter and the music, no one heard a thing.

Dunkirk, France
May 28th

The coast was lined with ships of every conceivable size and purpose. The massive behemoths of the British navy were moored as close as they could manage off Dunkirk. Yachts and fishing boats buzzed around them like flies, ferrying men back and forth from the shore.

France was lost. The Germans had conquered her unimaginably fast. The British Expeditionary Force and regular army soldiers who had fought valiantly to prevent it were now forced to withdraw. Dunkirk was the last bastion of fighting in France, where hundreds of thousands of warriors stood fast against the blitzkrieg. Though most of the fighting men were unaware of it, the British were evacuating without having informed their French allies. It was their only recourse, and though bitter, all involved were aware of it. There were more than a quarter of a million Allied soldiers at Dunkirk awaiting transport across the Channel. If there was any hope of rallying from the astonishing German victories to take back the continent, those men could not be sacrificed.

The call had gone out up and down the southeast coast of England. Every boat, large or small, was needed to ferry British and French fighters across the Channel, or from the shores of Dunkirk to the larger boats that could not come any closer. The response had been immediate and overwhelming. In the dead of night, men waited in the thousands on the coast for their turn. There were incidents of violence and ignoble behavior, but for the most part, they waited with grim determination.

There was a plan. Winston Churchill, the new prime minister, would not allow this to be the end of the war. The battle for France was lost, but as a nation, Great Britain was determined that there would be another. Men swam out to the vessels in the water by the hundreds, they floated on chairs and boards and bits of flotsam. All with the knowledge in their minds that it was not over.

They would return.

At least, that was the spin the captain of the *Seaspray* had put on it. Ned Jude was his name, and he'd been dredging the oyster beds near Burnham-on-Crouch in

Essex with his ship when the news had spread. Old Ned had dropped his work, refueled and set off across the Channel quick as could be. For the first half a day he had ferried a dozen men at a time across the water back to England. On the last trip, however, one of the soldiers had suggested it might be more efficient if he used the comparatively small ship to pick up men at the shore and deliver them to one of the navy ships.

"Felt like a damn fool, William, I can tell you that. It was the plain truth, and I should have seen it."

It was perhaps the fiftieth time Ned had said as such, but Spike nodded earnestly to the man as though he thought the old oysterman was doing a bit of difference; as though he cared. In a quiet moment, he confessed to himself that he did care, just a little bit. Not for the people, not that. He was a vampire, after all, and the behavior of humans who were not currently his victims did not interest him. But there was a part of his humanity that lingered, that haunted him like a phantom limb. The idea that the Germans might actually defeat the British Empire set his teeth on edge until he reminded himself that he was not supposed to care.

Cigarette clamped between his lips, Spike watched the churning waters ahead as they approached the shore of Dunkirk. The men were everywhere. A pack of fools were rowing a small boat out into deeper water, barely able to keep from hitting men who were swimming or floating in the surf.

"What a bloody circus," he whispered.

" 'Tis," Ned Jude agreed. "But we've all got our part to play, 'ey?"

"Oh, aye," Spike replied, surprised that the old skipper had heard him.

"Still," Ned said cautiously, "don't want to tell you your business lad, but takin' that girl ashore . . ."

The ruddy-jowled seaman shook his head and scratched at the white stubble on his cheeks. No other words were necessary.

"It's out of my hands, Ned. She's got three brothers taken prisoner in Rotterdam and she's determined to see them free. Believes Gerry'll take pity on her and her old mum, being without any man at all. We'll likely die, but neither one of us could face her mum if we didn't try."

Ned Jude scowled.

"We've got to try, old chap."

The skipper said nothing else but it was clear from his expression that he thought Spike and Drusilla would be killed by the first Germans they came across. If the story had been true, Spike judged the old man was probably right.

Let them shoot, he thought.

Drusilla came out of the cabin and stood silently beside him, the elegant blue dress beneath her heavy coat hinting at an aristocratic background that seemed to garner great deference from the seamen.

For once her face was grim and blank, no playful expression, no pout. She watched the exodus on the shore without comment or response. For his part, Spike wondered why he had bothered expending so much energy on the story he told the old man. He considered the possibility that he wanted to avoid having to kill Ned Jude, and then dismissed it. He was merely focused, that was all, intent upon their purpose and wanting to do nothing to slow their progress. Hunting in London had been simple enough, but this—hunting in conquered France—was something else completely.

"They're winning," Drusilla whispered beside him. "The mermaids all have guns and are watching over them."

He glanced at her, eyebrows raised. "How can they be winning?" he demanded. "They're retreating."

"Oh, but they're angry now, don't you feel it? It's like hornets in my eyes," Dru replied.

"God's truth, that is," Ned Jude rumbled beyond them. "'Til now our lads were fightin' for others, helping out their neighbors. This changes everything."

Spike marveled once again at the skipper's hearing. Before he could reply, however, Ned cut the engine and let the *Seaspray* drift. They had moved close enough to shore now that the nearest of the swimming soldiers had reached them.

"Lend a hand!" the skipper called to Spike, who was astonished to find himself doing precisely that.

After he had helped pull the first couple of soaked soldiers on board, however, the process took over. Men held on to the side of the boat as others climbed over them. Ned cranked up the engine and moved his ship closer to shore, and soon enough the *Seaspray* was full. The ruddy-faced skipper had a grave expression that was nevertheless filled with pride. He glanced at Spike, who had hoped not to have to get wet.

"Good a spot as any, Ned," Spike told him. He ducked into the cabin, pushing past soldiers who were astonished at the presence of Drusilla on the boat. For her part, his lover was smiling coquettishly at the battered troops. Spike grabbed the two bags in which they'd packed a few items of clothing and pulled her by the hand as he went back out onto the deck. When the soldiers realized they meant to get off the boat, they raised a furor, but the skipper informed them that the young couple was not to be dissuaded. He explained the predicament about Drusilla's three brothers, and the men all nodded gravely.

Ned got the boat close enough that the water was only up to Spike's chest when he jumped in. Drusilla was lowered gently over the side by several of the soldiers and then the boat churned away toward a naval vessel, so Ned could dump this load and then go back for the next.

They waded ashore amidst a dense forest of humanity. Now that he could truly see the numbers involved, Spike knew it would take days more before all the troops at Dunkirk could be withdrawn. He wondered if they had days to spare, or if the Germans would break down their defenses too soon. If so, there would be a massacre, with the blood and gore spread so thick across the landscape it would look like Hell on Earth. He was tempted to stay behind to see how it turned out, but they had places to be.

Orleans, France
May 29th

Drusilla was bored. The war ranged far and wide across France. The German army had split the nation in two and were trampling it underfoot. But by traveling at night on little used roads they had missed most of the carnage she had hoped to see. Thus far they had killed their fair share of both German and French soldiers at roadblocks and other spots along the way, and thus had acquired a cache of weapons and gasoline. But there was a kind of joylessness to the times in between that made her cranky.

It had been chaos and dread and terror at Dunkirk, a dizzying carnival of wounded men and wounded spirits that had been like an amusement park ride to her. Spike had been furious at the dozens of questions, the need for them to repeat the lies about her brothers in Rotterdam over and over just to get away from the retreating army. He wanted to kill and Drusilla would not have balked. She could envision the crescendo of death and viscera that would have ensued if they had begun to tear into the first of several hundred thousand soldiers. The sound of blood pumping through one excited soldier's heart had been almost too much for her, and Drusilla had started to stroke him to distraction before Spike intervened.

There had been a fight. The soldier's superior had been forced to step in. Drusilla had blown them both a kiss as Spike had dragged her away, chiding her. If she wanted Freyja's Strand, she would have to play along. A delicious thrill went through her every time she thought of that trinket, the necklace of the Brisings. Such an old bit of magic, such a wonderful toy. Oh, how she wanted it, sparkling there around her throat.

The British soldiers had given them a clanking truck that would have been left behind otherwise. Spike was even angry about that. They had killed for the clothes they were wearing and the valises that they carried, and he had so wanted to kill for transportation, after having been around so many humans at one time.

"What is it, Dru?" he snapped suddenly, as the truck bumped over the rutted road.

"Bored, bored," she replied with a wave and a pout. "There's no music at all now. I'm buried in the grave of this dull war."

Spike glanced sidelong at her, eyebrows raised. "You're not the only one who's bored, pet. Not to worry, though. Things'll get more lively soon, I promise. We've got a lot of Slayers-in-Waiting to kill, and I know how that pleases you."

Drusilla sighed. "I wanted whole vistas of war. Battle-fields drenched in blood from horizon to horizon as the sweaty, wounded men murder each other and the demons in their bellies spill out onto the ground. I wanted opera. Mushrooms grow in the shattered skulls of soldiers, and I wanted those too."

He sighed. "Look, if we pass a big battle in progress, I promise we'll stop, all right?"

"Mmm," she said, writhing pleasurably on the torn seat, sliding over to twine her fingers in his hair and scratch his chest. Spike barked in pain and shot her a withering glance before returning his attention to the road.

"Not now, Dru," he snarled.

"Come on," she wheedled. "You smell like chocolate. I want a taste. I want to be dirty, out on the ground under the moon. With my ear to the earth, I can hear the moans of the dying. They sound like crows."

Spike's eyes blazed and she could see he was tempted. A low chuckle rumbled in her throat.

Bright lights flashed through the truck's cracked windshield and Spike swore.

"Bloody hell. Well, Dru, at least you got your wish."

"Oh goody," she said in a throaty rasp.

He killed the truck's engine, then reached out to stroke her cheek. "You hungry, love?"

"Famished."

Drusilla opened the door and stepped out of the truck. The soldiers who ran toward them were French, and they held their weapons at the ready, wary of spies or German reconnaissance. Two of them stood in front of the truck while one went to the driver's side door and a fourth approached Drusilla, shouting at her to put her hands up.

She obeyed with a shy smile, but she continued moving toward him, weaving her body like a serpent, speaking to him in lilting French. Her fingers twirled in the air before her, as though she were Salome and this her last dance, and then her hands moved down over the peasant gown that covered the soft curves of her flesh. The two soldiers who stood in front of the truck at first frowned and called out for their fellow to be careful. But then they were watching her hands and eyes and the way she moved, listening to her voice.

"That's it, lovely fatted calves," she told them in English, eyelids fluttering lazily, contentedly. "Come to me."

The three were mesmerized. Fifty yards beyond them, where the two large trucks were pulled across the road, three or four other men smoked cigarettes and eyed the new arrivals carefully. They were paying particular attention to Drusilla. They were too far away to be hypnotized, but close enough for enchantment and temptation. She provided both.

On the other side of the truck, Spike offered the French soldier at the driver's window a cigarette. The man ignored him, glaring suspiciously. "Do you not see that we're British, Pierre?" Spike snapped, growing agitated. "Do I sound like a bloody Nazi to you?"

In halting English, the French soldier—who was a bit older than the average and had quite a bit of stubble on his cheeks—admitted that Spike did not sound like Nazi.

"Look, old man, the war is behind us," Spike said. "We're going away from it. Seems like a damned sensible course of action to me. Could we just get on our way, then?"

The French sergeant thought about it another moment and then nodded in agreement. He was about to say something when his gaze went across the truck to Drusilla and the men who were gathered around her, flirting with her, even rubbing against her. The soldier frowned.

Spike whipped open the door and knocked him back, then reached through the open window and ripped the soldier's gun from his hands before the man could even fall. With a short burst from the machine gun he perforated the fallen man's chest, then turned the gun on the vehicles that comprised the roadblock. Bullets ripped the air.

With a swift flick of her wrist, Drusilla tore out the throat of the man nearest her, then caught his body before it fell. Lithe and ghostly, it was easy for even Spike to forget her strength, but she turned the soldier around, got control of his gun, and then cut down the other two in front of her while using their comrade as a shield. She laughed as she did it. Gouts of blood from her human shield's torn jugular pumped from his throat to splash on the ground, and she stretched out her tongue to let the crimson flow spatter her mouth like a child catching snowflakes.

Drusilla paid little attention to the soldiers at the roadblock. There were three of them left alive when she was extending her tongue for that special treat. One of those grunted in surprise as a bullet passed through his forehead, blowing the back of his skull out in a shower of bone and brain.

"Damn it!" Spike shouted as a bullet tore through his ribcage. "I didn't want to get shot again."

Dru flinched and began to whine, as if the pain were her own. Her baby was hurt. Poor Spike. She turned to glare at the two soldiers who still lived, hiding behind one of the trucks.

"Naughty, naughty things," she said, her voice almost a groan, her features now contorted into the countenance of the vampire. "You hurt my baby."

She dropped the corpse from her embrace. Weaponless she began to run at the roadblock. They fired at her, but Drusilla moved so quickly, leaping from side to side, that not a single bullet touched her. Her hands went out to touch metal and she vaulted over the truck, rolled across the top, and fell on the men, talons whickering through the air as they slashed downward. The first man she blinded. The other died quickly, his neck broken by a simple twist. Spike stomped about petulantly, cigarette clenched between his teeth.

"All right, love," she told her man. "Drusilla's going to make you all better. Here, have a bite. It'll do you wonders."

Later, when they'd cleared off, taking the fuel and weapons the dead soldiers had bequeathed to them, Spike and Drusilla found a secluded villa and pulled off the road. They killed everyone inside, save for the elderly grandmother. She was blind and unable to walk and it was far more amusing to leave her alive. When they had drunk their fill of the family and taken all the baubles that sparkled enough to catch Drusilla's eye, they made love in a slippery pool of gore in a second floor bed chamber. She dug the bullet out of his flesh with her fingernails, then kissed and licked the wound until it was all better.

And then they slept.

Drusilla wasn't bored anymore.

Nice, France
June 2nd

It was hard riding up the hill to Monsieur Arno's villa, but the girl did not mind. The little road rose up parallel to the crashing surf of the French Riviera, and the view was astonishing. When she had been taken away from her parents to be trained by the Council, Collette Boisvert had never envisioned her preparation for the future would take place in such an idyllic location.

Nor had she imagined that, during that time, all of Europe would be at war. It seemed distant to her, and Monsieur Arno insisted that it was none of their concern; they were fighting a war that had been going on for ages, and would continue long after the present conflict had ended. But it was still a distraction.

Her parents were in Paris, and Collette feared for them.

The muscles in her legs had begun to burn and her lungs ached. Collette did not slow, however; rather, she sped up, putting every ounce of effort she could summon into pedaling the last quarter mile to her Watcher's villa. The girl lived in the center of Nice in a moderately appointed apartment provided by the Council, along with Sally, an older woman whom the Council had appointed as her chaperone. A young girl could not very well live alone in a villa on the Riviera with a much older man without raising eyebrows. Perhaps the locals would not have cared, but Collette's parents had been adamant.

She had decided that was all for the best, as Monsieur Arno enjoyed an active social life that included a great deal of wine and at least half a dozen different local girls that Collette had seen come and go from the villa.

Tonight was to be a celebration of sorts. Just lately they had been working to raise her proficiency with fighting staves as well as studying the various known demon species and methods of combatting them. It was all quite rigorous but she was up to it. This evening's dinner—no doubt to be accompanied by several toasts—was in honor of her completing her training in staves. Tomorrow she would move on to fencing, and she was excited by the idea of it. *The Three Musketeers* was her favorite novel. At night when she closed her eyes and put a name to the boy of her dreams, it was always D'Artagnan.

Collette was thirteen years old.

She left her bike on the grass in front of the villa. No one would be up here this late at night, and even if someone were to come by, she was hardly worried about thieves. The very idea seemed absurd. In Paris, things had been different. Being in Nice, spending so much time at Monsieur Arno's villa, was like stepping back in time.

LeBeau, the butler, met her at the front door. The man was insufferably smug nearly all of the time. He did not work for the Council but was rather a servant of the Arno family. Though he would never dare have spoken his thoughts aloud, LeBeau had never done very much to hide his obvious disapproval of the amount of time Collette spent with his employer. The girl thought that, this evening, the old man looked even more put out and censorious than usual.

"*Bonsoir,* LeBeau."

"Mademoiselle," the man sniffed.

"Monsieur Arno, *est-il la?*" she asked, merely to be polite, for she knew Arno was at home. He had invited her, after all.

"*La salle a manger,*" the butler replied curtly. He stood back to let her pass and Collette rolled her eyes as she walked toward the dining room at the end of the hall.

LeBeau closed the door behind her and went off into the bowels of the house to do whatever it was he did when not gruffly answering the door. Collette thought the rest of his job likely consisted of gossiping about his employer with the cook and the maid, but she said nothing to Arno. He would have been greatly saddened.

As she walked down the corridor toward the dining room, Collette heard the sound of a woman laughing, high and delicate, a light breeze jostling a crystal chandelier. She paused just outside the large wooden door. Within, Arno laughed as well. Collette closed her eyes tightly and her chin fell, just a bit. Their dinner. Their celebration. And he had forgotten, brought some perfumed trollop up from town. Her heart broke then; just a tiny crack, barely noticeable to any but herself.

With a sigh, she began to turn away. Then her disappointment was replaced by anger and Collette went to the dining room door and pulled it open. A slender, pale woman with cascading black hair sat too close to Monsieur Arno, sipping her wine and staring at him with wide eyes and a suggestive smile that said that *he* was the main course. Arno was quite obviously intoxicated, recounting some adventure or other in a drunkard's drawl. At the other end of the table sat a man with hair so blond it was white. He smiled warmly at the girl as she entered, and Collette frowned.

"You have a guest, Henri," the woman said, and her accent revealed her to be English.

Arno spilled his wine as he slid around in his chair. His face blossomed into an enormous grin when he saw Collette. He stood up and went to her, took her hand in his and grandly led her farther into the room. She tried to ignore the reek of the wine that had spilled on his clothing.

"My dear Collette," he said in English.

She was not certain if he spoke the language of his guests to impress them or because he knew that Collette needed to practice.

"Let me introduce you to my new friends. They so wanted to meet you, and I did not think you would mind adding two more to our celebration this evening. The young lady is Deandra and the gentleman is her brother William." He then regarded his other guests more closely. "My friends, this is the girl I have been telling you about, my young pupil, Collette Boisvert."

The blond man rose from the table, lifting a wine glass in the process. He began to move around the table, closer to where Collette and Arno stood. There was something about his smile, a kind of brutal sparkle in his eyes, that told Collette immediately that he was not what he appeared to be. This was a cruel man, she could tell that just by looking at him.

"Yes, congratulations," William said pleasantly.

He had a grin like a prowling cat, and Collette did not trust him at all. She could not understand why Arno would have invited such people back to his home. Then she noticed the woman again. Even now she was refilling Arno's wine glass. After that Collette understood perfectly.

"A toast, shall we?" William asked. "Now that you've finally arrived, that is." He moved closer, until he was standing only a few feet from Collette and Arno.

"We've been waiting for you."

Venice, Italy
June 12th

Alessandra Cavallaro lingered in the twilight realm between consciousness and death. She had long since lost the feeling in her arms and legs. Now the fourteen-year-old only felt heavy. So heavy.

She had been hung from the doors of St. Mark's Cathedral by heavy metal spikes—railroad spikes—that had been driven into her open palms and the tops of her feet. They had capered on the cobblestoned square at four in the morning, killing seven different people who had passed by and tried to come to her aid, and then they had stabbed her in the side with a long knife and knelt beneath her with their mouths open as if for communion. Or, perhaps more accurately, like besotted revelers falling open-mouthed before the open tap of a free-flowing beer barrel.

Only when the sky began to lighten and people began to emerge onto the open square before the cathedral did they at last withdraw. Alessandra could not move by then, not even blink. Her own blood, what remained of it, had begun to fill her lungs and chest cavity, and soon she was drowning in it, choking on it, tasting its copper flavor in her mouth. Her last coherent thought was a jolt of fear, wondering if somehow that would make her like them.

Warsaw, Poland
June 16th

Weeping, cradling his broken arm against his body as best he could in the makeshift sling he had fastened around his neck, Jozeff Strakus dragged the broken, mutilated body of Marya Bajdek half a mile to get her out of the filthy street. It was the only way he could be sure that the dogs would not get to her corpse.

After he had sent for help, Jozeff sat and stroked the girl's brown hair and shook with the power of the sobs that tore through him.

Marya Bajdek had been murdered at the age of eleven.

Chapter Seven

London, England
June 20th

The mood was more than somber in the building at the far end of Great Russell Street. It was funereal. British military forces had been absolutely routed by the Germans in France, hundreds of thousands forced to evacuate via Dunkirk, and now the barely solvent, rusting British Empire seemed the last bastion of freedom in Western Europe. How that had happened, and so quickly, beggared the imagination. Yet it had.

War. Parliament was retrenching. The people were gritting their teeth and angrily looking east for another chance at Adolf's men. Churchill was attempting to build a victorious war machine from the remains of years worth of overconfidence and torpidity. For it was clear that the Germans had only just begun. Hitler believed in a manifest destiny for his Third Reich, his so-called master race.

And if the British could not do better, that grotesque vision might well come true.

War. It was the only topic on the lips of His Majesty's subjects throughout Brittania, in bedrooms and boardrooms and pubs. Yet in the meeting chamber in the building on Great Russell Street, the war that was being addressed did not involve Adolf Hitler. The Nazis attacked with savagery and speed, but the war had not really come as a surprise save for those who had tried to pretend it was not on the horizon.

The Council of Watchers faced an even more insidious foe, an enemy who used deceit and the element of surprise, who struck from the shadows, an adversary who chose assassination and subterfuge over all-out combat.

A hideous evil. A devil, if ever there was one.

"It's Spike," Marie-Christine Fontaine told the Council's board of directors.

Their reactions were what she had expected. It had been difficult enough to deal with the savage attack upon their headquarters the previous month. Though the building was protected by wards and charms against magickal attack, over time security had grown lax. No one had ever imagined that vampires would have the audacity to attack the Council so directly, or that even the most naïve Watcher-in-Training would be stupid enough to be fooled into inviting one inside.

Already security was being checked and redoubled, the specific invitation for Spike and Drusilla sorcerously revoked, and additional measures put in place, both human and magickal.

The violation of the sanctity of the Council headquarters would have been horrible enough were it not for the events that had followed it, the month-long series of murders that had claimed both Watchers and the candidates they were training as potential Slayers. The search for such girls was ongoing, but in light of the recent murders, efforts had been made to speed the process, attempting to identify new candidates. Widening the net. With the recent murders, however, it had been deemed best to pinpoint the location of these girls but to hold off on contacting them or beginning their training until the Council could find the fiends responsible for the killings, and stop them.

Now the worst was confirmed.

"The same vampires who perpetrated the attack upon these premises last month are also behind the murder spree that has so profoundly affected us all. Given the pair's history, it was presumed that the attack was simply that, an assault upon the sanctity of the Council's headquarters, perhaps as a reprisal for past conflicts or—equally possible for these two—simply because they could.

"Since several of you have recently returned from excursions abroad, and might not have read my report on that attack, I will reiterate. Spike, also known as William the Bloody, has a very colorful history that includes the killing of a Slayer in 1900. His companion Drusilla is also his sire, and she was herself sired by Angelus. Drusilla is a formidable opponent in her own right, but reports indicate that she is quite deliriously demented, and therefore would likely lack the focus for either the earlier assault, or these recent murders, were it not for Spike's presence."

An elderly man with a thick gray mustache cleared his throat. When he spoke, he did not bother to take his pipe from between his clenched teeth.

"We're certain that Spike and Drusilla are also responsible for these recent killings? The Slayers-in-Waiting?" the man rasped.

"Quite certain, Sir Nigel," Marie-Christine said. "The two of them use one another's names freely, just as they did in my presence the night of their attack here. I had previously believed that their initial attack was prompted by an effort to dissuade the Council from its mission. The night Harold Travers was killed, Spike said he was delivering a message."

"From whom?" Sir Nigel barked angrily, and sat back in his high-backed leather chair.

"Another vampire? A collective of them, perhaps?" Marie-Christine suggested. "Only Spike himself can answer that question. There is another possibility, however."

"We're waiting, Fontaine," Sir Nigel replied, grimacing at her from beneath his bushy eyebrows.

"I have done a great deal of research into Drusilla's past, and Spike's history with her," she explained. "It is a tale of excess and whimsy. The tides have carried them, and the winds, but never a vendetta, as far as I can tell."

Sir Nigel scoffed at that. Though no vote had been taken, the old man seemed to have assumed the role of spokesman for the board, at least for the moment. He puffed on his pipe as he glared at her.

"These two vampires brought murder to our Council, came into this house and drew blood," Sir Nigel said gruffly. "The rogues delivered their message. But more than that, to be sure. After they killed, and after you and young John Travers were unconscious, they must have copied the list we had compiled of Slayers-in-Waiting and their Watchers, then put it back so we would be none the wiser. Until now.

"Thank God we've got at least one well-trained candidate who *wasn't* on the list. The ballerina, whatever her name is. The other Dane. If it comes to it, she may be our only hope."

The old man paled and glanced out the window to avoid meeting anyone's gaze. From the grief in his eyes, one might have thought his own children had been murdered. The sun shone brilliantly through the high windows in the chamber. The thick glass made everything outside seem warped somehow, a twisted version of reality. Marie-Christine thought that view quite appropriate. It was beautiful outside, and yet the world had been changed, distorted, by the horrors perpetrated by Spike and Drusilla.

"Liverpool. Nice. Venice. Warsaw," Sir Nigel grumbled, still not facing the rest of the board. "Murders so cruel, so vicious that other abominable deeds pale in comparison. If this is not a vendetta against the Council, Mademoiselle Fontaine, I would be grateful if you could tell me what else to call such depravity."

The old man's voice cracked as he spoke, and his jaw seemed to clench even tighter, pipe rigid between his teeth.

Marie-Christine searched the faces of the other members of the board, even as they nodded their assent. They were all haunted, almost traumatized by the events of the previous weeks. The war between nations seemed so distant for all of them in comparison to this. They had always known they were fighting a war themselves, the Council against the forces of darkness. But the darkness had never struck back with such forethought and intelligence.

Evil was rarely clever. It frightened, disgusted, and enraged every last one of them.

Marie-Christine took a breath. She did not want to speak the words that were on her tongue. But she believed them to be the truth.

"Fun, Sir Nigel," she whispered.

Finally the old man turned to stare at her, his abhorrence of the very idea etched within every line in his face.

"What the bloody hell did you just say?" he demanded.

She swallowed. "Simply this. I doubt there is any vendetta involved here. I believe that somehow, these two creatures were made aware of the existence of the list of potential Chosen Ones. Much as I know you are as appalled as I by the thought, I believe that their actions are motivated purely by their own amusement. It's nothing more than a lark to them."

Marie-Christine felt the ripple of anger and revulsion that went through the room. Trevor Kensington, by far the eldest member of the board, lifted his cane and rapped its brass wolf's head tip on the oaken table.

"That'll do, my friends," the old man wheezed. "That will do. If Mademoiselle Fontaine is correct then we waste time now, attempting to discern the objective of these murders. A lark! Damn them both to hell, I say. They're hunting our girls, and slaughtering the Watchers assigned to them. That is not what the Council of Watchers is used to. We are the hunters. The tables must be turned on these damned leeches straight away."

"I agree," Sir Nigel offered with a bit of bluster. "Word will be sent at once to France. The Slayer and the operatives with her shall begin the hunt for Spike and Drusilla immediately. Until such time as the Council orders otherwise, their destruction is to be the Slayer's sole mission."

Marie-Christine rose from the table feeling suddenly more energized. They had been made into victims, something very few opponents had accomplished over the centuries. It did not sit well with any of them, and now the Council would strike back.

"I shall see to it," she announced. Then she glanced about the room. "I shall also see that the other Watchers assigned to potential candidates be apprised of the situation so that they might see to the safety of their charges.

"Spike and Drusilla will claim no more blood from this Council."

Galdhöpiggen, Norway
June 20th

One of the panes of glass in the meeting chamber at the Watchers' headquarters in London was not made of glass at all. It certainly looked like glass, and it felt, save for a slight drop in temperature, like glass. But it would have broken much easier than a thick piece of glass, and if it were not constantly being replenished by the magickal spell that had created it—a spell that had been cast before any of the building's sorcerous defenses had been in place—it would melt very quickly when the sun shone upon it.

For it was made of ice. Ice and magic.

From his subterranean stronghold in the mountains of Norway, the demon lord Skrymir sat upon his high seat and stared at a block of ice in his hands, and he smiled. From time to time, as frost gathered on the surface of the ice, he wiped it away with the palm of his frozen hand. Sorcery offered a hundred different ways to spy upon distant events from afar, everything from crystal balls to scrying pools, but this had always been the simplest magic for him.

Ice magic.

In the block of ice before him, Skrymir could see the Council meeting as though he were standing just outside the window looking in. The words were muffled but he could make them out. The block of ice in his hands, for all intents and purposes, *was* the window into that room.

"Excellent," he whispered to himself, his voice like icicles breaking.

Scattered about the floor of the main chamber of his lair, his guests never paused in their hedonistic pursuits. And he would not ask them to stop. If he required it, they would die for him. Otherwise, he was content to fulfill their needs and desires. His servants were another matter entirely, both the troll-like stonecutters who were his own little soldiers and the lithe, dark creatures who performed those household functions that were required for the stronghold.

One of the servants paused as it passed, a platter of Vargas demon meat in its hands, and glanced at him curiously. "Did you say something, my Lord?"

"Nothing of your concern," Skrymir snapped.

He had the urge to destroy the darkling creature, but it had only wished to serve him. Skrymir allowed it to live. His attention was quickly drawn back to the ice window upon his lap, and he grinned again as he watched the directors of the Council mutter among themselves and then depart their meeting chamber. All was going according to plan. Skrymir would have preferred it if Spike and Drusilla had not revealed their identity so early in the game, but even that seemed to be working in the demon lord's favor. Given the vampires' reputation, the Council had easily dismissed the possibility that there was any greater scheme at work here.

They were unaware of their true enemy, and that had been Skrymir's goal all along. For eons he had lingered in his stronghold, his agents roving out among the humans, becoming his eyes where his magick could not reach. Skrymir now knew the location of nearly every object of arcane power in the world. His plans were falling into place. First he would destroy the Council, then he and his agents would gather every talisman and amulet and magickally imbued weapon on earth, so that none could stand against him, human or demon.

Then the war could truly begin. It might take eons longer, but Skrymir would return the world to another time, a darker age. The sun would dim and the land grow cold, and the old gods would return. And Skrymir would lead them all.

"My lord Skrymir?"

With a snarl, the ice demon turned his gaze upon the beast that stood before his throne. It was Paxel, a Yazi demon whose talents Skrymir had come to respect. Though the creature was built like a minotaur, Paxel found a way to disguise himself out among the humans, no easy feat for a demon of his size and with horns like a bull's. A glamour, Skrymir believed. Tiny magic, yes, but quite enterprising for a Yazi. Most demon species would not even have bothered. But Paxel had ambition.

"You know better, Paxel!" Skrymir scolded. "You are to wait until I note your presence before you address me."

"Yes, Lord Skrymir," the Yazi replied, snorting hot breath through his enormous bull's nostrils. "Apologies, my lord, but you asked for the report on the vampires as soon as I could deliver it."

Skrymir smiled. His scrying-ice was limited magic at best. A spell had to be created and maintained. It was wonderful for stationary observation, but worthless for roving surveillance. "Yes, the vampires," he said, the surface of his icy flesh rippling, crackling. "Where have my little pawns gotten to now?"

Paxel stood a bit taller, stomping his hooves almost unconsciously, the involuntary behavior of the beast he was.

"They are in Libya, my lord," the Yazi reported. "It appears they are hunting their fifth target."

"Fifth?" Skrymir asked, pleased. "Mmm. I wonder how many girls are on that list. How many possible future Slayers can the Council have identified? Ten? Twenty?

"No matter. Spike and Drusilla will kill them all. They are so very good at it."

Chapter Eight

Sandefjord, Norway
1880

With the long gray afternoon giving way to early evening, Christian Bornholm doffed his hat and used his sleeve to wipe the sweat from his forehead. He had a bit of trouble explaining to folks who knew him that the simple fact that he was an archaeologist, and this was his dig, did not mean he could avoid picking up a shovel. He knew men of his profession who took that approach, but Professor Bornholm had always felt he got more from his men if he joined them on the dig, mixed his blood and sweat and dirt and exasperation with their own.

Sometimes it paid off. Times like now.

"She's a beauty, professor," declared Henrik, a man in his late forties who had been with Bornholm for a dozen years, perhaps more. Henrik was a thickly muscled man with a broad back and a bit of a stoop from spending most of his life with a shovel in his hands.

"That she is, my friend," Professor Bornholm replied, stroking his grizzled beard, feeling the grit trapped in it.

"That she is. Now we must try to find a way to move her safely."

"A problem for tomorrow, I think," Henrik replied.

Bornholm glanced at him, saw the exhausted smile on his friend's face, and the two men laughed together. They stood there as the shadows lengthened and the other men passed on their way home. The diggers and the artifacts team the professor had put together all waved and called out to him and Henrik as they left.

Bornholm was drained, but quite pleased. They had accomplished something incredible.

"I think I'll head home as well, Professor. Aren't you coming?" Henrik asked. He glanced up at the darkening, overcast sky. "We were fortunate that the rain held off all day, but it will not hold off forever."

"In a bit," Bornholm told him. "I just want to sit here a bit. Besides, I've got to wait for the sentries to arrive. Can't expose a find this valuable and then leave her to fend for herself."

Henrik chuckled at that, patted the professor on the back, and then walked off toward the road to town. It was more than four miles, but they all walked the route regularly, as long as it was warm enough.

On the ridge of excavated dirt that ringed the dig site, Bornholm stood and stared proudly down at the most significant find of his career. The Viking ship had been built, he believed, between A.D. 820 and 850. It was seventy feet of solid oak construction, sixteen feet wide and only five feet deep. The shallowness allowed the Vikings to not only sail upon the ocean but to travel up rivers and fjords, aiding them immensely in both war and trade.

The vessel had been buried in blue clay for more than one thousand years, and was in extraordinarily fine condition. It would have had a sail, of course, but also the long oars of the age. At least sixty oarsmen would have been aboard, though half of them would have rested while the others rowed. Upon the ship Professor Bornholm and his excavation team had found several beds, two sleighs, a pair of harnesses for horses, a massive iron cauldron, and the bones of forty-one men, all of whom appeared to have been executed. Bornholm only wished he knew why. Another ship that had been unearthed in a blue clay burial mound only miles away had supposedly housed the body of a king, and its interment was an honor. But it seemed that in this case, the opposite was true. Whatever these Viking warriors had done, it had been despicable enough to warrant their deaths, and their burial with numerous runic inscriptions that must have been wards against unearthing them.

But why bury the ship as well? Unless it had something to do with their crime? They were not kings, but some kind of criminals.

Bornholm was more than puzzled by these mysteries, he was completely confounded. He would decipher the past, though. Of that he was quite certain. It was fortunate that he had such a generous benefactor.

Almost as though summoned, that very gentleman appeared beside Bornholm soundless as a ghost. The professor gasped and put his hand across his chest, so startled was he by the newcomer's arrival.

"Mr. Charn," Bornholm said quickly, flustered. "I had no idea you intended to visit the site this evening. I would have prepared."

Charn snickered. It was an unsettling habit. "I did not want you prepared, Professor."

The man had cruel eyes and was thin enough in body and face that it gave his overall appearance the unflattering effect of reminding those who came into contact with him of a vulture. For those who had ever seen a vulture, of course. But those carrion birds were the first thing Bornholm had thought of upon meeting Charn. The creatures that picked over the remains of the dead. That was Charn, all right.

Despite his wealth and his willingness to bankroll whatever dig Bornholm suggested, Charn was no archaeologist. His interest was in stripping historical finds of their valuables and selling them on some kind of black market. Bornholm did not know much, and wanted not at all to know more, but he had not liked Charn even before he realized what the man was up to.

Something about his eyes, and the sneer on his face. The way he snickered. As though he knew so many things Bornholm did not, and was playing the professor for a fool, somehow. Well, Bornholm knew what was going on, and he had made a decision to stick with it. At least the sites would be exacavated, discoveries would be made.

What were a few ancient trinkets among hundreds of one-of-a-kind archaeological finds?

Charn wore a heavy jacket and boots like the diggers wore, and he had on a hat though it was far from cold for this time of year. Despite his thinness, the man's hands were huge, with long thick fingers. It was so extreme as to almost be a deformity, Bornholm had always thought.

"So you're to remove the ship for transport tomorrow, eh?" Charn asked.

"Well, that depends upon how long it will take us to get it out of the hole. But soon enough," Bornholm confirmed.

With a little snicker, Charn turned to size Bornholm up with a cold stare.

The professor frowned, not understanding what had elicited this reponse. "We are moving as fast as we can, Mr. Charn," he said.

"I can see that," Charn agreed.

With a smile that he might as well have painted on, Bornholm regarded his benefactor again. "Have you given any more thought to that Egyptian excavation I was hoping to do next season? The funding?"

Charn ignored the question. "Did you find the chest down there aboard that ship?"

The professor sighed. "Yes, sir. Once the Viking remains were removed, we discovered the box beneath them. It has been left untouched as you instructed. I have either been present myself or had sentries standing guard ever since the ship was unearthed."

The smile on Charn's face was uncharacteristically warm. "Excellent," he said, and laid a powerful hand on Bornholm's shoulder. "A job well done, Professor."

With that, Charn started down the mound of dirt and into the hole dug around the Viking ship. Bornholm chafed at this breach of etiquette. It was his dig. This was history in front of them, and whatever came up ought to have been catalogued and analyzed by antiquities experts first. But Charn had funded this and many other digs, and the professor could not deny him. Had never been able to deny him, for Mr. Charn always wanted something from a dig, always had some rare knowledge of an item he expected to find with each new excavation.

So Bornholm said nothing as Charn descended the slope.

With a sudden jerk, as though he had struck some sort of invisible wall, Charn came to a halt, halfway into the hole. He stood perfectly still a moment, fists clenched at his sides. With the clouds so thick above, and the last light of day almost completely faded, Bornholm could only barely make this out. That thought led to another—where were the sentries?

"Bornholm!" Charn shouted angrily, without turning.

"Is something wrong, sir?" the professor asked. It was clear to him, though, that there was *something* wrong.

Charn turned to glare at him. "Get me the box, Professor."

He almost argued. A bit of rebellion rose up in Bornholm and he nearly told his benefactor to get the damned box himself. Why was it necessary for him to descend into that pit when Charn was halfway down there himself already? Then he thought better of it. It was only a small thing he was asking, really. Bornholm had spent weeks with a shovel in that very same spot, and he loved to be around the ship anyway. Only a small thing.

With a sigh, he started down the dirt mound as the darkness closed in. It was almost fully night now, and his eyes were adjusting. Though the clouds were thick, there were places where the light of the moon and stars broke through. When he passed Charn on the wall of the pit, he saw that the man's jaw was set in a grim line of fury. He hoped that he had not been the cause of Charn's anger. That would not bode well for the Egyptian project.

He paused briefly at the base of the mound, outside the ship. Wooden beams had been put in place to make sure it did not topple while the excavation went on. Makeshift stairs had been constructed to allow simple access to the vessel, and Bornholm went up them quickly. At the back of the ship was a large chest of wood and iron. There was no lock. Despite Charn's warnings, Bornholm himself had looked inside, and nearly wept at the sight of the wealth within. Jewels and medallions of gold, goblets and bracelets made of finer craftsmanship than should have been possible one thousand years earlier. Might well be impossible now. It was an archaeological find of enormous significance, never mind how rich it would have made him.

But Bornholm had learned not to question Charn. If he knew the chest was there, he likely had expectations regarding its contents as well. And in the past, more than once, the man had actually taken items from a dig only to return them to Bornholm later, dissatisfied in some way but eager to move on to the next.

Reluctantly he hefted the chest and carried it to the front of the ship, then over the side and down the steps. When he looked up he saw that Charn had not moved any closer but had also not retreated back to the top of the mound. He stared expectantly at the chest, and Bornholm was unnerved by the intensity of that gaze.

The professor lugged the box to where his benefactor stood, halfway up the slope, and placed it on a level place on the dirt in front of him. Charn frowned at him.

"A little farther please," Charn muttered.

Bornholm raised an eyebrow. The damned chest was right in front of him. Was the man so unreasonable that . . .

The professor glanced back at the ship, then down at the chest, and finally back to Charn. A flutter of fear in his heart made him swallow hard. The image of the man stopping on the hill, as though prevented from moving any closer, came back to him, and he thought once again about the men executed and buried here, wondering what horrible crime they had committed, what sin.

They were never intended to be found, he thought. *And if they were, someone made sure that certain types of people could not remove the ship. Or anything on it. Certain types of people.*

Or not people.

He stared at Charn, telling himself it was lunacy.

"Move the box farther up the hill, Professor Bornholm," Mr. Charn said calmly.

Bornholm bit his lip.

"Once you have done so, we can discuss the funding for your dig in Egypt."

The professor closed his eyes tightly, then, fear and loathing filling his heart, for he *knew.* Knew that whoever or whatever Charn was, the Norsemen who had buried this ship had never wanted him getting hold of it, or its contents.

It nauseated him, but Bornholm could not help himself. Charn was his benefactor. The Egypt dig might be the one that gave him the fame in his field that he had sought for so long. He bent and lifted the chest again, moved it several feet farther up the side of the mound, and placed it in the dirt again.

Charn grinned, but there was no trace of warmth in it this time.

"Well done, my friend. Well done."

The vulture of a man knelt and opened the chest. He glanced up once at Bornholm with suspicion and the professor knew that Charn had somehow sensed that the box had been opened. Still, he seemed satisfied. Bornholm watched as Charn rooted through the box, apparently unsurprised and unimpressed by the priceless contents. At the bottom of the chest he seemed to find what he had been seeking, and withdrew it, shaking it loose from the other contents with such carelessness that a large ruby fell in the dirt beside him.

"What is it?" Bornholm asked, voice cracking.

Charn stood, obviously quite pleased with himself. Entwined in his fingers was a long strand of gold. It was not a chain, exactly, for Bornholm could see no links. The thickness of it should have made the thing stiff and unpliable, and yet it hung loosely from Charn's fingers like a chain, a necklace. That's what it had to be, some sort of necklace. But despite its appearance the thing had to be made of links of gold so fine and so tightly interwoven that it seemed to be all of a piece, solid metal.

"None of your business, what it is," Charn replied pleasantly, even as he lifted the chain and slipped it around his throat, fastening it at the back of his neck.

"Sir, about the Egyptian project?" Bornholm ventured, still fascinated but not wanting the advantage of the moment to slip away.

Without warning Charn's hands lashed out, gripped Bornholm's throat, and began to choke him. The vulture's face transformed, then. Ridges appeared on his brow and his entire countenance was one of a savage beast.

"My God!" Bornholm cried.

Charn snarled, baring long fangs. Finally, Bornholm knew what it was he faced.

Or thought he did. For in that moment Charn's face changed again. The flesh was like liquid as it altered beneath the professor's terrified gaze. A moment later, Bornholm found himself eye to eye with . . . himself. His own visage had replaced Charn's and he was now staring at his own twin, a brutal doppelgänger.

Charn laughed with Bornholm's voice.

Questions rattled through the professor's mind, but he never got the chance to put voice to any of them. Charn's hands... his own hands... closed around Bornholm's throat, and with inhuman strength, began to twist.

Benghazi, Libya
June 22nd, 1940

The road was sand and dirt, packed hard by trucks and baked by the harsh and unrelenting sun. After dark it grew cold and the wind picked up, the sand blowing across the desert and scouring every surface with grit. The desert could preserve and it could destroy, much like the sun.

As Spike drove a newly stolen truck along the pitiful road outside Benghazi, heading east and deeper into the desert, he glanced from time to time at the moon. The familiar orb was high and fat and yet somehow distant and powerless, unable to offer its usual comfort.

He did not like it here. Not at all. The sooner they left northern Africa, the better, as far as he was concerned.

"Can you hear them?" Drusilla whispered beside him.

Spike glanced at her, then turned his attention back to the treacherous road. Drusilla leaned forward in her seat, staring out the filthy windshield at what she could see of the sky through the blowing sand.

"Hear what? Them in the back you mean?" He tilted his head toward the back of the truck to indicate their captives.

Drusilla ignored him, and Spike had known she would. He had loved her long enough to know she had certainly not been referring to the Egyptian Watcher and his Libyan trainee in the back of the truck. He half-believed that in spite of the blood pumping through their veins, the copper liquid that would make Drusilla mad with hunger, she barely remembered they were there. Humans—the living, breathing kind—sometimes seemed to exist only as ghosts to her. And the things that only she could see, the surreal whispers of other worlds and other powers, those were rich with life and power.

There were times when Spike envied her the color and vibrancy of the world in which only she could travel.

This was not one of those times.

"What are you yammering on about then, Dru?"

The truck hit a rut and they were both jostled. Spike slammed his knee on the bottom of the wide steering wheel and rattled off a few colorful curses. He was on a roll, in a hell of a mood, and flying along with the power of his anger and frustration and the queer dread that filled him.

Despite the rough ride, Drusilla had not moved so much as an inch. She also had not responded.

"Dru?" he prodded.

"Sssshhhhhhh." The sibilance of her voice filled the truck's cab, as if the sound itself were capable of magic. Slowly, she turned to regard him. "You're not being very nice. Later I'll have to punish you for that. Nasty boy. You really don't hear them?"

"Hear what?" Spike asked, grumbling but trying not to snap at her. At times Drusilla seemed impervious to his moods and at others it was so easy to hurt her feelings.

"Ancient whispers, brittle and cruel," Dru told him, eyes darting about as though a flock of birds were flying past the truck. "The world is older here, older than anywhere, I think. The dead were gods once, and stories and poems and songs. They don't even remember what it was like to have flesh. Only words and music and then memories. Not even that anymore. They're on the wind now, and in the sand, and get no more notice than that. Eternal and invisible.

"It's awful misery, Spike," Drusilla said, her voice rising, excited. "Suffering forever like that. It's a symphony."

She shivered with pleasure, and Spike smiled indulgently. Times like these he loved her most of all.

Still, her pleasure did not dismiss his growing unease about the desert. Despite that all of this was to acquire Freyja's Strand for her, Drusilla had grown bored with the hunt for Slayers-in-Waiting rather quickly. Spike did his best to keep it interesting for her, but the challenge was increasing.

There was a turn in the road ahead and Spike slowed the truck, but stayed straight ahead, bumping up onto the desert sand and driving. Drusilla began to hum something with a kind of ugly, inverted melody beside him and she kept it up for the hour during which he drove straight into the desert. The truck's tires were oversize and he had let some of the air out of them. The hissing of sand against the vehicle's undercarriage was almost as annoying as the whimpering that carried, at intervals, up from the rear of the truck.

When he judged they had traveled far enough—and enough of the night had passed so that he was anxious to begin the return trip—Spike stopped the lumbering vehicle and climbed out.

"Let's go, Dru. We haven't got all bloody night," he said.

She seemed to wake as if from a trance. "Oh, goody," she drawled, a girlish grin on her features.

The Watcher and the fifteen-year-old girl in his care were trussed and gagged, but their eyes were wide as they were dragged from the back of the truck. Spike did not bother being gentle with the girl, but Drusilla cradled the aging Egyptian Watcher as though he were an enormous infant. She cooed to him, whispering to him all the while of the agony he was soon to endure and how sweet it would be. He would plead for death, she promised, but there would be no one to hear.

The girl wept copiously as Spike and Drusilla stripped her Watcher bare and then drove long wooden posts into the sand, deep enough to hold him tight. They bound him to those posts, face up to the sky. He would be there when the sun rose, and for days and nights thereafter, more than likely. This far into the desert, it seemed inconceivable that anyone might come along to save him. He would die there, burnt and dehydrated by the sun.

But there was that small chance that he might be found. A tiny chance, but enough so that they did not dare leave the girl the same way. The Watcher was a bonus. It did not really matter if he was saved. The girl, though—her death was required as part of the bargain they had made with Skrymir.

Spike made certain they were within sight of her struggling Watcher. The man screamed through his gag as the vampire lovers embraced the girl from either side, holding her between them, each dipping their fangs into her throat on opposite sides. Together like that, sharing so intimately, they drained her in what seemed like no time at all.

They left her corpse next to the Watcher.

Before they went back to the truck, Spike stood and looked down at the man, whose eyes were wide and maddened.

"Sweet dreams, guv."

In the truck, on the way back, Drusilla hummed to herself quite contentedly. The song was far more melodic than the one she had entertained herself with on the ride out, and it gave her a little ripple of pleasure that made her shiver.

"Enjoying yourself, pet?" Spike asked.

Drusilla swung her head toward him and her hair fell across her face in a cascade of darkness. She gazed up at him from behind the curtain of her hair with a knowing look that she knew drove Spike wild.

"Don't give me that look, Dru, or I'll have to stop the truck right here. You know I can't resist you, and I'd rather not still be in the desert when the sun comes up, truck or no truck."

She gave him a mischievous grin. Then her mind wandered back to what had brought them out to the desert in the first place. "It was fun, seeing his eyes," she whispered. "He'll cook up nice, that one. A shame we couldn't stay to watch."

"If you say so, love."

Suddenly, as the wind might shift, her mood changed. Drusilla pouted, her head tilting away from her man, her hands coming up protectively in front of her face.

"Spike," she said tentatively, in that little girl voice that she knew could make him do nearly anything. "I'm bored."

With a shake of his head, Spike sighed. "Of course you are, Dru. What would you like me to do to alleviate that boredom? You want the damned necklace, don't you?"

"Oh yes," she said, excited again by the thought of sparkly things, the games they might play with the Strand, and the possibility of seeing her reflection. "I want it very much. You tell me I'm beautiful, but in my mind I have no face."

"Well then?"

She considered for a moment. "Thought I saw two girls in America on that list. I like America. Vulgar people there, and all so different."

Spike stared at her, ignoring the rigors of driving for a moment. "Bloody hell, Dru. We already agreed the only logical way to go about all this mess is to save the American girls for last. It'd be daft to go all the way out there and then back to finish the job."

Drusilla pouted, arms folded up beneath her chin, and stared out her window at the swirling sand. The truck rumbled on toward the road they had left, and the coast of Libya beyond that, and Spike grumbled behind the wheel.

"On the other hand," Spike muttered.

"Yes?" Dru asked quickly, smiling, turning toward him again and bouncing on her seat.

"Wherever our little murderous jaunts take us, we'll have to go back up to Norway to collect your birthday present when we're all done. Not to mention Skrymir doesn't want us killing the Slayer till we've done with all her substitutes. We stick around here we're liable to run into her before we're through. Maybe heading off to America isn't the worst idea."

"Do you really mean it, Spike?" Dru asked, deeply sincere.

Spike reached across the torn seat and entwined his fingers with hers. "I mean it, poodle," he announced. "America it is."

She grinned and clapped in elation. Then she looked at him sternly. "I'm still going to punish you later."

"Wouldn't have it any other way."

Briare, France
June 26th

The days had grown long and warm. A breeze rustled the trees that dotted the property of the small farm on the outskirts of Briare where they had hidden themselves away for several days. The sun sank lower on the horizon and the trees' shadows reached across the ground toward Sophie, who sat on the front steps of the house and sharpened the sword she had inherited from her father. As she bent to the work, she whistled a tune her mother had sung to her as an infant, barely aware that the music was in her head.

Sophie had grown restless. There had been fewer and fewer vampires abroad after dark, and she yearned to return to Copenhagen or at least to London. She felt she would be put to better use in either city. The operatives Haversham and Rubie had left earlier that day to meet with a contact who would bring word to the Council that they all felt it was time to move on. The war had fallen into a kind of lull, and so had the vampiric activity that had accompanied it.

Yanna thought it quite probable that the creatures were simply gone. Sophie agreed.

The vampires had not expected the fighting to end so quickly. The Germans had been too successful, from the point of view of the supernatural predators that had prowled the battlefields. Many of them had traveled great distances when the war broke out so that they could feast upon the wounded and the strays. France had seemed like a paradise for a few short weeks. Then Paris had fallen, the north of France conquered by the Germans. Under the leadership of Marshal Pétain the southern half of the nation, now referred to as Vichy France, had agreed to an armistice with Hitler. They had conceded the free half of the country to German dominance without any further aggression, without even burdening the Nazis with the effort it would have taken to send a conquering army south.

There was a resistance, of course. In occupied France, and in the south as well, there were those working as part of an underground to fight against the Nazis, to spy on them and sabotage their efforts wherever possible.

That was no help to the vampires. War was chaos. Victory was order, particularly under the Nazis. Under the focused light of order, the vampires would simply draw too much attention if they continued to hunt there.

So they left.

Not all of them, of course. But a great many departed France to return to their homes. Some, expecting the Nazis to continue west, had reportedly crossed the Channel to England.

Sophie had been sent to France to fight a war of light and darkness, but her war had moved on.

When she finished sharpening the sword she sheathed the blade and carried it into the farmhouse. In the kitchen, Yanna sat at a table cutting vegetables. Or she had been doing so when Sophie had gone out onto the steps. When the Slayer entered the kitchen, she saw that her Watcher was immobile, eyes locked on some far distant point, face expressionless. She was having another vision. Sophie knew better than to interrupt Yanna during one, but sometimes she could not help studying the Watcher when she was in such a trance. She was aware that, in some way, it was rude to observe something so intimate. Still, she stood in the kitchen for a few moments, studying Yanna's face.

Sophie frowned. Usually the woman was expressionless during her visions. This time, however, there was a small smile at the corners of Yanna's mouth and her eyebrows and nostrils twitched from time to time.

Without warning, Yanna's expression changed. She gave a little gasp and then slumped to the table, her forehead making a solid thunk on the wood, scattering cut vegetables and coming dangerously near the blade of the knife in her hand.

The knife clattered to the ground.

"Yanna!" Sophie cried.

Alarmed, she went to the Watcher and pulled her upright. Yanna's eyes were not closed as Sophie had expected, but heavy-lidded and vacant, as though she were almost asleep but not quite. Sophie had once destroyed a demon who had been addicted to opium. His expression, clouded over with the euphoria of the drug, had not been unlike Yanna's now. Blank. Gone.

As though her mind had traveled from her body and not returned.

Sophie's breath caught in her throat as she recalled that in her studies she had learned that it was not uncommon for seers to lose some of the perspective others had. Their visions were sometimes so real that over time they left those gifted with them divorced from the tangible world, unable to tell the difference. At best, this left them confused. At worst, totally unhinged.

If Yanna were beginning to show signs of such a development, Sophie would have to tell her, might even have to request a new Watcher. The thought of doing such a thing grieved her. But more importantly, she feared for her friend and mentor. If Sophie remembered correctly, the kind of detachment that often came with a seer's encroaching madness could lead to an indecisiveness that could be dangerous in their profession, as well as paranoia, neurosis, and even, in extreme cases, catatonia.

"Yanna," she rasped, emotion catching in her throat. "Please be all right. Please."

Her eyes burning with unshed tears, Sophie pushed stray strands of Yanna's usually meticulously controlled hair away from her face and shook the woman ever so slightly.

"Yanna!" she said, a bit more forcefully.

The Watcher inhaled deeply, as though she had been suffocating and was only now granted breath. Her eyelids fluttered and her gaze began to clear. Yanna blinked, shook herself a bit, and then glanced over at Sophie. When she saw that the girl had been studying her, the Watcher flushed as though embarrassed or angry. Sophie decided it must have been the latter.

"I'm sorry," she said quickly. "I just walked in a moment ago and you seemed . . . distressed. You were . . . gone."

"It was another vision," Yanna told her curtly.

Sophie nodded. *Yes,* she thought, *but was that all it was?*

Yanna took a deep breath, seemed about to chide Sophie for her discourtesy, and then sighed. "The vampire again," she admitted.

"Spike?" Sophie asked. "This is your third vision of him. Yet they're all so unclear. What do you suppose it means?"

"Fourth," Yanna corrected. "I wish I knew what it meant, truth be told. The visions are . . . unnerving."

Talk of Spike seemed to make Yanna fidgety and anxious. She glanced about the room a bit, scratched at her head, and her eyes took on a faraway look that was not unlike her expression during a vision. It was as though, even now, she was not looking at the room but at the remnants of her vision. At Spike.

"You said you saw him once before, but you did not tell me where," Sophie reminded her, mostly to get her attention. "Do you want me to stop asking?"

Yanna sighed and shook her head. "I only saw him for a moment. It was in 1929. I had just become a Watcher after years of training. I went out to celebrate with Edgar Somers, who had been my mentor in the Council. We walked afterward, hand in hand. I was . . . quite fond of Edgar. He was such a good man, and wise. A true scholar. He was attempting to catalog vampires and had been looking into the backgrounds of many of them."

"Including Spike," Sophie said softly.

Yanna nodded. "Edgar walked me home. I stood on the front steps of the building where I was staying in London and Edgar stared into my eyes. I closed them, thinking he meant to kiss me. He made the tiniest noise and when I opened my eyes, he was falling away down the stairs, dead. Spike stood before me. He kissed me, once, very softly. Then he was gone. His lips felt very cold."

"Oh my God," Sophie whispered.

"He is so very cruel," Yanna said, voice cracking with emotion. "Evil radiates from him. Yet he is also quite fascinating. So charismatic."

With a scowl, Sophie crossed to the table and sat down. She took Yanna's hand in her own and studied the older woman's eyes. "He is a vampire, Yanna. You do remember that, don't you? Your visions mean that we are likely to face him, and soon. No matter how charismatic he may be, he is a demon, a savage, brutal monster. Look what he did to your Edgar. We cannot afford to be fascinated."

Sophie hesitated, almost afraid to broach the subject. But she knew she had to. She did it gently.

"Wherever your visions take you, Yanna, you must come back from there. Back to me, to the duties the Council has given you. He may be there in your visions, but they are not reality. Merely a way for the power that gave you this gift to communicate with you. Spike is evil. If your visions take you to him, you must always come back. You must have the strength to come back."

"Yes, of course," Yanna said, waving Sophie's words away as though they offended her. "Do you take me for a fool? Spike must die. But there is no harm in studying a unique specimen. Edgar would have appreciated the need for observation."

"I suppose," Sophie allowed. But she saw the thoughtful expression on her Watcher's face and was not convinced.

Though neither of them was very good at it, they prepared dinner together. Haversham was really the chef among them, but he and Rubie had not yet returned and Sophie did not want to wait until it was much later before they could sit down for their evening meal. As luck would have it, the two Council operatives returned a mere ten minutes before dinner was ready.

The truck rumbled loudly as they drove it around the back of the farmhouse and into the barn. When Rubie came through the back door with his face pale and slack, Sophie presumed it had been Haversham's driving that had disturbed him so. But then the tall, neatly dressed Haversham entered as well, and Sophie's eyes went wide. Her heart began to race. Haversham wore an expression of total horror, and yet there was a grimly determined set to his jaw as well.

All thoughts of dinner dissipated.

"What is it?" Sophie demanded. "What have you learned?"

"We're not going back to England right away," Rubie replied, eyes blindly gazing about the kitchen. "Though we're not staying in France either."

Yanna rose and went to Mr. Haversham. She seemed perfectly fine, now, and Sophie wondered if she had over-reacted earlier, if her fears about Yanna's visions and increasing distance and despondency were unwarranted. She hoped so. And looking at her now, she could almost believe it. This was the Yanna she knew, direct and confident. The Watcher stood just in front of Haversham, staring up at his face to get his attention, tiny in front of this tall man.

"Please, Mr. Haversham, what has happened? Why do the two of you seem so grave?" she asked.

Haversham took a breath and nodded his head. "I'm sorry, Miss Narvik. It's only that some of them were my friends, you see."

"Some of who?" Yanna asked anxiously.

"The Watchers," Rubie explained.

Sophie studied the ruddy-faced little man and saw the anger begin to break through the grief that had overwhelmed him. Fury blossomed within him, set his teeth on edge, so that when he spoke again it was with a hatred she would not previously have been able to imagine him capable of.

"We have all been reassigned," he explained. "Haversham and I are to return to England. The two of you are to embark immediately for America. Your mission has become a singular one."

"America?" Sophie asked, startled. "What for?"

Haversham cleared his throat, face still etched with horror and disbelief. "Last month, a pair of vampires managed to get into the Council headquarters in London and murder two of its members. No one was the wiser at the time, but it seems they also copied the list of Slayers-in-Waiting."

Sophie frowned and shot a questioning glance at Yanna.

Her Watcher would not meet her gaze, but she did explain. "The Council expends a great deal of energy in identifying those girls around the world to whom portents and omens point as potential candidates to become the Chosen One. Those deemed most likely are sought out and trained, as I trained you, in hopes that the next time a new Slayer is Chosen, it will be one of those we have already trained. You'd be surprised how well that system works."

"My replacements," Sophie replied in Danish. "For when I die."

Yanna nodded. "Yes. That's exactly right."

The Slayer took that in, closed her eyes a moment, and then turned to the operatives again. "These vampires? They're killing the Slayers-in-Waiting, aren't they? And their Watchers?"

"That's right," Haversham confirmed.

"How many so far?" Sophie asked, stomach roiling with revulsion.

"Five candidates," Rubie replied. "Four Watchers. One of 'em lived. Well, six Watchers, counting the two in London. The Council's had scriers searching for them magickally, and operatives all over Europe trying to figure out where they'll go next."

"And they believe it's to be America," Yanna said, putting it together.

Sophie waited for more from her, but the Watcher said nothing. It was not unusual for her now. Some of her visions were quite direct and helpful, clairvoyant warnings of the future. Others were merely images, feelings, vague hints of danger. The visions of Spike had been like that, and there had been many. After each one, Yanna seemed to slow down a bit, and defer to Sophie more.

So be it, she thought.

The Slayer stood up from the table, carrying her father's sword in its sheath. "For us as well. We leave immediately," she said. Sophie strode toward the bedroom that she and Yanna had been sharing. Before she reached the door she turned to regard the Council men again. A question had occurred to her. One to which she was certain she already knew the answer.

"These vampires. What are their names?"

"The female is Drusilla," Rubie told her. "The male is called Spike."

"Of course," Sophie replied grimly. She felt a dire apprehension bloom in her gut, but when she glanced over at her Watcher she saw that Yanna's expression was very different. She seemed almost happy. Excited.

While the Slayer was filled only with dread.

Chapter Nine

Boston, Massachusetts, USA
July 6th

Her parents were dead.

Rita Gnecco stood panting in a darkened doorway on Hanover Street in the North End of Boston, tears streaming down her cheeks. Her parents were dead and it was her fault.

She had let the vampire in.

Most girls trained by the Watchers Council were removed from their families for a large part of that training. Family was a distraction, the Council insisted. Later on, should a particular girl be Chosen, it could put her family in danger and the fear of such a tragedy was a liability to a Slayer.

But the Gneccos had been a very close family. Rita's parents, Giovanni and Teresa, had immigrated to America from Genoa, Italy, with their own parents thirty years before. The North End of Boston was like a little piece of Italy itself. Every shop and restaurant, the butchers, the barbers, the priests at the many churches, even the postman, they were all Italian. It was a community that existed within Boston, but somehow outside of it completely.

It was home.

The Gneccos would not allow the Council to remove Rita from their home, or from the North End, for that matter. Instead, the Watcher Arthur Cabot was forced to make his home there among the Italian immigrants. It had suited him perfectly well, and the Englishman had made friends quickly.

Rita bit her lip at the thought of Arthur, and the memory of her parents' love for her. All of them were dead now, and only Rita remained behind. Alive. Though for how long, she could not say.

Rita huddled back against the door and tried to think. Her heart thudded in her chest and her mouth felt dry. A lance of pain shot through her temple and she winced with the onset of a devastating headache. One hand went up to her face and she steeled herself and willed the pain away. She could not afford to be slowed down now. He was coming for her, stalking her along the street. She could not see or hear him, but she knew she had mere minutes to figure out how to defeat him, to destroy him.

The bells at Sacred Heart Church rang twice. Two in the morning. In the recessed doorway, Rita stopped breathing a moment. The church. So close. Some vampires, she had been taught, would not dare enter a house of worship. But even if he followed her inside, there would be crosses there, and holy water. Weapons.

With one last deep breath and a silent prayer, Rita lunged from the doorway and out onto Hanover Street. If it had been a mere handful of hours earlier the street would still have been buzzing with life and she would have been able to find aid. But she dared not batter on some poor unfortunate's door for it would surely draw the vampire to her like a beacon.

"Reeee-taaa!" a singsong voice called behind her.

She bit her lip again, but did not turn. Rita dared not look to see how close the monster was. So quick, he had found her. It made her wonder if he had known she was there all along and was merely tormenting her now, extending her life for his own amusement.

"No," she whispered to herself, her breath coming fast, the tightness in her chest increasing. "No!" she cried out. She was determined that she would not die so easily.

With a burst of energy she increased her speed and sprinted to the corner of Hanover and Prince Street, where she turned left and started for the church at the end of the block. Weapons, she reminded herself. Sanctuary.

Down the street, in the cobblestone square in front of the church, she saw a policeman walking his beat. Just as she spotted him, the officer noticed her, saw that she was running. Even at that distance, with only the lights of the street and the stars, she could see the alarm on his face. He grabbed the night stick at his side and ran to meet her.

"What is it, miss?" he demanded. "What's—?"

His words cut off as he looked past her and saw the vampire in pursuit. Of course the policeman did not know that it was anything more than a man, frightening a young girl.

"All right, you!" the cop bellowed. "Hold it right there."

"No!" Rita snapped, terrified for the policeman. She grabbed him by the arm and pulled him backward. "He's not what you think. Come with me to the church. We can fight him there. If you try to fight him out here you'll die!"

The cop frowned, then chuckled at her hysteria. "You go along now, miss, and I'll have a talk with this fellow."

"No!" Rita shouted, but the policeman would not listen. He turned and calmly walked toward the vampire, who was running along the street and did not slow in the least.

With the pain of regret in her heart, Rita turned to flee. The church was so close now, just across the square. She heard the policeman cry out in agony behind her but did not slow. Her conscience would not allow her to see what had been done to him. She had tried to warn him; she truly had.

Her legs hurt from running so hard, but she bounded up the steps to the front of the church and a horrible thought occurred to her: what if the doors were locked. It seemed frighteningly possible at that moment. But when she hauled on the iron rings in the doors they swung wide easily. Rita did not bother to pause to pull them closed. Doors would not stop the vampire.

She only prayed that the church would have some power over it, make it hesitate. Rita ran halfway up the center aisle and paused, breathing hard, eyes darting about the huge structure for the monster. Nothing happened. Seconds ticked by but it did not enter the church. *A cross*, she thought. *Holy water.*

At the front of the church near the altar there were doors on either side. Beside them were small bowls filled with holy water. There were similar bowls by the doors she had entered through, but Rita did not dare go back that way.

The girl bolted toward the altar. She had nearly reached the front of the church when a stained glass window off to her left exploded in shards of multicolored glass and the vampire landed in a crouch less than twenty feet away.

Rita was in training. She was not the Slayer yet, if she was ever meant to be. And she was afraid. Startled, terrified, she screamed as she fled from him again. With a lunge, she reached the bowl of holy water by the door, reached into it with her fingers cupped . . . and found it dry.

Weeping, Rita collapsed on the floor just inside the door. The vampire paused in his approach and studied her, smiling cruelly. She looked up at his face, his oh-so-familiar, well-loved face, and her heart shattered.

"Arthur please," she begged her Watcher. "Do not do this. It isn't you. Please, God, remember who you are."

Arthur grinned. "This *is* who I am, sweet girl. *This.*"

He dropped to his knees beside her, reached out and grasped the sides of her face, wiped the tears from her cheeks, and then pulled her to him. His fangs slipped easily into the soft flesh at her throat.

Behind the vampire, Spike and Drusilla sat in a pew near the front of the church. He had his feet up on the pew in front of them, and Drusilla lay her head upon his chest.

"Beautiful, isn't it Dru?" he asked. "Are we having fun yet?"

"Oooh, yes," she cooed. "A wonderful bit of drama. Aren't we clever? I rather think we are."

The Atlantic Ocean
July 6th

On the deck of their passenger liner, bound for New Orleans, Yanna and Sophie stood together against the rail and watched the sun slipping down on the horizon. Yanna swayed and began to pitch forward with the swell of the sea. Sophie cried her name and wrapped both arms around her Watcher, then pulled them both down to the deck.

Yanna was in the throes of a vision . . .

. . . *church bells ring somewhere far off. Around her, strange birds call to one another in the swamp. The water is up to her knees and her bare feet are sucked into the muck below the surface with each step. She has somehow lost her shoes and can feel the slippery, grasping sludge pushing between her toes, closing around her ankles as if to trap her there.*

From somewhere behind her, Yanna can hear Sophie screaming for her to come back, crying out in frenzied tones. But Yanna presses on. She must. Spanish moss hangs from the trees that jut from the water and the small clump islands in the swamp. An enormous serpent slithers from one of those tiny islands and into the water. Its slithering makes odd patterns on the surface of the water for a few seconds and then it disappears into the murk.

Yanna is frightened of the snake, feels terror of it run throughout her entire body, and yet she wants to follow, to catch it, to touch its cold scaly flesh.

Ahead she can hear something thrashing in the water. A snapping and clacking that is unlike any other sound she knows. Though the mire under the water attempts to hold on to her she picks up her pace, wading swiftly through the swamp to a bit of soil above water level. There are trees and scrub upon it, and Yanna pulls herself up and peers through the vegetation.

Beyond the trees, two alligators savagely attack each other. There is already blood in the water. One of them is bleeding from a bite on its foreleg. Their tails slap the water. The jaws crack together and they tear each other apart. Bits of flesh are gulped down and blood flows freely until finally, at long last, one of them dies.

The other tears out the throat of the dead gator and Yanna feels a quiver of excitement in her secret heart, the most intimate place within her, and she cannot breathe.

It is terror, she knows. But it pleases her.

The surviving alligator slides beneath the surface of the swamp and glides about, sluicing the blood from its mottled skin. Slowly, but with obvious intention, it turns in the water and begins to swim toward land, toward Yanna. Only its reptilian eyes and the bump of its head are visible above the water until it reaches the tiny island.

Yanna knows she ought to run, yet she is frozen. She knows she ought to be terrified, and yet there is no fear. This ancient creature has a beauty she would never have expected to find. It lived and reproduced and killed in the dark places of the earth before primates evolved into humanity. Its blood runs cold, its heart is ice, it kills as a matter of instinct. It is a creature of cruelty, rage and murder, and it is natural and beautiful for all its terribleness.

The alligator crawls up onto a bare patch of earth beside the swamp, its cold, dead eyes capturing Yanna as though she were hypnotized. And then it changes. The alligator shakes itself once, and begins to stand. Its eyes remain the *same, they do not change, but its body . . . scales slough off white, marbled human flesh. Its snout draws back into the face until only the fangs remain to identify it as a predator.*

Its hair is white-blond, and it smiles . . .

"Yanna!"

Her eyes regained their focus and she saw that the sky was a deep, rich, twilight blue. Minutes had passed. Sophie knelt by her side on the ship's deck and stared at her in consternation.

"A vision," Yanna explained weakly.

"I know. I'm not blind," Sophie snapped. "They're getting stronger. And more dangerous. You cannot continue like this. I fear . . . I fear for you. If I had not caught you, you would have fallen over the rail and drowned."

Yanna took a quivering breath, well aware that Sophie's fear for her had little to do with the danger of drowning. "Thank you," she said. "I . . . I'm sorry. This isn't fair. I could endanger you if a vision came at the wrong time. In battle."

There was more to be said. As she gazed into Sophie's eyes, she saw that the Slayer knew it as well. Instead, they talked around it.

"It has never happened before, you receiving a vision during a battle," Sophie said, slowly, studying her sadly. "But it is something to consider. Do you feel that you are . . . up to a physical conflict?"

Yanna could not meet her gaze.

The Slayer stood up, unfolding her long legs and backing away to lean on the railing and look down at her Watcher. Yanna felt herself under the microscope of the girl's observation. Sophie ran her hands through her long blond hair in frustration, and then looked out to sea.

"You don't trust me," Yanna whispered. It pained her to speak the words, even more so because *she* did not trust *herself.*

The Slayer did not turn. "I fear for you," she confessed. "These visions, so many of them. And each time, you are . . . absent longer. It takes you longer to grasp your surroundings again. I worry that your dreaming self may be contaminating your judgment, that it might be clouding your mind. It's never been like this before. I wonder if you are somehow inviting these visions, creating them yourself without even being aware of it."

"Impossible," Yanna scoffed.

Sophie turned and stared at her, face etched with confusion. "Is it? Can you be sure? Your fascination with this devil worries me. He has slaughtered innocent young girls and many Watchers, people you knew. He killed a man you loved. Even now, he and Drusilla have probably killed that girl Rita, in Boston, and her Watcher. How much evil must they do before you shake this mist from your eyes?"

Yanna shook her head, prepared to deny the Slayer's accusations, but her mind went back to the vision, and the feelings she had had while watching the alligators tearing at each other.

With a groan she pulled herself to her feet and stood by the rail, chin raised proudly, to face Sophie. "Evil is the vampire's nature," she declared. "I do not claim to understand them. Yes there is something about this Spike that draws me, confounds me, even awes me, in a way no dark power or demon ever has. I cannot define what that magnetism is, except to say this: He rejoices in evil. I have seen him once, in the flesh. And I have seen him so many times in my head. Evil is ecstasy for him. There is so much joy for him in death and suffering that it undermines everything I have ever believed in."

Sophie stared wide-eyed at her mentor. Yanna understood the girl's confusion, though she could not assuage it completely. For all she knew of the dangers inherent in being a seer, she had begun to believe that what she felt was not madness, but an intellectual fascination.

"I would love to study Spike, Sophie. To understand him, and Drusilla, and all the rest," Yanna admitted. "But listen and understand: I know they are evil, that the abominations they commit must be stopped. Spike and Drusilla must die."

"They must," Sophie emphasized. "They cannot be allowed to survive."

Yanna nodded. "Savage beasts kill by instinct, but when they hunt human beings they must be put down. Whatever else vampires are, they are evil. I will not fail my duty to you, Sophie. I could never."

Sophie let out a trembling breath and pulled Yanna into her arms. They held each other as the last of the sun bled into the ocean and the moon shone bright above.

Yanna tried to tell herself that she had spoken true.

Chapter Ten

Batiste, Louisiana
July 13th

Even after dark it was sweltering hot. Sometimes the gators stayed down in the cool mud of the bayou for hours after nightfall. Unless they were being fed.

Batiste was a tiny little town in the middle of nowhere. It had a small school and a general store, though, and the houses were more than shacks, though the townspeople did get most of their food from the bayou. But the nearest post office was fifteen miles away in Catahoula. The nearest doctor as well.

Not counting gators, there were two hundred and eighteen living residents of Batiste.

And twenty-seven dead ones.

Only the old-timers could remember when the vampires had first come to the swamp town. For most of them, things had simply always been that way, with the largest homes at the edge of town occupied by dead men and women, shuttered up tight during the day. There were stories, of course. Legends about people from Batiste who had tried to burn them out, or just tried to leave town with their families still breathing.

Nobody even whispered about such things after dark, and even when the sun was out, it was never more than talk. Not now. For the stories always ended the same; ended with death and bloodshed that had been unnecessary. The people of Batiste led good lives, considering.

There were only a handful of rules. First, obey. Second, do not speak of the undead outside of the town. And finally, do not ever try to leave. In the early years, supposedly, many had tried to flee. Each night they were hunted and brought back to die in front of their families and neighbors. Soon enough, people stopped trying to run.

As long as everyone followed the rules, the people of Batiste were safe, for the vampires did not hunt in the town. That was their cardinal rule. Their master would not allow it. In fact, the farther from Batiste they hunted the happier he was.

It was a good life, in its way. Ironically safe. For the people of Batiste knew what lurked out there in the shadows, they lived with it every day, and they were protected from it.

Kakistos protected them.

An ancient vampire, he had come to the Louisiana swamps to escape the spread of the virus called humanity. It seemed to be infecting the whole world. Kakistos wanted a return to simpler times, to hunting and feasting and inspiring abject terror in human souls. In Batiste, he had everything he wanted and he knew he would be content to stay there forever. As such, he was fiercely protective of his territory.

With the heat at last beginning to dissipate, he sat in a chair behind the enormous plantation house he had forced his humans to build for him and looked out over the swamp to the bayou beyond. It had taken the people of Batiste seven years to build the house without anyone in the outside world any wiser. It was grand, and not merely by the standards of such poor humans.

"My lord Kakistos?"

He looked up. The vampiress before him was beautiful, her red hair falling all the way to her waist. The dress she wore was little more than a shift and it filled him with a great lust to see her like that. His hooflike feet clicked together as he sat forward to admire her.

"Alannah, isn't it?" he asked.

The vampire girl smiled. "There's entertainment available if you want it, sir," she informed him in the lilting accent of the area. She was a local girl, he recalled. He had found her in Lafayette and turned her himself, so taken with her had he been. But that had been a long time ago, and it was easy for him to forget.

"What is it tonight?"

"Young lovers from the city. Their car broke down, sir, so we offered them our special brand of southern hospitality. The gators are awful hungry, sir."

Kakistos smiled. "You make me proud, Alannah. Have I told you that?"

"You surely have, sir. You surely have," the girl replied and smiled, her fangs showing. "Before we bring the entertainment up from the pit, sir, we have guests. Visitors who wanted to beg a boon from y'all."

"I don't like visitors," Kakistos said, scowling.

The so-called visitors appeared behind Alannah with no more introduction than that. Surely they had been told to wait.

"We won't take up much of your time," said the male. "I'm Spike. Me lady love here's Drusilla. We're on a bit of a mission, see, but we heard right off when we came down here that this is your territory, and we weren't about to operate our little business transaction on your hunting grounds without your permission."

Kakistos studied them. He did not like the male, Spike. Not at all. He swaggered with arrogance, fairly burned with the energy of it. But the female, Drusilla . . . even as he examined her she smiled and batted her lashes coquettishly at him. Her hands moved like serpents in front of her, and yet she seemed almost unaware of them. She swayed as she moved closer to him.

"Spike's a bit rude, he is," she said, her voice low and soothing. She smiled suggestively. "He left out the most important bit. We've brought you a tribute, Kakistos. Juicy and rare. Twin boys, only thirteen. A single soul split into two, and the way the colors bend for them when they scream, and the clouds boil, they'll be quite a delicacy, I can promise you that."

Kakistos smiled at Drusilla, reached out and stroked her cheek. She rubbed against his hand and purred like a kitten. Her lover bristled but spoke not a word.

He glanced at Alannah. "The tribute?"

"As precious as she says," the girl confirmed. "The sweetest, pinkest young ones."

"Still . . ." the ancient vampire grumbled.

"Left something out," Spike said almost offhandedly. "Might help make up your mind. Girl we want, she's over in Lafayette. She's got a Watcher training her."

Kakistos stiffened. This was something else entirely. He attempted to hide how deeply this news disturbed him and failed. He wanted nothing to disrupt the paradise he had created for himself.

"A Slayer?" he asked.

Spike pursed his lips and tilted his head first to one side, then the other. "Not yet," he said slowly. "But you know what they say about weeds. Gotta kill 'em before they grow."

"I will take your tribute," Kakistos said sternly, but without hesitation. "You may hunt your girl. But I don't like you, Spike. It would be wise for you not to return to this part of the world in the future."

The blond vampire glanced around at the swamp and shrugged disdainfully. "Oh yeah, sure. It'll break my bleedin' heart, but you're the boss 'round here, eh? Not to worry."

Kakistos narrowed his eyes and glared at Spike. Was the Britisher mocking him and the world he had built? He could not be certain. Before he could inquire further, Alannah drifted before him in her flowing, gossamer dress and smiled.

"Something tells me you're goin' to want those twins first," she said, a gleam in her eye.

"Mmm. Yes. Let's see how they fare against my dear ones," Kakistos murmured.

Spike and Drusilla had gone on their way, but it no longer mattered. The arrogant one was out of his sight, and the problem of a potential Slayer in the area would be eliminated.

Kakistos's thoughts had turned to a far more important matter.

Feeding his pets.

Baton Rouge, Louisiana
July 15th

The train sat motionless in the station at Baton Rouge, just as it had for more than two hours as repairs were made to the engine. It had been another long, sweltering day, the heat flirting with the one hundred degree mark all afternoon. While repairs were made, the passengers were encouraged to get off the train and go to a nearby restaurant to have a bite to eat, maybe a glass of lemonade. Only a fool would have stayed on board the train in that brutal heat. The air was stagnant, no wind at all, and the windows on board the train weren't very big to begin with.

Now, though, the sky was bleached white as the sun fell on the horizon. Dusk was fast approaching and the conductor had still not rung the bell that would have indicated the train was ready to depart. No matter. They could not wait any longer.

"It's going to be hot," Bertram Martin complained.

"Yes," the Slayer replied. "Yes it is."

Eleanor Boudreau studied Sophie with a curiosity and awe she had never felt before, not even at the movie palace. The Danish girl was only a year older than she herself was, but Sophie was at least five inches taller, and so beautiful that being near her made Eleanor painfully self-conscious. There was also the devastating fact that Sophie was the Slayer. For a multitude of reasons, this unnerved Eleanor profoundly.

They walked toward the train and the four of them boarded a rear car. Miss Narvik—Sophie's Watcher—was first, followed by Eleanor and Bertram, her own Watcher.

Or he would be, someday, if she was ever Chosen. Sophie stood aside as the three of them went up into the train. Only then did the Slayer follow.

Inside their compartment, despite the heat, Miss Narvik closed and locked the door. They opened the window, but there was little breeze and Eleanor was already sweating profusely. Within the compartment it was at least fifteen degrees hotter than outside, but Eleanor knew better than to complain. Sophie and Yanna were there to protect her, after all. The way Bertram had explained it, only their timely arrival had saved her life. Other girls, other Slayers-in-Waiting as they called them, had been horribly murdered already.

Why me? Eleanor asked herself that question, but did not have an answer. It did not make sense. Not that she wished the older girl ill, but Sophie was the Slayer. It simply made no sense to Eleanor that anyone would want to kill her not for what she was but for what she might one day become.

One day.

They sat in silence in the stifling compartment and Eleanor studied Sophie closely. There was a pain in her heart and a sick feeling in her stomach that had nothing to do with the heat, but she could find no real explanation for it.

"Yanna," Bertram began, clearing his throat. "I understand the need for precautions, but must we suffer in this sweat box? Surely your scheme will be enough to throw these killers off. They're only vampires after all. Not terribly bright, are they?"

The Slayer and her Watcher had taken a ship to New Orleans before making their way up to Lafayette and locating Eleanor. They did not think it safe to return by the same route, so they were taking a train east from Baton Rouge to Charleston, South Carolina, from which they would sail to England.

"It isn't my scheme," Miss Narvik replied. "It is Sophie's. Should you ever be Watcher to the Chosen One, Bertram, you will eventually find that it becomes difficult to instruct them. Generally, the Slayer's instincts are best."

Bertram blinked and turned to Sophie, as if to reiterate his question. The Slayer gazed at him firmly.

"Mr. Martin," she said, "if you had read the reports about the activities of these vampires, you would not underestimate them. It may be uncomfortable in this car, but the sun is down, and it is better for us to be here together than out there in the dark."

Suddenly Sophie shifted in her seat and peered at Eleanor. The younger girl shied away, eyes downcast, deeply uncomfortable.

"Eleanor, you have been staring at me since this morning when we first met. Is there something you need? Something I can help with? You have questions?"

Very tentatively, Eleanor lifted her gaze and brushed her long black hair away from her face. Sophie watched her intently. The Slayer had such grim features, such cold eyes, that Eleanor almost could not bring herself to speak. When Bertram spoke her name, the word turned into a question. He was concerned for her.

"No?" Sophie prodded.

Eleanor swallowed hard. "Are y'all afraid?" she asked.

Sophie blinked in surprise. "That was not one of the questions I thought you would have. Of course I'm afraid. Though maybe not as afraid as I should be. So far these vampires have not come after me. I imagine that means that they are merely saving me for last. Once all the candidates who might replace me have been eliminated, they are sure to come after me."

With a shake of her head, Eleanor leaned forward on her seat to study Sophie even more intently. The Slayer also leaned forward, until the two girls nearly bridged the floor of the compartment between them.

"I don't mean just afraid of the vampires who are huntin' us. I mean . . . more than that. Just . . . are you afraid to be the Slayer? 'Cause I am," Eleanor confessed. Bertram seemed startled, but she ignored him. The only opinion that mattered now was Sophie's. "Here I am, bein' trained to replace y'all when you die. If I'm next to be Chosen, that is. But you're so nice to me, protectin' me, even though just bein' around me's gotta be a constant reminder of how short Slayers' lives usually are."

"Eleanor!" Bertram scolded her.

Yanna only watched Sophie expectantly.

For her part, the Slayer looked stricken, even a bit pale. She closed her eyes a moment, then got up and moved across the compartment to sit beside Eleanor.

"Yes, I'm afraid," she said again, though this time they both knew she was talking about something else. "It is hard to look at you and know that in some ways you represent my death. On the other hand, you are one of many. You are in far greater danger than I, at the moment."

A tiny smile played at the corners of Sophie's mouth. "There is also the fact that I do not plan to die."

Eleanor could not help laughing, and the distance that she had felt separating her from Sophie evaporated in an instant. In that same moment, the bell was rung to call the passengers back to the train. Less than fifteen minutes later, the whistle blew and steam hissed and the engine screeched as it hauled its coaches and freight cars out of the station.

At last, with the motion of the train, a breeze poured into the compartment and they all felt some relief. Outside the window, night had fallen. The lights of Lafayette disappeared quickly and then there was only blackness, save for the occasional railroad signal.

The two girls sat more closely together, and Bertram moved to the other side of the compartment to sit beside Yanna. As the Watchers conversed anxiously about the war in Europe and their own battle against the vampires, the girls got to know each other. Eleanor had grown up with just her mother in Lafayette and the idea that Sophie was an orphan from a place as distant and exotic as Denmark was amazing to her. To Eleanor, Denmark could be visited only in the pages of *Hamlet.*

Their bags were on the rack overhead. Sophie stood and went through them, then produced for Eleanor's wide-eyed admiration a sword that had been in her family for centuries, and which the Slayer had received from her own father. Its scabbard was decorated, and the blade itself was inscribed with designs and words in a language Eleanor assumed was Danish.

"It's beautiful," she said, running her fingers along the flat of the blade.

"And sharp," Sophie told her. "Be careful."

"You use this in battle?" Eleanor asked, amazed.

"I do."

The younger girl shot a nasty look at Bertram. "I haven't been trained to use a sword."

Bertram cleared his throat, looked nervously at Yanna, and then sat up a bit straighter. "Though decapitation is perfectly acceptable as a means of destroying vampires, and demons as well, facility with a sword is far lower on the scale of priorities than, for instance, the use of the stake or crossbow, or expertise in simple hand-to-hand combat. The stake is a crude but far more reliable weapon under most circumstances when it comes to vampires. You will be trained in swordsmanship, Eleanor, but all things in time, eh?"

With a small grunt of disapproval, Yanna looked at Bertram. "Sophie knew how to use a sword even before I was assigned to her. It is her chosen weapon because it means a great deal to her. And in her hands, there is no more efficient weapon."

"All well and good for her," Bertram replied snappishly. "But I say again, all things in time."

The Watchers continued to speak, but a new coolness had developed between them and Eleanor felt responsible. She sighed. Bertram had trained her well in the fourteen months they had had together thus far. She had learned proficiency with a number of weapons, but she did not have the supernatural gifts of the Slayer. Nor did she have the natural confidence that Sophie simply exuded, the swagger the other girl seemed to have been born with.

It made her realize something. Despite the fact that the Council of Watchers had identified her as a potential inheritor to the mantle of the Chosen One, Eleanor did not believe it for a moment. Nor had she ever, if she allowed herself a peek into her own secret heart. She was not the Slayer. She never would be the Slayer.

"Sophie," she said, leaning against the older girl, to whom she felt bonded in some way. "Tell me about bein' the Slayer. I wanna hear. About your life and the things you've done, the battles you've fought."

The Slayer stiffened slightly and then relaxed and allowed Eleanor to lean against her. When she began to speak, about an ancient vampire king named Gorm, Sophie seemed almost embarrassed by Eleanor's open admiration. Later, as Sophie talked about the war in France, Eleanor drifted off to sleep.

Sophie was dimly aware of the rhythm of the train rattling along the tracks. It was the staccato beat of her own heart, and the promise of a journey to safety. It was a comfort to her even as she slept sprawled across one of the seats in the train compartment, with Eleanor leaning heavily against her, also asleep. They breathed as one, and Sophie had one arm across the other girl's back as though they were sisters, just small girls overcome by a long day's travel.

From time to time the whistle blew. When the train switched tracks at a junction, each coach would shudder through the change. Sophie's scabbarded sword was tucked partially beneath her sleeping form. They were scheduled to make a stop in Montgomery, Alabama. Seventy miles outside of Montgomery, the train switched tracks again and their coach was jostled so violently that the sword slipped from beneath its owner and clattered onto the floor of the compartment.

Sophie snapped awake.

It was dark in their compartment but she could see well enough by the starlight coming through the window. Eleanor still slept heavily upon her. Across from them, she could see Yanna sitting primly upright, leaning against the wall of the compartment, also asleep.

Bertram was gone.

"Damn it," Sophie hissed.

Eleanor moaned in her sleep and squirmed, attempting to get comfortable in an inherently uncomfortable spot. With a grimace, Sophie slid out from beside the other girl and settled her down flat on the seat. She would wake Eleanor if it became necessary. It was possible Bertram had merely gone to relieve himself.

The scabbard of her sword did not seem to have been damaged, but she put off more than a cursory examination until after she had confirmed Bertram's safety. Sophie crouched beside her sleeping Watcher, her back to the window so that she could see the door.

"Yanna," she whispered harshly, and poked at the woman's knees.

The Watcher's eyes fluttered and then settled so that they were open barely a crack. "Sophie? What is . . . is something wrong?"

"Where's Bertram?" Sophie demanded.

"Bert?" Yanna murmured.

Then her eyes opened wide, her gaze darting around the darkened compartment. "Oh, no," she muttered in Danish. "We agreed to sleep in turns, so that one of us would always be awake. You don't think . . . he might have gone out just to—"

"That was my thought," Sophie told her, eyes still on the door as she fastened the scabbard to her belt. "But he would have waked you, wouldn't he?"

"Should have," Yanna agreed.

Sophie cursed in a low voice. Since the moment she had woken she had listened carefully to each sound that reached her ears. The rattling of the coach, the rhythm of the train upon its tracks, the whistling of the wind. That was all. The coach was completely silent otherwise.

Relenting, she reached across the compartment to shake Eleanor awake. The younger girl blinked sleepily and then, when she had focused and seen the expression on Sophie's face, she sat up quickly.

"Where's Bertram?" she demanded.

Sophie was blunt. "We don't know. Find weapons. Stakes if possible. It's too close in here for crossbows." She stared at Eleanor a moment, trying to think of something to say to calm the other girl, but then decided that perhaps that was not for the best. Instead she turned back to Yanna to find her Watcher staring at her expectantly.

So there it was. The Slayer had felt their roles reversing, felt herself becoming the leader, but the altered nature of her relationship with Yanna crystallized in that moment. Sophie had always imagined that one day she would take charge of herself, of her destiny and her mission, and Yanna become more advisor than teacher, but never had it occurred to her that this might happen not because she was ready to do so, but because Yanna was no longer fully capable of guiding her.

Sophie glared at Yanna, angry in spite of her love for the woman. "Lock the door. Stay here. Protect her."

With that, Sophie went to the door and opened it. It was not locked, of course, for Bertram would not have been able to lock it behind him. She paused a moment in the passageway outside the compartment until she heard Yanna bolt the door behind her.

The passageway was dimly lit by electric lights that flickered with every rattle of the train. No one else was about, but Sophie moved silently and cautiously along the row of compartment doors until she came to the rear of the coach. She tested the door into the next car and found it unlocked. The Slayer frowned. There was no room for error here. No second chances.

Sophie snapped the knob off the door. Nobody would be able to come into the coach from that direction without her hearing them. With a deep breath she stared down the long passageway at the opposite door. To her left there were only windows, looking out at the night. All the compartments were on her right. She went to the first of the compartments and held up her fist to rap on the door.

No, she thought. *No warning.* It would be easier to apologize for barging in than to suffer the consequences should she warn her enemies of her presence.

The blade of her sword hissed against the scabbard as she freed it. Then she reached for the handle. The door was unlocked. Sophie hauled it open and went in, sword at the ready, heart hammering in her chest.

The elderly couple who lay on either side of the compartment looked as though they might be sleeping, save for the odd angle of their necks and the fact that they did not so much as flinch at her intrusion. Sophie steadied her breathing as she glanced around the compartment. Once certain no one else was within, she turned her back upon the dead and quickly returned to the passageway so that she could not be surprised from behind.

So they are here, she thought grimly. *The time has come.*

The second compartment was completely empty. In the third were a pair of middle-aged men who by their dress she identified as traveling on business. These had been killed just as silently as the elderly couple, though the men had been bitten, their blood drained. The killers had painted a smiling face on the window in the dead men's blood.

Sophie swallowed hard and held her breath a moment. This was not what she was used to. Vampires did not usually behave like this. They were brutal, yes, but their savagery was obvious and swift. Even Gorm, who had been her nemesis, had never been very clever. Combat, that was what Sophie craved.

This skulking about had her every nerve crackling and her teeth on edge.

The fourth compartment contained the mortal remains of an entire family. Their corpses had been placed about the floor in a grotesque tableau, father and mother leaning against the outer wall of the compartment side by side, little boy propped between his father's legs as though they were watching a sporting event together. A babe only a few months old, swaddled in bloody linens, lay dead in its mother's arms, face pressed against her cold, exposed breast.

Sophie bit her lip and her breath hitched in her chest. All of the strength she had received from Eleanor's adoration was torn from her heart and replaced by dread and fear. Real fear, unlike any she had felt before.

Evil, she thought. *This is evil.* Most of the creatures she had fought before were simple, stupid, horrid beasts with monstrous intentions. But these two vampires were intelligent, they were toying with her, taunting her, showing her that she was alive only by their sufferance, for their amusement.

No, damn them. They won't be so amused when they feel my blade at their throats.

The next compartment was her own. The door was still locked. She made no sound, not even to let Yanna and Eleanor know it was she beyond the door. Instead she moved on to the next. There was only one more beyond it. As she reached out to open the door a new thought occurred to her.

What if it was Bertram they wanted? she wondered. *What if they are killing the Watchers, and the Slayers-in-Waiting are only a matter of convenience? What if they are already gone?*

She slid the door open. Bertram lay naked on the floor of the compartment with his chest torn open, and his organs placed around his corpse in a decorative circle.

A tiny "oh" escaped Sophie's lips and she felt as though she could not breathe. For the briefest of instants, the point of her sword drooped and wavered.

A hand lunged out from beneath the seat to her right, grabbed her ankle and yanked her leg forward. The Slayer struggled to free herself, lost her balance and tumbled into the room, falling upon Bertram's corpse, her left arm sliding into a coil of the man's intestines even as she gripped her sword in her right hand. She wanted to scream, but she dared not. Swift as she was able, Sophie began to turn, to draw herself up again.

Too late.

Spike was there, above her. He launched a hard kick that caught Sophie in the temple, the boot making a solid thunk against her skull. The blow rocked her backward but Sophie shook it off, rolled back and leaped to her feet, slick with Bertram's blood.

But Spike was gone. She saw the blond vampire grinning out in the passageway, and the almost ghostly countenance of his lover, Drusilla, beyond him. Then Spike slid the compartment door closed and there came the sudden sound of something hammering against the door.

"No!" Sophie screamed.

For she understood, immediately, what they were doing. It was a wedge. Perhaps more than one. They were banging wedges into the door to keep it from opening, to keep her trapped inside.

The scream that ripped from inside her was akin to that of a savage beast, a primal roar of fury and hatred. Her mind flashed through the abominations she had witnessed in the past few silent minutes and all the things these creatures had done to the Council. But foremost among the images in her mind was one of something that had yet to occur. Yanna and Eleanor, torn apart like poor Bertram, or set up in a mockery of life like the family in compartment four.

"Me!" she screamed at the vampires. "You're supposed to fight me!"

"Oh no," Spike whispered from the other side of the door. "We're not allowed to do that. Not yet. Apparently our . . . employer has something else in mind for you."

Then they were gone. Sophie stared at the door. Something broke inside her and she started screaming for Yanna and Eleanor to run, to escape somehow. Spike began to shout right along with her and to pound on the door to the next compartment, where the Slayer knew her friends huddled. They had weapons, she knew. Stakes, and perhaps some holy water. But against these two, she knew they had no chance.

Her hand felt almost numb as she looked down to see that she still held her sword. Her knuckles were white with the tightness of her grip.

With another scream, Sophie lifted the sword and drove it through the door to the compartment. Wood splintered and the tip punched through. She hauled it out, lifted the blade, and brought it down as though it were an axe, using all the strength of the Chosen One.

"I feel like an artist," Drusilla said airily, feeling the train as it rumbled over the tracks beneath her feet. "I've got all these lovely, bloody pictures in my head. It's absolute bliss to finally get them out, to sculpt them with mortal flesh."

With the Slayer locked in a compartment farther along the train car, they stood in the corridor in front of the door behind which her companions awaited her.

"You're gettin' pretty good at it, Dru," Spike told her. "Ought to start your own bloody museum soon. An exhibition of murder."

With a shiver of pleasure and a wild song burning in her, she turned to him with a suggestive smile. "Mmm, you always know what to say." Drusilla fell into his arms and licked the dead Watcher's blood off his face. "I need a little taste, Spike."

He grinned and shook his head. "I'd love to, poodle, but the Slayer's in the next room, remember? Later, though—"

"You'll hurt me?" Dru asked expectantly. "Make my flesh burn?"

"You'll burn like the sun," Spike promised.

With a sudden crack, the point of the Slayer's sword pierced the door to the next compartment. It was removed, and then the girl started to hack at the door with her sword.

"We'd best hurry, love," Spike said, frowning.

Drusilla smiled sleepily and turned her attention to the door in front of them, with the Watcher and the someday-Slayer beyond. She could feel them in there, feel their terror. It made her tingle.

"They're like kittens, Spike. I can hear them mewling in there, asking for a bowl of milk, for a little more life. I had kittens once. Lots of them. But every time I gave one a bath it would stop moving."

"I remember," Spike told her. "They weren't as slippery as your puppies. Now, shall we? The train is grunting along at a good clip, but if they break the window, they *could* jump."

"Oooh," Dru said angrily. "Bad kitties."

She felt her face change then, shifting into the primal visage of the vampire. Drusilla grabbed the door handle and turned it, easily breaking the lock. With a grin she slid the door open, quivering with anticipation. She felt like dancing.

Drusilla smelled the smoke at the precise instant in which she saw the flames. Even as she lunged into the compartment, the Watcher was in motion. The diminutive woman held an enormous torch in her hands, clothing wrapped around a length of wood that had to have been snapped off of a seat or the overhead rack.

Matches, Drusilla thought, in the instant in which thought was possible for her. All the weapons they had steeled themselves to face, and she had never even considered matches.

With a cry of defiance and terror, the Watcher drove the flaming length of wood into Drusilla's chest.

"Nooo!" Spike screamed behind her.

Drusilla blinked in astonishment, expecting her body to explode into a cloud of dust. But the Watcher had missed her heart. Drusilla lived.

She lived to suffer in blazing agony. Flames engulfed her clothes, scorching her flesh. Drusilla screamed with the pain, glanced wildly about in search of a way to put out the fire. Then the American girl grabbed her by the arm and yanked her forward. Drusilla's hair was ablaze, her mind reeling, and she lashed out like an animal, trying to free herself.

Too late.

With a burst of surprising strength the American propelled her across the compartment and into the window. Drusilla's face, amidst the halo of her blazing hair, hit the glass. In flames, crying out for Spike, she hurtled out into the night, hit the ground hard enough to snap bones, and rolled painfully for several yards before coming to a rest.

She lay very still.

Spike screamed his lover's name. The light from the flames around her disappeared the instant she crashed through the window, and the locomotive rattled on.

"You stupid cow!" Spike roared at the American girl.

The Watcher faced him, a stake in her hand. She quivered in fear as he took a snarling step closer to her. The would-be Slayer lunged at him with a stake but he slapped her down, hard enough to split her cheek over the bone, to make her bleed. When he looked back at the Watcher and saw her, wide-eyed and wavering, he blinked in astonishment. Then Spike began to smile.

"Yeah," he said with a pompous drawl, his lip curled back. "This is the big bad you're dealing with now, love. Is it the pain you like?"

She flinched, and drew back a bit.

"Yanna?" the American girl whimpered, holding her bleeding face. "Do something!"

"You don't know what you're talking about!" the Watcher screamed at him, her skin flushing darkly.

"Don't I?" Spike asked, putting all the insinuation he could muster into his voice. "I asked if you liked pain, you silly cow. 'Cause there's going to be quite a bit of it 'fore I'm through with you."

"Yanna, kill him!" the American girl screamed. "Kill him now!"

"Ah, she's not likely to, are you love?"

Spike moved closer, reached out to touch the side of Yanna's face, to push aside a hair that had come loose from her taut braid. The Watcher only flinched and closed her eyes. She quivered.

Then she snarled, her eyes popped open, and she lunged at him. "Monster!" Yanna screamed.

Spike batted the stake out of her hand and gripped her by the throat. The American girl started to rise but he turned to her, the face of the vampire now, and snarled. She fell back onto the seat and wept.

"Got yourself a little thrill, don't you?" Spike whispered. "Hate yourself for it, maybe even want to die for it, but it's there. Another day I might even have indulged your fancy. But you just set fire to the woman I love, so I'm afraid I have very hard feelings on the subject."

He dipped his mouth to her throat and sank his fangs into the soft flesh there. Her blood flowed into his mouth and he began to suck.

The sword punched through his back from behind, piercing his heart cleanly. Spike arched his back and screamed in pain, then staggered forward, knocking the weakened Watcher down. The sword was yanked out of him hard and he turned to face the Slayer.

Now his own knees were weak. He stood with his back to the shattered window, the wind buffeting him, almost strong enough to knock him down. The metal blade would not kill him, but no vampire could take such a wound and not be staggered by it.

"*Spike*. If you've killed her . . ." the Slayer began, but could not find any more words.

He glanced at the Watcher, unconscious on the floor. "Look," he snapped, "she set my girlfriend on fire, right? Not exactly the neighborly thing to do. And she's not dead. Just down a pint or so. She'll live."

"You won't," the Slayer vowed, eyes flashing in the starlight streaming in through the broken window, sword gleaming with blood.

My blood, he thought angrily.

"I couldn't take your head with you bent over like that," Sophie told him. "And before you caught me by surprise. But we're face to face now, vampire. Try me. The wind will take your ashes."

She was perfect. Spike was amazed by the girl, captivated by the long blond hair that swirled behind her with the wind. She was tall and lithe and moved with unnatural grace. A dancer, he decided.

"Come then," the Slayer barked.

And for the first time, he sensed the fear she had been hiding so well.

Spike grinned. "Another night," he promised.

Then he turned, grabbed the jagged edges of the broken window, slicing into his palms, and thrust himself out into the darkness. Even as he fell, struck the ground painfully and rolled over stones and scrub brush, he could hear the Slayer screaming in frustration behind him.

Another night.

Chapter Eleven

London, England
July 17th

For hours, automobiles had been coming and going along Great Russell Street, coming briefly to a stop at the far end to discharge passengers before moving on to unknown destinations. Many others arrived on foot. By five o'clock in the afternoon the Council's London headquarters was host to the largest gathering of Watchers and operatives seen within its walls in many a year. The table in the fourth floor meeting chamber had been moved back against the far wall and still there was barely enough space for the fifty-odd people standing shoulder to shoulder in the room. Perhaps two dozen others stood in the hall outside the chamber. Most of those in the corridor were Watchers, as it had been made quite clear that the operatives took precedence at this meeting.

There was plenty of grumbling about that, to be sure. The Watchers disliked the idea that mere employees of the Council should be given priority over them under any circumstances. To appease them, several of the directors made room within the meeting chamber by standing out in the corridor themselves. No one could complain outright about their place in the pecking order when the elderly Trevor Kensington stood in the hall alongside them, leaning on his wolf's head cane.

Though evening approached, it was stiflingly hot outside. For once the windows in the meeting chamber were wide open, and eavesdroppers be damned, as far as Marie-Christine Fontaine was concerned. Sweat beaded on her forehead, chest and arms, but she did her best to ignore it, to maintain some semblance of dignity. She stood at the far end of the room, behind the table, with the crush of human beings before her and Sir Nigel beside her.

It was an honor for her, to have been chosen to speak for the board of directors during this crisis. But she also felt that, in some ways, the other members of the board had picked her because she was the only one among them who seemed to have a grasp on the situation. They were all still reacting to the predations of Spike and Drusilla, but Marie-Christine had begun to urge them to take real action, to do something about it.

Sir Nigel moved up close to her. "I must tell you, Mademoiselle Fontaine, that I am still quite dubious about this course of action," he said in a low voice. "It would be exceedingly detrimental to the Council if our enemies perceived this as a sign of weakness."

It was all Marie-Christine could do not to roll her eyes and sigh. *Image,* she thought. *Our people are dying and he is concerned with perception.*

"Sir Nigel," she whispered, "if we do this right, our enemies will never learn of it. And if we do not do it at all, I don't think I have to warn you of the possible outcome. If the Slayer cannot stop Spike and Drusilla, we may soon be dipping from a dry well. We do everything in our power to see to it that each new Chosen One has received at least some training before she is called. When unknown girls are called, they tend to have even shorter life spans and give way, relatively quickly, to one of the girls we have already begun to prepare. But if these two vampires kill all the girls we've trained, we will be in for a succession of Slayers ill-equipped and unprepared for the role. Imagine the damage to the Council's image if that should occur."

Marie-Christine was pleased to see the grimace on the old man's face. Her words had had the desired effect.

"Shall we begin?" she asked, trying to hide the plea in her voice. The sooner they were out of the room, the happier she would be. The heat was pressing in on her and a dull ache throbbed in her head.

"By all means," the old man said, voice low and gravelly. "Let's get on with it before they begin to faint."

With his approval, she forged ahead, explaining the circumstances that had led to such a grim gathering. Wave after wave of shock, anger, and bewilderment ran through the men and women before her. There were many familiar faces in the crowd, but at the back of the room, near the windows, she saw one face she had almost hoped would not appear to her. John Travers, whose father Harold had been her friend and confidante, wore a dark expression as she discussed Spike and Drusilla with the others, relating the events surrounding his father's death.

Poor man, she thought.

Young Travers saw her watching him and his eyes flared with sudden anger before he turned sullenly away.

Marie-Christine took a deep breath. Several hands shot up during that tiny moment's rest, but she ignored them. Now was not the time for questions. Not until she had told them what was expected of them.

She pressed on.

"The Slayer has recovered one of the girls on our list. She and her Watcher are transporting her from America at this very moment. But there are eleven other girls on the list who still live. It will take the vampires days to return to Europe. We must take advantage of that time to gather the remaining candidates and bring them back here to London, where they will be kept under Council protection at all times until this crisis has been resolved. Nearly all have been contacted of course, though the war has necessitated communiqués in some instances. We have suggested they move to alternate locations and await the arrival of an escort.

"To that end, all Council operatives presently in Britain have been accounted for. Recovery teams of three each will be formed and sent out to bring back these candidates. The rest of you will remain on assignment here, working in shifts along with Watchers currently in London to fortify and safeguard this building, and to convert some of our larger rooms into temporary sleeping quarters for the candidates and for many of you as well.

"A team of operatives will also be selected to hunt for Spike and Drusilla. Something the Slayer will continue to do as well."

Hands shot up again around the room. Marie-Christine hesitated, but finally called upon Kenneth Haversham, whom she had met on several occasions and of whom she was rather fond.

"Mr. Haversham?"

"Yes, ma'am. Well, it just seems to me that by consolidating in such a way, we're providing our enemies with a single target. Feels a bit like the American story about the Alamo, to be honest. Wouldn't it be better if we split up into teams to protect these girls where they are?"

Marie-Christine nodded. "I see your point, Mr. Haversham, and it is something the board has discussed. These vampires would happily slaughter half a dozen of our people at a safe house in Vienna, for instance. And, no offense intended to your prodigious talents, but they have proven themselves quite capable in that area. I doubt, however, that they would dare make an attack on these premises again when they would have to be aware of the kind of force they would be pitting themselves against. And if they did . . . well, clever and brutal as they are, there are only two of them after all."

Sir Nigel cleared his throat. "Indeed. Only two against you lot, operatives and all. I rather hope they do come at us then. We'll be rid of them right off, then, and not have to be concerned about them in future."

Other operatives still had their hands raised, along with several Watchers.

"Right then, move along," Sir Nigel said gruffly.

The hands went down. Marie-Christine was relieved.

"All right. I'm going to run down a list of team assignments for each of our candidates. Team leaders see John Travers for documents and itineraries."

With a quiet sigh, she wiped the sweat from her brow with a handkerchief. Then Marie-Christine began to go down the long list of assignments for those in the room. Ten minutes or so into it she glanced up and saw that young Travers had left the room. Given his organizational role in this effort she realized he must have relocated to another room for space. Still, it concerned her that he was not there. She had come to feel very protective of the man in the wake of his father's death.

When it was all over, and the operatives and Watchers had dispersed to prepare for their various journeys and other responsibilities, she sought John out and found him in a second floor office going over a stack of assignments by the light of a green glass lamp.

A light tap on the open door drew his attention, but when John looked up at her, Marie-Christine almost wished she had not interrupted him. Ever since his father's murder, the young man had burned with an inner rage that overshadowed his grief. She had known that his fury was partially directed inward, for John blamed himself for not being able to prevent Spike and Drusilla's attack. Now, though, all that anger seemed to have been burned out of him, leaving only deep, abiding sorrow.

"John?"

"Miss Fontaine. Can I help you with something?" Young Travers sat up straighter, composing himself as best he could.

Marie-Christine's heart broke for him. She mourned his father's passing as well, for she had loved the man in her way. But John was his son and it was far from equivalent.

"Not at the moment, thank you. I was . . . I had thought that you might like to talk. About your father. I don't mean to presume, but if you ever need to unburden yourself . . ."

She let the rest of the sentence go unspoken, her words hanging in the air between them. John frowned, his brows knitting, and he seemed pained even by her raising of the topic. He closed his eyes and composed himself, then fixed her with a steady gaze.

"I want to do something," he said firmly. "Something *more*. I would like to be assigned to one of the retrieval teams, to be in the field. I need to take a more active role."

"You're a Watcher. Not a field operative," Marie-Christine replied. She moved farther into the room and sat down in a chair by the desk. John seemed uncomfortable when she reached out and took his hand, but soon relented. Some of the anger in him drained away in that moment. "Council operatives are vital to what we do, but good Watchers are essential. I understand your anger and your despair, John. I do. I have lost a great deal in my life, and I confess I was more fond of your father than I ever admitted to him while he was alive."

The young man blinked in surprise, and Marie-Christine smiled.

"The Council needs young men and women of distinction. Your father served with great dignity in this war against the darkness. As your grandfather did before him. We have lost a great many Watchers in recent weeks. Good ones. Courageous and brilliant people. Our ranks are thin, and we cannot afford to lose even one more, either to death or to the rolls of our operatives.

"I'm sorry, but no."

Travers hung his head, but his eyes did not seem to focus on anything on his desk. Marie-Christine wanted to say more, but could think of nothing that would assuage the pain John was feeling. She stood, paused a moment, and then went out into the corridor.

"Miss Fontaine?" he called after her.

She turned and was pleased to see that though the sadness remained in his features it had been joined by a new resolve.

"Thank you," he said.

"Your father was very proud of you," she quietly replied. "I expect he would be even more so today."

Geneva, Switzerland
July 21st

On the hills of the right bank of the Rhône River, which cut right down the center of Geneva, lay a maze of cobblestone streets and narrow stone steps called the Old City. The Old City was centuries old, and built without any prescient knowledge of what the future would bring. The narrow passages were built for walking and for wandering, with antiquarian bookshops, quaint flower shops, and candlelit restaurants.

In one such restaurant, Charles Rochemont sipped at his French wine and tried to control the trill of excitement running through him. His companion, Ariana de la Croix, had never looked so beautiful. Despite the war, there were still pleasures to be had in life. Ariana wore a beautiful pale blue gown and her hair was done up on her head so that strands of it cascaded down in front of her face. She herself was flush with the tingle of anticipation.

But Ariana was not his lover. Indeed, Charles considered it fortunate that, for a girl of sixteen, she was capable of appearing much older. Otherwise he would have feared they might have drawn undue attention out together at night like that.

Charles had taken only a few sips from his wine glass, and had eaten lightly. Ariana had done the same, though now she lifted her wine in a silent toast. A coquettish smile touched her lips but he knew there was no real flirtation there. Only the excitement of the moment.

They had found a vampire.

Though he had not cleared it through the Council, once they had discovered the vampire lurking in the Old City, Charles had determined that Ariana should have her first experience with a kill in the field. He had only been her Watcher for nine months, but there was something so magical and electric about her that he could not conceive of any other girl taking up the mantle of the Chosen One when next the need arose. She was, in his estimation, an extraordinary girl.

"To your big night," he said in French.

Ariana glanced shyly away, though the smile never left her lips.

When the vampire stood up from his table across the room, hand in hand with the young woman he had been romancing, Ariana did not react. But she noticed. Charles watched her in fascination as she tracked the vampire in her peripheral vision. She would make an excellent Slayer, he thought. He had never seen a girl so naturally imbued with the skills necessary for the duty.

"Let's go," she said, reaching out to take his hand.

He had already paid for dinner, so Charles did not argue as she led him out of the restaurant and into the winding labyrinth of the Old City. For nearly ten minutes they walked hand in hand, wearing the pretense of lovers, behind the vampire and his intended victim. Past the Cathedrale St.-Pierre they walked, and on through the city until they came to the *promenade de bastions,* where portions of the fortifications from the age when Geneva was a walled city still remained.

The vampire veered off, then, directing his intended into the darkness where the crumbling wall stood. The creature was dapper and swarthy, and the girl giggled as he led her to her death. Charles and Ariana kept walking, his arm around her, as she leaned her head dreamily against his shoulder.

After a count of ten, they glanced around to be sure that there was no one else to see them, then turned and ran for the opposite side of the crumbling bastions. They moved silently, just as he had taught her, and when he glanced over, Charles saw that Ariana already had a stake in her hand. His heart surged with pride.

There came a small yelp of alarm from the darkness beyond the wall, and then a whimper of pain. Ariana dashed ahead. Charles wanted to call out a warning to her to wait, but he dared not warn the vampire that she was coming. As he watched her outstrip him, he grew anxious, having second thoughts now that the moment was upon them. Though she was in training, Ariana was not the Slayer. She did not have the abilities nor the stamina and healing powers that the Chosen One received.

She knew to wait for him. He had instructed her that they must do this thing together, simply because she was not the true Slayer yet. But now she had become overwhelmed with her excitement, perhaps even her need to please him, and he feared for her.

With a burst of reserve energy he had not realized he had, Charles sprinted to catch up with her.

As Ariana rounded the edge of the wall, he was on her heels. By the time she paused in sight of the vampire, Charles was by her side. He was her Watcher. She would not face the darkness alone.

Ahead, against the wall, the swarthy vampire nuzzled the throat of his victim. Her blond hair tossed from side to side as she thrashed, trying to escape him. Ariana and Charles moved more slowly, spreading out somewhat, and now Charles took his own stake out from inside his jacket.

Ariana's foot kicked a rock and the creature looked up, features contorted into the demonic countenance of the vampire, eyes blazing, fangs bared in a hiss.

"Leave her, vampire," Ariana instructed, her voice regal and commanding.

Yes, Charles thought. *She will be an extraordinary Slayer.*

He grinned as the vampire cursed, testing the feel of the stake in his hand, risking a quick glance at Ariana. There was no smile on her face. Only a grim determination.

When Charles looked back, the blond woman had moved away from the wall. But something was wrong. She did not run, nor scream. Instead, she snarled and her face *changed.*

"Oh, no," Charles whispered. He moved toward Ariana, keeping his eyes on the two vampires. "This was a mistake. Let's go, Ariana. Slowly."

"You're not going anywhere," the swarthy vampire told them, his words punctuated by a low, snuffling laugh.

Ariana did not even look at Charles. "We can do it. You've trained me well enough, Charles. Don't lose faith now. They're hellspawn. Whatever the odds, we cannot simply ignore their presence."

Charles nodded. She was right. It had been a mistake, coming out here, risking her in this way. Stupid. But they could not flee now, and leave the predators to go about their business. Nor did Charles believe, in his heart, that they would be allowed to go.

The vampires had stood regarding them with curiosity. Special attention was paid to the stakes they both held.

"What are you supposed to be?" the female asked disparagingly.

Inspiration struck Charles. If he could intimidate them, that might be the advantage he and Ariana needed.

"She's the Slayer," he said.

The male laughed. "Oh, is she? Met a girl who thought she was the Slayer once. It's just a myth, you fool. No matter what she's told you."

Charles paled. He had never imagined this. While most humans believed vampires were merely legend, it had never occurred to him that some vampires might believe the same about the Slayer.

"Are you going to be jealous?" the male asked his female companion.

"Not at all, darling," she replied with a gruesome smile. "She's a pretty thing and you're welcome to her. Besides, the man's handsome as well."

Ariana shot Charles a quick glance. "Come on, Charles."

He nodded. "Kill them," he said.

The vampires were both grinning cruelly as Charles and Ariana rushed toward them. Their fangs glistened in the moonlight and Charles found himself almost entranced by them. He faltered, and hated himself for the sudden streak of cowardice in his heart. Then it was too late, for the vampire girl was on him. He tried to bring the stake up into her chest but she slapped it away, grabbed him by the hair and hauled his head back to get at his throat.

As he tried to fight her off, he caught sight of Ariana and the other vampire. She had succeeded in burying her stake in his chest, but had missed his heart. Now he drove her to the ground and fell upon her. She was skilled enough, but he was simply too strong. Charles saw the vampire sink his fangs into her pale flesh, and he screamed.

There was a tiny sound and the vampire girl he struggled with exploded in a cloud of dust. Stunned, he turned around just in time to see a tall, thin, well-dressed man stand over Ariana and the vampire with a crossbow. The man fired a bolt into the other vampire's back, piercing the heart, and the creature burst into a pile of ash that showered down onto Ariana.

Charles ran to her. Her neck was bleeding, but she seemed otherwise unhurt. Ariana looked at him, eyes shining with her fear. Then she embraced him tightly.

A moment later the tall man cleared his throat. Charles helped Ariana to stand and face him, only to find that a second man, shorter and wide around the middle, had joined them. He also carried a crossbow and Charles realized that the stout one had saved his life.

"Thank you, gentlemen," Charles said in a tremulous voice. "To whom do we owe our lives?"

"My name is Haversham," said the tall man. He gestured to his partner. "This is Mr. Rubie. Council has sent us to collect yourself and Miss de la Croix, Mr. Rochemont."

Charles nodded grimly. He had thought as much, and the repercussions chilled him.

"What you saw here, gentlemen ... well, it wasn't what it appeared. Mere coincidence, really."

"Really?" Rubie asked, a quizzical expression on his face. "That's funny, 'cause it looked to me like you was giving your charge here a bit of a test run. If I know my Watcher business well enough, which I can't really claim I do, that'd be quite a bit premature, wouldn't it? For a field test, I mean?"

"Please, gentlemen," Ariana began. "You mustn't—"

"P'raps you'd best stop right there," Haversham interjected. "As long as you're both all right, and we're all headed back to London anyway, I'd be of a mind to keep a firm rein on my curiosity, wouldn't you, Mr. Rubie?"

Rubie regarded Charles harshly, and the Watcher sighed. He deserved the man's scorn, for putting Ariana's life in jeopardy. But the stout man nodded.

"I don't see any reason we can't keep this to ourselves."

"Oh, thank you both," Charles said, weak with relief. "For this, and for our lives."

Haversham's features hardened. When he spoke again, it was in a grave tone. "Don't thank us yet, Mr. Rochemont. Neither one of you is safe yet. None of us are. Save your gratitude for when you sleep your first night in London.

"Until then, be more cautious than you have been, sir. There are hunters in the dark, and your girl here is the prey."

Ariana's eyes widened with alarm, but the Council operatives said no more. Charles felt an awful chill pass through him. As they walked back to his rooms, the Watcher peered into every shadow. Though he wished she would walk beside him, Ariana strolled along between Haversham and Rubie. She no longer trusted Charles to guide her and keep her safe.

He had never felt so ashamed.

The Atlantic Ocean
July 25th

A few hours before dawn, Drusilla stood at the very back of the deck of the *Madrid,* a passenger liner bound for the southern coast of Spain, and gazed down at the ocean churning behind the fat-bellied ship. Though it was midsummer, there was a chill to the wind this late at night and this far out to sea. Drusilla made no sign that she felt it, nor any motion at all, for that matter. She stood at the rail, rigid and still. Her eyes did not move, not even a blink, and her chest did not rise even with the semblance of breath. In the moonlight her skin was gossamer and pale, thin blue veins ran through it like marble.

Any crew member or sleepless soul who had passed her during those moments of reflection would have thought her dead were it not for the impossible fact that she was still on her feet. For long minutes, near an hour, she stood frozen, watching the tumultuous sea.

The dead bobbed and swirled in the wake thrashed up by the huge liner, a grotesque ballet of corpses on the water. The ocean swells were salt-tipped gouts of blood, crashing over the bodies and painting them in crimson. Hundreds of cadavers, thousands of dead men and women and children. As the vessel pressed on through the night it carved through the dead like an icebreaker clearing a shipping lane through the Arctic.

Below them, beneath the menagerie of rotting, sodden flesh, lay a cemetery of iron and steel. To Drusilla's eyes the warships and submarines looked like enormous tombstones. It was so cold and still in the depths, broken only by the scream of tearing metal, the ghosts of explosions that haunted the bottom of the ocean.

Beside her, Spike lit a cigarette, then tossed the match off the back of the ship. The flame sputtered out long before it reached the bloody sea.

"You all right, pet? Thought you'd have come in 'fore now."

For the first time in an hour, Drusilla blinked, but she did not turn away from her vigil, nor did she respond.

"Come on, Dru. Come inside. You look like a bleedin' scarecrow or a flamingo or something, standing back here like that. You were any more stiff they'd strip you down to show your Bristols and nail you to the front of the boat like on them old Viking warships."

Drusilla turned at last to regard him. As if that motion was all that was needed to break her trance, she began to sway a bit, out of synch with the swell of the ocean. Her eyes did not focus on Spike, nor anything else for that matter. She was adrift, haunted, a ghost even to herself.

"Too much blood," she whispered.

"What's that?" Spike asked. "I'm surprised at you, poodle. Never thought I'd hear you complain about having too much of anything." His smile was sly and suggestive.

"Down there," she said, returning her attention to the churning water below.

Spike glanced down at the ocean. "I don't see anything, love. Course that's not all that unusual, is it? My Dru has always been able to see a damn sight better than the rest of us. What is it this time?"

"The war," Drusilla whispered. "It's beautiful in its way. Death always is. I don't want to be sunk again, Spike." As she said this last, she glanced back at him as though he were the one responsible for the sinking of the *Aberdeen* months earlier, and now he must be punished.

"It'd be damned inconvenient," Spike observed.

"We should have kept our submarine," Drusilla reminisced, her gaze drifting off again, lost in memory.

Spike shrugged. "Didn't seem practical at the time. Besides, those boys had their own agenda, remember? Funny thing about Nazis. Turn 'em into ravening vampires, some of 'em don't seem all that different from when they were alive. Anyway they're likely at the bottom of the Atlantic about now and if not, odds are they will be long before the curtain's drawn on this lovely little war."

Drusilla tilted her head and looked out over the ocean again. The blood and the dead were gone and now there was only the water. It made her think of alligators, and alligators made her think of Louisiana. Drusilla did not like to think about Louisiana. She shuddered. Though her skin was all healed now, it felt sometimes like there were thousands of tiny insects, squirming maggots, under her skin. After she had been burned, when her charred and cracked flesh had been flaking off and even the coolest breeze had pulled at the edges, that had been the feeling. Insects.

"You're my warrior, aren't you Spike?" she asked, in a voice so low she thought even the wind must have barely heard her.

But Spike did.

"Course I am, Dru. When you want me to be. Sometimes you like to do the ripping and tearing on your own, right? But when you need your black knight, here I am."

"You'll kill that Slayer, then, and let me watch? I want to see her eyes when you do it."

"It'll be my pleasure, Dru. Got to keep to our side of the bargain, though. Do in all the someday Slayers first, then the real thing. Love to have another crack at that girl, and the other, too. The American. Damned embarrassing, that was. Not to mention inconvenient."

They both fell silent again a long moment. Drusilla felt the wind tugging at her hair, whipping it around her face, and she closed her eyes to enjoy it a moment.

"Do I like Spain?" she asked at length.

"Don't you remember?" Spike shook his head. "The bullfighter and his daughters in Barcelona that time?"

Her smile was wicked, her eyes focused at last. Her laugh was a trilling moan of pleasure. "Oh, yes," she murmured. "I love Spain. I liked America too. Not the South but the rest. Do you think we'll ever go back?"

Spike stood by her and slipped an arm around her back. He kissed her on top of her head. "Whatever your black little devil heart desires, Dru. Always."

Galdhöpiggen, Norway
July 27th

In his frozen lair, Skrymir spied upon the Watchers Council through his icy scrying glass, and he nodded his head in satisfaction.

Everything was proceeding according to plan.

Chapter Twelve

Barcelona, Spain
August 4th

All day the sun had been so hot that the air had stagnated over the city. As night fell, a breeze kicked up, carrying the spicy scents of cooking across the city. Somewhere, down in the streets of Barcelona, music played loudly, drifting up to the small, heavily shuttered villa that Spike and Drusilla had appropriated from its owners several days earlier.

The aging couple who owned the place lay dead in a second floor bedroom and the heat from the previous days had caused them to decay quickly. Of course the vampires did not need to breathe in, to smell the stench of the rotting corpses, but sometimes one or the other would forget.

The worse the smell became, the more it reminded them that they had been in Barcelona too long. They had searched the city from the Gothic Quarter to the Barceloneta, the harbor neighborhood where the fishermen lived. From their villa in the shadow of the fortress on Montjuïc, they had spent each night slipping through the city in search of the girl. She had not been at the address noted for her on the list and no one had seen any sign of her or her Watcher.

Spike stood in front of the villa and watched the night come alive in the city to the north. He was greatly troubled. The girl in Louisiana had escaped them, but not before the little bitch had set the torch to Dru. The girl could not realize it, but if she had simply let Drusilla burn instead of tossing her out the window—where she could roll in the dirt until she put the flames out—his baby might have died that night. Dru's flesh had healed in just a few days, of course, but she had seemed off since, distant and unreadable. And this lurking around Spain was not helping a bit.

Spike knew what would do the trick, though. The American girl was not really to blame. It was that Slayer, Sophie. He was certain they would meet again, and when they did, Spike would make the girl suffer, make her scream. Skrymir had instructed them not to kill the Slayer until he sent word that they were to do so. But ol' Frosty never said they could not torture the girl.

"That'll be just the thing," he whispered to himself, nodding.

He searched his pockets for cigarettes and then remembered that he was out. Even as he cursed the luck of it, he heard the door open and Drusilla floated up beside him and lay her head on his shoulder. Her fingers traced the line of his jaw, then moved around to twirl in the hair on the back of his head.

"My poor Spike, you're so tense," she whispered.

Drusilla leaned in to nibble at his ear, but Spike barely responded.

"She's not here, is she, Dru?" he asked. "Isabel Cortés is gone."

"Had a dream today," Drusilla replied quite matter-of-factly. "A city full of Bengal tigers, and all of them were hungry."

Spike nodded. "That's what I thought. I'd like to think it's coincidence, but I'm afraid those self-important poofs at the Council may've actually taken some action here."

Drusilla pulled him around to face her. His chin was tucked down so that she gazed up at him. Her eyes were clearer than they had been since Louisiana, perhaps long before that.

"I want my necklace. I want to feel its power on my flesh, hear it whisper the secrets of the old world and old gods. I want to see my face, Spike, and any other face my whimsy gives me. Freyja's Strand belongs to me. I deserve it."

Spike nodded slowly, a grave expression on his face. "And you'll have it, pet. It's only a matter of time and persistence, and we've an endless supply of both. We'll find the little lambs we can, then go back and see Skrymir. I don't fancy another walk up that mountain before we have to. This is his plan; if it goes bollocks-up that's his fault, not ours.

"Now then, where would you like to go next?"

Drusilla made a trilling noise in her throat, a small smile on her face. "What about Prague?"

Spike shuddered. "I've been sort of putting off Prague. Rather not go back there until we have to."

"Hong Kong?"

With a frown, Spike glanced down upon the city again. "I don't know, Dru. It's a hell of a trip, isn't it?

Wouldn't mind so much if I could be sure that girl would be there, but after this . . . I think we'd best concentrate on the continental lasses and then report in."

"Mykonos? The sands are lovely."

"Right, then!" Spike said happily. "Greece it is."

London, England
August 7th

The pristine blue sky was tarnished only by chalky traces of cloud that seemed so forgotten and haphazard they might have been left behind by an absentminded god. A breeze rippled the surface of the lake in St. James's Park, urging on a toy boat carved of wood. From a nearby bench, Sophie watched the little boy who must have been the boat's skipper chasing after it along the shore of the lake, crying out in glee at the boat's progress and terror that he might never get the vessel back. Beside him a large man with a handlebar mustache grumbled as he took off his shoes and cuffed his pants, prepared to wade in after the boat.

Sophie watched in silent amazement.

Lovers had set out picnic lunches on blankets scattered across the park. A pair of giggling children played with a dog nearby under the watchful gaze of their mother. The heat of previous days had abated for the moment, and the weather was nothing short of perfect.

A crystalline day, worth preserving forever. And Sophie marveled to find that those around her seemed actually to believe it could be done, that by some miracle the day could go on forever, could be encased in amber or frozen in time. The war lingered, threatening far worse than any approaching storm. Her own war, and the lives of those Slayers-in-Waiting yet to be brought to London, weighed heavily upon her. So much so that she felt in some way a black spot upon the otherwise unsullied perfection of the day, as if she might infect those around her with her terrible knowledge.

It was illusion, of course. They knew at least enough about their own war to know the beauty of the day, the carefree hours they would spend in the park that day, was fleeting at best. Yet they went on as if these were the only moments that mattered.

Sophie watched the grumpy man with the handlebar mustache splash into the lake, soaking himself up past the knees, and a new thought occurred to her. An impossible thought to a girl who had been raised to war as she had.

Maybe they are, she thought. *Perhaps this, all of this, is the only bit that really does matter.*

The man with the handlebar mustache shook his head in exasperation and laughed as he waded back to shore, rescued boat in his rough hands, to be greeted by his cheering son.

Sophie found herself laughing softly at the picture they made. But slowly, the smile drained from her face.

All of this was possible for them, but not for her. The duties of the Chosen One prevented such carefree moments. It was her obligation to keep the darkness at bay for no other real reason than so that lovers could picnic and fathers play with their sons on the green grass of St. James Park, and not think about the horrors that lurked just out of sight, waiting for an opportunity to strike. She could not protect them from the Nazis. But she could keep the monsters at bay.

Thus she sat alone, a stone's throw from Buckingham Palace, and waited for Yanna to return from her meeting with the Council. It had been made clear, and quite firmly, that her presence was not required at that meeting. Sophie was more relieved than offended. Though she had enjoyed Eleanor's company on their voyage from America, she needed to clear her head. The park had afforded her the opportunity she had sought, but now that her head was clear, the thoughts that began to fill it were even more morose than ever.

Her worst fears about Yanna had proven true. Not perhaps the madness some seers were prone to, but certainly a slow separation from reality. How else to explain her inability to act when Spike threatened her? The Watcher's visions had so polluted her waking mind that it infringed upon her rationality. Yanna had a chance to kill Spike, and failed.

All the more reason for Sophie to stay away from the Council headquarters. She had carefully weighed her duties, knew that it was incumbent upon her to report her Watcher's condition, and purposefully decided not to do so. Yanna was ill. Her mind was not right. But Sophie would not abandon her to the Council. Yanna might no longer be able to engage in combat or to lead, but she was a brilliant woman with an extensive knowledge of the creatures of the dark. Sophie would keep Yanna with her, as an advisor, and also to watch out for the one person in her life she could think of as family.

Yanna had failed her, but Sophie could not hate her for it. She could only mourn what they both had lost, and pray that now the conflict with Spike, which had prompted so many visions, had come and gone, Yanna's mind would not deteriorate any further.

"Sophie."

The Slayer looked up to see Yanna hurrying toward her along one of the paths through the park. In dynamic contrast to the way in which Sophie had allowed herself to relax, Yanna seemed wound up more tightly than ever, her braid severe, her clothing drab and functional, almost as though it were a reaction to her recent loss of control. Even as she thought it, Sophie realized it must be true.

Yanna's expression, as she approached, betrayed the anxiety she obviously felt.

With a tiny smile of affection and concern for her mentor balanced by trepidation, Sophie unfolded herself from her perch on the bench, pushed her long blond hair away from her face and moved to meet Yanna along the path.

"Was it as bad as all that?" she asked her Watcher.

Yanna came to a halt in front of her. She seemed about to say something, then paused. "No. No, it was as I expected."

Sophie glanced away. The words sounded hollow, but she could not imagine what reason Yanna would have for lying to her. After a momentary pause to compose herself, she regarded her Watcher steadily.

"What now?" she asked, the transition of leadership in their relationship still eminently clear. "If I am to understand things correctly, all but the most distant . . . candidates on that list have been retrieved and are either here in London already or on their way."

Yanna nodded. "The candidates in Moscow and Hong Kong have been informed that they are to be on alert until further notice. The Council believes that Spike and Drusilla will attempt to complete their extermination of candidates in Europe before venturing so far afield."

"But all of the others are here now," Sophie reasoned. "Though I suppose it will take some time for them to realize that."

"Not all," Yanna explained.

Sophie frowned. Somewhere nearby she heard a child laugh loudly, but it did not draw her attention any more powerfully than the songs of birds in the trees above her head.

"Council operatives spotted the vampires in Barcelona. Of those remaining on the stolen list, the nearest would be in Greece. The candidate there has yet to be informed of the danger."

"Why?" Sophie asked. Then a horrible idea played at the back of her mind and a wave of nausea swept through her. "Please tell me the Council hasn't left her out there on purpose, as bait."

"Nothing of the sort!" Yanna protested, scandalized. "The girl's family insisted she remain on Mykonos, the island of her birth, for training. Her Watcher apparently convinced them to allow their daughter to go to Athens with him for several weeks to study certain texts and journals the Council preferred he not take to the island with him. She has not returned and their precise whereabouts are unknown. It seems our friends Mr. Haversham and Mr. Rubie have been dispatched to Mykonos to retrieve the girl the moment she returns to her home."

"If Spike and Drusilla don't find her first," Sophie said grimly. Then she regarded Yanna levelly, and put voice to the question that gnawed at her. "If that was the purpose of your meeting, why couldn't I attend?"

Yanna blinked, taken aback by the question. She vacillated for a moment, absently rubbing her neck where

Spike had bitten her, drunk of her. Sophie caught her gaze again and held it.

"What is it, Yanna? Why would they exclude me? With all we are going through now, this is hardly the time for there to be more secrets between us."

For a moment Yanna looked almost angry. Sophie understood. They had quite purposefully avoided discussing what had happened on the train back in America. Yanna's hesitation to kill Spike had almost cost them all their lives. It was obvious to Sophie that even that had not cured the woman of her dangerous fascination with the vampire, nor of the dementia that had overcome her. Sophie wanted to bring an end to things quickly, to give Yanna's mind a chance to heal.

Yanna was far from insane, nor was she fully engaged with the world around her any longer. It was a dangerous state, and made them both more vulnerable. But Sophie refused to abandon Yanna now, when her former mentor needed her most.

"Yanna?" she prodded. "Please?"

"I have not had any visions of him since the last I told you about," Yanna insisted. "I keep no secrets. I swear to you that I will not fail you, or the Council, again."

Sophie took Yanna's hand, grief in her soul. "I trust you. I need to trust you," she said, pained by the raw truth of it. "All the more reason for you not to keep anything from me now."

"It's only to save your heart," Yanna said quickly, the secret crumbling within her. "The Council can be blunt and hurtful, cold and uncaring. But in this instance they were protecting you. The headquarters has many guests at the moment, Sophie. Eleanor is only one of the potential candidates residing there now. They hoped to avoid any discomfort for you by keeping you away from these girls who might one day take your place."

Sophie swallowed. A chill ran through her and she found that her head had begun to ache ever so slightly. "Do you think my shell so brittle?" she asked.

"It isn't—"

The Slayer held up a hand to interrupt her. "It's all right. I understand." She took a long breath. At length she regarded Yanna again. "And what of us? What next?"

Yanna studied the Slayer's eyes, reached out and laid a hand upon her shoulder. "We go hunting again. We'll start in Mykonos. The vampires will have no way of knowing if we have removed the candidate there or not."

Sophie considered that a moment. "Greece makes the most sense for them now, but it isn't as though logic has ruled them thus far. What if Greece is not their destination?"

"Operatives have been set in place to observe the other locations from which candidates have already been removed. We *will* find them, Sophie. However long it takes."

Sophie nodded. Each lost in her own contemplation, they walked along the path and out of St. James Park. In front of Buckingham Palace, the guard stood stiff and unresponsive as ever. It occurred to the Slayer that those men in their tall, black-furred caps and bright red tunics were lifeless as corpses, with only their upright position indicating that they were alive at all. It was an errant thought, ricocheting through her mind and out again too quickly almost to register, but it made her shiver just the same.

Despite Yanna's confidence, Sophie suspected that once the vampires realized that the candidates had been recalled they would disappear forever into the darkness. If this slaughter of theirs was whim, it could end just as suddenly as it had begun. They could very well get away with it.

No, she vowed to herself. *No, they will not. Not after all they have done.*

Then, to her disgust, she realized a terrible truth about herself. Though the very idea of it repulsed her, and though Yanna had vowed that it had not been the Council's plan to do so, Sophie had indeed begun to think of the girl on the island of Mykonos as the perfect lure set out to trap these animals.

Intentionally or not, the girl was bait.

Mykonos, Greece
August 15th

On a hill overlooking a fishing village of cottages the sun had bleached as white as the bone-hued sand of the shores of Mykonos, there sat a small house as pale as the rest, only a bit larger. Paradise, many would have said of that island, but to the people of Mykonos it was only home.

In that small house, as sunlight spread long shadows across the island in the waning afternoon, Spike and Drusilla lay naked together on a mat on the floor, breathing heavy more from habit than from the exertion of their lovemaking. They lay on their sides, facing each other, and Spike ran a hand along the contours of his beautiful love's porcelain flesh, still cold in spite of the heat.

With a mischievous grin he traced the bloody wounds on her breasts and belly that he had given her. There was

one on the soft underside of her left breast that had made
her giggle with pleasure, and he cherished the echo of
that sound in his head. For his own part, Spike would not
be able to lie down on his back for the rest of the day,
perhaps the night as well. Dru had torn deep furrows
from his shoulders down to the small of his back and
Spike had screamed with the pain of it, and simultaneously lost control of himself.

They were more spent, more content as lovers, than
they had been for quite some time. It was this damnable
quest that had distracted them so much, Spike knew,
but he would not voice those thoughts to Dru. It was
for her, after all. She would have Freyja's Strand, whatever it took. She wanted it simply to be playful, of
course, to wear different faces, and as a weapon against
their enemies, wherever and whenever they might present themselves. Being able to look like anyone was a
valuable bit of magick.

But she also wanted it simply to see her face, to
remember what she looked like. It was perhaps the most
lucid desire she had expressed to him in some time. And
he could not blame her. Her beauty was exotic and magnificent, and it was one of the curses of their existence
that she could not see it.

Spike loved Drusilla with his whole self. He might tear
at her flesh, bruise her tender body, but only when it was
what she desired, what she craved as part of their lovemaking. Her eyes and mind saw a reality unlike that
which everyone else could see, but that was one of the
things that made him worship her so fully. She drifted,
often, in a state akin to trance, but Spike chose to think of
it as enchantment. Drusilla was his baby, his mad, fear-
less girl, and he cherished her. Every drop of blood he

spilled was for her as much as it was to feed his own hunger.

"You *are* a wonder, Dru," he told her, admiring the whole of her.

"You made me sing," she told him. "Did you hear? The song was all through me. All thunder and strings. Did you hear?"

"Oh yeah. How could I not?"

With the heat of the day warming them, even through the walls and ceiling, they lay there for what seemed hours. Spike felt himself begin to drift off and might even have fallen asleep for some time, though he could never be sure.

When the door crashed open, ripped half off its hinges, the light streamed in and burned his back. Spike grunted with the pain, rolled out of the way of the splash of sun, and leaped to his feet. Drusilla was already up, crouched catlike, ready to defend herself.

In the open doorway stood a tall man in black pants and a white shirt. A fellow Englishman by the look of him. He held a crossbow and pulled the trigger even as Spike's eyes adjusted to the light. The bolt shot across the room, straight for Spike's heart, but the man had given him too much warning. Spike dodged.

"You're Council, I expect," Spike said.

"Ken Haversham, at your service. Though I didn't expect to find you starkers," the man said pompously.

Spike hated pompous, particularly in men who were trying to kill him.

"You didn't expect to find us at all, you stupid git. You got lucky s'all."

"I'll say. Glad I got a chance to have a look at her before we marched you out into the sun," Haversham replied, gesturing toward Dru with a knowing grin.

Spike snarled, his features shifting to those of the vampire without his even realizing it. "Enjoy the view, then, old man. But we're not marching anyway. You think we didn't know you'd be coming? That once the nice old couple who owned this place didn't show up in town a few days it wouldn't draw attention. We've been waiting on you, see."

"Like hell!" Haversham snapped, but it was obvious Spike's words had an effect on him. He stood in the sunlight, safe from them, as he nocked another bolt into his crossbow.

"Can I get the toy?" Drusilla asked, a little girl pleading for a pony. "Can I?"

"By all means," Spike said.

Dru padded deeper into the house and into a bedroom where they usually slept. Spike heard a splintering of wood and a crash, and turned quickly to glance down the short hall. When he turned back, Haversham was already firing at him again. The crossbow bolt cut through the air and it was too late to dodge. Without thinking, Spike whipped a hand up to block it and the bolt punched through his palm and out the back, grinding against the tiny bones of his hand.

"Son of a bitch!" he shouted. He turned to Haversham, eyes blazing, and moved toward the man. "That hurt."

"That sound in the back?" Haversham began, arrogant as ever. "That was my partner, Mr. Rubie. By now your little succubus is nothing but—"

"I found it!" Drusilla called sweetly from the back room.

"You were saying?" Spike asked.

Haversham faltered, mouth open slightly. Drusilla pranced out into the front room, holding her prize by the hair. It dangled there, encrusted with dried gore.

"Rubie?" Haversham asked, fairly choking on the word.

"Are you blind, gov? Your partner's dead enough, I'd wager. But that ain't him. Take a better look."

Spike circled around to one side of the door, even as Drusilla held up the disembodied head. Haversham seemed to waver, to sway the way Dru so often did.

"It's her, isn't it?" he murmured. "The girl. Valerie."

"We're way ahead of you, *Ken*," Drusilla cooed. "But don't be a little baby about it, all right? You're going to get a consolation prize."

As she said this, she let the head dangle beside her and she posed for him, seductive and sweet and extraordinary. Haversham shuddered, but could not keep his eyes off her.

Spike roared as he dove sidelong across the patch of light thrown by the shattered door, tackling Haversham and driving him into shadow. They tumbled together on the floor and the Council man shouted in defiance. He scrabbled behind him and pulled out a stake he'd secreted away there, and Spike broke his arm for his trouble, the stake clattering to the floor.

Haversham screamed.

Spike stood up, leaving him there to stalk the floor a moment. Drusilla lingered near the door—though out of the light—to be certain the man did not attempt to escape. With a snarl, Spike stood over him again.

"I've burnt my arse, thanks to you," he growled, lips curled back to reveal his fangs.

Haversham whimpered. "I . . . I don't understand," he whined. "If you'd already killed her, why did you stay?"

"We needed a bit of a vacation, didn't we?" Spike asked idly. He turned to Dru. "Poodle, hurt him."

With a sweet smile she knelt by Haversham, draped her body across his and dragged her silken hair across his face. As she performed that sensual act, she sank her fangs into the soft flesh of his cheek, and tore.

Haversham screamed again.

Drusilla withdrew.

Spike crouched beside the broken and bleeding man, his face reverted to its human appearance, and smiled quite amiably. "Now, Ken," he said. "You are going to tell us which of the Slayers-in-Waiting have been taken back to London, and which are still wandering about. When you've told us what we want to know, we'll kill you. Until you do, well, we won't *let* you die, no matter how much you beg."

Chapter Thirteen

Mykonos, Greece
August 18th

The sun was cruel. It glared mercilessly down upon the island through a sky burned clear of clouds or any moisture at all. Though there was wind off the ocean it did little more than scour the village and its people. It was only a few degrees shy of one hundred, close enough so that merely breathing the superheated air was enough to scorch your throat. The entire island seemed drained completely of color and life, as though the very earth had been exsanguinated along with the young girl, the girl whose parents had wanted her to stay close by, though the Watchers Council told them she might be the one, she might be Chosen.

Sophie and Yanna stood at the side of a dusty dirt road that made its way gradually into the hills above the village, far from the blue-green brilliance of the ocean below. The wind kicked up the dust of the road and Sophie covered her nose and mouth the best she could, slitting her eyes as she peered down the road, through the heat haze rising above it, for the funeral procession. The church was down there, itself just as bleached and lifeless as the rest of the village.

They could hear the bells.

Yanna was silent beside her, and Sophie did not blame her. It had been made clear that they were not welcome at the service. It pained her greatly to know this, but the Slayer could not have said she was surprised. No matter what the reality of the situation, to the dead girl's parents all that mattered was that outsiders had come to their village and brought death and terror in their wake. Their daughter had been bled dry and then decapitated, her corpse left to rot.

Sophie remembered having thought of the girl, Valerie Vourtsas, as bait, and shuddered with guilt and horror. Though there was nothing she could have done to save the girl, she could not shake the feeling that she was somehow culpable, almost as if she had been with Spike and Drusilla when they had performed their latest atrocity.

They could not have known that Valerie and her Watcher, a Brit named Donald Morgan, had returned from Athens even before Haversham and Rubie had arrived on Mykonos. That Spike and Drusilla had executed both the Slayer-in-Waiting and Morgan and then simply lay in wait for the Council operatives.

Sophie had asked Yanna why. Why would they have waited? What did they stand to gain? The answer, when it came, was so obvious that Sophie felt embarrassed she had not seen it. The vampires knew the Council was gathering its flock and needed to discover which of the targets on their list was still unaccounted for.

Fortunately, according to what she and Yanna had learned in England, Sophie knew there weren't any more. Valerie had been the last. Cold comfort to the girl's parents.

Almost as if it were an apparition summoned by her dark ruminations, Sophie saw the funeral procession appear over the edge of a hill, on the road leading from the village and the church to the cemetery at the top of the hill. The church bells still tolled with haunting and nigh-impossible slowness, the mournful sound carrying up to them. Now, though, even over the sound of the bells, there came the chanting of the priests and the wailing of the mourners as the funeral procession came on.

In the dust swirled up by the scorching breeze, they looked like ghosts themselves, wan spirits in agony as they marched forever in the purgatory of grief. A strong man walked in front, an enormous crucifix hugged to his chest, almost large enough to be Christ on the way up Golgotha. Behind him were two priests in black vestments that hung low enough to drag on the dusty road, their tall black hats trailing long veils on the backs of their heads. Their faces were lined and weathered but their voices were clear and strong as they prayed loudly in Greek. A younger man in black, possibly also a priest, waved an iron censer back and forth across the road as if the smoke from its burning incense could cleanse the path for the dead girl.

Six large men with the look of fishermen acted as pallbearers, carrying the ravaged corpse in its coffin along the road. Behind them was the girl's family, also dressed all in black, wailing and crying out to God loud enough to drown out the prayers of the priests as they grew nearer. Finally there came the rest of the mourners, every soul from the village below, and each one of them draped in black.

As the procession passed, Sophie found herself unable to tear her gaze away from the dead girl's mother. The woman had to be supported by her husband and a tall boy who could only be her son. She cried as though her heart were being torn from her chest, and Sophie realized that in a way it had. It was so very foreign to her, for she had lost her parents so young that the aching loneliness remained but the real pain and tragedy of it usually escaped her.

The ghosts in mourning made their way along the road, ignoring the dust from the road that gave them the aspect of spirits. Once more struck by a wave of guilt Sophie glanced down at the sun-bleached dirt road and thought of war. Hitler had not reached this place yet. The Nazis' war to conquer Europe might never get this far. Mykonos was thus far untouched by a conflict that was consuming the world. But that did not mean war had not come to this little island village. It had. The war against darkness had touched these people, and it had cost them.

"Sophie," Yanna whispered.

The Slayer looked up, blinking against the harsh sun, and saw that they had been noticed. The grieving mother was glaring at them. With a cry of fury the woman broke away from her husband and son, away from the procession taking her only daughter to her final rest, and swept across the road toward them. Every muscle in Sophie's body tensed. She wanted to withdraw, feeling now like not merely an intruder but some sort of perverse voyeur. But it was too late. Valerie's mother lifted her black veil to reveal a face as lined and weathered as any of the fishermen. Her eyes blazed with hatred and grief, and her eyes were red and moist, but there were no tears.

Hatred. The woman blamed them. Never mind the corpses of Haversham, Rubie, and Morgan, awaiting return to England for burial. It was her daughter in that coffin, her daughter whose head had been torn from her body. To her, Sophie and Yanna were the Council. To her, *they* had killed her little girl.

Four feet from where Sophie stood with her Watcher, the woman stopped, hacked something up from her throat, and spat a bullet of yellow phlegm into the dirt at their feet. Then, with a final, hateful glance, she returned to the procession. They continued up the dirt road as it wound up the hill. The wind kicked up again, swirling dust into the insufferable air, and the receding mourners were ghosts again.

Down in the village, the church bells had stopped ringing.

Sophie felt the first hot tear spill down her cheek, cutting a clean line through the grime from the road on her face, and then she began to weep in earnest. After a moment, Yanna reached out to her and pulled her into an embrace. They stood like that for several minutes until Sophie finally insisted they get off the road. She did not know how long the funeral would take and she had no desire to be there at the roadside when the mourners returned.

London, England
August 20th

The fourth floor meeting chamber in the house on Great Russell Street had been utterly transformed. The table stood against the wall opposite the windows, chairs stacked atop it. The rest of the room was now occupied by two rows of cots and upon those cots, nine young girls who feared for their lives.

In the second cot of the second row, Ariana de le Croix slept fitfully, shuddering beneath the rough sheets, and not because she was cold. On the contrary, it was warm and stuffy inside that converted chamber, now more akin to a barracks. Ariana murmured, face contorted into an expression of fear and disgust.

In her dream, she was already dead. Dead and buried and risen again, and hungry for blood and life and screams.

The girl's eyes snapped open and she felt as though she could not take a breath. It made sense, in those mist-shrouded moments just after waking from a nightmare. She was dead, thus she could not breathe. Perfect sense. But her heart hammered painfully in her chest, pulse racing so fast she thought she might burst, and then she knew she was alive and her breath came back to her in heaving gasps.

Ariana did not scream, though she felt the urge to do so. Instead she covered her mouth with one hand and shuddered into a series of sobs, despair overwhelming her. When she could control her body, though not yet her tears, she managed to sit up on her cot. She looked around the sterile room with its stifling, stale air, and tried to slow her breathing, to get more control of herself. It was dark, save for the light from the city outside the windows.

In that pallid illumination, she glanced around at the other girls. Ariana's native language was French, but the Council required Slayers-in-Waiting to learn English. Unfortunately, some of the girls had only just begun to study that language, and so she had not been able to get to know them at all. Others had become almost instantly like sisters to her. On the cot adjacent to hers in the next row was Eleanor Boudreau, who hailed from America. She was a smart, serious girl who, nevertheless, seemed inclined to watch out for the others in an almost motherly way. Down the end of her own row, farthest from the door, Isabel Cortés lay on her back with her limbs splayed wildly about her, mouth open, sleeping as peacefully as an infant. The girl was from Barcelona, spoke English only a little, but had quickly become Ariana's friend and confidante.

Part of her wanted to wake the other girls. Ariana would not feel so alone then, so vulnerable. As she sat in the dark she felt as though she were being watched, that there were things lurking out in the shadows of the night that were stalking her. The terrifying truth was that, in a sense, it was true. A tingle ran up her spine and she shuddered, and fresh tears sprang to her eyes.

If she were to wake Isabel and Eleanor, she would not be alone with her fear. And yet in some way she felt that whatever cruel evil menaced her as she sat on the cot in her thin white shift was no threat to the others while they slept. But if she woke them . . . it could take them then. Her fear could cost them their lives. Absurd, she knew, but she realized she had to master those fears on her own.

There was another reason she did not want to wake them, however. Ariana feared that if she did she might reveal to them the embarrassing truth, the way in which she and her Watcher, Charles, had almost thrown their lives away through arrogance. Their respect was important to her, and she planned to hold that secret close to her heart forever. Together they talked about so many things, but not that. Instead, she prodded Eleanor to talk about the Slayer, whom only she among them all had met. It was a fascinating subject, though a morbid one as well. For one of them to become Slayer, Sophie Carstensen had to die. It was an unnerving thought.

Ariana was also fascinated by her discovery that not all of them wanted the job. Isabel seemed to have accepted that possibility only because if she was Chosen, and given the gifts of the Chosen One, it would be ignoble of her to refuse. Others dreaded the possibility more outwardly but had been almost coerced by the Council, their obligations explained to them.

Others wanted it badly. But none so badly as Ariana. Ever since she had learned about the Council, and the Chosen One, she had hoped that one day the duty would fall to her. Now, though, her fear had given her second thoughts. That, and the fact that now that she had met someone to whom the Slayer was a real person, it seemed hideous to wish for another girl to die so that she might be Chosen.

It was all so confusing.

Once more she looked around at the other girls. Not for the first time, she thought how fortunate they all were to have survived this long. They were being hunted. Unless Sophie caught up to Spike and Drusilla, there was no indication of when that would cease to be so.

I can't live like this, Ariana thought, arms wrapped tightly around herself, cross-legged on the cot. *I can't stay here forever, just being afraid.*

Softly, she whimpered.

Even as she did, she heard a click as someone turned the doorknob, and a squeak as it began to open. Ariana stiffened, her dream coming back to her suddenly. Wide-eyed, she stared at the light from the hallway that appeared in the opening. Then there was a face there, and she sighed with her relief. It was a familiar face, kind and warm.

"John," she whispered.

Gently, so as not to wake the others, John Travers stepped into the room and over to Ariana's cot.

"What is it?" she asked worriedly.

"I'm on watch," he told her. "I heard . . . I thought I heard you cry out. Are you all right?"

In the dark, she studied the way the lights from outside glinted off his eyes, and the firm cut of his jaw. He was at least seven or eight years her senior, but Ariana thought John Travers the most handsome, intelligent, and soulful man she had ever met. She searched his gaze for something more than just quiet concern and was saddened to have found nothing.

"I . . . had a nightmare," she whispered. "Silly, I know."

"Anyone would have nightmares with all that's going on," he comforted her, patting her hand sweetly. "Between our own crisis, the losses we have suffered, and the war on, I've had more than my share, I dare say."

Ariana nibbled her bottom lip thoughtfully. She knew what he meant. The Nazis had been bombing the south of England regularly for at least a week. Nobody knew if they would target London next, but there was a great deal of suspicion that it was only a matter of time.

As if he could read her thoughts, John leaned forward to catch her eyes. There was a bit of a smile at the corners of his mouth and she was happy to see it there for it was a first in the brief time she had known him.

"Trust me, you're in more danger from German bombs than vampires here. The appropriate spells have been cast to prevent them from entering again, and there's a veritable battalion of Watchers and operatives here to protect you."

Ariana smiled in return. She glanced about the room and shuddered once more. "Do you think I could sit watch with you for a bit?" she asked, pleading with her eyes but keeping her voice steady. "I don't think I could go back to sleep just yet and I'd like some company, just to talk to someone."

John blinked, a bit surprised. But then his sweet smile returned. "It would be my pleasure, Miss de la Croix," he told her.

She pulled on the robe that lay at the foot of the cot, then took the hand he offered her and rose to her feet.

"Please," she said. "Call me Ariana."

Athens, Greece
August 23rd

The sky was an ugly gray. The rain drizzled as though it were reluctant to fall, seeping out of the sky. Sophie and Yanna sat across from each other in a dingy taverna eating tzatziki and souvlaki, and wishing the time would pass more quickly.

In a sense, theirs was a victory. Though many had died, others had been saved and Spike and Drusilla had been thwarted. But Sophie could not allow herself even the tiniest feeling of satisfaction. Not with the aftermath of Valerie Vourtsas's death so fresh in her memory, and particularly not with the vampires still on the loose.

All the joy had been leeched from her, the same way that the rain and dingy skies had stolen the life from the day. Even the food was tasteless to her, as if the rest of the world only existed in a kind of ephemeral shade of reality.

When Sophie had left her souvlaki untouched for several minutes she began to feel Yanna's gaze upon her. She glanced up to find her Watcher staring at her forlornly, worry clearly etched upon her brow. The Slayer spoke first, however.

"Do you think they'll try?" she asked obliquely. "Do you think they'd be that daring?"

Yanna shook her head slowly. "I do not dare try to predict them," she replied. "My instinct says no. That Spike and Drusilla will content themselves with the anguish they have already wrought and go about their business. But would it surprise me if they attacked the Council directly? Not at all."

Sophie felt her own expression harden, her jaw set angrily. *Damned Nazis,* she thought. For it was the war that had held them up so far. They dared not return to England across the continent, and it had taken days, even after the arrival of the operatives sent to retrieve the corpses of the Council men on Mykonos, to line up a freighter willing to carry them to Great Britain by sea. Even then, the ship's captain had made it plain he would sail 'round the southern tip of England and make port on the western shore, away from the German bombers.

The need to return to the house on Great Russell Street, to be there in case Spike and Drusilla dared the unthinkable, pulled at her. Though their departure was mere hours away, Sophie mentally urged the operatives who must even now be loading coffins on board the freighter to move ever faster. It was day, but with the dark sky and the rain and the candles guttering weakly on each of the taverna's tables, it felt as coldly ominous as the lonely predawn hours ever had.

Suddenly determined to be off, Sophie pushed back her chair and stood. "We should go. If they're prepared to depart sooner, I want to be there and ready to leave."

The eyes of the mostly Greek clientele seared her, she was so out of place with her long legs and blond mane. Sophie ignored them as best she could; her long skirt and dark blouse had been enough of a compromise with the attitudes of the locals. She had a small handbag with her, and as she slipped its strap over her shoulder she realized that Yanna had not moved to respond. Not an inch.

"Yanna?" she began, glancing at the Watcher.

The woman's green eyes were glazed and empty. She sagged in her chair, head lolling slightly sideways.

"Not now. Not another one." Sophie cursed under her breath and went to her mentor's side to make certain she did not fall over. A minute passed, perhaps less, before Yanna's eyelids fluttered and it was clear the vision was over.

But it was several minutes after that before the Watcher's eyes began to focus again. It was the longest Yanna had ever taken to recover from one of her clairvoyant episodes, and Sophie's heart broke a little more as she considered the ramifications of that.

"Another vision?" Sophie asked quietly, though she knew the answer.

Yanna nodded. Her pallor was ashen, the skin around her eyes crinkled in dismay, her lips pursed as though she might speak. Instead she shook her head.

"What was it?" Sophie asked worriedly.

After a moment's pause Yanna let out a long, resigned sigh. There was pain in her eyes when she regarded Sophie again.

"Please sit," she said, an ache in her voice Sophie had never heard before.

Her anxiety growing, Sophie did as she asked. "I am here with you, Yanna. Focus on me. Remember who you are," she said softly, laying a hand over Yanna's on the table. "Now what is it? What did you see?"

Chin raised, expression grim, Yanna closed her eyes a moment, then almost seemed to shudder as she opened them again. "We cannot return to London. Not yet. It will be hard traveling in the midst of the war but the Germans have their sights set on England now and France is a dangerous but less volatile place. We have contacts with the French underground as well, and that should help."

"I don't understand," Sophie said, with a shake of her head. "Where are you suggesting we go?"

"Home," Yanna replied. "We must go to Copenhagen."

Sophie smiled, a warmth spreading within her to cut the chill dread within her. As sudden as it had come, however, the smile was erased by the grave expression on Yanna's face. The question was on Sophie's lips—*why?*—but even before she could voice it, she had the answer.

"There's another Slayer-in-Waiting there," Sophie said, her voice barely above a whisper. Her frown deepened as she stared at her Watcher. "But she wasn't on the list."

To her credit, Yanna did not look away from Sophie's intense gaze. "That was the Council's decision. The girl in Copenhagen was kept off the list completely with the idea that, should her existence somehow become known to you, the knowledge that a candidate to become Slayer upon your death was so close by, there in the city with you, would dishearten and demoralize you."

Sophie glared at her, stomach churning with anger. "You deceived me."

"A sin of omission," Yanna replied, though not lightly. "I did as I was instructed. The odds are greatly against this girl becoming the next Slayer in any case. It was thought that no good could come of your knowing."

"Oh, I can see that," Sophie said, voice dripping with venomous sarcasm. "Particularly now that that secrecy could cost the girl her life. I presume that your vision showed that she was in danger?"

Yanna nodded. "Spike and Drusilla are on their way to Copenhagen even now. They must have learned about her from poor Mr. Haversham."

Emotions swirling in her head, a pain thrumming in her heart, Sophie stood up again. She felt destiny rushing toward her, dark and inescapable. Sophie did not look at Yanna, nor did she even notice the other patrons in the taverna now.

"Come, then," the Slayer said, her voice a low growl. "Let's go home."

Chapter Fourteen

Paris, France
1912

It was spring in the city of lights. Even long after dark, the air was filled with the scent of flowers in bloom and the lilting laughter of couples in love. But nowhere in Paris was more alive after dark than Montmarte. The artists who painted on the cobblestoned streets in the square at the top of the hill had folded up their easels at dusk, but the street performers, the jugglers and flame eaters and mimes, were still about.

On the corner in front of the grand white façade of Sacre Couer a lone figure stood and caressed music of eternal beauty from a single violin. At tiny cafés in and around the square, young Parisians drank wine and debated literature and philosophy. And in an alley not far from the apartment where he had lived for eleven years, Charn ran his fingers over the supple flesh of a nineteen-year-old painter's model who dreamed of becoming an actress, even as he drained the blood from her veins.

She writhed beneath his touch and her skin cooled.

Nearby wine glasses clinked together in a loud and drunken toast, and raucous laughter followed.

Charn knew he should have brought the girl home, but she was simply luscious and he could not wait. There were times when he could be almost infinitely patient. But when it came to pretty girls, Charn simply could not help himself.

He slid her corpse to the ground, laying it across the rear stoop of a building. When he straightened up, he was no longer Charn. Thanks to Freyja's Strand, he wore the girl's face.

With a slightly drunken giggle, a sound that could only have come from her throat, Charn emerged from the alley, red-faced and flustered, looking for all the world like a young girl just back from a quick grope, or even a little more.

The vampire swayed her hips and smiled her smile and ran her hands through her hair. It was all him. All the Strand. The Brisings had crafted an extraordinary trinket indeed. Charn walked across the square, stopping to run his fingers across a juggler's face, then to blow kisses to the man playing the violin. The violinist stopped the music to catch them, and many turned to see why he no longer played.

What they saw was the beautiful, flirtatious girl, with her high, infectious laughter. She sauntered into the café and a group of young people, students perhaps, called out to her with a name Charn did not know. Regardless, he used her hands to wave back, then held up a finger, letting them know he would be right over. *She* would be right over.

Charn left the outdoor patio café and went around the corner and into the shadows. Once out of sight, he willed his body back to its original state, felt his features changing again. Anyone who might have seen the girl go off with him had now also seen her come back without him and go on along her way. The deceit was pleasurable, but that was only part of the thrill for him. Charn simply enjoyed studying the different ways people looked at him when he wore various faces. He also enjoyed seeing his own image reflected in a mirror; his, and those he adopted. That was another function of the Strand, negating the portion of the vampire's curse that prevented him from seeing himself.

When he returned to his apartment, he wanted to take the dead girl's face again, to see what she looked like in the light, to know her from inside her skin.

The violin music had started up again and it seemed to swirl in and out of the back streets. Charn walked a short way down the long, steep hill that led away from Montmarte and overlooked the rest of Paris. The view was exquisite by day or night. He had chosen an apartment with a window looking down from the hill for just that reason. If he stood back and away from the sunlight that streamed through it, Charn could admire the city in all its splendor.

By day.

At night he played, drank, and caroused. At night he hunted.

A cruel smile still splayed across his features, Charn turned left, stepping over a broken patch of cobblestone and entering the narrow street where he lived. His apartment was only a short way down on the right, on the top floor. The other tenants in the building were delightful creatures, including a seemingly ancient artist and sculptor, and a pair of women he was certain were not auntie and niece as they claimed.

But then, as Charn always said to himself, he was a murderer, so who was he to judge?

He snickered to himself at the thought, and wondered if he ought to have them all up to his rooms some night for cocktails. It really would be the neighborly thing to do.

The front stoop was just ahead and he was savoring the taste of the supple girl's blood in his mouth when he sensed motion on the other side of the street, across from his building. Alarmed, Charn turned and stared into the shadows between two sets of stairs.

Something moved.

In the moonlight, he could only make out the shape of a man, a silhouette, and where his hands should be, long glistening talons like knives.

"Show yourself, fool," he demanded with false bravado. "You are in error, attacking me upon my doorstep. Let me see the face of him whom I am about to destroy."

The figure stepped forward, out of the shadows and into the light thrown by the moon and the street lamps. He wore a hat with its brim pulled down low, and a long coat that made him little more than a cipher unless one saw him up close, as Charn now did.

Run, he told himself. *If you want to live, then run.*

But he could not. The terror was so deep within him that his legs would not obey that command. He could not move.

"Old Ones, protect me," Charn whispered, closing his eyes part of the way, not wanting to see his fate coming but not courageous enough to simply let it come.

The demon laughed heartily, the motion shaking tiny jagged shards of ice off his face and hands. They fell to shatter on the cobblestones with a sound like muted chimes. Sparks of flame burned in the frozen sockets of his eyes, and he moved closer to Charn.

And then he grew.

Only a little. Not so much that a passerby would see him from behind and not still think him human. Just enough to give Charn an inkling of his true power, to confirm that the myths surrounding him were true.

"Lord . . . Lord Skrymir," Charn stammered. "I . . . didn't think you ever left your stronghold now. I thought—"

"You thought very little," Skrymir replied, his voice the sound of ice splintering when the spring thaw arrived. Then he laughed, low and deadly. "You really are a fool, Charn. Zweig might have been an annoying, runty little creature, but he was *my* creature. An errand boy, perhaps, but one of *my* errand boys. And there is the small matter of the dagger he was carrying, a bit of history, that blade. Belonged to Darius himself, upon an age. Are you an idiot, Charn, to think I would not discover you were responsible? You, whose love of antiquities is so well known?"

Skrymir had not touched him, but had moved closer as he spoke, his voice almost hypnotic. The cold that emanated from him was enough to chill the vampire's bones. At length, the demon reached out with his sharp, frozen talons and grabbed Charn's chin, puncturing his flesh as he did so.

The vampire flinched, but Skrymir only grasped harder and lifted his chin so he could glare down into Charn's eyes.

"That was *not* a rhetorical question," the ice demon snarled.

"I . . . you . . . what I mean to say is that you had not been seen in so long that no one could be entirely sure you still lived. There are many who still believe that you are just a myth, so long have you been buried up in that stronghold of yours."

Skrymir's eyes flared up with colorful flames. "I've been busy," the demon said, rasping voice almost a whisper. "I have ambitions, Charn. They take up all my time, all of my attention. I do not appreciate being distracted from those ambitions, not even for a trip to this lovely city of yours. Do you understand me?"

"I swear, Skrymir, I didn't even know you were alive," Charn said quickly, expecting at any moment the final blow to fall.

Skrymir could easily tear his head off.

Instead, the demon leaned down to glare directly at him. Even the flames in his eyes were cold as ice.

"You will return what you stole," Skrymir whispered, a deadly promise in his tone.

"Y-yes, of . . . of course," Charn agreed quickly, sensing that his life might yet be spared.

"You will swear fealty to me, and take up Zweig's work in his absence. You will also make reparations for the loss of Zweig in the form of a tribute."

"I will. I swear to you, I will," Charn vowed. "What can I give you as tribute? Anything. If I don't have it, I'll get it."

Skrymir smiled at that and retreated a step, crossing his arms to regard Charn thoughtfully, as though considering. But even from his expression, Charn suspected that the demon had known exactly what he wanted all along.

"The necklace," Skrymir told him. "The necklace of the Brisings. It is mine."

Charn stiffened. *The Strand.* He wanted the Strand, the thing that gave him a reflection, that allowed him to live inside other's lives, to be seen with, and out of, other eyes.

Charn pulled himself up to his full height and lifted his chin in defiance. "I spent decades hunting for Freyja's Strand. I will give you any tribute you ask, but not this one. You'll have to kill me to get it."

Skrymir's frozen brows furrowed together, tiny spikes of jagged ice jutting up above his eyes. "If you say so."

And he did.

Copenhagen, Denmark
August 30th

Spike was in a foul mood. If the Nazi propaganda could be believed, the war against Britain was going well for the Germans, with England being torn up by Luftwaffe bombs every night. Here in Copenhagen, the arrogant German soldiers goose-stepped along the streets in formation, and there were armed sentries everywhere. The city seemed to have been allowed to carry on its business, but only under the watchful eyes of Uncle Adolf's goons.

The Danish people continued to live, but it seemed to Spike that they hesitated with every breath, fearful that it might be the last.

They were all cattle, of course. Germans and Danes alike. But Spike had been born, raised, and killed in England. The demon within him was as British as if hell itself were part of the King's Empire. The idea of bombs raining all over England did not sit well with him.

Which might have explained all the Nazi corpses.

In a second floor office only a few blocks from Town Hall Square—an office that had housed Bernstorff Textiles before the Nazi occupation had led to Bernstorff abandoning his business—Spike and Drusilla lounged in high-backed leather chairs. In his hands Spike held a German Mauser rifle. From time to time he would lift the bolt-action rifle and aim it at one of the half-dozen dead German soldiers in the room. There were no bullets in the weapon, however. He liked the way the trigger felt against his finger and knew he would be too tempted to fire it, drawing unnecessary attention.

With a simple pull of his finger, Spike dry-fired the weapon at the still-helmeted head of a German corporal, his uniform stained with the soldier's own blood.

"What the hell are we doing here, Dru?" he groaned.

With a sigh he laid the rifle across his lap, then spun around in the chair to regard her. She looked beautiful in the moonlight streaming in the office window. Delicate and fierce as she licked blood from her long fingers, spending perhaps a bit too much time in that operation once she had his attention.

"Ever watch a kitten clean its paws, Spike?" Drusilla cooed suddenly, her voice so wispy and languid it seemed to come from somewhere else, as if carried into the room on moonbeams.

"I'm not in the mood," he said flatly. "We know where this girl is supposed to be. We've checked out her place; we know she still lives there. So how come we haven't managed to run her to ground yet? It's been three days."

"Aren't you having fun, Spike?" Dru asked, hurt. "I like playing with the toy soldiers. They're so serious all the time."

Spike hung his head. Sometimes there was simply no talking to Drusilla. They had spent the past three days sleeping in the Bernstorff Textiles office and wasted the nights by attempting to track down this final candidate for Slayer-hood while entertaining and sustaining themselves by torturing and killing Nazi soldiers.

While there was something to be said for that latter bit, Spike was growing frustrated with their search for the girl. During the day they had to be quiet because of the other offices in the building, and the people who still worked in them. It did not help that he wondered what would happen after they found her.

He had realized even back on Mykonos that once they killed the Danish girl they would have to return to Skrymir's Norwegian stronghold with the job not completely done. It would be madness to attempt a full scale attack on the Council headquarters in London with a complete complement of Watchers and operatives there. That news had certainly thrown a spanner in the works. Skrymir could not possibly expect them to throw their lives away for him, but they couldn't very well complete their part of the agreement now, either. Could be it was time for them to kill the Slayer, but they'd had no word at all from the demon yet as to how they were to proceed.

The last thing he wanted was to climb that mountain again and find that Skrymir still had work for them to do. But if the demon did not contact them, he knew they really had no other choice.

"What is it, love?" Drusilla asked. "What's got my man all growly?"

"It's all bollocksed up," Spike replied, shaking his head. "I mean for you to have that necklace, Dru. After all the trouble we've gone to, Freyja's Strand'll be yours if I have to kill the Old Ones themselves to get it."

Drusilla made a little whimpering noise, rose from her chair with a creak of leather and springs, and floated across the office, her gown luminescent with the glow from outside. As if on fairy's wings she settled to the ground before him, kneeling in front of Spike and laying her cheek upon his lap, eyes gazing up at him lovingly.

"I like pretty things," she whispered. "Gleaming and golden, silver and jewels as well. But I like that you'd kill to get them even more. My big bad Spike will get the necklace, I just know it. A present for Dru. And Dru has a present for you, too. A naughty one."

Spike wanted to grunt at her again and tell her he was not in the mood. But the way she looked at him . . . he had meant what he said. Whatever it took to get Freyja's Strand from Skrymir, he was willing to do it.

"What might that be, pet?" Spike asked.

Drusilla's dreamy smile spread even wider, and then suddenly faltered. Her eyes rolled up in her head and she began to quiver. Her hands fluttered at her sides and she twitched once. Then she stood and gazed at him with blank eyes, as though staring right through him.

"My, you are a pretty one, aren't you?" Drusilla said, her tone cruel and insinuating. She walked to the office window and looked out at the night. "The moon is bleeding," she said without turning. "There's dancing and crying, and there's a castle. The girl has ghosts all around her; they're her family, and when she holds the sword all their hands are upon the hilt."

Drusilla hugged herself then, rocked forward on her toes and ran her fingers up to her shoulders and then back down again. Spike laid the rifle down and rose from his chair. She turned to meet him.

"What girl?" he asked. "The one we're after?"

With her eyes drifting from side to side, face tilted demurely downward, Drusilla looked lost. Then her smile slowly returned.

"Not that one, though I saw her, too. She's a dancer, the girl we're after. We'll find her, Spike. But we aren't the only ones looking. The Slayer, that one that hurt you, with her blond hair and whore's lips, she's coming here. Coming home."

"Home? You mean she's from Copenhagen?" Spike asked.

"Oh yes. They all know her 'round here. All the dark things do."

Spike grinned.

His mood was improving.

Copenhagen, Denmark
September 1st

In a beer house on Hammerichsgade, Drusilla and Spike sat close together and whispered to each other, talking about old times. Drusilla had never been one for nostalgia, never really had the memory for it. But there had been some moments between them that Spike enjoyed reliving, and she didn't really mind. The Boxer Rebellion was one. Their trip to Venice right around the turn of the century was another, when they'd gotten in dutch with one of the demon families running the city and had to play them off one another to get out.

They never talked about Angelus, though. At least not much. It was almost as though he were a ghost lingering with them, something they were aware of but did not want to give power over them by acknowledging it. He had disappeared off the face of the world, or so it seemed. It had been decades since either of them had seen him. But Drusilla was sure she would have known if he were dead.

That was the problem with reminiscing. Even when they did not talk about Angelus, he haunted them. Drusilla loved Spike now. But Angelus would always be her first. Sometimes, she knew, Spike had a difficult time dealing with that.

Drusilla thought of Angelus often, and she thought that Spike could sense it when she did, for he always tried to distract her then, get her mind on something else.

Like now.

"What do you suppose was up with that ugly bloke in Louisiana and his alligators?" he asked her in a low voice.

"Pets. He's a bit lonely, that one. Makes the aloneness easier to bear, having pets about." Drusilla tilted her head to one side in thought, exposing the soft white flesh of her throat. The light from the candle on their table flickered, throwing shadows about.

Absently, Spike patted the pockets of the dark suit he had appropriated from a man he had correctly judged as just about his size—he'd gotten good at it over the years. Drusilla tended to kill women whose dresses were a bit too large for her. Not that she really minded, particularly in velvet.

From his left breast pocket, Spike produced a silver cigarette case. He slipped it out and pulled out a cig, then snapped the case shut and returned it to the same pocket. The cigarette perched between his lips, he bent to light it off the candle, puffing a few times to get the tip burning. He drew in a lungful of smoke as he sat back, then let it out with satisfaction.

Drusilla watched the entire process, enchanted by the confidence, the arrogance that informed his every move. He was powerful, was her man. Save when it came to dealing with her. Between them, Drusilla would always have the power. Spike loved her too much to ever really be in control. It excited her, having that power over such a wild beast, but there were times when she wondered if it might not one day become tiresome.

"This is taking longer than I thought," he told Drusilla. "Almost makes me wonder if we're wrong about our man."

Drusilla gazed at him beneath long black lashes. Then she glanced across the beer house, with its many tables and the heavy stench of Danish beer and ale. There were a trio of German soldiers in full uniform in the far corner, and a fourth stood by the door, eyeing the patrons. He had come in with the others but was apparently the lowest ranking among them, for it had fallen to him to make certain there was no trouble.

But Drusilla was not looking at the soldiers. Rather, her attention was drawn by a tall, muscular man with shaggy red hair and a beard. His name, if the good-natured bellows of several other beer-drinkers on hand were any indication, was Thorvald. They had spent the better part of an hour waiting for him to leave with the drunken woman to whom he whispered in a far corner. She giggled appreciatively from time to time.

"You're staring, Dru," Spike warned her as he sipped at his beer.

With a tiny shrug, Drusilla turned back to him. "He looks like a Viking."

"Could be he *was* a bloody Viking," Spike reminded her.

Over in the corner, Thorvald helped his ladyfriend on with her coat. Drusilla raised her eyebrows. Spike dropped the cigarette into his beer, and rose slowly.

When Thorvald and the girl slipped out the door past the lone sober German soldier, Drusilla and Spike were perhaps five seconds behind them. Outside the street was dark. Somewhere not far off Drusilla heard someone shouting in German and the pounding of many sets of leather boots on the street. Even farther away there was a short spurt of gunfire.

A spy, she thought. *Or just someone who said something they shouldn't have.*

Not that it mattered. It was hardly her concern. Right now their only interest was in Thorvald, the first vampire they had located in Copenhagen. Drusilla kept her arm around Spike and they stopped to kiss and caress from time to time as they walked the streets, but always they stayed aware of Thorvald's presence and location.

When he disappeared, they moved swiftly, specters in the shadows. For the most part, vampires moved like human beings to avoid undue suspicion of their true nature. But at that moment as they hurried to determine where Thorvald had taken his conquest, any onlooker would have seen their speed and nimbleness and known they were something other than human. Vampires. Demons. The people of Copenhagen, however, would hardly have been surprised. They were growing quite familiar with the idea of demons in the midst.

It was a narrow alleyway off the road that would allow deliveries to the butcher shop around the back. Drusilla and Spike kept close to the walls of the alley as they traveled to the back of the shop. In a darkened area behind it, they found Thorvald feasting on the girl. There was blood all over his mouth and beard.

"Ooh, he's quite sloppy, isn't he Spike?" Drusilla asked, tone rife with her disapproval.

Thorvald looked up at them, down at the girl, then dropped her and bolted. They caught him a moment later. With a ferocious growl he struggled as together they drove him against the back of the building. His nose broke where it splayed against the brick.

He bucked. Thorvald was strong and very large and he managed to throw both of them off. Spike leaped back, ready to go at him again, but Drusilla only took one step away. With blood on his lips and staining his beard he looked like an animal as he lunged at her.

But Drusilla was stronger than she looked.

She grabbed his arm, flitted down and under and behind him, then snapped it with a single tug. Thorvald roared his pain before Spike was able to dive at him and clamp a hand over his mouth.

"Another sound and the Nazis will be on to us," Drusilla chided him, as if he were a badly behaved little boy. She snarled at the big vampire in disgust. "Is that what you want?"

"Looks like you've got a nice setup here," Spike added. "No reason to change that if you cooperate."

Though there was hatred in Thorvald's eyes, there was logic as well. Spike took his hand away from the bloody mouth.

"What do you want?" Thorvald demanded in passable English.

"The world," Drusilla told him. "Every bite."

"Who's the big noise around here?" Spike asked. "Cock o' the walk. The boss?"

Thorvald shrugged. "Used to be Gorm. Everybody knows that."

"And what happened to Gorm, my darling?" Drusilla asked.

"The Slayer got him," the red-bearded vampire replied. He frowned then and studied them. "Who are you?"

"Meet the new boss," Spike said happily.

Thorvald seemed about to argue when Drusilla wrenched his arm back again. He bit right through his lower lip trying not to scream. Drusilla nodded her approval.

"You're a tough one all right," she said. "Think we may have use for you." Drusilla moved closer to Thorvald then, pressing her body against him from behind. Even as she did that, she kept hurting him.

"Now then, my sloppy boy," she whispered. "It's time to tell us everything there is to know about your little Slayer. She's coming home, you see, and we want to have a bit of a party for her when she gets here."

Copenhagen, Denmark
September 3rd

Whatever joy the German occupation siphoned from the city, they had not managed to steal it all. There was still pleasure to be found in art and in elegance, and both were in great supply at the Royal Theater. Danish nobles and members of parliament ignored the hard truth of the times, that their pride and dreams had been taken from them. They sat in their boxes at the theater, the men grand and dignified in their best suits and the women resplendent in their fairytale gowns.

The orchestra played the music of angels and on the stage, like the seraphim themselves, the dancers performed a ballet that offered the audience a brief escape from their captivity. Only the soldiers strategically scattered throughout the theater, weapons at the ready, shattered the illusion.

"Something almost mournful about the proceedings here, don't you think?" Spike asked.

They sat in a box near the back of the theater dressed in finery still warm from the flesh of the couple they had killed for it.

"I think they're lovely," Drusilla purred, eyes riveted to the dancers upon the stage, reacting with little oohs and giggles and near-silent scoldings as the ballet unfolded. "That one's like a little doll. Could I have a dolly like that, Spike? You must find me one."

Spike leaned backward in his chair and slipped an arm around behind Drusilla, caressing the back of her neck. He watched the girl who had gotten Dru's attention, a lithe little thing not more than sixteen. The dancer's name was Ilse Skovgaard, and it was she they had come to the theater to see.

"You'll have your dolly, Dru. Soon as we settle down in one place long enough I'll have a nice little ballet dancer made for you," he promised. Then a devilish smile blossomed on his chiseled features. "Till then, though, what do you think about playing with the real thing for a bit?"

Chapter Fifteen

London, England
September 7th

It was a bit hazy that Saturday afternoon, the temperature warm but not uncomfortably so. Marie-Christine Fontaine sat reading Milton in the parlor on the first floor of the building on Great Russell Street. On the other side of the room the ancient Trevor Kensington played what seemed an eternal game of chess against Sir Nigel Rathbone, who sputtered and fooled with his spectacles and blew out a blast of brandy-scented air every time his opponent made a move.

In the corner, the pendulum on the grandfather clock ticked slowly back and forth. They were generals in a war, all three of them. Their troops were, for the most part, rallied about them in that very same building, waiting for word, waiting to be deployed, waiting for an attack.

The armory had been raided. There were no weapons on the walls for decorative purposes any longer. All had been cleaned and honed for use. Axes, crossbows, stakes, swords, even guns. There was no way to be certain what form the attack would take, but they were certain that it would come.

Marie-Christine had never approved of the use of seers. Their predictions were so vague. But in this instance she was grateful that the Council had several in its employ.

From somewhere upstairs came the sudden but pleasant distraction of violin music. One of the girls played, though she could not recall which. John could have told her. Young Travers seemed to have appointed himself personal guardian and protector of the Slayers-in-Waiting, though their Watchers fancied that post for themselves of course. He had taken a particular liking to the Swiss girl, Ariana de la Croix. Marie-Christine approved. The girl was headstrong, but competent and dignified. A bit young for John, but time would pass.

It always did.

Only this afternoon, it seemed to be passing at a snail's pace.

"Checkmate," wheezed old Kensington.

"Damn you, Trevor," Sir Nigel cursed. "How can you be half-blind and still beat me at chess?"

"Goes to show how awful you are at it, eh old chap?" Kensington snickered, took hold of his wolf's-head cane and rose to his feet. Grinning, he walked away with more energy than he had when he had sat down for the game.

"Where are you going? We've only just begun," Sir Nigel called after him.

"Tea. Got to have a nice cup of tea. Since none of the help have bothered to offer one, I thought I'd best go make it myself."

Her book held up to hide her face, Marie-Christine smiled. Sir Nigel cursed loudly several times.

"Up for a game, then, Mademoiselle Fontaine?" he asked at length, forcing a lightness into his tone that she suspected was feigned so as not to frighten her off.

She lowered the book. "Thank you for offering, Sir Nigel, but I think not. Chess has never been my game, I'm afraid."

"Precisely the point, my dear," Sir Nigel revealed.

Marie-Christine smiled but made no move to rise. She heard voices in the foyer and looked up to see the Spanish girl, Isabel, speaking with one of the operatives on sentry. After a moment Isabel smiled sweetly at the man and then entered the parlor.

"Excuse me, Miss Fontaine," she said, her English much improved in the brief time since she had arrived in London. "You said about the books?"

"Of course," Marie-Christine replied. "Come in, Isabel." She had nearly forgotten her offer to lend the girl several books so that she could continue to work on her language skills.

She slipped a finger into *Paradise Lost* to keep her place, and stood up as Isabel approached. Just then there was a ruckus in the foyer as the front door was thrown open and the operatives guarding it shouted in response.

"Back up, you idiot, and let me in."

The voice belonged to John Travers.

"You gave us a shock, Travers, that's all. You should know better, tense as things are 'round here," chided one of the operatives.

"You want a shock, Williams," John retorted. "Take a look out the front door."

Marie-Christine glanced at Sir Nigel. As one, they moved swiftly into the foyer with young Isabel in tow.

When she saw John's eyes, Marie-Christine felt tendrils of fear encircle her heart.

The young Watcher turned to Williams. "Get everyone on the upper floors to come downstairs. Interior rooms only. Stay away from the windows. Move! Now!"

The two operatives started up the stairs, two and three steps at a time, calling out loudly for everyone in the building to move. John turned to Sir Nigel then.

"With all due respect Sir Nigel, whatever magical protections we have available to us, now would be the time to use them."

"My God, John," Marie-Christine rasped. "What is it?"

In response, Travers simply reached for the front door, opened it, and stepped outside. She followed, Sir Nigel behind her. Her first thought was that the sky had begun to darken rather earlier than she had expected. Then she turned her eyes heavenward.

German aircraft filled the sky, blotting out the sun. Layer upon layer of them, a mile and a half high, and as far as the eye could see. Hundreds of enemy planes, like a plague of locusts, so many that the entire eastern horizon was covered with them, a curtain being drawn across the sky.

"Merciful Lord," Marie-Christine whispered.

Then the bombs began to fall.

Galdhöpiggen, Norway
September 7th

Though the wind howled across the face of the mountain, in its stone bowels all was silent save for the whimper of captive humans who had yet to achieve the good fortune of death. In the main chamber of his stronghold, Skrymir sat upon the bone-and-ice throne that had been constructed for him in another age and fumed impatiently. The many guests who benefited from his generosity had been instructed in no uncertain terms that they would not be welcome over this long afternoon and evening. Hedonists that they were, they had taken that as a cue the previous night to engage in even more debauched revelry than was common for them.

All for the better, Skrymir thought. Most of them were still in their guest quarters recovering. His servants had been instructed to see to them in his absence, should he be gone for very long. The demon doubted that would be the case, however. Everything had gone as planned. If all went well he would return long before the next dawn with a great deal of blood on his hands and news that would cause a celebration like no other.

It was a thought that should have brought a smile to his icy features. But he was tired of when and if and how. Skrymir had proven himself infinitely patient over the course of many, many centuries, but now that one of the vital components in his dream was about to come to fruition, he allowed himself the luxury of frustration and impatience.

Flames flickered in metal lanterns that hung from the ceilings. In their cages, the two or three surviving humans groaned. The mindless demon he had imprisoned had died days before, but he could not spare a thought for new entertainment. Not now.

In a way, the silence in the enormous, ice-columned chamber was astonishing. Twelve gnarled Nidavellir knelt in a half circle around Skrymir's throne, iron breastplates gleaming, two-headed war axes sharp and at the ready. Though they were fully awake and alert, their eyes were closed and their breathing slow and steady as they meditated before battle.

Skrymir had used his ability to manipulate the ice to enlarge his scrying glass. It stood twenty feet from his throne, eight feet high and eight feet wide. Around its base the ice had built up so that it would not topple and shatter. That would be disastrous. To that end his servants had been instructed to keep the guests out of that chamber, and he had set loose his gryphon to pad around the enormous room and to kill anyone who entered it without his permission. The massive creature had the head, wings, and forelegs of an eagle, with the body, tail, and hind legs of a lion. It was not the most intelligent beast he had ever seen, but it would serve to guard over the scrying glass until Skrymir's return.

The glass. Or rather, the icy window through which he magickally observed the goings on in the meeting chamber at the Watchers Council headquarters in London. He had stared at that frozen surface for days upon days now, had received reports from his agents all over the world, monitored their efforts as well as the progress of the war in Europe. Now, beyond the glass, he could see four of the young girls, the Slayers-in-Waiting. There was a man there as well, a Watcher. Two of the girls were talking and laughing, smoking cigarettes. A third lay in bed reading. The fourth argued with the Watcher at the far end of the room, though Skrymir could not make out the words.

They did not matter, of course.

Shortly, they would all be dead.

The time had come. The Germans were about to bomb London. Skrymir knew the moment was at hand but as the seconds and minutes ticked by, he grew more agitated. Without him even truly being aware of it, his body endured subtle changes. His wings ruffled and crackled, their frozen edges growing sharper. The jagged spears of ice that hung beneath his arms and jutted from his elbow and back lengthened and sharpened. Within his icy form, the glowing green mist that was the core of him churned with the tumult of his anticipation, growing and extending. His talons and teeth grew longer as well.

One by one, the Nidavellir opened their eyes, sensing the change in their master. They were an ancient race, and he their even more ancient god. They were perfectly attuned to his needs and commands and eager to spill blood in his name as their ancestors once had—the blood of his enemies, and their own as well.

Suddenly the chamber echoed with shouting and a loud but muffled bang. The sounds were from entire nations away, filtered through the ice window of the scrying glass. Skrymir narrowed his eyes and gazed at the scene unfolding within the Council headquarters. The door to the converted meeting room had been thrown open. A man stood in the doorway shouting that the Slayers-in-Waiting and the other Watcher should follow him, that they had to take cover. The German planes were attacking.

Perfect. Ever since the war in Europe had begun, and the fierceness of the German war machine revealed itself, Skrymir had known that it was only a matter of time before the Nazis bombed London. A happy coincidence. His plan would have worked without it, but now not only were his targets all in one place as he had arranged, but their world was in chaos, the bombing creating utter pandemonium.

Now was the time to strike.

He watched with pleasure as the girls looked up in astonishment. Before they had time to react, the building shook slightly and the sound of explosions could be heard in the distance.

The girls—these humans trained to one day perhaps take up the mantle of Slayer—screamed. All four of them shrieked in naked fear and rushed for the door, the male Watcher following along behind them.

"Now," Skrymir growled. "Follow me."

With a single flap of his mighty wings, green mist swirling within his icy frame, Skrymir propelled himself from the throne and landed with a crunch upon the stone floor of the chamber. He stood before the scrying glass and allowed himself a moment to gloat.

"Now," he whispered to himself. "Now it begins."

Skrymir touched the ice, staring through the window as the girls ran from the room in a panic. With the tiniest mental command, the ice withdrew, seeming to melt away to the edges of the scrying glass. Instantly he felt the warmth of that room in London, so far away . . . close enough to touch. For the window on the other side had also disappeared, the ice opening to allow its master to pass. He had created this window, this passage, before the Council had installed wards against magick in its headquarters, and had replenished it time and time again. It was a hole in their defenses. Likely the only one.

But Skrymir would only need one.

With a roar, the ice demon lunged forward, again powered by the strength of his wings. A rush of frigid mountain air swept along with him and Skrymir entered the fourth floor meeting chamber at the headquarters of the Watchers Council as easily as moving from one room to the next. With a clamor of grunts and snarls and war cries in a language not heard by human ears in generations, the Nidavellir followed, leaping down from the window to the wooden floor with a thunder of heavy boots.

Skrymir bellowed once more, a throaty roar of pleasure. The Council building shuddered again with the pulse of falling bombs, and the explosions continued to erupt in the city outside, the devastation matching his own urge toward destruction.

Skrymir took only one glance at the room. After all, he was intimately familiar with it after all this time, with the meetings that had once been held there, and with the girls who now bedded down there each night. The huge table, thrust into a corner, the chairs piled atop it. The cots and bedclothes, the girls' things, the weapons of their training. One blink, and he had seen enough. The demon turned for the door through which the girls and their Watcher had raced only moments before. Skrymir allowed his right arm to dangle by his side as he moved, and the ice shifted and re-formed, talons becoming scythes.

Cots shattered as he brushed past them and the Nidavellir were no more cautious. He could hear the German planes flying, could even hear the British RAF pilots firing at them as the bombs fell. Fires already burned across the city and the scent of the blaze came to them, swirled with the wind from his mountain stronghold that still blew through the open passage. It was chaos. Beautiful and pure.

Skrymir reached the doorway and slammed through it, tearing the door off its hinges and shattering the frame, sending splinters of wood flying into the corridor beyond. From there he could see down the stairs, where the Watcher who had been the last of them to leave was still hurrying to what he thought would be safety.

"Good Lord!" the Watcher cried, choking out the words.

With a thrill racing through him, the mist that was his essence swirling within, Skrymir crashed through the railing above the stairs and swept down upon the Watcher. He brought the scythe-fingers of his right hand down and sliced the man clean through with each one. Chunks of flesh and bone slapped to the stairs and thumped down several steps.

Farther below there was even more screaming. Several of the Slayers-in-Waiting were near enough to see what had happened. On the third floor landing, a pair of Watchers stood slack-jawed, staring in horror and awe. Skrymir gloated for a moment at the weaponless fools.

Then he leaped for the girls. As the Nidavellir tramped down the stairs in his wake, Skrymir extended a single spear of a finger and spiked it through the skull of the nearest girl. She did not have time to scream. With a rustle of his wings he lifted her up and then dropped her to tumble down the stairs.

"Kill them!" Skrymir howled. "Kill them all!"

Outside the building on Great Russell Street the bombs continued to fall. Within, the screams grew louder, ice started to form on the walls, and the blood began to flow.

Copenhagen, Denmark
September 7th

It pained Sophie to walk the streets of Copenhagen and to feel the city's broken spirit. To an outsider it would barely be noticeable. The German soldiers were omnipresent, of course, but beyond that, the world moved along. Autos still ran, businesses did business, even restaurants and beer houses were still open. But a cloud of oppression, the knowledge that they were no longer free, that the royal family no longer ruled the kingdom of Denmark, hung over Copenhagen like the smoke from a funeral pyre.

The Slayer would not bow to that oppression. She would do nothing unwise, nothing to compromise herself or Yanna or their mission. But she walked with her head high, bolstered by the nobility and dignity of her ancestors. Though it was still day and she risked being discovered, beneath her long coat, on the strap that went around her neck and shoulder, she wore the scabbard and carried her father's sword proudly.

They had been there for two days. The night before she had been forced to kill a pair of Nazi soldiers in order to prevent her own arrest. Sophie felt no remorse.

Seeing her city this way, for the first time she truly felt as though she were fighting two wars simultaneously. *I cannot afford to lose either.* As she moved surreptitiously along a narrow street not far from the river, she vowed to herself that when Spike and Drusilla were dead, or the Council decided the crisis was over, she would see to Yanna's condition and state of mind, and then return to Copenhagen and use her skills against the Nazis.

"For King and Council," she had always said. But the kingdom had always come first in that phrase. When the Germans had been defeated she would return to do the Council's bidding. But not until.

She paused and turned to wait for Yanna to catch up. Sophie had urged her to remain at Ilse Skovgaard's apartment. They had arrived in Copenhagen to find the girl missing, but no one knew what had become of her. She was a ballerina of some repute, apparently, despite her youth. But she was also a Jew, and many thought she might have tried to flee in secret as many Jews had done, now that Hitler's barbaric treatment of the Jews made it unsafe for them in any German-occupied land.

Sophie was uncertain. Ilse might have fled, but if so, why do it without notifying the Council, who would certainly have helped her? And where had her Watcher gone? No, it seemed more likely that vampires had gotten to the girl, but Spike and Drusilla had never been subtle before.

Yanna had been pursuing the issue of the underground, and the escape of Jews from Denmark. Meanwhile, Sophie did what she had been Chosen to do. She hunted vampires. There were surprisingly few to be found, and she knew it was not merely because she had slain Gorm earlier that year. Many had left the city to avoid the German soldiers. Others, those hardier, or more foolhardy, had stayed simply to prey on German soldiers.

In two nights, Sophie had dusted three. None of them had a clue about Ilse, or about Spike.

But the last one had mentioned another vampire, an ancient giant of a leech named Thorvald.

"Are you ready?" she whispered to Yanna.

With her hair a bit wilder than usual, stray strands floating around her face after breaking free of her tight braid, Yanna seemed more than a little out of sorts. But she merely pressed her lips into a thin line of grim focus and nodded. After all that had happened—and now this latest bit of information withheld—a wall had been built up between them. Sophie still felt responsible for Yanna, but she did not know if the gulf that had been created between them would ever be bridged again.

I should have forced her to stay behind, Sophie thought grimly. But it was too late for regrets.

Sophie swept her long blond tresses back with one hand and unsheathed her sword with the other. She traced the ancient symbols inscribed there with the tips of her fingers and closed her eyes for a moment of silent prayer.

"Let's go."

When she moved to the rear door of the squalid flat that Thorvald had been said to live in, Yanna was right behind her. With a single kick, Sophie smashed in the door. It hung loose on its frame and she rushed into the room, illuminated only by the gray light filtered through the clouds outside. It took a moment for her eyes to adjust.

"Yanna, stay still," she rasped.

On the other side of the rotting, damp, and fetid room stood a massive, long-haired, red-bearded vampire. From the description she had been given she knew it must be Thorvald.

The vampire held Ilse Skovgaard by her dark hair with one hand. Thorvald's features were ridged and cruel, his eyes glowed yellow in the dark and he clutched her belly with his free hand, holding her against him. Ilse was weeping openly and copiously.

"You are the Slayer," Thorvald said in old Danish. "I managed to avoid you all the time you were here before."

"And yet now you confront me without fear."

Thorvald only smiled, and the expression was that of an old wolf's through the heavy beard.

"Ilse, you'll be all right," she told the girl.

The tiniest glimmer of hope flashed in Ilse's eyes.

Then Thorvald dipped his face to her neck, ripped her throat out with one quick snap of his powerful jaws and spat out the torn flesh. He leaned forward to let the girl's hot blood pump into his face and he opened his mouth so that it spattered on his tongue.

Yanna screamed and went to rush the vampire, crossbow raised.

Sword in her right hand, Sophie held out the other to stop her. Disgust and hatred filled her, rage enveloped her soul, but she kept her cool. Yanna's safety was paramount. Something more than murder was happening here. Sophie took several cautious steps toward Thorvald and the vampire had such arrogance that he did not even pause in his drinking of Ilse's blood.

"I'm not even going to cut your head off for that, Thorvald," she snarled at him. "Instead, I'll cleave your arms and legs from your body and leave you a mewling, helpless, starving thing, a creature to be despised even by others of your kind."

That got the vampire's attention. It even seemed to unnerve him. Then Thorvald's gaze ticked past Sophie, and he smiled as though relieved. Though alarmed, she dared not turn her back on him.

Until she heard the voice.

"Bloodthirsty little bitch, aren't you?" She knew that voice. *Spike.*

Sophie spun, ready to attack, knowing that Yanna would loose a crossbow bolt at Thorvald in the same instant, that together they would prevail. This was what she had come for, to destroy Spike once and for all.

But Yanna would never release the bolt. She no longer held the crossbow. Spike had her by the throat, from behind, and the image of Thorvald tearing out Ilse's throat was too fresh in Sophie's brain for the Slayer to do anything but freeze, even if only for a moment. Spike smiled sweetly. His eyes seemed to have illumination unto themselves. His white hair shone almost like a halo.

"How did you follow? It's the middle of the day." Sophie studied him, trying to hide the fear she felt for Yanna, trying not to see the way her Watcher slumped into Spike's arms, as though surrendering to a destiny she had accepted long ago.

Fight him, damn you, Sophie thought. Yanna would not meet her gaze, but Sophie could see that her eyes looked empty, hollow. She was nothing but a marionette now in the vampire's clutches.

"Looks like rain," Spike explained. "Nice and cloudy. And down this end of town the buildings are close together, lots of alleys. Convenient, actually. You can walk about all day down here."

Spike kissed Yanna's cheek but gripped her throat even more tightly. "Simple enough to get you both where I wanted you," he said. Then his voice dropped to a whisper. "And you, Yanna. Did you think I'd forgotten you? Your man Edgar was a pebble in my boot, dearest. He needed to be removed. And you were so sweet then. Took me a bit to recall why I knew your face, but it came to me. Got a hell of a memory, I do."

Yanna only whimpered softly, her mouth open into a tiny O and her eyes locked on Spike's. She looked almost as though she thought he might kiss her.

"Let her go!" Sophie cried, bringing her sword up again, ready to attack.

Spike thought about it a moment. Then he shrugged. "Sorry but no." With a grunt he spun Yanna and slammed her head into the wall hard enough that she slumped down in his grasp, unconscious. But Spike did not drop her, nor did he slow down. Instead he hauled her up with all his vampiric strength, threw her over his shoulder and sprinted out into the dingy gray light, sun blotted out by the clouds. He kept to the shadows thrown by the buildings, even though it was overcast. Taking no chances.

The urge to follow Spike, to save Yanna, was so powerful that Sophie did not turn in time. She knew Thorvald was there. Felt his evil presence and the weight of him as he lunged for her. The huge vampire drove her to the ground beneath him, grabbed her by the hair and moved in to bite her. She still gripped her sword, but could not manage an effective blow, trapped as she was.

"I will not run from you," Thorvald snarled.

Raging like an animal herself, Sophie darted her own head up and sunk her teeth into the flesh of Thorvald's cheek, tearing at it with her incisors. They were not fangs, but they tore flesh.

Thorvald screamed in surprise and pain and Sophie bucked him off, then leaped to her feet, bringing her sword around again.

"Where?" the Slayer demanded. "Tell me where he's taken her and I'll spare you."

"The lair of your old enemy," Thorvald said immediately, hand clapped to his wounded face, staring at her still as though she were the monster rather than he.

For just a moment they faced each other, Sophie breathing hard more from fury than exertion.

"You're not really going to spare me, are you?" the vampire asked, resigned.

The blade of her ancestors whistled through the air in a clean arc. Thorvald's head bounced once on the filthy floor before turning to dust along with the rest of him.

Chapter Sixteen

London, England
September 7th

There was blood on the ice.

Skrymir glanced down at the human blood that was smeared on his long, frozen talons and dappled across his icy shell and he uttered a guttural noise that was more snarl than laugh. Still it was a sound of pleasure, for it had been far too long sitting in that damned stronghold since he last had the joy of slaughtering human beings who had not been brought to him as prisoners. This was better. Much better. For eons, it seemed, he had been patient. And more patience would be required before he was through.

But at this very moment . . . bloodshed. Glorious murder.

The sounds of war and terror echoed in the streets of London. Hundreds upon hundreds of Luftwaffe planes dropped bombs. Fires burned on the east side, raging high as though angry at the aircraft that buzzed above. The Royal Air Force was retaliating, but it was too little, too late. The Blitz had come, and London would never be the same.

In the house on Great Russell Street, the walls shook with the force of explosions not far off. The focus of the attack was a ways off but that did not stop bombs from going astray and falling nearby. Skrymir exulted in the chaos and the screams, both out in the streets of London, and there in the headquarters of his most hated enemies, the Council of Watchers.

In the short hall on the third floor, Skrymir stood fast against an onslaught. He had come down the central stairwell from above to find a handful of Watchers and Council operatives already standing in opposition to his attack. His gnarled, armored Nidavellir foot soldiers followed him down. The Council's defenders did their best with the weapons at their disposal. Large chunks of ice had been hacked from Skrymir's shoulder and one of his talons sheared off by the sword of a Watcher.

The man now lay broken and twisted in a pool of his own blood on the floor between Skrymir's massive legs, spectacles broken and hanging loose from one ear. It was his blood that adorned Skrymir's hands.

"Die, demon!" shouted another man, a swarthy Watcher with a large mace in his hands.

There were four others there in the hall, two with crossbows, one with an ornate dagger, and the last with an ugly, oily smelling pistol. The pistol was Skyrmir's primary concern. Crossbow bolts flew at him and past him. One of them punched through the cheek of a Nidavellir, but the little beast simply tore the offending shaft from its flesh.

Doors along the corridor and at its far end began to open. Other men appeared, also armed. Skrymir sensed that there were more, in the rooms beyond. He thought he glimpsed the barrel of a machine gun and he knew that the men armed with more conventional weapons were operatives, not Watchers. Those were the ones he had to avoid.

It seemed as though the air itself froze for a moment. The sounds of aircraft and exploding bombs, even of screams and shouts on the floors below him, simply stopped. In that moment, Skrymir's smoky essence roiled within its icy shell, and his frozen form rippled and changed. By instinct he pulled moisture from the air around him and his icy flesh erupted with even more jagged protrusions, including a pair of enormous, curving horns that were heavy upon his brow.

The fear in the humans' faces was plain, but so was their resolution.

From the second floor came a shout of fury and alarm. Behind him the foot soldiers snorted and stamped, filled with bloodlust. Skrymir looked past the mace-wielding Watcher before him and beyond two other men to meet the confident gaze of the man with the pistol. The weapon came up, barrel aimed directly at Skrymir. The demon lord was not afraid, but he did not know enough about guns and did not wish to learn.

The swarthy one with the mace lunged at him. The sounds of the world outside began again. An air raid siren. A staccato run of explosions from far off, then another close by. Windows shattered at either end of the hall.

The mace swept through the air.

The pistol was leveled, the operative holding it pulled the trigger.

Skrymir rose up. With the talons of his right hand he tore off the arm of the Watcher who attacked him with the mace, sending flesh, bone, and weapon sailing over the railing and down onto the stairs leading to the second floor. With his left hand he grabbed the swarthy Watcher by the head and lifted him up.

So swiftly did he move that the bullets fired from the operative's gun punched into the Watcher's body, where Skrymir held it before him as a shield of flesh. The body jumped obscenely, amusingly, and then Skrymir threw it at the others in the hall.

Two of them fell, scrambling with their weapons, caught between the urge to attack and the instinct to save themselves. Either way, it was too late for them. The Nidavellir behind Skrymir could not do their duty trapped in this narrow passage. Their master had to clear the path and clear it he did. Even as the man with the pistol leveled it at him again, aiming quite carefully for his eyes, Skrymir trampled the men on the floor with his icy hooves. Amidst their screams of agony he turned, raised his wings and lashed out.

One frozen wing cut into the wall, battering portraits from their hooks. The other wing, crackling with the constantly shifting ice, slashed out and easily sliced through the flesh and bone of the operative's neck. Fresh blood gouted from the beheaded corpse's neck and spattered Skrymir's wings even before the head tumbled to the floor and rolled toward the open door at the end of the hall.

Skrymir bellowed, rage and bliss surging within him, wrapped in a dance of emotion he had not felt the likes of for centuries.

"He's killed them!" shouted a Watcher from one of the side rooms. "We've got to stop him before he reaches the girls!"

"Yes! By all means, stop me!" Skrymir roared, even as he trampled the wounded and dying Watchers that were beneath his hooves. The walls shook again, but this was his doing, not that of the German bombs.

This was war. Nothing else mattered, not even the human conflict taking place simultaneously out in the city.

"Go!" Skrymir commanded, holding out a hand to point past the railing to the stairs leading downward.

With a chorus of murderous, bestial assent, the gnarled little warriors obeyed. They did not bother with the stairs. Rather they simply rushed the railing, shattering through the wooden balusters and crashing down onto the stairs, leaping one after the other, axes flashing as they thundered down after the Slayers-in-Waiting and their protectors.

Wolves in the fold.

"Come then!" Skrymir shouted. "Give me your lives!"

And they did. Watchers shouted with fury and fear as they clattered out into the hall. Skrymir counted at least five males and three females. Four of the men were operatives, armed with guns. Two of them were armed with machine guns. Of the Watchers, the demon recognized Abram Levin and Charles Rochemont from spying on the goings on in the house for so long.

Levin stepped forward. "No farther!" he shouted.

At his signal the others raised their weapons. The operatives aimed their guns, but did not fire. Rochemont held an ancient longbow far too unwieldy for the close premises, but it was steady in his hands and the arrow head was wide and gleaming with a razor edge. The man was a fool. Arrows might have harmed his Nidavellir, even killed them, but they would have less than no effect on him.

"You have made a grave error, demon," Abram Levin told him as the Council's defenders gathered closer around Skrymir. "Did you think we would not be prepared for an attack? The Board of Directors suspected that the vampires' predations were only preamble for some more sinister scheme. Now you have revealed yourself as its author—"

Skrymir laughed. Greenish flames flickered from his eyes, a fiery emulsion from the mist at his core. "I'm sorry," he said, snickering and glaring at each of them. "This is how you prepare? To do what, other than die at my hands?"

Charles Rochemont took a single step back, wrist not even quivering though he still held back the string on the longbow. "Appearances can be deceiving, Skrymir."

The demon flinched.

"Yes, I recognize you. Some of us are warriors. Others are scholars. You have been gone long enough to have attained the status of myth once more, but I recognize you. We may not be able to defeat you, or at least not without a great deal more blood, but we are prepared. Withdraw now, before we discover precisely how well."

Skrymir stared at him, incredulous. Another ripple went through him, a crackling of shifting ice. With a sudden snarl, Skrymir thrust out his right arm and his talons stretched, lengthening impossibly as the moisture was sucked from the air around him to add to his body mass. His jagged fist punched through the chest of one of the machine-gun-wielding operatives and he tore the screaming man's heart out, cutting the scream off abruptly. A momentary torrent of bullets ripped the ceiling and then were cut off as instantly as the dead man's scream. The gun clattered to the floor.

The others attacked. Crossbow bolts flew. Bullets punched the air. Skrymir wrapped his frozen wings around his body as a shield. Machine-gun fire shattered his wings and they fell in pieces to the floor. The demon roared in pain, but that sacrifice bought him precious seconds during which he lashed out and knocked one operative through the shattered railing to break his neck on the stairs, squashed the skull of another against the wall, and disarmed the third. Enraged he swept through them. His arms became scythes. Bones were shattered, some were cut. Blood flew and Skrymir sang a melody not heard upon the face of the Earth since Woden walked the world.

Abram Levin began to withdraw. "Keep back," he shouted to Rochemont, the only other survivor save himself. "Leave it to the others now!" he called out.

Skrymir flicked out a hand and with the swipe of a single talon across the man's eyes, he blinded the Watcher forever. But he left the man alive.

Fuming, eyes blazing with flickering greenish flame, Skrymir rounded on Charles Rochemont. He shuddered and the ice that had made up his wings was drawn to him, absorbed once again into his form, emerging from within as jagged spikes on his back. His horns grew and he stood, suddenly, several inches taller. He was forced to crouch in the hall, towering over Rochemont, who quivered as he stared at the demon.

"You have not loosed your arrow, Watcher," Skrymir said, his voice filled with insinuation, for he deemed the man a coward to simply stand there and watch as his fellows were massacred.

"I have one task, demon. I have had failures in the past and I will not allow another," Rochemont said courageously, stretching his neck but keeping his gaze steady. "For the moment, I wait."

"You die," Skrymir told him, confounded by the fool's inaction.

There had been a great clamor below. Screams and shouts of men and women. Girls. Slayers-in-Waiting, Skrymir expected. But also the shattering of furniture and impact after impact upon the walls. Now, though, up from below there came a wail of agony unlike any he had ever heard before. Voices in unison, exploding with pain. The voices were not human.

Over the distant noise of planes and bombs exploding he could hear the sound of heavy blades striking flesh and clanging off of armor, and the pounding of booted feet upon the stairs.

A Nidavellir screamed in a language older than man as it struggled to climb the stairs. It cried out like an infant as it slowed, halfway up. Skrymir saw it emerge into his field of vision and his anger was matched only by his disgust. It was one of his foot soldiers, of course, but unrecognizable. The little beast was on fire, deep blue flames engulfing its body, burning high and bright and smoking oily black sulphur. It was not natural fire, but a magickal inferno that engulfed the beast. Its face had already begun to melt off its knobby, misshapen skull.

A madness swept through Skrymir, a lunatic fury like nothing he had ever known. All of his careful planning, all of his misdirection and the cleverness for which he had congratulated himself, and the arrogant human pigs of the Watchers Council had known it! Whether they had sensed it, learned of it through their supernatural intrigues, or simply used logic, the eyeless, mewling Watcher on the floor had not lied.

They had been expecting him.

"Damn you!" Skrymir screeched as he took a step toward Rochemont.

The Watcher's legs quivered and tears formed at the corners of his eyes. He saw hell itself coming for him, Skrymir knew. And he was right. The fear in Charles Rochemont was wondrous to behold.

But Rochemont kept his hands steady. The arrow did not so much as twitch. The Watcher held his breath and loosed the arrow. It flew across the hall, slicing the air. Skrymir ignored it. A tiny little blade, what harm could it do? At the last moment he saw the runes etched into the metal head of the arrow, but in his maddened state he ignored the alarm that sounded within him.

The tip of the arrow burned through the ice at his midsection. Skrymir reached out and tore the bow away from Rochemont, then impaled the Watcher with the length of curved wood before kicking him with a frozen hoof hard enough to send him pinwheeling back and out through the shattered window to fall to his death three stories below on the stone steps of the building.

The arrow burned him.

It had melted the icy shell around him but it did more than that. The second its metal tip cut deep enough to reach the green vapor at his core, that mist ignited with blue flame. His true self was on fire.

Skrymir screamed loud enough to blot out the war beyond those walls. The floor shook. Ice cracked and sloughed from his form. Water trickled from his limbs and he began to melt. Panic ran through him as the fire burned the vapor that composed his true body. The magickal flame consumed part of him and it was as though a limb had been sheared off.

"Noooo!" the demon cried in a frenzy.

He collapsed. The ice melted away where the arrow had entered and the shaft clattered to the floor not far from the broken and bloody corpses he had trampled a minute before.

The vapor began to leak.

Skrymir roared again. Steeled himself for the pain. He concentrated and with a loud crackling noise, the ice that made up his shell shifted again, dramatically. The portion of his midsection where his misty flesh burned was suddenly cut off from the rest of his vapor-form by walls of ice. The center portion of ice surrounding the burning vapor, a dying portion of himself, was cut away and fell to the ground, melting quickly and producing a trail of smoke.

Magick.

The demon was on his knees, bent over, hands clasped across the enormous wound in his frozen shell even as ice cracked and shifted to fill the hole. With the wound closed, Skrymir shuddered once, then stood and examined the carnage that surrounded him. It was only the beginning. Cries of agony shouted in ancient tongues rose from the floors below and the demon stood up to his full height once more.

"Prepared," he snarled quietly. "They thought they were prepared for me."

Skrymir sprouted wings once more, frozen shell cracking and re-forming, stealing moisture from the air. Hooves splintering the wooden floor, he ran to the end of the hall and threw himself out the shattered window. Wings spread, he soared high before turning back upon the headquarters of the Watchers Council and diving toward a window on the second floor.

The sky above him was dark, blotted out by the specter of war, by the seemingly infinite sweep of bombers and fighter planes that slashed the heavens. He could hear screams echoing across the city, could smell the fires burning not far away.

This, he thought. *This is the way the whole world will be when I am through. Hell on Earth.*

Copenhagen, Denmark
September 7th

Sophie Carstensen was seventeen. She had barely noticed the passing of the days, but the week before, on August 31, she had turned seventeen.

Her breath plumed in the chill air but she made no sound as she slipped across the land surrounding Christiansborg Palace. Months had passed since she had experienced her greatest victory here, the defeat of the vampire king Gorm. It had been a lifetime. Denmark was no longer ruled by the royal family but by Nazi conquerors. The palace, where so many of the functions of Danish government had been carried out before, had more than its share of German soldiers marching about the grounds.

Another time, in another world, perhaps even had she still been the girl who had triumphed here earlier in the year, Sophie might have done things differently.

This day, this long afternoon, the Slayer was ruthless.

She moved across the palace grounds like a sliver of moonlight, a ghost against the pale light. It was sometime after five o'clock. Eleven German soldiers died upon her sword for no reason other than that they were the enemy, that they had invaded her homeland, and that they stood in her way. Stood between her and the shattered woman who was her only true friend in the world, her Watcher, Yanna Narvik.

Silent and murderous, Sophie found her way to the hidden entrance to the ruins of Bishop Absalon's castle, the remains of a time forgotten, upon which the palace had been built. Gorm had made his lair there, and Sophie could not stop herself from wondering how Spike and Drusilla had come to do the same. They must have learned of it somehow, perhaps thought that it held some special dread for her.

They were wrong. The mad, flitting Drusilla, a nightmare creature of dark fairy tales, and her lover, the swaggering Spike, had badly miscalculated. Sophie had grown tired of obeying the Council, of blindly following their edicts and leaving her homeland to the predations of monsters far more numerous than vampires. Had they disappeared into legend, lurking amid the human populations of some other nations or continents, she would have let them go, no matter what they had already done.

But now . . . in a narrow passage of stone, with only a torch flickering in a wall sconce for light, Sophie paused, finding herself suddenly weak. Without her parents, Yanna was all she had. If she were to lose her Watcher, the Slayer knew she would truly have lost everything.

With a single breath, she calmed herself. Both hands were firmly wrapped about the hilt of the sword of her ancestors. In their name, and in the names of King and Council, but more than anything for Yanna, she moved more deeply into the vampire lair, eyes ticking right and left. The sconces would not be lit if the place were abandoned. Not that she had even considered the possibility. They were here.

They were waiting.

Something shifted in the shadows of a narrow tunnel off to her right. A vampire, tall and thin with a mane of wild hair. A Dane, just as she was. Sophie turned quickly to meet the attack. Her blade whistled as it sliced the air, the only sound before it cut cleanly through the vampire's neck. It was dust before it could fall to the uneven stone floor.

Two others approached from behind her, coming into the lair just as she had. Perhaps Spike had thought she might become frightened and try to leave.

If so, he was a fool. Yanna had become obsessed with him, arrogant and handsome and clever and vicious. Spike was all of those things. Perhaps now, Sophie thought, Yanna would have realized the depths of his evil. Or perhaps that had been his allure all along.

The newly arrived vampires were dispatched even more quickly than the first.

Her resolve even stronger, her jaw set, expression grave, Sophie moved along the dimly lit corridor of crumbling stone. With a toss of her head she swept her hair over her shoulder. Her legs were slightly bent, even as she walked, prepared for combat at any moment.

Without further incident, she found herself entering the same chamber where she had killed Gorm. The tapestries and paintings were gone, likely stolen by Gorm's followers after their master's death. Candles burned upon iron stands and torches flared in sconces on the walls on the side of the room nearest her. On the far side, there were only shadows and ghosts of shapes and images flitting in the darkness that might have been tricks of the light upon her eyes.

Long blade held out before her, Sophie slid into the chamber, into what might as well have been a spotlight given the strategic lighting in the room. Nothing moved. The chamber was silent. Then there was a muffled cry, a whimper.

Yanna.

"I've come," Sophie said bitterly, her voice echoing in the room. "I would ask you to free her but I know that you won't. You want to kill me. Come and kill me, then. If you can, she'll die. And if you fail, I'll take her away with me."

From the shadows came the sound of giggling. Then a voice. "You can't take her away. She's my little dolly. We've had the sweetest tea party."

Sophie shifted, eyes peering into the darkness. She shivered at the madness in that voice. Suddenly she could see the pale ghostly face of the vampire emerging from the darkness into the flickering candlelight. Drusilla's face was framed by lustrous, raven black hair which seemed part of the darkness itself.

"Make no mistake," Sophie told her, "I will kill you. You and that devil of yours."

Something rustled in the dark behind Drusilla. Muffled cries told Sophie that it was Yanna there, bound and probably gagged as well. She flinched.

"Moths fly toward the flame," Drusilla whispered, and it carried throughout the chamber, dark and seductive and totally insane. "Wolves bay at the moon. Fascination in the sparkle of moonlight on a razor's edge. She loves him, you know. I sensed it the first time we crossed paths."

Drusilla's hands fluttered before her face, fingers twirling in some perverse pantomime. A thin smile flickered in the half shadows behind her hands.

"She loves him," the vampire repeated. She tilted her head to one side and regarded the Slayer steadily. "Naughty, naughty. I like her, though. The more I tortured her, the more I hurt her, I think she only loved him more."

Sophie would not allow her lip to quiver. Her teeth ground together. But she could not stop the single tear that welled in the corner of her left eye and slipped down her cheek.

Drusilla disappeared into the darkness for a moment. When she emerged once more she was dragging Yanna by the hair. Never had it taken so much effort for the Slayer to hold herself back. But she waited. Yanna cried out in pain against the gag in her mouth. Then Drusilla dropped her and, astonishingly, removed the gag.

"Yanna?" Sophie ventured, gaze roving about the room, searching the shadows for Spike or other vampires in his employ.

The Watcher turned her eyes up. She wept openly, though barely seemed to notice her tears. Her gaze seemed hollow and distant, and she rocked ever so slightly. Her right cheek was cut open and there were slashes and burns on her face and neck. The bruising was so severe that the left side of her face was swollen and black.

Sophie could see that both her arms were broken. More damage she could only guess at. All of that, the two vampires had accomplished in a few short hours.

"Go," the Watcher whispered. "Go now, Sophie. Run fast and far. I am already dead."

Sophie stiffened. Her sword rotated in her hands as she flexed her arms and wrists. A cold certainty had filled her, though she fought against it. There was only one reason Yanna would tell her to go, to run away like a coward.

She's had a vision, Sophie thought. *I'm going to die.*

"You're really quite beautiful, you know," Spike said, just a voice in the shadows. "It's going to be a bloody crime to tear you apart."

Slowly, as though strolling through a park on a romantic evening, Spike stepped into the light. His smile was charming, his manner pure whimsy.

"But we'll do it," he promised. "Oh yeah. We'll do you up right, little girl."

London, England
September 7th

In the foyer of the house on Great Russell Street, Ariana de la Croix stared in horror as the corpse of a gnomish, leather-skinned, armor-clad warrior crashed through the wooden second story railing, engulfed in blue flames, and tumbled to the stairs, only to roll to a stop two feet from where she stood. Its body was a blazing husk by the time it came to rest, eye sockets empty, face charred down to bone.

"Nidavellir. So it really is him, as the seers suspected," Marie-Christine said, then tugged on Ariana's arm. "Come. We must go down into the basement."

Angrily, Ariana pulled away from her. Her expression was almost feral as she stared up the stairs, wincing at the sounds of battle that came down from above. Sir Nigel, one of the Council's board of directors, was just down the hall, urging Eleanor, Isabel, and the other girls to flee into the basement with John Travers and several other Watchers. An operative named Gillian Partington stood with Miss Fontaine and the two women were adamant in trying to pull her away.

"Where's Charles?" Ariana shouted, rounding on them. "He should be here. He's my Watcher."

"And he would want you to be safe," Miss Fontaine told her sternly. "You must come along, Ariana. With the Germans attacking, the basement is the only—"

"Don't treat me as if I'm a child!" Ariana screamed at her, almost snarling. "What's happening upstairs has nothing to do with the Germans, nothing to do with the British either. What's upstairs, that's the real war! The one we've been trained for. But you want to hide us in the basement."

Her words echoed down the hall, drawing the attention of the other girls. Eleanor Boudreau, the American girl, was the first to begin to move back toward her. Sir Nigel blocked her way but Eleanor slipped past him. The others followed.

"Don't you understand that we cannot afford to lose you?" Miss Fontaine pleaded.

"Damn you!" Ariana snapped. "I am not yours to lose. If there are demons up there, and they are too much for all of you, then they're going to get us anyway. We have a better chance if we work together."

She stepped in close, staring at the older woman eye to eye. "Charles Rochemont is up there. My Watcher. I will not let him die for me without at least giving him the respect of standing by his side."

A strong hand gripped her shoulder, and Ariana was spun around and then driven, hard, back against the front door. The handle jabbed her lower back as Gillian held her there, pinned by the throat.

"Chances are you're too late with Rochemont. He was up on the third level. Likely he's already dead. You, on the other hand, are alive. And whatever Mademoiselle

Fontaine and the other directors instruct you to do, that is exactly what—"

Ariana pummeled her in the face with a swift punch, then followed through with a blow to the gut before kicking Gillian to the ground. The operative groaned, wiped blood from her mouth and reached for the gun she wore in a holster beneath her coat.

"Gillian, no!" Miss Fontaine cried.

The operative never touched her gun. Eleanor Boudreau and Isabel Cortés grabbed her from behind. Isabel whispered to her in Spanish, but Eleanor had her eyes on Miss Fontaine.

"Ariana's right. You've trained us to do a lot of things, Mademoiselle. But you never trained us to hide. We won't do that," Eleanor told her.

Behind them, Sir Nigel cleared his throat. He was about to protest. John Travers, the handsome young Watcher she had come to admire very much, spoke up first.

"Don't do this, please, Ariana. Eleanor, you know better. The directors know what's best for you and for the Council. People are dying upstairs to protect your lives. If you throw them away, their deaths will be meaningless."

"Their deaths will mean less than nothing if we all die, John," Ariana told him, though she spoke more gently to him than to any of the others. "It's all we know how to do."

Ariana and the other girls moved quickly through the first floor, arming themselves with weapons taken from displays and from the few Watchers who had been prepared to stay with them in the basement. Ariana herself took up the axe from the tiny monster's corpse on the floor. With six other girls following her, she headed for the stairs.

John glanced once at Marie-Christine before follow-ing, a grave expression on his face.

There were two more dead Nidavellir at the top of the stairs, but that was nothing in comparison to the carnage that greeted them when they reached the second floor landing. Strewn up and down the hallway, lying half in and half out of various rooms, were broken and bleeding corpses. Most of them were the Nidavellir, but at least five were human. Watchers and operatives Ariana had known, or at least greeted at breakfast or dinner in the house since she had arrived. The human dead were a far more horrible sight, not merely because they were people instead of monsters, but because of their wounds. One man was impaled upon a broken baluster from the rail-ing at the top of the stairs. A woman Ariana knew only as Katherine had one of the dwarf-warriors' axes lodged in her skull, her eyes wide and dull and dead. Others had limbs severed or their viscera strung out from enormous abdominal wounds.

Isabel cried out to God and muttered a prayer, though she was on guard for more attackers. Several of the girls backed away slightly, even taking a step or two down the stairs. One of them fell to her knees and threw up. Eleanor stood stalwartly at Ariana's side, and John came up right behind them.

The battle was not over, but near enough. Two of the gnome-creatures still stood, their axes over their heads, their armor singed but not burning. They looked older than the others, grizzled and even more gnarled. Gnashing their teeth, they moved toward the lone sur-viving Watcher on this floor.

His name was Trevor Kensington and Ariana thought he was the oldest man she had ever seen. He was also, she now saw, the most powerful. For as Mr. Kensington muttered words in a guttural language under his breath, his arthritic fingers contorting and sketching symbols on the air, blasts of blue flame swirled out from his hands to engulf the Nidavellir.

Simultaneously they burst into flame, shrieking in agony as death claimed them. Mr. Kensington staggered backward until he hit the wall and he leaned there for support, rheumy eyes watering, breath coming too fast. He was weak, and growing weaker. He had been extraordinary a moment before, a vision of magickal power, of arcane sorcery. Now he was merely a very old man once more.

"I don't understand," Ariana said, glancing from Kensington to John, who came up next to her in the hall. "Is it over?"

Mr. Kensington looked up at her. His skin was pale and wrinkled and drawn back over his face so that he looked like little more than a shroud-covered skull.

"It's just beginning," he rasped, wheezing.

From the end of the hall there came a roar. The window was already broken, but the frame shattered as well as an enormous winged demon made of ice barged through it. The creature was like nothing Ariana had ever seen. All jagged ice and horns, wide wings popping as the ice shifted inside it, a green mist floated at its core and its eyes burned with green fire.

It laughed, and Ariana felt so cold she wondered if its ice had extended out to envelop them all.

"Skrymir," Mr. Kensington said. Weakly, he forced himself to stand erect once more.

"Kensington?" the demon asked, sounding almost amused. "Will you never die?"

"Not today," the ancient Watcher promised. He lifted his hands and began to mutter in that guttural tongue again, fingers twisting into impossible configurations.

With a flash of one icy razor-sharp wing, Skrymir the demon cut Trevor Kensington in half. The old man's corpse fell forward, slamming to the floor with enough momentum that the top half of his body tumbled forward and over the broken railing to fall down to the stairs, then roll into the foyer below.

Ariana heard Miss Fontaine and Sir Nigel crying out in alarm and grief. Steeling herself, she hefted the battle axe she had taken from the dead monster and stepped forward. Eleanor, Isabel, John Travers, and several other girls followed. She could hear some of the other Watchers from downstairs running up behind them to help.

The ice demon's frozen tongue snaked out and slid over its lips. "Ahh," it said, staring at the girls. "The main course."

Chapter Seventeen

Copenhagen, Denmark
September 7th

Spike felt good.

After all the traveling they had done, killing the girls and their Watchers had become almost tedious. It had hurt the Council, that much was true. And for a while their creativity and Drusilla's wonderland of an imagination had kept it interesting. But that part was over.

No more Slayers-in-Waiting. No more knocking about with Skrymir's mysterious mission. Time to kill the Slayer and then go demand Freyja's Strand from the ice demon.

Head cocked to one side, he stood with his back to the shadows. To his left, Drusilla held the Watcher by her hair, the tortured woman whimpering with each twitch of his lover's hands. Before him at the center of what remained of this ancient castle, in the midst of the arena Spike had prepared for her, stood the Slayer.

She was a beautiful creature, this Slayer. Breathtaking, really. Her hair was fine spun gold and it hung over her shoulders in natural curls. Stray strands of hair partially obscured her face and made her look mysterious, all the more beautiful, and far more deadly as she eyed him steadily, her sword firm in her hands. She wore a long cotton dress, almost featureless save for the modern collar. It was blue, almost black in the blaze of illumination in that dingy chamber. Her legs were long and lithe, tan from her travels. She stepped out of her shoes and stared at him with soulful eyes, as though she were preparing to make love to him rather than cut his head off.

Spike licked his lips. He had been aware of the girl's penchant for swordplay and had armed himself accordingly. He held a long sword, half-forgotten, in his right hand. As he studied her, he set its tip onto the stone floor and rested his hand upon the hilt as though it were a cane or walking stick.

"You are something, aren't you?" he asked her. "Sophie, isn't it? Last Slayer I killed wasn't near as pretty. Deadly little thing, but not quite as stirring, if you know what I mean."

He could hear Sophie's breathing from across the room. Steady and deep. She moved a step or two to either side, taking his measure. Up until he'd mentioned that other Slayer. Then her eyes had widened just slightly.

"They didn't tell you that part, did they?" Spike asked, gleefully. He stood up a little straight, pompous as could be and enjoying himself. "Course it's been forty years. I hope I haven't lost my touch."

Sophie's blade wavered just slightly, catching the light from the torches on the wall behind her.

"Nice sword, by the way. Oughta fetch a lovely price. If I don't decide to hold onto it, of course." Spike studied her, frowning. "You're a bit too quiet for my taste, girl." He glanced at Dru. "Hurt her."

The Slayer flinched.

Drusilla did not respond. Spike looked over at her, a bit surprised. Drusilla glared at him, feeling hurt and petulant. She tugged hard on the Watcher's hair. Yanna cried out in pain but Drusilla had replaced her gag and she could voice no other protest. Not that it would have done her any good.

Drusilla imagined that her eyes were the sun, and where her gaze touched Spike, his flesh burned.

"What is it, Dru?" he asked a bit tiredly.

Furious, she glanced away. When she turned back to burn him with her eyes again, her mind was filled with thoughts of punishment. "You're flirting with her."

Spike's eyes widened. "Bollocks, Dru, I am not. Just savoring the moment is all."

"The air gets all pink when you look at her. I don't like it," Drusilla said firmly, pouting a bit.

"All right, poodle, not to worry. The air'll be nice and red in a moment, won't it? You know you're my only girl," Spike told her, shooting a cautious glance at the Slayer. "We'll just move things along, shall we?"

With that, Drusilla stopped pouting and allowed a tiny smile to touch the edges of her mouth. She tugged harder on Yanna's hair and the Watcher yelped, but only a little. The woman's eyes gazed past and through Drusilla, as though she were not even there.

Dru hated that.

"I don't like your eyes," she said, quite matter-of-factly. "I think I'll pluck them out."

The Slayer moved then, her sword whickering through the air. She cut through the broad chamber as though she herself were a weapon. Drusilla glanced at her and gave a dismissive wave. As she expected, Spike was there in an instant, his sword clanging loudly off the Slayer's own blade.

The girl twisted, then spun back and away from them, ready to continue. But the air around her had gone from pink to deep, deep blue, tinged with streaks of red. Blood and darkness.

"Let Yanna go," the Slayer demanded. "If you let her run, I vow to you I will not even fight you. My life is yours, just let her run."

Spike frowned, then snickered a bit. "You don't really think we'd go for that one, do you? Not like you Slayers are known for keeping your end of a bargain. Particularly with us . . . sharp-toothed lads. Make a deal with you? Bugger that."

He took a step toward her, picking up his sword and laying it across his shoulder like a lady with a parasol. The Slayer reacted, slipping sideways across the floor like a dancer, sword tilted to one side and up, ready to attack or to parry a blow.

"You know what I think, Sophie, dear? I think you're afraid of me. Not that I blame you. I am a nasty old sod after all. The big bad. You've been following us 'round the world, haven't you? You've seen what we can do. Now herself over there has had a vision, hasn't she? You know what's to come, what's to become of you. Might as well put your neck in the noose, love."

"I'll say it one, final time," Sophie told him, nostrils flaring, chin high, baring the soft flesh of her long neck. "Let her go."

Spike grunted. No trace of a smile remained on his face. "Now you've gotten me angry." He looked at Dru. "Poodle?"

Drusilla studied Yanna's eyes with an oddly disturbed expression on her face, almost as though she felt insulted somehow. Then she slammed the Watcher's head back against the stone floor with a resounding crack.

"Yanna!" the Slayer cried, eyes darting from Spike to Drusilla, her expression desperate.

"Ooh, I like the sound of that!" Drusilla cried happily. She let the woman slump to the ground and clapped her hands giddily. Then she knelt primly on the ground and crossed her hands on her lap. "Go on, then," she told Spike. "Kill her, like you promised. I want to watch."

"You always did like to watch," Spike told her lovingly.

Then he turned his full attention on the Slayer. He saw it in her eyes in an instant. She was over the edge. The girl had probably not even bothered to see if her Watcher was still breathing, if the woman's chest still rose and fell. It did. But the Slayer was much too far gone for such thoughts.

She was pure rage now. That, and fear. Much as she tried to hide it, he could practically smell the fear off her.

"Last time we met you caught me unaware," Spike told her. "No chance of that now, girl. You know how it's got to end."

"Come then," Sophie said, nodding for him to approach her. "Let's end it."

Though she spoke in words close to a whisper, there was a queer echo in the chamber. Spike paused for a moment, studying her, listening, eyes darting around the ruins. It was as though they were not alone, as if some other presence lingered in the shadows beyond the light of candle and torch and in the space between the collapsed stones, some expectant force, watching them like a flock of carrion birds.

It unnerved him.

Then Sophie shifted slightly and he saw the flame reflecting off her moist eyes, saw the trepidation there, and suddenly he felt he could smell her blood. His lip curled up in anticipation and he shook off the feeling that had come over him. The girl was a tasty little treat, and he was going to break her up like kindling. Slayer, sure. That meant she was dangerous. But she was on edge now, desperate and enraged and afraid. Some of them were tougher than others and he thought another day Sophie Carstensen might have done him in instead of the other way around, might have hacked off his head the way she wanted so badly to do.

But not today.

With a shudder, Spike changed. He wanted the girl's blood coursing down his throat and that desire sent an electric surge of adrenaline through him. He felt his fangs elongate and ridges form on his forehead and around his eyes. He grinned and brought his sword up in front of him.

It had been as though a clock ticked somewhere nearby, as though by some tacit agreement they spent those seconds studying one another. Then, as if the clock had stopped, they surged forward.

Spike heard Drusilla whimper with anticipatory pleasure, and that sound drove him all the more. The Slayer snarled as if she were a beast herself and edged in toward him.

Sophie's heart thundered in her chest, her pulse racing, adrenaline pumping through her. Yet somehow, she felt calm. Her breathing was steady and easy, and her movements confident and swift. The chamber had once been decorated in luxury and was now empty as a tomb. She tried not to let that analogy resonate within her, but it was difficult not to consider.

Exhaustion frayed the edges of her mind as well as her nerves. Fear for Yanna's life and the fragility of her mind had her off guard. And as much as she had tried to deny it to herself, the swath of death Spike and Drusilla had cut across Europe had intimidated her. So many had been murdered, and in such brutal fashion. They seemed unstoppable.

Which was absurd, of course. They were vampires. And she was the Slayer.

"Come on, then," she taunted Spike as he edged around her warily. "Kill me."

"Don't mind if I do," he chirped happily.

With a roar and a powerful swing, Spike leaped in, pivoted on his leading foot, and brought his blade down at an angle clearly meant to hack her in two. Sophie's heart fluttered in her chest and she held her breath as she grabbed the flat of her sword near the tip and used it almost like a staff to block the blow.

The clash of metal reverberated around the chamber and the strength of the blow sent a painful quiver running up her arms to her shoulders.

Spike was far from done.

He moved in again, swinging the blade down in a similar attack. Sophie used her own considerable strength to bring her sword around in a fast arc, moving closer to him rather than away. She parried his blow, but kept going, inside his defenses. Her sword strike had carried her hands around to protect her, but she stepped in even closer and slammed an elbow into Spike's face.

There was a satisfying crack as his nose broke. It would heal, of course. But only if she let him live that long. Spike staggered back, a few drips of blood on his upper lip.

"Oh, that smarts, young miss," he said, grinning evilly, the handsome, charismatic Englishman no longer even visible beneath the face of the vampire. His tongue lashed out and he tasted his own blood.

With a roar, he came at her again, more cautious this time. Their blades flashed in the candlelight, metal clashing, ringing and resonating through the chamber. Drusilla whistled and applauded and cried out happily. The lunatic propped Yanna up, dead or unconscious, and used her hands to applaud and to cheer as though she were some kind of puppet.

Sophie ignored her. Spike attacked again and again and the Slayer studied him, and waited. She grew tired, waiting for an opening. Her limbs were heavy. They moved in and out of the shadows, between columns of stone and around iron candle stands.

Her opponent paused to regard her. "You're not bad, you know that?" he said. "It won't save you, but I thought you'd like to know."

The Slayer kept silent. He was taunting her, trying to draw her into making a fatal mistake. She would not do that.

But she made him think she had.

Spike backed Sophie toward a fallen stone column, hoping to trap her there with her back to it. Sophie leaped up on top of it, knowing he would take that moment to attempt to end it. He feinted with his blade at her left side, a move he had almost succeeded in catching her off guard with several times.

Sophie also feinted. She let Spike think she was going for it. The vampire reversed direction, spinning inhumanly fast to bring his blade all the way around in a wide arc that would have cut her in two where she stood atop the fallen column.

Drusilla cried out in lustful triumph. Spike had the Slayer exactly where he wanted her to be.

Or he would have, if she had been tricked by his feint.

When he reversed direction, bringing his blade around to finish her, Sophie leaped up, the top of her head nearly grazing the ceiling of the chamber. Spike had nearly completed his turn, blade coming around for the kill, when Sophie snap-kicked in midair, her boot caught him in the face, and Spike's head rocked back hard. Off balance, he lost his sword and went down in a heap on the stone floor.

Her heartbeat thrummed in her chest. Desperate to finally have her vengeance upon the beast, for Yanna, for herself, and for all the others who had died at his and Drusilla's hands, Sophie swept down upon him with her sword swinging 'round like the Reaper's scythe.

"She's not dead."

Though she spoke barely above a whisper, Drusilla's voice carried through the chamber, like the distant burbling of running water or the hiss of a snake in tall grass.

Stunned, Sophie froze, paralyzed by the import of those three words. She glanced over at Drusilla to see that she still had her Yanna puppet in her arms. In that same instant, Drusilla raked her talons across the Watcher's cheek, and Yanna's eyes snapped open. She cried out in agony, and then fell silent and still again.

It did not matter. If Sophie did not kill them, Yanna would be dead soon enough. Victory was her only hope. She knew that, but Drusilla's distraction had cost her precious seconds, broken her momentum. When she turned to look at Spike again, the vampire was reaching for his sword.

"No!" Sophie cried.

Too late.

Even as she brought her blade down at him, Spike scooped his weapon up by its handle and rolled out from under her blow. Then he was on his feet again. It seemed to Sophie that he was moving even faster than before. It was impossible, and yet there it was. Unless of course it was she who was slowing down.

"Right, then," Spike sneered. "Let's have a sip."

Spike gazed into the Slayer's eyes and was certain he saw the light fade from them, the brilliant spark of life and righteousness diminish. He brought his sword around in a deadly arc, but the girl parried easily. The metal blades scraped together and the sound echoed off the stone walls of Absalon's fallen castle. He ducked, spun, and came up with the sword again in an arc meant to slash open her side. Sophie blocked the attack with enough strength to turn his sword away.

The Slayer feinted toward him with her own blade. Spike might not have fallen for the deceit but the desperation he saw in her eyes made him too cocky. There was a little trickle of blood running down her chin where she had bitten through her lip in concentration. The sight of that blood, and the scent of it, mesmerized him for an eyeblink.

Long enough for her to cut him.

The point of her sword impaled him, thrusting five inches into his gut before withdrawing. Spike cried out in pain and bent over slightly. Sophie took a single step back, brought the blade up, and swept it across in an arc that would have taken his head off if he had not blocked it. Which he did.

With his arm.

"Damn you!" he bellowed.

The blade bit into his flesh and cut to the bone. Only the fact that he was in motion stopped it from breaking his arm. Blood slipped from the wound as Spike took a few angry steps back.

Hatred, rage, and even bloodlust burned in the Slayer's eyes.

"You're an arrogant bastard," Sophie told him. "Maybe not so arrogant now."

Spike grimaced, stretched his neck a bit, then grinned. "Gave me a bit of a scratch, I'll give you that. Got a bit ahead of myself, maybe. But don't let it fool you. We're done here." He moved around so that a tall iron stand upon which sat a trio of burning candles was between them. His view of her was interrupted by the flames, which seemed to frame her face, then to burn it.

With a snarl Spike kicked the iron stand over, the candles tumbling toward her, the fire licking her blue dress. The material did not catch, but it was enough of a distraction. Spike lunged for her, she dodged graceful as a dancer, spinning out of his way, but he had watched her move. He anticipated her escape, and swiftly moved to meet her. Before she could bring up her sword he slashed her across the back, cutting cloth and flesh.

Fresh blood flowed, soaking her dress and dripping down her long, tanned legs. Sophie screamed and spun to face him. She stood up straight, courageous and still intent upon his death. But he saw it in her eyes again, even more than he had before. The way they darted around, she had the look of a victim now, the eyes of prey, and he knew he had her.

Drusilla applauded happily, cooing her love and calling out exhortations and promises of what he would have of her when the girl was dead.

"I'll teach you the songs the stars sing, Spike. You're my wonderful champion. Knight in blood-spattered armor," she murmured dreamily.

Suddenly there came a scream. The Slayer's name. Her Watcher had come fully awake and seen the blood streaming down the girl's legs and knew that her vision was becoming reality. Drusilla went to bash her head against the stone again but Spike glanced quickly at the precious love of his dark heart.

"No," he told Dru. "Let her watch. Just hold her there."

Even with broken limbs the older woman thrashed as though having a seizure. Spike focused his attention once more on the wary Slayer who even now circled around, trying to keep out of his range. Her eyes ticked right and left looking for an opening, a way in for her blade, a way to kill him.

"It's over for you, girl," he told her, his voice low and insinuating.

To her credit, despite the pain and growing weakness from her wound, Sophie said nothing.

Spike stalked her across the chamber and she retreated toward the dark edge of the room. She never reached it. With a devilish grin, eyes glowing yellow in the torchlight, Spike stepped in close to her. He even let her swing her sword in attack, a blow he easily parried. He spun her blade around, guarding against it, and then slid in close to her, inside her guard, and drove her hard against the stone wall. Half her face was illuminated by the torch off to Spike's right, and the other half was in almost total darkness.

He dropped his sword and gripped her right wrist, the one in which she held her weapon. Staring deeply into her eyes, a delicious thrill running through him, he snapped the bones. Sophie dropped her sword but did not cry out. Instead she bit even more deeply into her lip.

Spike leaned forward and licked the blood from her chin.

To her credit, the Slayer did not cry.

She tried to fight him.

"Now, now," Drusilla called. "None of the naughty bits or I'll have your guts for garters."

"Not even a little kiss?" Spike asked. "The special kind."

"Oh, well that's all right then," Dru replied, satisfied.

Sophie fought harder and Spike slammed her hard against the wall. Her skull banged off the stone and her eyes lost some of their focus. With a smile and a shudder of pleasure—and to the gag-muffled screams of the Watcher and the giggles of his lover behind him—Spike sank his fangs into the Slayer's throat and drank deeply of her.

He feasted upon her blood until she died in his arms.

When it was over he simply let her drop. He had felt a certain respect for her while she lived. But now . . . she was just another corpse. When he turned, Drusilla rose from her crouch and they met at the center of the room.

He slipped his arms around her, and she him. He felt the velvet and lace that sheathed her body, and he felt the svelte power beneath the fabric.

Her face changed, and he gazed upon her beautiful vampiric countenance and thought he had never wanted her so much. Their lips met, fangs biting each other's lips, just a nip. Spike had held some of the Slayer's blood in his mouth, and now he pushed it into Drusilla's mouth with his tongue, and she sucked it from him with great fervor. It was their greatest kiss.

Moments later, he lay his forehead against Dru's and gazed into her eyes for what seemed an eternity. Then he recalled the Watcher and glanced over to see the woman crumpled upon the floor.

"Did you kill her, then?"

"Dolly?" Dru asked, confused. "She was a bad dolly, but no. She just stopped moving. She was quite naughty, and perhaps she knows she'll be punished."

Together they went to stand over Yanna and gaze down upon her. The woman looked up at them, eyes wide and afraid but without any conscious thought or recognition.

"She's gone mad, I think," Spike said, a bit surprised but not unpleasantly so.

"How sad," Drusilla said, voice tinged with profound sympathy. "Nothing to be done about the mad except to pity them."

Spike agreed.

They left her there.

Yanna lay on the cold stone and wept, but her mind truly was gone. She no longer even knew what she was crying for. Outside, the night came on and the gray sky faded to black.

Chapter Eighteen

London, England
September 7th

It all happened so fast.

Ariana watched in horror as the demon Skrymir tore open a Brazilian girl she had spoken to only twice. His long talons, like daggers made of ice, ripped her chest and abdomen open and her viscera spilled out onto the floor. But Skrymir did not stop there. He grabbed another girl by the face and dashed her body so hard against the wall that the snapping of her bones was like wind chimes.

"Ariana!" John Travers cried, trying to pull her away. "We don't have a chance. Come away, now!"

But she could not. Though she had been trained to combat the forces of darkness, and schooled in their nature, never in her wildest dreams had she imagined the existence of something like this. Demons were real, yes . . . but how could she conceive of true evil until it stood, fuming, emanating the chill of its cruel and frozen heart, eyes blazing with sinister intent.

How can I fight such a thing? Tears threatened at the corners of her eyes as Ariana realized that she must fight it, no matter the inevitable consequence.

"I will not run," she told John, her own gaze locked upon the demon's eyes.

"Ahhh," Skrymir said, almost relieved. "A brave one."

Perhaps fifteen feet separated her from the demon. Ariana felt John pulling at her again but she shook him off. Vaguely she was aware that for him to concentrate his concerns so much on her that he must care for her. It registered, for she cared for him as well. But he should know that she could not run, could not turn away from the presence of such evil.

Skrymir's wings rippled and spread wider, ice scraping the wall on one side and cracking the railing on the stairs on the other. Eleanor and Isabel and two other girls stood between them, but Ariana felt, somehow, that the fight had come down to her and the ancient beast, this darkling god from out of northern myth. The world seemed to slow around her. Her physical sensations intensified, so the leathery handle of the axe in her hands was rough but comfortable—it felt powerful in her hands. Even as she took a step toward the demon, Ariana saw another girl attack Skrymir, a morningstar in her hands. It was Beatrice Lizotte, a shy girl with a sweet smile from Nova Scotia in Canada. She swung the spiked mace around on its heavy iron chain as though she were a warrior out of legend, but there was terror in her eyes.

Skrymir tore the morningstar from Beatrice's hands, then struck her with it, the spiked ball hitting her in the shoulder with a crack of bone. The girl screamed and went down, and the demon lashed out with a single hoof that sent her crashing through the broken balusters and tumbling down onto the stairs that led to the first floor.

Perverse as it was, Ariana thought of her as lucky. For Beatrice might yet live.

Grim-faced, she glanced at John. "Are you with me?" she demanded.

His own expression just as grave, John nodded. Then he moved to stand just beside her, though it was clear from his body language that he would have liked to stand in front, to shield her from the horror that stomped toward them on cloven feet.

Eleanor and Isabel, both armed with swords, attacked together. The American girl was batted aside easily, though she rolled with the blow. Ariana admired the move; the girl had been well trained.

Skrymir brought the morningstar down to crush Isabel's skull. Isabel brought her sword up to clang against the weapon's chain and held it fast. The ball and chain wrapped once around the sword, and then extraordinary things began to happen. Isabel flicked her wrists and used the sword to yank the morningstar from Skrymir's grasp. She tossed the weapon away even as the surprised demon brought his right hand around in a swift arc, foot long, razor sharp ice talons extended to cut her to ribbons.

With her eyes shining brightly as though in a nigh-upon religious fervor, Isabel lifted her sword up before her with both hands to deflect the blow, knocking Skrymir's arm away before spinning in a vicious little arc and hacking into the demon's frozen gut hard enough to crack the ice and send shards flying.

Skrymir roared in pain and astonishment.

"My God!" Ariana cried. "How did she do that?"

John was grinning madly. "She's been Chosen!" he said loudly. "She's the Slayer!"

The demon knew it, as well. For he took two steps back to regard the girl again. Now Isabel stood between Skrymir and the others, the survivors, which included a trio of frightened girls, four young Watchers, and the handful of older Watchers and other girls who waited down on the first floor.

"Damn you, Spike!" the demon roared.

Ariana was confused. She was also, in truth, slightly disappointed. *It should have been me,* she thought. *I felt it, somehow, the moment of choosing. It should have been me.*

A tiny wisp of green mist drifted from a crack in the demon's gut before the ice sealed it off again. Ariana frowned and studied that crack. It was true that something swirled within the creature's icy form, like poison gas or smoke. Somehow, that point at the demon's midsection was vulnerable.

Isabel stood tall before the creature. She seemed to have a kind of gleam or polish that she had never had before, as though she crackled with the energy of the Slayer. With a shout of vengeance, the girl from Barcelona moved in to attack once more, sword held high. But she did not attack the demon's torso. And it was clear that Isabel did not have much training.

Swiftly, yes, and powerfully as well, Isabel hacked at Skrymir. With one stroke she chopped two talons from the demon's left hand. With another she carved a chunk out of his shoulder. A third blow lopped off one of Skrymir's massive horns, cracked his icy skull and sent him stumbling backward, wings coming up and around him to act as a shield.

Isabel approached with all the strength of the Slayer but with little caution. With the demon crouched within the shell that his wings created around him, she stood there, in the middle of the hall, and brought the sword down again and again, hacking away at the ice wings that protected the evil one.

Eleanor was the nearest to the Slayer. She was bruised and battered but otherwise all right. When she saw what was happening, she shouted out immediately. Ariana did the same. Their voices merged into one as they cried out for Isabel to take care.

In the pause between one sword stroke and the next, when Isabel had lifted the blade above her head, Skrymir's wings opened and both hands shot out almost faster than Ariana could see. The demon gripped both of her wrists in one massive hand and crushed the bones to powder. Isabel screamed, but her voice was cut off when the demon lunged forward with its open maw filled with jagged, frozen fangs and tore out her throat. Steaming blood melted his ice just a bit where it spattered his body.

With a roar of pleasure, Skrymir dropped the corpse of the Slayer and rose to finish what he had begun.

Ariana stood paralyzed, waiting for the choosing to happen again, waiting to become the Slayer.

Waiting.

Skrymir stormed toward her, massive hooves stomping, cracking the wooden floor, talons flashing through the air as he reached for her. Ariana stopped breathing. Her heart beat wildly and she closed her eyes.

Waiting.

She felt the cold of the demon's icy claws as they sliced the air near her face, but by then she was falling, tumbling to one side. John drove her across the hall to slam into a partially open door into an elegant bedroom. She hit the floor and all the breath was driven from her. Her axe thunked to the floor inches away from her and even at an angle it cut through the wood and stayed there, blade dug into the floor.

John was on top of her.

Ariana looked up at him, saw the fear in his eyes, and realized it was for her. Only for her. This brave man had never been afraid for himself. That new understanding struck her profoundly, but there was not time even to ask herself what it meant to her. Someone else screamed out in the hall. One of the Watchers, one of John's friends, was dying out there. Perhaps more than one.

Though his look told her he might have wished to linger, John stood up quickly and reached for his own dropped weapon. Ariana leaped to her feet, anger and fear and determination coursing through her, revitalizing her. She wished that it were more than that, more than emotion and adrenaline, but she knew that it was not.

As she tore her axe from the wood floor, she marveled at how sharp its blade was. Magick. It had to be. No man-made weapon had ever been honed to so keen an edge.

John was at the door before her. From out in the hall there came the clang of metal. He paused at the door and glanced back at her.

"Eleanor," he said. "It's Eleanor."

For a moment Ariana did not understand what he meant, and wondered if Eleanor had been killed. Then the two of them moved out into the hall, weapons at the ready, and she saw what had happened. Eleanor, with her superior training, ducked, dodged, or simply outpaced every one of Skrymir's attacks as the demon attempted to destroy her. The girl's blade whickered through the air with blinding speed and she chipped away at the demon.

Eleanor Boudreau was the Slayer.

Once again, Ariana's first, bitter thought was, *it should have been me.* Instantly, she pushed the thought away. Eleanor was her friend. There were better reasons as well. Ariana had no doubt that of all the Slayers-in-Waiting who had been forced to hide out together in the fourth floor room of the Council headquarters, Eleanor was the best candidate. She had received excellent training, but she had also been an excellent student.

Now here was the truth of it.

"You are swift, girl, and clever," Skrymir thundered, attempting to lash out at her with his hooves. "But I am older than legend and I have been waiting for this day. I will not allow you to steal it from me."

Eleanor avoided his attack once more. Skrymir tried to catch her with his wings and Eleanor did the impossible. Rather than try to escape again, she stood fast, then brought her blade around with such power that she shattered the demon's wing. Skrymir roared his fury.

He slashed at her with his talons again. Eleanor avoided the blow but could not dodge in time to escape being battered by Skrymir's raised hoof. The Slayer was thrown backward and hit the floor, doubled over in pain. Eleanor was up quickly, but she was moving slower now. She would heal, of course. Ariana knew that. But not instantly. And Skrymir was not likely to give her time.

With a sudden twirl, Ariana turned and kissed John on the cheek, hefted her axe, and—as Eleanor rose to meet the demon's renewed attack—followed the Slayer into battle.

Eleanor attacked again. Ariana stood back, keeping the Slayer between herself and the demon. She watched and she waited, in case Eleanor met the same fate as Isabel . . . in case she were called after all. Skrymir cried out as Eleanor impaled him with her sword, and when she withdrew the blade it was followed by another puff of that green smoke.

Skrymir shuddered almost imperceptibly and grunted. Eleanor ducked inside his reach again and tried to stab once again. But this time Skrymir was too quick for her. The demon slammed a closed fist down onto Eleanor's wrist, breaking her arm. The sword fell to the floor. The demon struck her again, his massive fists covered with jagged ice stalagtites that punctured Eleanor's shoulder and back. One punched through her upper arm enough to pierce the skin on the other side, protruding bloodily.

Skrymir was bent over the Slayer, forcing her to the ground, rearing back his fists to pummel her again.

Ariana knew one more blow might cost Eleanor her life. But she also knew that she had to take that risk, had to wait . . . wait . . .

The demon struck again, hunched over the broken body of the Slayer. Silent, furious, Ariana stepped in close to Skrymir and, with a single swing of the darkling axe, cleaved the demon's icy skull in two. Screaming, Skrymir reared up on his hooves. Ariana pulled the axe back and it came away smoothly.

Green mist leaked from the shattered ice of Skrymir's skull. The demon clamped both hands on its head. The green flames that flickered from its eyes dimmed slightly, even as it began to glance around for the source of this attack.

Blood, Ariana thought. *It's like blood. Or even worse.*

With Skrymir standing up to his full height, in the second it took the demon to heal the massive wound in his skull, she swung again. This second blow was sideways. She stood as if chopping down a tree, and brought the axe around with all her might. It struck the same spot where the crack in Skrymir's torso had been, the spot she had thought was vulnerable. He had been wounded there before, at least once, probably more.

The axe shattered his midsection completely and the demon collapsed to the floor, broken in two like a porcelain doll.

It flailed out with wings and hooves and talons and Ariana stepped back to avoid its death throes. She grabbed Eleanor and then John was beside her, and the two of them hauled the injured Slayer away from the broken demon. Already, Eleanor was recovering, ready to fight again.

But the fight was over.

Green mist curled from the two shattered halves of Skrymir's body and the ice that made up the top and bottom halves of his body began to truly freeze, to become nothing more than lifeless, though horrifying, sculptures carved of ice. The mist drifted toward the shattered window the demon had come through.

Ariana watched it in fascination. It was in that moment that she realized something else. The bombs had stopped. The air raid on London was over, at least for the moment.

The city was devastated. The damage had been done. Yet somehow she knew that this attack might be the very thing that steeled the British people for the war, forged within them a determination that would carry them through to victory.

The last of the mist was leaking from the upper half of Skrymir's body. Even the demon's face seemed nothing but ice, now.

"That was amazing," Eleanor told her. "You saved us."

Ariana shook her head. "You saved us. I simply waited for the right moment."

John Travers smiled and reached for Ariana's hands.

Close by there came the sound of ice shattering. Ariana whirled around to watch in horror as spikes of ice shot into the air from the broken form on the floor. Almost like massive icicles, straight and sharp tentacles, they seemed to chase after the mist. There were half a dozen at first, then a dozen, in a circle around that mist. Then the air between them, as though charged with a current of freezing cold, quickly turned to ice, forming a long cylinder of a shell around the green mist that was the essence of the demon Skrymir.

It fell to the ground with a crack but did not break.

Then it changed, altering its form, until they were looking at the face of Skrymir once again.

But a Skrymir reduced in power and stature so that the demon was no larger than Ariana herself, perhaps even a bit smaller. It glared at her and at the others, then stepped forward without a word until it reached the shattered remains of what it once was.

It began to absorb the ice into itself, building its mass. Its back cracked and wings sprouted.

Ariana hefted her axe.

John stepped in front of her, sword raised.

The demon ignored them all. With a roar of humiliation and pain it beat its wings and pushed off the floor. Skrymir flew above them, small enough to be out of reach after taking them by surprise. The demon flew to the landing and then up to the third floor. Then it kept going.

"Where's it going?" Eleanor asked.

"However it got in, that's how it will get out," John replied.

Together, they ran after the thing, up two flights of stairs. Eleanor, with the gifts of the Slayer at her disposal, pulled ahead and reached the fourth floor fully a dozen steps ahead of them. It did not matter. By the time Ariana and John caught up to her, at the door to the meeting chamber that had turned into the girls' quarters, a massive ice tunnel that had opened from the windows on one wall was shrinking quickly.

It narrowed, the room returning to its original state, the windows intact, until there was no trace at all that the portal had ever been there.

John stepped into the room. Eleanor and Ariana followed.

"He's really gone," Ariana whispered.

"But he didn't finish the job," John said. "He survived. It might take a long time for Skrymir to recover from the damage the two of you did to him today, but he survived. This is not over. The Council is in ruins, but we must survive. And we must be more vigilant than ever before."

Ariana frowned, studying the windows. One of the panes of glass did not look exactly right. She stepped forward and reached up to touch the glass. She had to stand on tiptoe to reach it.

"What are you doing?" John asked.

"It's cold," Ariana told him. "This is not glass. It is ice."

Eleanor, the taller of the two girls, stepped forward and punched the ice pane out of the window, shattering it instantly.

"Vigilant," she said, turning to Ariana.

The two girls embraced. John laid a hand on Ariana's shoulder. All through the house were the corpses of their friends and associates. The carnage had to be removed. But members of the Board of Directors had survived. It would be up to them to decide what to do next.

"I was so afraid," Eleanor whispered into Ariana's ear.

"Me too."

Chapter Nineteen

Helsingør, Denmark
September 8th

Even before the arrival of the German army, the old port of Helsingør was a quiet city. At war, the day-by-day life of the city went on, but after dark Helsingør was absent the spark that conquest stole from so many places. Celebrations were not unheard of, but under the watchful eye of the occupying German forces, they were muted at best.

It was a clear night and cold. The sky sparkled as though the stars themselves were frozen, and across the Øresund channel that separated Denmark from Sweden lights could be seen burning in the night. To the people of Helsingør, looking out across the water, it might have seemed that those warm lights were a beacon, a declaration that here was a refuge, a sanctuary from the cruel fist of Nazi Germany.

In truth, those lights were a taunting lure, inspiring fantasy, for Helsingør's sister city, Sweden's Helsingborg, lay across waters prowled by German ships and submarines.

There was nowhere to run.

For a human.

Spike and Drusilla had slipped out of Copenhagen just after dark. Not far from the lair they had made for themselves in the bowels of Christiansborg Palace they had stolen an automobile and simply driven north. Just outside the city they came upon a road block and without any discussion of strategy, slaughtered the soldiers who stopped them there.

There was an officer among them. The uniform did not fit Spike very well but he had managed to keep it mostly free of bloodstains. Drusilla remained in the crimson velvet and lace she had come to favor. His new uniform would be enough of a distraction to buy them the little time they needed. They fed, gorging themselves on Nazi blood to the point where they allowed themselves the luxury of twenty minutes to simply recover from that numbing pleasure.

After they were sated and strong, they moved their few things from the stolen car to a German army truck. Spike glanced at his papers, which identified him as Franz Gruber, and nodded contentedly. They would not fool anyone, but they would get him close enough for the kill.

Drusilla helped him pile the bodies in the back of the stolen car and drive it off onto the farmland west of the main road. It would remain undiscovered until dawn. More than enough time.

It was not very long before they came to Helsingør. There was a checkpoint on the road just outside the city, but it consisted of four sleepy soldiers. The one who asked for his papers only glanced at them briefly before turning his gaze upon Drusilla. He eyed her hungrily and she smiled shyly, knowingly, naughtily. The soldier smiled enviously at Spike, handed back his papers and slapped the side of the truck for them to continue.

The vampire had never had to speak a word of German.

Spike would have killed them all if necessary, but in a way, he was glad it had not come to that. Much better to get in and out of Helsingør quietly. Also, his mind was preoccupied with thoughts of Skrymir and the necklace of the Brisings. His body felt charged with power he had felt within him only once before. He had killed a Slayer and drunk her blood, a powerful thing.

Yet now that it was done he recalled Skrymir's warnings and realized that killing the girl might have been foolhardy. He and Drusilla had not, technically, kept up their end of the bargain. One way or another, however, he would see to it that Skrymir kept his.

So it was that they traveled mostly in silence, even as they approached the harbor area of the creaking, old port city.

"It's like a bloody ghost town," Spike said, frowning as he peered through the windshield, bent forward slightly. "Haven't seen a soul about who isn't in uniform."

Drusilla did not respond. As he slowed the truck and turned to drive along the wharfs where fishing boats and military vessels were moored alongside one another, Spike glanced over to see her sulking, arms crossed, staring wide-eyed off into some infinite universe only her eyes could see.

"Don't be like that, pet," he chided. "Look, we're on the last leg of our little journey here. We do a quick jaunt across the sound here, ramble about the Northland, do a bit more mountain climbing, we'll see our old mate

Skrymir and get your sparkly trinket, and everybody's happy, yeah?"

With a dour expression, Drusilla regarded him out of the corners of her eyes. Spike wondered if she felt the same concerns as he did about Skrymir coming through on their deal, or if she had simply intuited his own thoughts on the matter.

"I don't want to ramble anymore," she said, in a hurt little girl voice that both irritated and enthralled him. Drusilla pouted and her hands came up to twirl and dance in front of her face, as if she were caressing the air, or painting it with colors only she could see.

From what Spike knew, that last might not be far from the truth.

"I'm tired of trucks," she said grumpily, her lower lip pooched out. "We've driven smelly, noisy, falling-apart lorries halfway 'round the world this trip. They make my eyes hurt, and my head's all static. When we're done with the demon, I don't want to ride in trucks anymore. Not ever."

Spike downshifted and the gears ground on the truck. He braked and it shuddered to a smelly, noisy halt. He understood this new aversion of Drusilla's completely, but it was not as though they had had much choice. The easiest thing would have been to say nothing, or simply agree to her condition and let it go. But Spike felt, somehow, as though he had let her down.

"Come on, Dru. It's not that bad. And what else were we to do? We're in the middle of a bleedin' war, aren't we? You want to be inconspicuous, the average luxury auto just isn't gonna do the job, right?"

"No more trucks," she said simply.

"After we get Freyja's Strand, then, all right? My baby says no more trucks, then that's it. No more."

"Even the road hates them. And the fumes make the air scream."

"Can't have that," Spike agreed.

Drusilla seemed to perk up then. She sat up a little straighter and a tiny smile touched the corners of her mouth. Her hands stopped fluttering and glided across the cab of the truck to touch Spike's arm. Her fingers traced their way up to his face where she stroked his cheeks and nose, ran her fingertips over his closed eyes and then slipped them into his mouth. Spike kissed her hands and ran his tongue along her fingers.

He felt a surge of desire and reached out for her. As he did, though, his eyes flickered open and he had to force himself to remember where they were. There was rarely a bad time or a bad place for the two of them to ravish one another, but this was an exception.

Twenty yards ahead there was a small building. Once upon a time it had probably been the harbormaster's office and quarters. Now it was a guard shack for the German soldiers who had been assigned to watch over all of the vessels that went in and out of the harbor. Even now, a quartet of soldiers eyed the truck warily as they approached from the building. Two had machine guns out, though the man in front, probably the ranking officer, had only his sidearm. Several others on watch along the wharfs were also moving cautiously toward the truck, machine guns held ready.

"Damn," Spike muttered. "We drew a bit more attention than I'd hoped, just sittin' here like a pair of idiots."

Drusilla ignored his words and the danger that surrounded them, her hands trailing down his body, fingers tracing his most sensitive spots, those she knew quite intimately. "And no more war, either," she whispered. "It's gotten inside me now. Through my eyes and ears and nose, leaking through my skin. It can be a great deal of fun, war. But I've had my fill for a while. I think I should like to go to South America after all. The humans are so pretty there, dark and glistening flesh. And they celebrate the dead.

"They'll love us in Rio, Spike. I just know they will."

The officer with the gun tapped its barrel on the driver's-side window. Spike rolled it down and the man barked at him in German. The vampire smiled. With a sudden lunge he grabbed the man by the throat with one hand and yanked the gun away from him with the other. He shot the German officer in the head and tossed the gun on the seat. The other soldiers opened fire and the windshield and passenger window exploded in a shower of glass shards. He and Drusilla ducked.

Spike started up the truck. Drusilla grabbed the gun, grinning at it as though it were an infant child. With the truck in gear, Spike drove right through the small building at the end of the wharf. The roof collapsed down upon them but three walls remained standing.

It was dark in there.

The soldiers came in after them.

Twelve minutes later they were putting out to sea in a small fishing boat that had been converted to use by the German army. German ships in the harbor weren't likely to stop one of their own. Spike cursed angrily as he steered the vessel. There were bullet holes in his uniform and bloodstains all down the front of it.

That was all right, though. Sweden was only three miles away. And he was sure he could get another when they docked.

London, England
September 12th

The dead had been removed from the house on Great Russell Street. Some of the damage had been repaired. No one in London paid any mind. The rest of the city had its own problems, with the Luftwaffe continuing to prey upon Londoners. The blitz had started on September 7, but that was only the beginning. Hitler's plan regarding the British had become painfully clear. He meant to bomb them into submission.

But the German leader did not understand the English. That much was clear. If he had, he would have realized that with every bomb that fell, every son or daughter killed, every building razed to the ground, the people of Britain grew ever more resolute. He hoped to crush their spirit. Instead, he had given them the tool for an unprecedented unification of purpose: hatred.

What was meant to be the final blow in a war that had been filled with German conquests was, rather, the first salvo in a new war. A war Adolf Hitler could not win.

Within the walls of the headquarters of the Watchers Council, a similar atmosphere had developed. The call had gone out to Watchers who had retired, as well as to the families of those who had served in the past but were now gone forever, and to Watchers already serving as scholars or trainers far abroad.

Come home.

The war had claimed many casualties and it was time to rebuild, to bolster the ranks. Skrymir was defeated but not dead. Spike and Drusilla had disappeared. The forces of darkness thrived out there in the night, and the Watchers Council must oppose it.

Still, there was much to do. According to reports from operatives working in secrecy in Copenhagen, Yanna Narvik had been found wandering the streets after curfew and nearly shot before it was realized that she was quite mad. She was in a Danish asylum, and would remain there until the Germans were driven back, or the Council managed to arrange a surreptitious release that would only mean moving her to an asylum here in London.

There had been no word of the Slayer, or the discovery of her corpse. The mere fact that Eleanor had been Chosen was enough to confirm Sophie Carstensen's fate, but efforts were being made to establish the chain of events that led to her death and the whereabouts of her body.

Those members of the Board of Directors who had survived had a Herculean task ahead. Council losses had been catastrophic. The process of rebuilding would take time they could not truly afford. Training and education were sorely needed, and there were not enough trainers and educators left to go around. But somehow, they would prevail.

We will prevail, John Travers told himself. Though the vow was not only to himself, but to the spirit of his murdered father, whom he firmly believed was watching over him, even now.

The room on the fourth floor had been returned to its original purpose. John stood outside the meeting chamber beside Ariana de la Croix, and struggled against the urge to reach out and clasp her hand, to comfort her. He believed that Ariana would not mind. In truth, he felt certain she knew that he had feelings for her, and that she also cared for him. But now was not the time.

They had been there in the hall, staying well clear of the damaged stairwell, for nearly half an hour when the door at last opened and Marie-Christine Fontaine appeared from within, looking as haggard and tired as they all felt. The woman whom his father had so admired—and whom he knew had felt the same in return—smiled kindly at John. In that moment he thought they both felt a resurgence of their initial grief at his passing. In the depths of that grief his loyalty to the Council had been forged anew, stronger than ever before. Harold Travers had given his life to the Watchers Council, quite literally.

John would do the same.

This was a war never to be taken lightly. The things in the shadows were never to be underestimated, their capacity for evil never forgotten. The rest of the world was ignorant, yet it was that very ignorance, and innocence, that the Council was sworn to preserve.

"You may come in now, John," Marie-Christine said softly, her voice a bit raspy, perhaps on the verge of a cold. "The directors have agreed to speak to you as well, Ariana."

The girl smiled cautiously and reached for John's hand. She took it and squeezed, just for a moment, before letting go. Marie-Christine clearly noticed, but if she thought there was any impropriety in the gesture, she gave no sign of it.

John stood aside to let Ariana precede him into the meeting room. The window had been repaired, and he was glad. He had no desire to be reminded any further of the horrors that had taken place in that building or that particular room, and even less interest in recalling the demon's escape.

His attention was drawn to the long table at the center of the room by the sound of Sir Nigel clearing his throat. The old man seemed to have shrunk in John's estimation, to have collapsed in on himself in some way. He had been old before, but never had seemed less than hale and hearty. Now there was a sunken quality to his countenance, and his eyes were moist all the time.

But when he spoke, his voice still held all the power it had always had.

"Please sit down, Mr. Travers. Miss de la Croix."

Ariana looked nervous. She glanced over at John and he tried to reassure her with a slight nod. There were only five Watchers in the room aside from himself. There were two men beside Sir Nigel. Both were retirees who had been called back into the fold. The other new face was a woman John had seen before, but only briefly. She had apparently been on a research trip to the South American rain forest during the entirety of those dark days of 1940. Giles was her last name, he thought, though they had never been introduced.

All five directors were seated on one side of the table, and Marie-Christine gestured for them to sit on the other side. John first pulled out a chair for Ariana, and then sat down beside her. He could practically feel the nervous energy pouring from the girl.

"Mr. Travers," Sir Nigel began, "first let us say how sorry we are for the loss of your father. It is a sentiment we have likely expressed to you before individually, but at this time we find ourselves particularly missing his wisdom and sage counsel."

"Thank you, Sir Nigel."

"It is our hope, young man, that you may one day sit at this table in a more official capacity," Mrs. Giles told him. "Your family has been involved with the Council for generations. Your recent actions would have made Harold exceedingly proud."

John flushed a bit and repeated his thanks.

"We have a great deal of business to conduct, so you'll pardon us if we dispense with certain niceties in the processing of your request?" Sir Nigel ventured.

"Of course," John agreed.

As one, the entire Board focused their considerable attention upon Ariana. The girl stiffened slightly, shifting in her chair, but she did not drop her gaze. She looked at each of them in turn.

"We have a difficult road ahead of us," Sir Nigel said. "I am certain you are aware, Mr. Travers, of the trials that await the Council. New Watchers need to be recruited and trained. New operatives hired. A massive search must be made for potential candidates we ascertain might one day be Chosen to become the Slayer. I don't believe I have to tell you how unlikely it will be that such information will ever be released to any hands but those of the directors."

This time, however, Sir Nigel did not wait for a response. He had, indeed, dispensed with the niceties.

"You are a very young man to be charged with this task, John, but we place our faith in you as your father's son, and as a bold and decisive man of action. The directors have decided to place you in charge of the hiring of new agents for our operations branch."

John blinked, nothing short of astonished. "Sir Nigel, I . . . I am honored, but are you certain that is—"

"We would not have given you the assignment if we were not confident of your abilities," the old man interrupted. Then his gaze turned to Ariana. "The situation regarding Miss de la Croix is less clear."

Ariana pursed her lips, a bit angry, a bit defiant, but she said nothing.

"Your Watcher is dead, Miss de la Croix. We are sorry for that loss, yours and the Council's. We are also grateful for your exemplary performance in the fight to repel the invasion by Skrymir and his Nidavellir minions. You may not have been Chosen, but you acquitted yourself as well as any Slayer might have hoped to in that battle."

"Thank you, sir," Ariana said.

Her voice shook, and John wanted to touch her arm, just to steady her, but he knew it would not be appropriate. Not in front of the directors. Particularly not now.

Sir Nigel sat forward, frowning as he studied her.

"Am I to understand, from Mr. Travers's written report, that you want to become a Watcher?"

"Yes, sir," Ariana said immediately, happily. "It is my fondest wish."

"But you are still a potential candidate; you may yet be Chosen," Mrs. Giles added.

"Yes, madame," Ariana replied. "I would continue training as a Slayer for at least one year to eighteen months, until the Council determined I was past the point where I was likely to be Chosen. During that time, though, and starting as soon as possible, I would like to begin studies to become a Watcher."

For what seemed a very long time, no one spoke. John understood why. As far as he knew, this was the first time such a request had ever been made. Several Slayers-in-Waiting who had not been Chosen had been *asked* to join the Council as Watchers over the years, but he had never heard of one who had made the request herself.

At length, Sir Nigel let out a long rasping breath. He glanced at the other four and in turn, each of them nodded. Marie-Christine was the last to give her assent and she smiled at John as she did so.

"We are agreed," Sir Nigel declared. "You are a courageous and quick-witted young woman, Miss de la Croix. We would be proud to count you among our number. You will continue your training as you suggested, but you will also embark upon your studies immediately. For the time being, Mr. Travers will act as your Watcher as well as beginning your education."

Ariana blushed a moment, glancing away.

"I will oversee your unique situation myself," Sir Nigel added. "I have no doubt that you will continue to prove quite an asset to the Council."

John knew it would be a great deal of work, handling his many assignments. But he also knew that everyone involved would be working tirelessly to save the Council. Plus he would have all the time in the world to spend with Ariana. That was the best of all, for he had admitted to himself the previous morning that he was falling in love with the girl.

For her part, Ariana was obviously excited and pleased, but was unable to prevent herself from blurting out the one, final question that was on her mind. She had asked John, but he did not have an answer.

"What about Eleanor?" she asked. "Where will she be sent? Who will be her Watcher?"

"Ariana," Marie-Christine chided. "This is really not the time, nor is it your place to—"

"Actually, Miss Fontaine," Sir Nigel interrupted, "the girl's question is quite pertinent."

Marie-Christine frowned as she looked at him.

"She and the Slayer have become close. Miss de la Croix merely wishes to know if they are now to be separated,"

Sir Nigel said kindly. "The answer is no. The Slayer will remain here in London for the forseeable future. As her own Watcher was also killed, you are indeed correct that a new one must be appointed. Given our current circumstances it is vital that this Watcher be the best the Council can provide. That is why the Board of Directors—or most of us, in any case—have determined to assign Miss Marie-Christine Fontaine to the Slayer as her Watcher."

John blinked in surprise, then turned to see that Marie-Christine looked even more astonished than he did. Another first, as far as he knew, assigning a member of the Board to be the Watcher for the current Slayer.

Extreme measures, true. But as he looked at the faces gathered around that table, as he thought about how brave and skilled Eleanor Boudreau was, and how wise her new Watcher, as he considered the courage and beauty and intelligence of the girl beside him, the girl with whom he would be spending nearly all of his time from then on, John was gifted with a tiny flash of pre-science of his own.

They would do it.

Somehow, they would find a way.

It was all going to work out just fine.

Galdhöpiggen, Norway
September 14th

It had all gone to hell.

The diminished, weakened Skrymir sat upon the high chair in his throne room, a mere shadow of his former self. With his essence partially dissipated, his control over the ice was minimal. He could not summon the moisture with the power he had once wielded and so his body, the frozen shell he wore, was a sliver in comparison to the hideous, horrifying, masterful visage he had once presented.

Torches burned to light the chamber. Several living humans whimpered in agony within their hanging cages. The gryphon still lazed by the throne, chained there and apparently still content. Darkling servants still bowed in obeisance whenever they were in his presence—but he knew they whispered about him when they left the room. All of his many guests, his "friends," had departed soon after his return from London. They had seen him, sensed the depth of his defeat, understood how wretched a creature he had become in just a very short time, and they had promptly abandoned him. With barely a whisper of good-bye, and not a moment of consideration for his injuries or desires, his guests went down the mountain and returned to the world. Better to face a continent at war than have to look into the eyes of one so ruined.

For ages, Skrymir had plotted. Once upon a time he had held true power in his grasp. Godhood. Thousands upon thousands worshipped him. Then there came a new age of reason unto man, and Skrymir had withdrawn, confused, disheartened. When once again he emerged and began to learn about the world of man, he determined to take back what he had once had, and more, to create a realm of chaos and evil, all under his rule.

It required centuries of observation, the building of a network of advisors and observers, agents of darkness abroad in the human world, and the creation of an elite personal guard. Among the races of demons that still walked the earth, as well as among the vampires and other monstrous tribes, he had earned respect, even awe. His plan hinged upon one thing and one thing only—if he could rid the world of the Watchers Council, destroy the Slayer and many of her heirs, throw the forces of light and order into total disarray, then the forces of darkness would be his to command.

He would truly have been the Lord of Demons.

Now he was nothing. A pitiful recluse, broken and battered, given an ignominious defeat by the Council, by the Slayer, and by a young human girl with no real power whatsoever. His Nidavellir were wiped out, slaughtered by a human mage who had lived long past his time. Perhaps a dozen of the creatures—those too young or stupid for him to trust enough to take along with him in battle—still lived within the walls of Skrymir's stronghold. And even they were unlikely to remain for very long.

Only the darklings would remain faithful, and then only because the lithe, deadly servants had nowhere else to go and no awareness of any life except catering to the needs of their lord.

Someday, far in the future, he might find within himself the strength to rebuild. Patience had always been among his greatest assets, along with cunning. This time, however, it seemed that Skrymir's cunning had failed him. As had his patience. He had made a grievous error, thinking that he might speed up his plan by utilizing the vampires who had appeared upon his doorstep half a year before. It had seemed propitious at the time, a perfect opportunity.

Ironic, he thought, that only at the end would his patience fail him.

It was not that Spike and Drusilla killed the Slayer. That had been his intention all along. It was simply that they killed her too soon. Timing was everything. In this case, it was the timing that had devastated his plans and nearly cost him his life.

There in the half-light, with the sound of the snoring gryphon and the groans of the suffering humans for company, Skrymir enveloped himself in his thoughts, his regrets and the seeds that would become his plans for the future.

When a trio of darklings slipped into the chamber and approached, eyes downcast, then dropped to their knees before him, Skrymir frowned. With a low rumble to his voice, an echo of the power he had once had, he bade them stand and speak their minds.

"My lord," said one, its voice like the shush of snow and ice rolling down the mountain, just before an avalanche, "you have . . . visitors."

The other two flinched, and Skrymir realized they had chosen the third to speak. To put itself in the way of his anger. And angry he was, but not at them.

"They dare?" Skrymir asked, quivering with rage. Though it shot sharp jolts of pain through him, the demon began to absorb the ice around him, growing larger and more deadly. Small horns grew in size upon his forehead. His icy fangs lengthened and Skrymir cringed in agony as the effort took its toll. He looked more formidable, but he could barely stand. Only fury drove him on.

"After what they cost me, after breaking our bargain, they dare ask for an audience?" the demon snarled.

The darkling shuddered, eyes still downcast.

Skrymir's eyes widened as he looked at his servants and realized the truth. Alarmed, he looked around the room.

"An audience?" Spike asked incredulously, stepping out of the darkness of the tunnels off to the right, with Drusilla just behind him. "Who do you think you are, you silly git, the bloody king of England?"

Drusilla, resplendent in fine crimson velvet, slipped up beside her lover and eyed Skrymir dangerously. "I've come for what's mine," she said. "My birthday's long past and I want my present." The beautiful vampire girl's features changed, then, to the hideous visage of the demon within her. She tilted her head to one side and smiled grotesquely.

"Now."

Chapter Twenty

Galdhöpiggen, Norway
September 14th

The mountain wind whipped through the caverns, and deep within the bowels of Skrymir's stronghold, it sounded like distant screams. Spike slipped an arm around Drusilla and stared at the ice demon. Off to the left, humans in cages cried out for the vampires to save them, which Spike thought was fairly amusing. The darkling servants he had bullied into announcing their arrival had fled in terror, which Spike thought said an awful lot about their faith in their master at the moment, or lack thereof.

Skrymir's eyes crackled with green flame and the demon snarled, baring a mouth full of long, ice needles.

"You dare much coming here," the demon said, and despite his diminished stature, his voice was as unnerving as it had been the first time they had met. Each word resonated deeply in the chamber.

Spike reached inside his jacket and pulled out a pack of twenty silk cut cigarettes. "Now that's not very nice, is it me ol' mate? If I was the sensitive sort, I might have my feelings hurt." He tapped one of the cigarettes out and placed it in his mouth to dangle from his lips as he searched his pockets for the metal lighter he always carried. "Thing is, Skrymir, we've done a job for you, and time's come to make good on your end of the deal."

The chamber was filled with a familiar crackling noise as the demon rose from his throne and shuddered. The horns on his head grew, curving around and down. Skrymir's icy shell cracked and re-formed, jagged edges appearing where there had been none. But even as this happened, the demon seemed to wince in pain, the expression on his hideous face reflecting his discomfort.

"You look awful, old boy. Something wrong?" Spike inquired innocently, though he had a fair idea by now what exactly had gone wrong.

"There were Nidavellir guards and another frost giant guarding the entry to my stronghold," Skrymir rumbled, taking a threatening step toward them. "I cannot believe the two of you . . . you mad, bumbling things . . . managed to kill them all."

Drusilla giggled. She stepped away from Spike and twirled, a little girl's dance, all fluttering fingers, across the stone floor. She grabbed a tall iron stand upon which burned nine black candles, and spun around it.

"We didn't have to kill them all, silly," she said. "Only the giant and two or three of those ugly little dwarves. The others were happy to leave. I blew them kisses as they went."

She stopped, suddenly, and her face hardened again. It was as though she were noticing Skrymir for the first time. "There are echoes all through the caves down here," she whispered. "Every word you have ever spoken still lives inside these walls, bouncing around, and I can hear them all at once, an eternity of anger and cruelty."

Drusilla spun again, but only once, to move back to Spike. "He doesn't like us, you know," she told her lover.

Spike laughed. "I'm crushed. Really."

The demon roared and stomped toward them on frozen hooves. Spike did not even flinch as Skrymir poked him with a sharp talon. The demon's claw cut through his shirt and jacket and flesh and drew a drop of blood. Spike only regarded him with a pleasant, innocent expression.

"You were to await my instructions!" Skrymir howled furiously. "I have planned for centuries, slowly and carefully weaving a web out of nothing but promises and pain. You were given a simple mission to carry out. Kill the girls but leave the Slayer alive until I ordered her death."

"Never been much for orders, really," Spike said, frowning. "Look here, though, we killed all those girls, stole that list. We jumped the gun a bit on the Slayer. Sorry about that part. But we did our bit, so hand over Freyja's Strand and we'll be off, right? You can get back to your plotting. Everybody's happy."

Skrymir froze then. Quite literally. The ice demon became completely still. Only the flickering of flames from his eyes and the churning of the green mist within him revealed that he was still alive. Spike glanced at Drusilla, who was batting at something in the air like a kitten attacking phantom catnip. He frowned.

"Right, look Skrymir, I'm not going to ask again."

"I don't have it," the demon confessed.

Spike blinked. "I'm sorry. Got a bit of wax in my ears, I think. What was that last bit?"

Skrymir sighed. Drusilla scratched the air and hissed like an angry cat. She moved toward the demon menacingly.

"I did have it, once," Skrymir revealed. "I gave it to a Xharax demon as a gesture of goodwill in order to make a mutual defense treaty."

"You had the necklace of the Brisings?" Spike repeated, astonished. He waved his hands in the air. "But you just gave it away. Just like that? To a Xharax demon, who I might remind you, aren't exactly known for their reliability? What did you think would happen when we came back looking for our agreed upon reward?"

Skrymir smiled then, but it was a bitter expression and it bared his needle teeth. "Truthfully? I never thought you would survive. Though I assumed that if you did, by the time I saw you again I would have already become perhaps the most powerful demon in the world, leader of an army of darkness. I would have simply had you killed."

"But you lost," Spike said grimly.

The demon did not reply at first. Skrymir would not even look at them. At length, he did turn his gaze upon the vampires. There was a desperation on his features that was only partially masked by his blazing eyes and ferocious countenance.

"I will rebuild. I will start again. The two of you were responsible for the loss of centuries of work, but for an immortal, that is only a setback. You owe me. I also owe you, I admit. There is only one way for us both to get our due and that is for you to join me in my quest for dark supremacy."

Spike's eyes widened and he stared at Skrymir for a moment, awaiting the punch line to what he thought was a colossal joke. When none seemed forthcoming and he realized the demon was serious he laughed heartily.

Skrymir did not like that. "How dare you laugh at—"

"Oh shut your gob, you bloody git," Spike snapped dismissively. "Here's what we're going to do. You've been parking your ugly old arse up here for ages. I'd wager you've got quite a treasure trove of goodies and powerful artifacts stored away somewhere. Give us a guided tour, let us have our pick, and we'll be on our way."

He turned to his lover. "That suit you, Dru?"

She pouted a moment, glaring angrily at Skrymir. Finally, her eyes drifted and she gazed into the darkness. "It isn't my reflection, but it'll do, I suppose. Better be something special for your princess, though."

"Nothing but the best. Right, then, shall we get to it?" Spike asked, smiling again at Skrymir.

The demon chuckled. "Kill them," he growled.

Spike was in the middle of taking a long and satisfying drag on his cigarette. He was a bit tired, his clothes torn from the fight with the frost giant and the Nidavellir just to get in here. He figured it was all over but the shouting.

The gryphon surprised him. He had forgotten all about the sleeping creature. At Skrymir's command the creature's eyes popped open instantly. Its massive wings beat the air and it easily snapped the chain that held it to Skrymir's throne. The demon laughed as the giant creature with its lion's body and eagle's wings and head leaped fifteen feet to drag Drusilla down to the floor, tearing at her with its claws and snapping at her with its enormous beak.

Drusilla did not so much as whimper.

"You bloody bastard!" Spike screamed. He did not even feel his face change, the fangs elongate, as he lunged at Skrymir.

The ice demon brought his elongated, jagged talons up to protect himself, slashing at Spike. With a grunt, Spike dodged the first attack, then he launched a high side kick that shattered the demon's frozen jaw and cracked his neck. A long, jagged fracture appeared on Skrymir's throat. Roaring in pain and humiliation the demon brought his right hand up to impale Spike on the four long spears of ice that his fingers had become. Spike felt his flesh tear, felt one of his lungs punctured and two of his ribs break.

Lip curling in disgust, he sneered at Skrymir. "Call off your puppy or I'll rip your head off."

Skrymir laughed and shoved his talons deeper into Spike's chest. "You'll do nothing but d—"

Spike was not about to let him finish that sentence. With all his strength he took hold of Skrymir's frozen arm and used his free fist to batter it at the shoulder. The ice cracked, Spike twisted, and the arm came away, followed by a tiny stream of green smoke. The wound sealed, but not before Skrymir cried out and staggered backward in shock.

Glaring furiously at the demon, Spike pulled the talons from his chest. Then he took a single step forward and began clubbing Skrymir with his own arm. The demon's horns shattered under his onslaught, and the crack in his neck deepened.

Spike dropped the arm and it shattered into a thousand shards. He pumped all his energy into another hard kick, ignoring the pain in his chest, and his foot struck Skrymir's chest. The demon stumbled backward and crashed into his throne, sending the chair tumbling from the dais. Spike was upon him in an instant, his own yellow eyes glaring with months of frustrations and fury unleashed.

"You've ruined my baby's birthday," Spike snarled.

Then he reached out, grabbed Skrymir by the stumps of his horns and twisted with all his might. There was a deafening crack that echoed throughout the chamber and the demon's neck split. Spike tore Skrymir's head off.

The fire in the demon's eyes died in an instant.

Green smoke drifted from the massive, unsealable wound where his head had once been attached to his neck. Skrymir's essence swirled in the air a moment before the mountain wind whistling through the caverns whipped it around and then sucked it away, off into the darkness.

Spike grinned, hopped up and down a moment with exhilaration. "Heh," he chuckled to himself. "So that's what it feels like to kill a myth. I like it!"

Suddenly remembering Drusilla, he spun in alarm, calling out her name. He need not have worried, however. On the other side of the cavern, his sweet love sat against a stone column with the gryphon beside her, its head resting comfortably on her lap. She cooed to it and stroked the feathers of its eagle head. Her velvet gown was torn, as was the flesh beneath, but she barely seemed to notice.

"You all right, pet?" Spike asked, concerned for her wounds.

"We're just fine, aren't we, Francis?" Drusilla whispered, speaking mainly to the gryphon.

"Francis?" Spike asked, incredulous.

Dru looked at him. "He's really very sweet, once you get to know him. Speaks only in kisses, though."

* * *

They spent the day exploring the stronghold and enjoying Skrymir's holdings. The last of the humans was tortured and feasted upon. The darkling servants who had hidden throughout the confrontation out of a sense of self-preservation were very cooperative once they realized their master was dead and the gryphon had chosen Drusilla as its mistress. They raided the place, of course, and were not at all surprised to find that Skrymir did, indeed, have a great many treasures, including ancient works of art and texts stolen from the library of Alexandria before it burned. None of those were small and light enough to carry down the mountain.

Several of the larger gems fit nicely into a pouch, however. There was one other item they took, a thick ring of gold that fit snugly around Drusilla's upper arm. According to the darklings, this was Draupnir, forged by the Nidavellir in an age before man. It had various magickal properties of course, but Drusilla was only truly concerned with the way it sparkled in the firelight. All in all, she was very pleased with the eightieth anniversary of her rebirth as a vampire.

When night fell once again they departed the stronghold, bundled in clothing stolen from German soldiers all through their trek to the mountain. It was difficult going, as it had snowed all that day, but Drusilla sang softly as they started down the mountainside. Skrymir was dead, the Watchers Council was in tatters, and both of them were blissfully happy. Spike felt more relaxed than he had in months. He smoked incessantly, studied the stars in the clear night sky, and held Drusilla's hand when they reached the more difficult portions of the hike down.

"Beautiful night, isn't it, poodle?" he asked, when they were perhaps a mile from the truck they had left hidden at the base of the mountain.

Drusilla giggled, singing a bit more loudly. She pulled him to her and wrapped herself around him impossibly tight. Her cold blue lips stung his ear and his throat, and her teeth nipped and nuzzled at him.

"Happy birthday, Dru," Spike whispered. "So it's off to Rio now, is it?"

"Oh, Spike, you really do know how to show a girl a good time," she cooed.

Then Drusilla pushed him roughly down to the ground and began to undress him. They made love, there in the deep snow, and laughed all the while. When Dru nipped at Spike, and scratched her nails down his back, it was so cold that the blood would not flow, not even a drop. Cold enough to kill, but Spike and Drusilla were already dead.

And yet, they had never been more alive.

About the Author

Christopher Golden is the award-winning, *L.A. Times*–best-selling author of such novels as *Strangewood*, *Straight on 'til Morning*, and the three-volume *Shadow Saga*. His other works include *Hellboy: The Lost Army* and the *Body of Evidence* series of teen thrillers (including *Thief of Hearts* and *Soul Survivor*), which is currently being developed for television by Viacom.

He has also written or co-written a great many books, both novels and nonfiction, based on the popular TV series *Buffy the Vampire Slayer* and the world's number-one comic book, *X-Men*.

Golden's comic book work includes *Batman: Realworlds*, *Wolverine/Punisher: Revelation;* stints on *The Crow*, *Spider-Man Unlimited*, *Buffy the Vampire Slayer;* and *Batman Chronicles;* and the ongoing monthly *Angel* series, tying into the *Buffy* television spinoff.

As a pop culture journalist, he was the editor of the Bram Stoker Award–winning book of criticism *CUT!: Horror Writers on Horror Film* and co-author of both *Buffy the Vampire Slayer: The Monster Book* and *The Stephen King Universe*.

Golden was born and raised in Massachusetts, where he still lives with his family. He graduated from Tufts University. He is currently at work on *Prowlers*, a new horror series for Pocket Books. There are more than three million copies of his books in print. Please visit him at www.christophergolden.com.

Buffy the Vampire Slayer™ ANGEL™

While helping a friend search for her lost brother, Buffy is drawn into a dangerous web of intrigue. Meanwhile Giles and the rest of the Scoobs are on the trail of a shadow stalker—a trail that leads straight to the city of Angels....

Someone is kidnapping the children of the rich and powerful and sending them off to another plane. With the lives of the kidnapped teens and one dangerously talented young woman at stake, Buffy and Angel venture off into the uncharted dimension to do battle....

UNSEEN

An epic trilogy that crosses the lives of Buffy, Angel, and their respective cohorts as they battle the forces of evil....

#1-The Burning
#2-Door to Alternity
#3-Long Way Home
By Nancy Holder and Jeff Mariotte

Published by Pocket Books

. . . A GIRL BORN WITHOUT THE FEAR GENE

FEARLESS™

A SERIES BY
FRANCINE PASCAL

FROM POCKET PULSE
PUBLISHED BY POCKET BOOKS